D1020299

WAKING THE DEAD

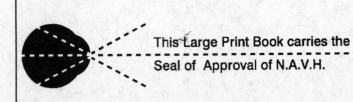

This Large Print Book carries the
Seal of Approval of N.A.V.H.

WAKING THE DEAD

HEATHER GRAHAM

THORNDIKE PRESS
A part of Gale, Cengage Learning

GALE
CENGAGE Learning·

Farmington Hills, Mich • San Francisco • New York • Waterville, Maine
Meriden, Conn • Mason, Ohio • Chicago

GALE
CENGAGE Learning

LIBRARY OF CONGRESS CATALOGING-IN-PUBLICATION DATA

Graham, Heather.
   Waking the dead / by Heather Graham. — Large Print edition.
      pages cm. — (A Cafferty & Quinn novel) (Thorndike Press Large Print Core)
   ISBN-13: 978-1-4104-6757-7 (hardcover)
   ISBN-10: 1-4104-6757-0 (hardcover)
   1. Good and evil in art—Fiction. 2. Large type books. I. Title.
PS3557.R198W35 2014
813'.54—dc23   2014002132

Published in 2014 by arrangement with Harlequin Books S.A.

Printed in the United States of America
1 2 3 4 5 6 7 18 17 16 15 14

In memory of my in-laws, Angelina Mero Pozzessere and Alphonse Pozzessere, who first introduced me to Massachusetts, wonderful Italian food — and the historic and incredible city of Salem.

And to Dee Mero Law, George Law, Doreen Law Westermark, John Westermark, Kenneth Law, Bill, Eileen and Eddie Staples, and "Auntie Tomato," Gail Astrella. Thanks for the very strange, fun and quite incredible road trips to Salem!

PROLOGUE

June 1816
The Shores of Lake Geneva, Switzerland

Lightning flashed, creating a jagged streak in the angry purple darkness that had become the sky — day and night at once, or so it seemed.

Henry Sebastian Hubert hunched his shoulders against the strange chill that permeated the evening. The sky's darkness was never-ending; the rain and the cold were foreboding. He'd heard that in America, there had been June snow in some of the northern states. Here, in Geneva, it always seemed dark, damp and wretchedly cold — but certainly no worse than it had been in England.

Another twisted arrow of light slashed across the eerie black sky, illuminating the lawn that stretched before the lake. Percy Shelley, Claire and Mary Godwin, and George, Lord Byron had arrived. Mary was calling herself Mary Shelley on this Continental jaunt but Shelley had a legal wife in England. Claire — well, Claire was Claire. He could hear her laughter as they approached, high-pitched and sounding rather forced.

The young woman tried so hard. She'd been Byron's lover in London, and did not seem to understand that Byron sought nothing more permanent. But through Claire, Byron had met Shelley, and his admiration for Shelley was complete and enthusiastic. And among their foursome, Claire was the only one who spoke French decently, making her a definite asset.

Henry was enamored of them all. "There they come," he said aloud. "The brilliant, the enchanted."

Behind him, he heard a strange sound and turned. Raoul Messine, the butler who'd come with the castle, was also looking toward the water.

"You were about to speak?" Henry demanded.

"No, *monsieur.* It is not my place."

Henry stared at him. Messine was thin as a stick; he had a pinched face and resembled a skeleton in black dress wear. He had served the late Lord Alain Guillaume and, Henry had been assured, was the finest servant to be found. Of course, Lord Guillaume had been a hedonist — and some said that Raoul Messine provided him with any pleasure his heart desired. Alain Guillaume had met with an early grave, drawing his sword against authorities who'd been sent to search for a missing servant. Afterward, Messine had properly interred his master in the castle's crypt. Henry had rented the castle from the lord's son, Herman, who had moved to London years before his father's death and preferred to remain there. Apparently, the son had taken after his mother and had no interest in his father's cruel pleasures.

Messine suited the dreary stone walls of the castle, blackened with growth and age.

"Speak — as if it *were* your place!" Henry insisted.

Messine shrugged. "The *depraved*," he said. There was something strange about the man's eyes. He said the word *depraved* as if it were a compliment.

To Henry, both the word and the tone seemed odd coming from a man who had served the likes of Lord Guillaume. Unless he'd *enjoyed* serving his master — and perhaps taking part in his exploits? Henry didn't know yet, but he was curious.

"They simply discard convention, my dear

fellow. That is all," Henry said. "They have great minds and great imaginations!"

"Indeed, sir, and you are their equal — with your paintbrush," Messine told him.

Hubert wasn't sure he could begin to equal the brilliance of Shelley in any measure, but he was grateful that the man had come with his interesting party of guests.

A moment later, those guests dragged their small rowboat ashore — Claire still laughing. Covering their heads with shawls and jackets despite the fact that they were already drenched, the four of them ran toward the great gates to the small, fortified castle Henry had rented.

The House of Guillaume was nothing like the beautiful Villa Diodati Lord Byron had taken near the water, nor did it in any way resemble the massive and beautiful Castle Chillon across the lake. Originally built during the Dark Ages, around 950 AD, when the area had been under the control of the Holy Roman Empire, the castle had drafty halls. The rooms were small and sparse and only one place, the south tower room, gave him enough light to paint. It was a wretched rental, but at least the enclosure no longer housed farm animals. But Guillaume offered four strong walls, four towers and a small courtyard that led to a keep with a majestic hall and a number of usable rooms. As long as Henry's servants kept fires burning constantly, it was bearable.

And, most important, he had lured George, Lord Byron, here — along with Percy Bysshe Shelley and his young lover, Mary Godwin. The party also included Mary's stepsister, Claire, who had surely come in hopes of regaining her place as Lord Byron's mistress, and the striking young John Polidori, a writer of sorts himself, but hired by Lord Byron as his personal physician.

What made the castle an exceptional choice despite its discomforts was the impression it allowed him to give others — that he was a moody artist making his name in the avant-garde world, where the dark side of human nature, religion and science were intriguing the finest minds of his day.

Thanks to family money, he could afford this place. Nothing better, perhaps — but the castle sufficed.

"Henry!" Claire was the first to greet him, running to where he stood at the gates, throwing herself in his arms. She was soaked and didn't care in the least that she dampened him, as well.

He gave her the mandatory hug and stepped back. "Welcome!" he called cheerfully as they ran up. "Welcome, welcome, get under the portcullis, my friends, and we'll make a dash for the house! I'm so glad you've arrived!"

"Did you doubt us, dear fellow?" George asked, giving him a hug, as well. The hug was enthusiastic; he wasn't sure if George was testing him. Lord Byron enjoyed outrageous behavior, although he toned it down in London, lest his words not receive the respect they deserved when he voiced his opinions in the House of Lords. He was often condemned for his poetry, ostracized by society — and yet his political rhetoric sometimes held sway.

"We're delighted to see you, Henry," Mary said. She had such a sweet smile. While she'd chosen the bohemian lifestyle — running off to the Continent with Shelley when he was legally married to another woman — there was still a sense of charm and old-fashioned morality about Mary. Henry was in love with her himself, he realized. "Any outing is exciting these days," she went on. "The weather is so very dreary."

"Yes, man, and we're quite frozen solid," Percy said, slipping his arms around Mary and grinning at Henry. "You've a fire, I believe."

"A big fire, and a great deal of delicious,

mulled brandy," Henry promised. Messine had already sent two other servants down to the lake. They'd gather his guests' luggage from the boat.

Henry greeted Polidari, who was bringing up the rear, carrying his own bag.

"It will be good that I am a physician, since we'll all be catching our deaths of cold!" Polidari told them.

They raced across what had once been the inner courtyard and was now the only courtyard that led to the giant double doors and the hall. Raoul Messine was there, and he held the doors open for them, handing warmed towels to the sodden guests as they made their way in. Henry followed last, closing the great doors as he entered. Mary was already before the fire, wrapped in the towel, a delicate tendril of damp hair resting upon her pale cheek. At least the hearth was massive and the fire burned warmly. But even with the fire and the many lamps set in sconces around the hall, the castle seemed dark, shadowed, forbidding.

"I love this glorious and faded homage to a day gone past!" Byron announced. He dried his hair as he looked around. "Ah, suits of armor standing guard, macabre paintings of lords and ladies long dead, shadows here, there, everywhere. How fit-

13

ting that we should come here to work, old friend, for you've heard of the task we've undertaken?"

"Ghost stories," Henry replied.

Shelley nodded. "We are to create creatures of the eerie darkness within our souls, faces so horrid that not even a mother could give them love . . . scenes so terrifying that none may escape. Mary had a dream — she's writing her dream. I'll take that brandy, Henry, my friend. Brandy has a way of setting the mind to sights within it!"

"Henry, you *must* write a story," Mary said. She touched the edge of one of the swords on the wall and said, "Ouch! Oh, indeed, these remain ready for battle!"

"Ah, my love, this was a fortified castle in the Dark Ages — filled with torture and screams!" Shelley teased her, taking her hand. "You're bleeding."

"Just a drop," Mary insisted. "Nothing of concern."

"Blood! Ah, as this great ruined hulk of an old edifice deserves. Or so we would say in our stories!" Byron said.

"They've got me working on one," Polidori told Henry. "You, too, must be seduced into the madness of this circle."

Claire whirled around the hall before the fire. Her clothing was still sodden and clung to her form, tempting the eye, and yet, Henry thought, Lord Byron seemed displeased rather than tempted. Of course, he'd heard that Byron would bed anyone who was pretty enough and that he tired of his conquests — male and female — as quickly as he enjoyed them.

"Henry *is* an artist!" Claire said. "George Byron, you paint with words. Henry uses a brush."

Byron pushed by Claire to stand near Mary and Shelley. "Yes, indeed," he declared. "Henry is a true artist. And he must join us in our madness, and while we create stories of normal circumstances suddenly distorted, out of focus, corrupted by monsters, he must do so on a canvas!" Byron paused to kiss the finger Mary had pricked and met her eyes. "He must paint with rich colors and darkness — as we do with words. Ah, yes, he must paint . . . with the color of blood!"

They were asking him to join their private yet so privileged adventure.

"It's a challenge I should love!" Henry assured the group.

"What shall he paint? Oh, what shall he paint?" Mary asked.

"He need but gaze around this castle," Shelley said. "There, above the fire! That old baron looks like a skeleton ready to step out of the portrait and into this very room. And there — the way those figures hold the armor, as if they could come back to life and cut down everyone before them. Ah, the tapestry with the saints bending down to succor the lepers! Those poor, vile afflicted beings could run wild in starvation, and rip the damsels helping them asunder."

"The swords above the fire!" Claire exclaimed.

"The gauze curtains," Mary said. "I see in them a ghost."

"A creature that rises from the sea or falls from the heavens?" Byron asked. "A tree being, with skeletal fingers that reach out to entangle in a young girl's hair . . . and curl around her throat? What kind of monster, Henry, shall you paint?"

Henry smiled. "I shall paint deceit — and with it, the worst monster I can conjure up."

"And what will that be?" Polidori asked.

"Man," Henry told them. "The depth and darkness and depravity of the human soul. I shall let the very devil into my heart and mind, and he shall teach me!"

"Ah, wickedness. Wickedness is in the mind!" Mary declaimed. "And the soul that is bathed in blood!"

Beyond the castle walls, lightning struck

again. The fury of the thunder that followed caused the very earth to tremble.

"Then, dearest Mary, I shall paint with blood," he promised. "And with all the dark despair that ever have lived within these walls. Yes, I shall paint with blood."

CHAPTER 1

The house was off Frenchman Street, not a mansion and not derelict. It sat in a neighborhood of middle-class homes from which men and women went to work every day and children went off to school. The yard was well-kept but not overmanicured; the paint wasn't peeling, but it was a few years old. In short, to all appearances, it was the average family home in the average family neighborhood.

Or had been.

Until a neighbor had spotted the body of the woman on the kitchen floor that morning and called the police. They'd entered the house and found a scene of devastating chaos.

Michael Quinn hadn't been among the first to arrive. He wasn't a cop, not anymore. He was a private investigator and took on clients, working for no one but himself. However, he maintained a friendly relation-

ship with the police. It was necessary —
and, in general, made life a hell of a lot
easier.

It also brought about mornings like this,
when Jake Larue, his ex-partner, called him
in, which was fine, since he was paid a
consultant's fee for his work with the
police . . . and his personal pursuits could
sometimes be expensive.

"You know, Quinn," Jake said, meeting
him outside, "I've seen bad times. The days
after the storm, gang struggles in our city
and the usual human cruelty every cop
faces. But I've never seen anything like this."

Jake — Detective Larue — was sent on
the worst and/or most explosive cases in the
city . . . or when something bordered on
the bizarre.

Jake was good at his job. He was good at
it, Quinn had long ago discovered, because
he'd never thought of himself as the be-all
and end-all. He took whatever help he could
get, no matter where he got it. That was how
cases were solved, and that was why he was
willing to call Quinn.

Good thing he was back in the city, Quinn
thought. He'd just arrived a few hours
earlier. Danni didn't even know he was back
after his weeks in Texas — he'd meant to
surprise her this morning.

Quinn looked curiously at the house. "Drug deal gone bad?" he asked. It didn't seem like the type of home where such a thing happened, but there was no telling in that market.

"I'll be damned if I know, but I doubt it. Get gloves and booties. We're trying to keep it down to a small parade going through," Larue said.

Quinn raised his brows. It was almost impossible to protect evidence from being compromised when that many people were involved. But Larue was a stickler; he'd set up a cordoned path to the porch. There were officers in the yard, and they were holding back the onlookers who'd gathered nearby. The van belonging to the crime scene techs was half on the sidewalk and cop cars crowded the streets, along with the medical examiner's SUV. The only people who had passed him were wearing jumpsuits that identified them as crime scene investigators.

"Dr. Hubert is on," Larue said.

Quinn liked Ron Hubert; he was excellent at his job and looked beyond the norm when necessary. He wasn't offended when another test was suggested or when he was questioned. As he'd said himself, he was human; humans made mistakes and could overlook something important. His job was to speak for the dead, but hell, if the dead were whispering to someone else, that was fine with him.

"First things first, I guess. The entry hallway," Larue said.

There was no way to avoid the body in the entry hall. The large man lay sprawled across the floor in death. Hubert was crouched by the body, speaking softly into his phone as he made notes.

"The victim is male, forty-five to fifty years. Time of death was approximately two hours ago or sometime between 6:00 and 7:00 a.m. Cause of death appears to be multiple stab wounds, several of which on their own would prove fatal. Death seems to have taken place where the victim has fallen. There are abundant pools of blood in the immediate vicinity." He switched off his phone, stopped speaking and glanced up. "Please watch out for the blood. The lab folks are busy taking pictures, but we're trying to preserve the scene as best we can. Ah, Quinn, glad to see you here, son." Pretty much anyone could be "son" to Dr. Ron Hubert. He was originally from Minnesota and his Viking heritage was apparent. His hair was whitening, but where it wasn't white, it was platinum. His eyes were so pale a blue they were almost transparent. His dignity and reserve made him seem ageless, but realistically, Quinn knew he was somewhere in his mid-sixties.

"He was stabbed? Have you found the weapon?" Quinn asked.

"No weapons anywhere," Larue answered. "This is — we believe but will confirm — Mr. James A. Garcia. His family has lived in the area since the nineteenth century. He inherited the house. He was a courier who worked for a specialty freight company."

"The woman in the kitchen, we believe, is his wife, Andrea. It looks as if she was slashed by a sword," Hubert said. "Make your tour quick, Detective," he told Larue while nodding grimly at Quinn. "I need to get the bodies to the morgue."

Quinn accompanied Larue to the kitchen. He couldn't begin to determine the age of the victim there; only her dress and the length of her hair suggested that she'd been a woman. To say that a sword might have been used was actually a mild description; she looked like she'd been put through a meat slicer. Blood created a haphazard pattern on the old linoleum floor and they moved carefully to avoid it. "There's more," Larue told him, "and stranger."

Upstairs, another body lay on a bed.

"Mr. Arnold Santander, Mrs. Garcia's father, as far as we know. Shot."

"Gun? Calibre?"

"Something that blew a hole in him the size of China. And there are two more."

Another bedroom revealed a fourth body — this one bludgeoned to death. Quinn couldn't even guess the sex, age or anything else about the remains on the bed.

"Maggie Santander, the wife's mother," Larue said.

The fifth body was downstairs by the back door. Compared to the others, it was in relatively good condition.

"This one is a family aunt — Mr. Garcia's sister, Maria Orr. What I've been able to gather from the neighbors is that Maria Orr picked up the Garcia children to take them to school. She was the drop-off mom and Mrs. Garcia was the pickup mom. Maria often stopped by for a coffee after she took the kids to school and before heading to her job at a local market. Mrs. Garcia was a stay-at-home mom and looked after all the children in the afternoon."

Quinn hunkered down by the body and gingerly moved the woman's hair. He frowned up at Larue. "Strangled?"

"That's Hubert's preliminary finding, yes," Larue replied.

Quinn stood. "No weapons *anywhere* in the house? The yard?"

"No. Obviously, the techs are still combing the house. I have officers out there questioning neighbors and going through every trash pile and dump in the vicinity and beyond. The city's on high alert. I'm about to give a press conference — any words of wisdom for me before I cast everyone into a state of panic?"

One of Larue's men, carefully picking his way around the corpse, heard the question and muttered, "Buy several big dogs and arm yourself with an Uzi?"

He was rewarded with one of Larue's chilling stares. "All I need is a city full of armed and frightened wackos running around," he said. "Quinn, what sort of vibe are you getting here? Anything?"

Quinn shrugged. "Was there any suggestion that they could have been into drugs or any other smuggling?"

"The poor bastard was a courier, a baseball coach, a deacon at his church. The mom baked apple pies. No, no drugs. And it sure as hell doesn't look like one of them killed the others and then committed suicide."

Quinn spoke to Larue, describing the situation as he understood it. "The grand-

25

parents were in bed — separate beds and rooms, but I'm assuming they were old and in poor health. The wife was cleaning up after breakfast, while the husband appeared to be about to leave the house. I think the aunt had just arrived and saw something — but didn't make it out of the house. She was running for the rear door, I believe. You'd figure she'd be the one shot in the back, but she wasn't. She was caught — and strangled. The different methods used to kill suggest there was more than one killer in here. What's odd is that the blood pools seem to be where the victims died. No one tracked around any blood, and there are no bloody fingerprints on the walls, not that I can see. Yes, we have blood spatter — all over the walls." He shook his head. "It should be the easiest thing in the world to catch this killer — or killers. He or she, they, should be drenched in blood. Except . . . your victim trying to escape via the back hallway was strangled. There's no blood on her whatsoever, and you'd think that if the same person perpetrated all the murders, there'd be blood on her, as well. Unless she was killed first, but that's unlikely. It looks like she was running away."

"So, the bottom line is . . ."

"Based on everything I'm seeing, I'm going to suggest more than one killer," Quinn said. "Still, they should be almost covered in blood — unless they wore some kind of protective clothing. Even then, you'd expect to find drops along the way. It seems that whoever did this killed each of these people where we found them — and then disappeared into thin air."

Larue stared at him, listening, following his train of thought. "You didn't tell me anything I don't already know," he argued.

"I'm not omniscient or a mind reader," Quinn said.

"Yes, but —"

"Your men should be searching the city for people with any traces of blood on them. It should be impossible to create a bloodbath like this and *not* have it somewhere. And the techs need to keep combing the house for anything out of the ordinary."

"This much hate — and nothing taken. Implies family, a disillusioned friend . . . or a psychopath who wandered in off the street. They say this kind of violence is personal, but there are plenty of examples to the contrary. To take a famous one, Jack the Ripper did a hell of a number on his last victim, Mary Kelly, and they believe that his victims were a matter of chance."

"They were a 'type,' " Quinn reminded

him. "Jack went after prostitutes. What 'type' could this family have been? My suggestion is that you learn every single thing you can about these people. Maybe something *was* taken."

"Nothing seems to have been disturbed. No drawers were open, no jewelry boxes touched."

Quinn nodded, glancing at his former partner. Larue was in his late thirties, tall and lean with a steely frame, dark, close-cropped hair and fine, probing eyes. There were things he didn't talk about; he was skilled at going on faith, and luckily, he had faith in Quinn.

"That's why I called you," Larue said. "I'm good at finding clues and in what I see." He lowered his voice. "And you, old friend, are good at finding clues in what we *don't* see. I'll have all the information, every file, I can get on these bodies in your email in the next few hours. Hubert said he'll start the autopsies as soon as he's back in the morgue."

"Mind if I walk the house again?" Quinn asked him. "There's something I want to check out."

"What's that?"

"Like I said, I'm surprised more blood wasn't tracked through the house. But what

I do see leads back to James Garcia."

"One would think — but you're trying to tell me that James Garcia butchered his family — and came back to the hall to slash himself to ribbons?"

"No, I'm not saying that. I agree with you that it's virtually out of the question. I'm just saying that the only blood trails there are lead back to him. There's no weapon he could have done this with, so . . . that tells me someone else had to be in the house. They got to the second floor first and murdered the grandparents, headed down to the kitchen and killed the wife, then caught either the aunt or James Garcia. But you'll note, too, that there's no blood trail leading out through the doors. Like I said, whoever did this should have been drenched. It seems obvious, but surely *someone* would've noticed another person covered in blood. Yes, this is New Orleans — but we're not in the midst of a crazy holiday with people wearing costumes and zombie makeup. And even if the killers *were* wrapped in a sheet or something protective, it's hard to believe they could escape without leaving a trace."

"What if they had a van or a vehicle waiting outside?" Larue asked.

"That's possible. But still . . . I'd expect

some drops or smudges as the killer headed out. I'm going to look around, okay?"

"Go for it — just keep your booties on and don't interrupt any of my techs. Oh, and, Quinn?"

"Yeah?"

"Thank God you're back."

Quinn offered him a somber smile. "Glad you feel that way."

He left Larue in the hallway, giving instructions to others, and supervising the scene and the removal of the bodies.

At first, Quinn found nothing other than what they'd already discovered. Of course, he was trying to stay out of the way of the crime scene unit. They were busiest in the house; he knew they'd inspected the garage but concentrated on the house, so he decided to concentrate on the garage.

He was glad he did. Because he came upon something he considered unusual.

It was in between two cans of house paint.

He picked up the unlabeled glass container and studied it for a long time, frowning.

There'd been something in it. The vial looked as if it had been washed, but . . .

There was a trace of red. Some kind of residue.

Blood? So little remained he certainly

couldn't tell; it would have to go to the evidence lockup and then get tested.

He hurried back in to hand it over to Grace Leon, Larue's choice for head CSU tech when he could get her. She, too, studied the vial. "Thanks. We would've gotten to this, I'm sure. Eventually we would've gone through the garage. But . . . is it what I think it is?"

He smiled grimly. "We'll have to get it tested. But my assumption is yes."

The giclée — or computer-generated ink-jet copy — first drew one's gaze from across the room because of its coloring and exquisite beauty.

Foremost in the image was a dark-haired gentleman leaning over a love seat where a beautiful woman in white lay half-inclined, reading. He could be seen mostly from the back, with only a hint of his profile visible, and he presented her with a flower. The scene evoked the type of mysticism and nostalgia that could be found in the work of the pre-Raphaelite painter John Waterhouse.

Movement, *life,* seemed to emerge from the image. It was complex; the viewer felt a sense of belonging in the scene, being part of a living environment.

Behind the love seat was a great hearth,

like that in the hall of a medieval castle. Above the hearth was a painting of a medieval knight, sans helmet; to each side of the image were massive plaques that bore the coat of arms of the House of Guillaume, with crossed swords below each. To the left, a massive stone staircase went up to the second floor and to the right, a hallway leading to another region of the castle, presumably the kitchens. It was guarded by a pair of 1500s suits of armor, standing like sentinels. And yet it felt like a scene of modern — nineteenth-century modern, at least compared to the medieval background of the castle — bliss.

Near the couple, on a massive wooden table, a boy of about twelve and a girl of maybe eight engaged in a game of chess. On the floor, a smaller child played with a toy. The pigments used were striking — even in the print, which was a copy of the original. Crimsons were deep and used throughout; the castle was dark and shadowed but the shadows were tinged with the same crimson and offset by mauves and grays. The little girl's clothing added a splash of blue. Just inside the giant doors to the far left in the painting, a silver-colored wolfhound barked as a proper butler opened the door to official-looking men about to make a call.

The allure of the courtly man and the beautiful woman first entranced the viewer. The scene was so lovely, so romantic.

The painting didn't, at first glance, seem to fit the title chosen by the artist — *Ghosts in the Mind.*

But then, even as the viewer studied the beauty and serenity of the scene, his or her perception of it would begin to change. If he or she shifted to a slightly different angle, looked at the painting from a different perspective, the hidden details became evident.

Beneath her book, the woman held a dagger. While he offered a rose to the woman, the man concealed a pistol behind his back.

A closer look revealed that malevolent, cunning eyes gazed out from the helmets on the suits of armor, both of which stood on pedestals but with swords in their hands.

The chess pieces had faces, alive and screaming.

The child on the floor played with a guillotine. What had appeared to be roses strewn over rushes on the floor were dolls — and their decapitated heads.

"Danni! Danni Cafferty, how are you? And Wolf!"

Danielle Cafferty turned as Niles Villiers,

owner of the Image Me This gallery, came toward her. Wolf, to her the world's most impressive pet, was seated by her feet. He was about the size of a small freight train but Wolf and Niles knew each other and Niles didn't so much as blink; well-behaved pets were welcome in his gallery.

And Wolf allowed himself to be petted and crooned to. He even thumped his tail for Niles.

"I love this dog, Danni," Niles said. "But I thought he actually belonged to your friend, Quinn? Haven't seen him around in a while."

"He has business in Texas," Danni explained. Niles looked at her a little sadly. "Too bad. I like that Quinn. Great guy. So the guy leaves you, but you get the dog?"

Danni started to protest; Quinn hadn't left her. After the case involving the Renaissance bust and the cult that had nearly formed in the city — the case that had brought them together — they'd both been afraid they'd gotten too close too fast. As a result, they'd decided to move slowly.

Quinn had gone to Texas a month ago to help the force there. He'd done it before when asked by law enforcement friends — or friends of friends — in other places. Usually he was only gone a few days. This time it seemed he'd been gone forever. But he'd made a decision never to leave her without Wolf. There was no question; the dog would lay down his life for her.

"At least he's an amazing dog!" Niles said.

"He sure is."

Niles greeted her next with an encompassing hug. She accepted it warmly. Niles was not only a friend, he'd been kind and generous enough to let her show her own art at his gallery on Royal Street. Image Me This was just a block and a half down from her own antiques and curio store, The Cheshire Cat. "Thanks for coming today," he said.

"You know me, Niles. List a gallery showing and I'll be here."

A waiter went by and Niles snagged two champagne flutes, giving one to her. "I did especially want you to come. You add an aura of the sleek and beautiful — of modern sophistication."

Danni smiled at that. "Niles, you should've told me I was supposed to be sophisticated. I'd have worn something other than jeans."

Niles waved a hand in the air. In a suit himself, he was extremely handsome, with his striking hazel eyes and olive skin. He was tall and slim, every inch the regal host. "My dear, even wearing a plastic garbage bag, you'd walk with an aura of mystery and class — and it doesn't hurt that you have a wolf at your feet. People are looking at paintings, but they're watching you, as well. And if *you* shop here, they'll think it's the place to buy."

"Hmm. Thank you. However, I think most of the credit goes to Wolf," Danni said. She set one hand on Wolf's head. Sometimes people gave her a wide berth — they were afraid of the dog. But he was so well-mannered that they usually asked if they could pet him. Wolf was, when not fiercely defending his family, a truly loving dog. Even if he was part wolf, as his name suggested.

Niles took a step closer to her, sipping from his champagne glass. "I have some wonderful original oils at this show, and, of course, I'd love to sell them. But a house in Paris was recently authorized to create giclée copies of *Ghosts in the Mind*. They're beautifully done, from the original, of course. Giclée is a way for people to own incredible works of art without having to rob banks or be millionaires themselves, and honestly, the quality is so good, it's almost impossible to tell the copies from the original."

Danni smiled. "That's not entirely true.

Yes, done well, they're as exact as you can get, but prints still don't compare to the real thing."

"Okay, maybe not, but . . . they're striking on a wall."

"And you can sell a lot of giclée copies and make money and survive, and I'm all for it," Danni assured him. "As long as the artist isn't cheated."

"Danni!"

"Oh, Niles, I'm sorry. I didn't mean that."

He grinned back at her. "When are we going to have another show of your paintings?" He shuddered. "Now that horrible case with the cult is well behind you."

Danni shrugged. She'd actually been working the past few weeks. Working on her painting — and on her life. It was barely a year ago that she'd discovered her father had led a secret existence before his death — and that she'd inherited not only his earthly goods, but his rather unearthly ones, as well.

Niles was referring, of course, to the case that focused on the bust of Pietro Miro. She'd known nothing about the nature of real evil when she'd first become entangled in that situation, and now she knew too much. Her father hadn't just been a collector of the priceless and unusual; he'd also been a warrior of sorts, saving others from the forces of evil. It made her feel, at times, as though she was dreaming about an odd graphic novel in which she simultaneously played a role. Before that strange case last year, she would never have believed that evil — or the wicked intentions of others — could reside in an object like Pietro Miro's marble bust.

"Sorry," Niles said quickly. "Maybe I shouldn't have asked. That nasty mess with the cult wasn't that long ago. And you were close to several people who turned out to be involved."

"I'm fine. That's all over. Billie, Bo Ray and I are doing well at the store," Danni told him. "And I'm always grateful for your interest and support, Niles."

"So. I have all these beautiful pieces in here — gorgeous street scenes, paintings of musicians so good you can practically hear them, the Mighty Mississippi, Jackson Square, the cemeteries and the French Quarter — and you head right over to the giclée of *Ghosts in the Mind.*" He raised his brows. "Back to *your* work for a minute. Let me remind you that we haven't seen anything in almost a year."

"I've been working. I don't have anything ready yet," Danni said.

"Well, let us know when you do. You're good," he added. "So is Mason. He just hasn't had the chance he needs. But his time will come . . . Meanwhile we can admire the giclée. It *is* beautiful. At a distance. And everyone's drawn in. Hubert was a talented artist, and this piece is different, even for him. He was fascinated by the dark side of things, but rarely did he come up with something that teased the eye with such exquisite beauty — only to display such wickedness in the, er, details?"

Danni nodded. "His *Weeping Angel at Dusk* is sad and dark, I guess, but very beautiful."

"You know something about the artist, right?"

"I was an art major, remember? I don't know too much, and he didn't paint that many pieces, since he died so young. But he's considered a relatively minor artist. He's hardly ever mentioned these days."

"That was true until recently," Niles said. "Because, of course, *Ghosts in the Mind,* his most famous work, went missing for years and was only discovered a few months ago — and sold at auction. There's a story to that, of course, but as to Hubert, well . . . like you said, he died young. We might have had so many more wonderful pieces had he lived longer. His use of perspective was extraordinary. Not many artists could create completely different images, pictures within pictures, in such an effective way."

"If I'm remembering my art history correctly, the original was oil on canvas and was painted in Switzerland during the summer of 1816. The world endured what they now refer to as 'the year without a summer,' " Danni said.

"Apparently, a natural climate change at that time was enhanced by the eruption of a volcano — Mount Tambora in the Dutch East Indies," Niles explained. "I got interested in this stuff because of *Ghosts in the Mind,* so I've been reading about it. Anyway, the volcano erupted in 1815 but the fallout changed the weather and the atmosphere all over Europe, even a year later. It snowed in June! In the United States, too," he said. "Anyway, that terrible weather caused a great many miserable days, but also brought about this wonderful, chilling piece of art."

"Don't forget, Mary Shelley's *Frankenstein* came out of that summer, too."

"Yes, yes, of course! And it was influenced by the fact that scientists all over were playing with electricity. Mary was familiar with some of the greatest scientific minds of her time. It's a brilliant book," he said in a reverent voice. "One that looked at what life was and what it wasn't . . . just like this painting looks at the masks we wear on the outside while we hide our real thoughts on the inside. Most critiques have agreed that this was Henry Sebastian Hubert's finest work. Pity, pity, pity!"

"He died by his own hand," Danni murmured.

Niles shook his head dismissively. "So said the bumbling authorities back then! Tragically, he was found in the tower where he was painting, seated before his masterpiece. They said it was poison. What did they know?" Niles demanded.

Danni laughed. "Probably a lot more than we suspect. Remember, anatomy was the rage back then. Corpses were stolen for dissection. . . . Burke and Hare were busy digging up corpses to sell and then killing people for the money their bodies would bring. They —"

"That wasn't until later," Niles interrupted.

"Yes, but they weren't the first," Danni said. "Different countries had different laws on acquiring corpses for medical purposes and learning about anatomy and so on. The thing is, by the early 1800s, doctors and scientists had been dissecting cadavers for centuries. Medical people couldn't cure most diseases, but they'd certainly learned about anatomy. Still, you have a point — he might have been poisoned and they might have missed it. But since Hubert was alone when he died, his fingers curled around the wineglass that held whatever toxin it was, I'm sure they were right, and he committed suicide. The poor man couldn't run to a doctor and get a prescription for an anti-depressant. Yes, it's a tragedy. Sadly, history is full of such tragedies. Shelley drowned in a lake and Byron was only in his thirties when he died. Mary Shelley lost three of her four children at very early ages — it was *all* very sad and tragic."

Niles still didn't seem convinced that anything was as sad as the death of an artist.

"So, did someone just license the painting for giclée reproduction?" she asked Niles.

"Like I was saying, the painting disappeared soon after Hubert died, reappeared in some kind of storage, in England, then ended up in a museum in France. It disappeared again during World War II."

"This sounds familiar. Wasn't it stolen by the Nazis?"

"Perfectly true!" Niles said excitedly. "It

seems an old Nazi war criminal died in Brazil within the past year, and the painting was found wrapped and buried in a vault. The Brazilian government returned it to the French museum, but the museum's having hard times and gratefully put it on the auction block. No one knows who purchased the original yet. These things can be so hush-hush and done through corporate names and all that. But the new owner authorized a gallery to make a copy, and from that copy, they were allowed to do a giclée limited edition of two thousand. And —" he lowered his voice as if he were speaking to a coconspirator "— there's a rumor that the purchaser was from here — from NOLA! I was incredibly lucky. I scored a hundred of them for the gallery. I've already sold sixty-six."

Danni studied the copy of the painting again. It was as interesting, as rich, as complex, as the human/monster tale about Dr. Frankenstein's creation.

"Shall I save one for you?" Niles asked.

Danni wasn't sure. On the one hand, the giclée of the painting *was* beautiful. It was also terribly dark and seemed to be a warning regarding human nature. Did a man smile and offer a rose while thinking of murder? Were children innocently playing, already on the way to cruelty and a callous disregard for life?

A lady in an elaborate feathered hat swept by to gain Niles's attention; he excused himself to Danni, winking as he did so. "I'll save one!" he promised.

"Great. Lovely. I can keep it with the coffin and guillotine and shrunken heads down in Dad's collection," she muttered to herself.

"Hey, Danni."

As she turned to leave, she almost crashed into Mason Bradley, Niles's sometime-salesman and sometime-artist. Mason's forte was restoration and he was very good at it. Like most artists, he worked on learning his own style by studying the masters and occasionally making copies. He was thirty-eight, tall, blond and handsome, and was working on establishing himself and making a name in the French Quarter by painting cemetery scenes. He had a special style, realistic yet slightly exaggerated, that made his paintings both poignant and eerie.

"Mason, hey, how are you?" she asked.

"Great, thanks. How about you? Are you doing any work? I know it's been hard for you since your dad died."

"I'm doing okay."

"I see you've got the dog — Wolf, right?"

Mason smiled at the dog but made no attempt to touch him. She wondered if he was afraid of Wolf or simply wasn't fond of dogs.

"Yes, Wolf."

"Well, I guess you got something out of the relationship when Quinn left. If you need to talk, get some coffee, go for a drink — have a shoulder to cry on — well, I'm here," he told her sympathetically.

She bent her head and couldn't help smiling. "I don't need to cry. Honestly. Quinn and I . . . He's in Texas."

"I'm glad. You deserve someone who . . . well, someone who's a little more . . . stable."

"I'm just fine, Mason."

"Enjoying the art of Hubert, I see."

"There's . . . nothing quite like it, is there?"

Mason stared at the giclée and nodded. "The story is that it was Hubert's entry into the 'ghost' contest that went on during the summer that wasn't a summer — that Lord Byron challenged him to paint something as frightening as anything they could write. He did a damned good job."

"I agree. Oh! Mason, I'm seeing more and more of your cemetery prints out there! You're doing great. The paintings are wonderful — and I'm delighted that the prints seem to be everywhere."

"Yes, but the paintings themselves don't always sell. People don't necessarily want to pay for an original. So I'm still a struggling artist, you know how that goes," Mason said. "But at least I'm not a starving artist." He took her empty champagne glass. "I guess I should get back to selling. I know we'll keep one of the Hubert giclées for you. Hey," he told her, lowering his voice as if sharing a confidence. "There's a rumor that the collector who bought the piece is here — right here in New Orleans!"

"Niles mentioned that."

"It's such a unique object," Mason said reverently. "Anyway, my dear friend, remember we love you, Niles and I. And don't forget, if you need me, I'm here!"

"Thank you." Danni smiled as Mason hurried away to attend to another customer and then found herself turning back to the giclée.

It was surpisingly difficult to tear herself away from *Ghosts in the Mind*. Determined, she finally did. Billie McDougall — her Ichabod Crane/Riff Raff lookalike and helper in all things — had been running the store alone. Bo Ray Tomkins, their clerk, hadn't been with them long, and generally worked on their bookkeeping and inventory, although he also assisted with sales when necessary. Billie didn't care if he manned the counter on his own, but still, she'd been gone for a few hours.

Danni waved a goodbye to Mason, who returned the gesture, and stepped out onto Royal Street, Wolf at her heels. The sun shone down on handsome balconies, some still wearing their Mardi Gras apparel or banners and ribbons and signs. Some sported chairs and plants with vines that seemed to trickle down, adding to the faded elegance that was so much a part of the French Quarter.

But just as she started to head back to her own shop, Wolf began to bark frantically and pull at his leash. He was very well trained, but so excited she was afraid he'd drag her across the street.

"Wolf!"

Then she realized that a figure was standing there, watching her.

He was wearing a light casual coat, perfect for the spring weather. It hung nicely on his six-four frame. He wore sunglasses and a brimmed hat, which hid his short sandy-blond hair and hazel eyes. But he smiled slowly, and she'd know that smile anywhere . . . just as she knew him.

Her heart quickened, and she felt exhilaration sweep through her.

She was deliriously happy to see him.

And yet . . .

His appearance made her tremble. *Was he back because he lived here, because he wanted to see her?*

Or was something about to happen?

Quinn.

Quinn had returned.

CHAPTER 2

Danni meant to greet Quinn with decorum. He'd been in Austin at the request of a friend in the police department there. She'd read what she could on the internet about the murder and spoken to him a few times on the phone, but they had determined that they weren't going to call each other every day, that they were going to take it slowly as far as their relationship went. They were both well aware that they'd face difficult situations as time went by.

The hell with decorum.

"Quinn!" She shouted his name and barely checked the road for cars before she went streaking across it.

The dog beat her to him. Wolf knew not to jump, but maybe he'd decided the hell with decorum, too. On his hind legs, the dog was the size of the man. Quinn gave him loving affection, calling him an old mutt, and then became the master, ordering him to sit. Wolf seemed to understand that he'd been assigned to watch Danni; Quinn would always be his real master.

So the dog and I both just wait for him to come back, Danni thought.

When Quinn looked at her, she tried very hard not to smile, to let him make the first move.

Then she couldn't resist anymore and threw herself into his arms. He caught her, lifted her, pulled her tight against him and met her with a kiss.

It was a decorous kiss, really.

However, some fool walking around them muttered, "Get a room!" And then someone else said, "Oh, Robbie, check that out!" and then a third person, presumably Robbie, said, "Hey, it's New Orleans!" Someone else sniggered and added, "But Bourbon Street's one over!"

Danni and Quinn listened, they laughed and they drew apart, still holding hands, looking each other up and down as if a few weeks could have changed the other and anxious to see that it hadn't.

No harm had come to Quinn, Danni concluded. He was perfect or, at least, perfect to her, over six feet, and as muscular as an athlete. His hazel eyes were vibrant, so alive, so well set in the classic structure of his face. He had a great jaw — a really great jaw. Square, the kind that made him appear to be in control on every occasion. And yet he had sensuous lips and the ability to laugh. She smiled, remembering a time when she'd actively *disliked* him. But that had been right after her father had died — and before she'd known exactly what her father had left her.

She pulled away, studying him. "Texas?" she asked.

"Very strange," he told her. "And sad."

"But it was solved?"

He nodded. "But there was really nothing *unusual* about the situation. It looked like the guy had killed himself. He had a vial of sleeping pills and a bottle of beer at his side, and there was no forced entry — nothing to indicate anything other than suicide."

"But you already knew it wasn't suicide."

"Yeah. The guy had been married for thirty years. Everyone thought that he and his wife were as happy as could be. They had a grown family, and husband and wife were both due to retire. But it turns out that he was the family dictator and had verbally abused them all for years. Still, the wife took it. But then he started using a cream for low testosterone and, apparently, the cream caused the wife to grow a beard.

I guess that was the final straw for her. He was sitting around watching TV and yelled at her to get him a beer. She brought him a beer, all right, and filled it up with the sleeping pills. She did everything correctly, called the police, said she'd been asleep and she came out and found him and . . ." He stopped to take a breath. "And she killed a man who'd probably dominated her and in a way tortured her for most of her life — because she just couldn't tolerate the hair on her face. Davy, the cop in Texas who called me, didn't like it from the beginning but couldn't prove she'd done it. When we did prove it, I don't think he was particularly happy."

"What'll happen to her?" Danni asked.

Quinn shrugged. "Hopefully, the courts will take her life into consideration."

"How *did* you prove it?"

"We went over and over the evidence. Her fingerprints were on the beer can, but of course they were on all the groceries in the house. Eventually, I simply asked her — and she broke down. It was probably a matter of timing, because Davy had questioned her repeatedly. When I asked, she was ready to confess. The woman wasn't a career criminal or a psychopath. She just couldn't take his abuse anymore."

Danni nodded. She'd greeted him; now she stood on the street feeling a little awkward. "So, you're home."

His eyes touched hers. "You told me to go," he reminded her softly. "You said we needed to make sure we were good at being apart."

Danni lowered her head and nodded again.

I wasn't good at it at all!

"So, yes, I went when a friend called. We solved the situation. I'm grateful, and I'm home. Except that I'd hardly gotten back before I was called in on a case here," he said.

"Oh?" Danni asked. "By . . . Larue?" When he was a cop in the city, Quinn had been partnered with Jake Larue. She was well aware that Larue kept a lot of his thoughts and opinions to himself, but if there was some out-of-the-ordinary crime, he knew he didn't have the special skills to comprehend what was behind it.

He *did know,* however, that there was something different about Quinn, and he was quick to call him when the situation warranted extra eyes — eyes that might see more deeply.

"Yeah, I'd only just dropped my bags at the house when he called. When we're off the street, I'll explain."

She heard the gravity in his voice. "Okay. Want to go to the shop?"

"I was on my way," he told her. She liked his awkward smile. "I drove back into the city and acted like a nice normal human being, thinking I wouldn't bolt over and scream your name like a character out of a movie. But what were you up to? Did I stop you from doing something?"

"I was just at my friend's gallery down the street — Image Me This," she said.

He glanced past her shoulder. "Ah, being an artist!" he teased.

"I do that now and then."

"Anything interesting there?"

"Very interesting. He has a number of pieces on display by local artists, and a remarkable giclée reproduction that's never been licensed before."

He was still looking at the gallery. Maybe he wasn't in any rush to tell her about this latest instance of man's inhumanity to man.

"Giclée?" he asked.

Danni explained, adding, "Giclée comes from *gicleur,* the French word for nozzle or spray. The term came about in the early nineties when certain specialized printers were developed. Want to see?"

"Sure."

"Good. I can show Niles and Mason that you didn't dump me, leaving me with the dog to soothe my broken heart."

"You're the one who thought we needed to take it slow."

"And you agreed." Danni hesitated a moment. "I still feel that way, except . . ."

"Except?"

"I'm not sure yet. You're here now. I'm glad. And I'm darned happy to go back into that gallery with you."

"Should I fawn all over you?" he asked.

"No, you should act normal!"

He reached out and took her hand and they headed across the street. Danni smiled, a sense of well-being washing over her.

Along with another chill.

Quinn was back.

And already . . . he'd been called in on something.

But she was pleased to walk into the gallery with Quinn. It had grown busier since she'd left. Of course, it was a Saturday morning in spring, a beautiful season in the city. A time when tourists loved to come. But spring-breakers tended to hang out more on Bourbon Street than in the galleries on Royal. However, Niles ran his business well and managed to attract a number of them.

Danni walked Quinn over to the Hubert giclée, Wolf trotting politely beside them. Quinn paused, frowning as he studied it. "It's a beautiful piece. I don't quite get . . . oh."

His frown deepened as he saw the image within the image, saw the weapons, saw how the children played.

"Wow." He turned to Danni.

She smiled in response. "There's a fascinating history to the real painting. Hubert was part of a very bohemian crowd in the early 1800s. He was friends with Byron, Shelley and crew. I don't know if you recall, but Mary Shelley wrote *Frankenstein* after she, Percy Shelley, Lord Byron and another man, Dr. Polidori, spent part of an exceptionally overcast, cold summer together in Switzerland. Anyway, it was dark and gloomy and they read old German ghost stories and came up with their own. They went to visit Henry Sebastian Hubert, the artist, and talked him into joining their game. But while they'd describe a scenario with words, he'd do it with paint."

"The guy was obviously talented."

"He was, but he died soon after painting this."

"He might've been one sick puppy, too, psychologically speaking. How did he die?"

"He was found in a tower room in the medieval castle he'd rented, staring at the painting — this painting — dead. He'd taken poison," Danni told him. "Or . . . some believe he'd been *given* poison. No one could ever prove it either way."

"Hmm. He might've been a victim of depression. Or he might have had more enemies than he realized. Or — another possibility — he might have overdone the drugs and alcohol. What do you think?"

"I've taken a lot of art history in my day but I never had a class in which anyone could explain the mysteries of the human mind. And if scientists could figure *that* out — well, the pharmaceutical companies might go out of business!"

Quinn frowned again as he looked at the painting, angling to one side.

"What?" Danni asked.

"Hubert," he said. "I suppose it's a common enough name."

"I'd say so."

"French in origin?"

"Probably," Danni said. "Hubert was an English citizen. His father was an Englishman. His mother was Norwegian. But even by then, names could be deceptive. The French lived in England, the English lived in France, and had for centuries. Plus, people vacationed all over. Why the interest in the name?"

Quinn raised one shoulder in a shrug. "This sounds funny, of course, because we all wish there wasn't any need for medical examiners, but my favorite M.E. in the city is named Hubert. You've met him."

"That's right!" Danni said. "I hadn't thought of that." It was her turn to shrug. "But there are Quinns and Caffertys all over, too, and we don't know about the majority of them. If we *are* related it's from hundreds of years ago."

"I'm just curious," Quinn said. "I left Hubert a little while ago. Now I'm seeing a painting by a different Hubert."

"Odd coincidence, I guess."

"Michael Quinn!" Niles seemed to float across the room as he came toward them. He squinted at Danni, as if unconvinced that she'd told him the truth before. "You're back in town. Lovely. Are you here for long?"

"I'm not sure, but I always come back. New Orleans is home. I have a house in the Garden District, Niles."

"Yes, of course, I'd forgotten," Niles said. "But you're here now. In my gallery. What do you think? Isn't the giclée just incredible?"

"Yes," Quinn murmured. "Incredible . . ."

"I told Danni I'm saving one for her. I'll get it wrapped up for you tonight, Danni."

"Uh, thanks. That's great," Danni said. She didn't want to decline the giclée; it was beyond doubt a piece by a famous — and infamous — artist. And it was decidedly unique. Unusual.

It was also creepy, and she had enough creepy in her life.

But Niles was beaming, so glad he could provide her with such a treasure, and she had no intention of hurting his feelings.

"How do you tell a copy from the real thing?" Quinn asked.

"For one thing," Danni replied, "Copies likes this — giclées — are numbered. The one on the wall is number 480 out of 2000."

"Yes, it's like buying a print — except better," Niles crowed.

"I see. More or less," Quinn said. "No, I do understand, and a copy would work just fine for me. Sadly, I don't know that much about art."

"Well, copies of all kinds *are* fine. Ah, but to have the real thing . . ." He sighed. "Well, anyway, I don't. Someone rich does. Hey, enough about other artists! When she's ready, Danni will do another show here," Niles told Quinn.

"Let's hope," Quinn said, meeting her eyes, "that she'll be ready soon."

They left after exchanging goodbyes with Niles and walked down Royal Street toward *The Cheshire Cat,* Danni's shop and home. Although she'd gone away for college and at various times had her own apartment, she'd moved back into her childhood home for good when her father died.

And when she discovered exactly what he'd kept in the basement.

She and Billie had recently restructured the shop area of the eighteenth-century house. She'd created a beautiful life-size image of a banshee for a jewelry line she was selling for a friend, and it was near the entry, with its various Celtic designs. She'd also added shelving for her "Gargoyles!" collection. Naturally she offered the customary New Orleans souvenirs — Saints T-shirts, beads and gris-gris bags and a line of "Voodoo for Love!" voodoo dolls that were adorable. You pricked the cloth body with a little needle that tattooed a kiss onto it for luck, love, happiness. . . .

But some things in the store had stayed the same — the replicated King Tut mask, for one, the cardboard cutouts of Bela Lugosi as Dracula and Vincent Price as Dr. Phibes and a few other pieces. Mostly, she sold specialty items, including antiques. The store was always spotlessly clean, slightly Goth, slightly vampire-themed — and as much fun and as intriguing as she could make it. When buyers stopped in, they could spend a dollar for a few plastic beads or a fortune for real art, antique pieces or jewelry. Danni's father — cast by the fates from the Highlands of Scotland to New Orleans — loved his adopted city. Shops should be different and unusual, he believed. Places people wanted to come back to, just like they wanted to come back to Bourbon Street for revelry, Frenchman Street for great local music, Jackson Square for art. . . .

The Cheshire Cat was special, Danni thought. Her father had purchased the building when he'd fallen in love with her mother. The place had been a home in the early 1700s, one of the only structures to survive the fires that had nearly destroyed the city later in the century. It still had a courtyard and the typical U or horseshoe shape of so many New Orleans homes and she loved every inch of it.

When she and Quinn entered, Billie was sitting behind the counter, actually a glass display case for jewelry. He'd been reading but when the door opened and he saw

Quinn, he jumped to his feet, hurrying around. "Quinn, you're back, man!" After years in the United States, Billie's Scots brogue remained strong.

He pumped Quinn's hand, stood awkwardly for a minute, then threw both arms around him. Then he quickly stepped back, his expression anxious. "Oh. Oh?"

Danni understood the way Billie looked at Quinn. He was glad to see him; he was afraid to see him. While they'd had some quiet times over the past months, if Quinn was here, *something* could be going on. And, given that Larue had already called him, something was. . . .

"I got back last night. Finished in Texas," Quinn said. "I came in really late so I went straight to my house."

"Everything all right?" Billie asked.

"It was last night. But this morning . . . bad scene in the city. A family massacred."

"Oh," Billie said. "Oh." His shoulders slumped. "I haven't seen the news today."

"It might have been a domestic situation," Quinn added.

Billie was obviously skeptical. "Domestic, eh?" He turned to Danni. "Bo Ray took a breather — he's gone to pick up some groceries. As soon as he's back, I say we walk over to Natasha's and after that, we get Quinn to tell us what went on at the 'domestic' situation."

Quinn glanced at his watch. They could just have called Natasha, but it would be better to see her. "Sounds like a plan, Billie. But I say we meet here after seven, when the shop closes. If Bo Ray's buying groceries, we can whip up something to eat and I'll tell you what I know — which might be a little more than I know now. I'm due at autopsy. I didn't realize I'd spent so much time looking at art."

"Looking at art?" Billie repeated.

"One piece in particular. It's a very . . . unusual piece," Danni said. "But we're getting a copy. It's a giclée."

"A what?"

"An ink-jet copy — almost as good as the original." Quinn winked at Danni. She doubted he'd been familiar with giclée prints until that day.

Billie just shook his head. Danni smiled. She loved Billie; he'd been devoted to her father. He was devoted to her now. And to The Cheshire Cat.

"It's a pity we looked at art for so long." Quinn said, his lips twitching with humor — and a secret message meant only for her.

She grinned wickedly, indulging him. "Go. We'll see you back here."

He nodded, turned to leave the shop. As he did, he nearly bumped into Bo Ray Tompkins, a young man who now worked at the shop as a clerk and bookkeeper. He'd been a suspect in their first investigation. Now, he was clean of drugs and grateful, and a reliable member of their staff.

Bo Ray was excited to see Quinn, too. He almost dropped the grocery bags he was carrying. Quinn grabbed and saved one and they all wound up on the counter.

"Quinn!"

Bo Ray said the word with such adulation that Danni had to laugh. He hadn't even noticed she was there.

"Bo Ray, great to see you!" Quinn said. "Things are going well?"

Bo Ray looked over at Danni. "You bet — Danni's the best. And Billie, too, of course! Hey, I'll have a Scottish accent myself in a few more weeks!"

Quinn laughed. "See you all tonight," he said, and headed out.

"He's really back!" Bo Ray said, delighted. Clean-shaven, his hair still on the long side, his clothing clean and neat, Bo Ray was darned good-looking. He was excellent with their customers, too, charming them easily. Danni's philosophy — which had also been her father's — was that they did far more business by making people like the shop than they did by trying to sell things every minute. That way, people remembered the place; if they weren't ready to buy, they came back. If they just wanted to look, they were welcome. "Ohhh!" he said, his mouth a circle. "Does that mean . . ."

"It means he finished working in Texas, but there's been a murder here — several murders, a family — and he's going into autopsy."

"Ohhh," Bo Ray said again.

"Maybe not 'ohhh,' " Danni said. "Bad things happen in any big city. Drug deals go wrong and we sure as hell haven't stamped out domestic violence. Anyway, I'll get Natasha over for dinner tonight. Then we'll talk."

"And we're just . . . We're just supposed to keep working until then? Keep the shop open? Smile and greet customers? Act like nothing's happened?" Bo Ray asked.

"Exactly," Billie said, clapping a hand on Bo Ray's shoulder. "Now, get the groceries into the kitchen. You're messin' with the gargoyles here!"

Danni laughed. "Children, play nicely. I'm leaving now to drop in on Natasha." Wolf barked. She could swear the dog understood her words. Wolf loved Natasha and the courtyard at her shop.

"Oh, Wolf, I'm sorry. I want you to stay here and help the boys, okay?"

Wolf whined; he not only loved Natasha, he took his role as Danni's bodyguard seriously.

She stroked his head and slipped out the door, leaving the dog with Billie and Bo Ray.

Danni walked down to St. Ann and then up toward Bourbon to Natasha's shop.

Quinn was taken directly back to the largest autopsy room at the morgue. Ron Hubert was already at work. The doctor's assistant offered Quinn a gown and mask — suggesting he'd definitely need the mask — and led him in.

The five bodies had been cleaned and prepped and were in a row on scoured steel autopsy tables. The scent of disinfectant was heavy in the air, but it didn't dispel the metallic scent of blood. The smell of decomposition already sat beneath that of the chemicals.

Hubert, his face protected by a full-cover plastic mask, stood by the body of James A. Garcia. The Y incision had been made and Hubert was recording his findings in an even, modulated tone that was picked up by the hanging microphone above the body.

He reached into the pocket of his white medical jacket to switch off the procedural recording as he saw Quinn walk into the room.

"You got here fast," he said.

"No time like the present," Quinn remarked. "Anything?"

"Well, as you can see, I've just begun the preliminaries. Jackson and Coe, two of my assistants, have bathed and prepped the bodies and so far I've made a few observations. Strange, my friend, strange indeed. I feel as if I've been cast into a gruesome version of the board game Clue. Follow me, and I'll explain," Hubert said.

He stopped in front of another gurney. "Andrea Garcia, I believe, was the first to be attacked. She was in the kitchen — and it's my contention that she was assaulted by a machete or a sword. The blade was long and broad. There are no defensive wounds on her hands or arms so I don't think the poor woman had the slightest idea that she was about to be attacked."

He moved on. "This was Maggie Santander. Since she was viciously bludgeoned to death, we see very little of her face. Oddly, I'm almost certain that both women died first. Usually, a murderer like this would dispatch the men immediately, wanting to disable the stronger of the victims so they wouldn't have to tackle them in a fight. What she was struck with I don't know — a heavy object. I haven't found splinters or metal chips or any telltale sign of the weapon used."

Quinn felt his jaw tighten; what had been done to the grandmother was gut-wrenching. She really had no face. "Luckily, my boy," Hubert said, "I believe she died instantly. The blunt force crushed her skull and bone shards went into the brain. However," he said, moving again, "her husband died the most easily — a single gunshot dead-center to the head. No bullet in him or found at the scene, according to the police. But I still say he was lucky. He probably never knew what hit him."

"Small mercies," Quinn said.

"In this situation? Yes." Hubert walked on to the next table. The woman lying there was pale and ashen; her lips were a sickly shade of blue. Hubert opened one of her eyes. "Petechial hemorrhaging in the eyes, the bruising around the neck. As we'd ascertained at the scene, this young woman was strangled and with great force. But I've looked at the bruising with a microscope. She was manually strangled, but there's no indication whether the killer was left- or right-handed. As you saw at the house, it *appears* that she walked into the midst of the carnage and was caught before she could escape. Now, let's return to Mr. Garcia."

Hubert went back to the first body. "Here's where it's curious. Mr. Garcia was right-handed. It almost looks as if the wounds were self-inflicted. See how the cuts are on the left side of the body? And the deeper wounds, the stab wounds, are all toward the left. Even where his throat is slit. It *could* indicate that the man took a knife or a similar blade himself and swept it across his own throat in a left-to-right motion. There was also a great deal of blood on his right hand. However, at that point, he would've instantly lost so much blood that I estimate death would have occurred in under a minute — certainly not enough time to stash the weapon. And, of course, he couldn't have gone far," Hubert added dryly.

Quinn stared at him. "So?" he asked.

"So, I'm the medical examiner. You're the investigator."

"What you're telling me is basically impossible. And yet based on what you've said — and what we discovered at the house — it *looks* like James Garcia got hold of a machete or a sword and sliced his wife to pieces in the kitchen. Then he moved around the house, dripping blood, found a heavy object and killed his mother-in-law with it, then found a gun and shot his father-in-law. After that, he headed downstairs, and strangled Maria Orr. Then he walked down the hall and stabbed himself several times before cutting his own throat and dying." Quinn shook his head. "Pretty damned impossible. I don't buy it."

"Me, neither."

"So, there *had* to be someone else there."

"That's what I'm assuming. Especially since there are no weapons."

"So, someone went to the house with weapons, gave them to James Garcia, who murdered his family and committed suicide, and then took the weapons away?" Quinn asked cynically.

"That's how it seems." Hubert sighed deeply. "But, as I told you, I'm the medical examiner. You're the investigator."

"Has Larue been here yet?"

"He's due anytime."

Quinn felt a chill seep slowly into him. There was obviously something not right about the situation; Larue had known that immediately and that was why he'd called Quinn.

70

"Are you waiting for him?" Hubert asked.

"No. There's not much point. I'm sure he's working on backgrounds, but I don't think this is about drugs, or a family feud or anything . . ."

"Ordinary?"

Quinn felt his brow furrow as he studied the bodies, then glanced back at Hubert. "Odd. You see a macabre game of Clue. I saw a strange painting this morning — or a copy of it — that this brings to mind."

"Oh," Hubert said. "Yeah. The Henry Sebastian Hubert. *Ghosts in the Mind.*"

"You know the painting?" Quinn asked.

"Of course."

"Of course?"

"Believe it or not, I do enjoy art," Hubert said. "But that's not why I know that particular painting."

"You *are* a descendant?" Quinn said.

"Sure am," Hubert said, grimacing.

"But . . ."

"I don't know how many 'greats' I am. The man was as bohemian as his friends. He had a wife he left in London. She had a child. That child had a child — you know how it goes. Anyway, my grandfather came to Minnesota and that's where I lived until I came here. But, yes, I'm a descendant. And I'm sure of my facts because my mother was something of a family historian."

"Now that's a bizarre coincidence!"

"What's really bizarre is that you saw the painting — or a copy of it. Hubert was talented but became obscure. I guess there's been a revival of interest in his work, especially that piece. It has a long tangled history."

"I heard some of it, and *tangled* is an understatement," Quinn said. "Did you know there's a copy — a giclée — at a shop on Royal Street?"

"Interesting. I'll have to go by and see it. But right now I have a lot of work to do. Is there anything else I can tell you?"

Quinn shook his head slowly. "No, not now, thanks, Doc. I'll see Larue later and find out what he's learned so we can decide how we're going to pursue this."

Hubert nodded grimly. "Get this bastard — whether he killed the family, which is the most likely, or forced Garcia to kill them. He's evil. Totally, heinously evil. Get him."

Quinn left, stripping off his gown and mask. But as he hurried down to the street and his car, he found his mind twitching in different directions.

A game of Clue.
A painting of domestic bliss that wasn't.

And someone — *something* — evil and alive in the city he loved.

CHAPTER 3

Natasha, also referred to as Mistress Labelle, was a renowned voodoo priestess in
the Quarter. Danni had known her as long
as she could remember — and loved her
like a wonderful, eccentric aunt for every
one of those years.

These days she realized that Natasha had
more than just an understanding of people.
Natasha's faith was strong. She knew that
spirits traveled in the world — and everything wasn't plainly visible for the eye to
see.

But Natasha also lived in the real world.
Her shop was filled with wonders. The scent
of incense flowed throughout; there were
handcrafted masks on display, along with
other artwork, jewelry and all kinds of gris-
gris, since Mistress LaBelle catered to tourists, as well as the devout of her flock.

Natasha had a trusted wingman — Jeziah,
who was at the counter when Danni entered

the shop. He looked up when the door opened. As a few tourists clustered in a corner, choosing a mask, Jeziah smiled at her.

Jeziah was often quiet and stoic but he saw everything that went on around him. Danni knew that he gave his total loyalty to Natasha; Jez, she thought, could have done anything in life. He was intelligent and compassionate. He was also striking, his skin a beautiful dark shade and his eyes a brilliant green. Jeziah moved fluidly and with purpose and seemed able to converse on any subject. He was a good friend to have.

"She's waiting for you," Jez told her before she'd come even two feet into the store.

"You're kidding me," Danni said.

Jez shrugged. "Do I ever kid? She had a dream about you."

"Oh?"

"She's waiting."

Danni could quiz him, but she knew he wouldn't say any more, so she merely thanked him and walked out to the court-yard.

There were many beautiful courtyards in the Quarter. Danni particularly loved Natasha's. Plants grew everywhere, adorned with wind chimes and dream catchers. She kept candles burning by her wrought-iron table, since she gave readings there, usually at night. She was pricey when tourists came calling, but a session with Mistress LaBelle was considered a coup.

Natasha didn't rise when she saw Danni arrive. She beckoned her to the table where she sat, a burning sconce on either side.

Danni took the seat opposite her. Natasha had set out two cups of tea.

"Where's Wolf?" she asked.

"With Billie and Bo Ray," Danni said, shaking her head. "How do you know when I'm coming?"

Natasha met her eyes. She was beautiful in a grand way, with nearly perfect bone structure and an ageless face. Tonight she wore a red-and-orange turban that complemented her orange robe and dark mahogany skin.

"The air tells me, child. The air . . . you can feel the crackle when something's up in the city." She paused. "I've also seen the news. There was a massacre today."

Danni nodded. "I don't know much about it yet."

"But Quinn was there, at the site."

"Yes. That's why I'm here. He thought you might want to come to my place around seven. We'll have a meal and talk about it. We —"

"Drink your tea," Natasha interrupted.

"Pardon?"

"Drink your tea."

Natasha was renowned for her palm reading, her insightful reading of tarot cards — and tea leaves.

Danni shouldn't have been surprised by Natasha's insistence. One way or another, she could "read" any situation.

"Drink up. I have to see what there is to see."

"This isn't like the situation we had with the bust last year," Danni said "There's no object that we know of associated with any of this. Quinn was called in by Larue. It may not have anything to do with me."

"There's going to be an object. We just don't know what it is yet. So drink up."

Danni sighed but dutifully drank the tea. When she'd finished, Natasha took her cup and studied the leaves. She shook her head and made a tsking sound; before Danni could groan or ask what she'd seen, she leaned back in her chair, eyes closed.

Then her lids opened, but her eyes were rolled back and only the whites were visible. Danni was about to spring to her feet, about to call for Jez. But before she could,

Natasha started speaking. "So much darkness! I see that the day is dark, there are clouds, and there is no rain, and then there is rain — thunder and lightning! Death spewed from the earth, darkness covered much of the globe. In the shadows, in the corners, in the most stygian places . . . evil was born. There was one who knew, and he guided the other, and there was a bright stain of blood against the darkness . . . and it's coming here. It's coming to New Orleans."

Natasha's head fell forward. Danni did spring to her feet then, rushing around to touch her friend. Natasha lifted her head and stared at Danni.

"Are you all right?" Danni asked urgently. "I've never — I've never seen you do anything like that! What's going on? Do you know what you said?"

Natasha patted Danni's hand where it lay on her shoulder. "I'm fine . . . and yes, I saw . . . I heard my voice. This has happened to me a few times. . . ."

"You might need a doctor, Natasha —"

"I'm fine, Danni. Sit, please."

Danni took her seat again, studying Natasha worriedly. Her skin had grown a little ashen, but she appeared to be in control.

"What did that mean?"

"It means that something very, very bad is in the city. It's a good thing Quinn's back. We'd have to send for him if he wasn't," Natasha said.

"But . . . what is it?"

"I don't really know. I just saw the sky, and it looked as if there'd been a great storm, and then there *was* a great storm . . . but when the rain went away, the sky was still dark."

"Okay . . . we'll check the weather?" Danni said hopefully.

Natasha gave her a disapproving frown. "Something is coming," she repeated. "And I don't think it's another storm, another Katrina. Storms are real. They kill, ruin, devastate, but we know them. They're forces of nature and they can be understood. This is different."

"Did you see anything else?" Danni asked.

Natasha was silent for a minute.

"Natasha!"

Natasha nodded. "I saw . . . you."

Quinn was eager to get back to The Cheshire Cat and Danni when he left the morgue, but before he'd gone very far, his phone rang. He answered on his hands-free unit. It was Larue.

"Where are you?" Larue asked.

"Heading back to the French Quarter. Hubert said you were due at autopsy," Quinn replied.

"Yeah, well, there's been another situation."

Quinn's grip tightened on the wheel.

Five already dead and there was another situation?

He had to clear his throat before he could speak. "How many?" he croaked.

"Nobody's dead. This is different. Can you get to the station?"

None dead. He let out a sigh of relief.

"Uh, sure."

Twenty minutes later he arrived at the station. Larue was there to meet him at the reception desk.

"What took you?" he demanded irritably.

"Uh, let me see? This area is filled with one-way streets, construction — oh, and we block off a few of our one-way streets now and then to accommodate fairs, wine tastings and musicians? Oh, yeah, and then there are the tourists who wander into the street. I always try to avoid hitting them."

Larue wasn't amused. "My office. Come on."

Quinn followed Larue down a hallway to his office. As usual, a few of those who'd overpartied were being booked, some still grinning sloppily, some sobering up far too quickly and realizing the trouble they'd gotten themselves into. There was one kid, wearing a college football jersey, Quinn was sure he recognized.

"Up-and-coming quarterback," he said quietly as they walked. "What did the kid do?"

"Thought one of the horses being ridden by a mounted patrol officer was making fun of him," Larue said.

"And?"

"He punched the horse."

"Horse okay?"

"Yeah, the kid will be, too. His parents are coming down."

They went into Larue's office. A man in uniform was sitting in front of Larue's desk, his head in his hands. He glanced up when Quinn and Larue entered the room.

The cop was about forty and appeared to be in generally good health. Except that he looked haggard and drawn, as if he hadn't slept for a week straight and had faced every demon in hell. Quinn thought he seemed familiar. He also looked as if he'd been in a fight; there were scuff marks on his clothing and a bruise under his eye that promised to become a massive shiner.

Larue sat on the corner of his desk.

"Quinn, this is Officer Dan Petty. Dan's been with the force for fifteen years. He's received medals for his extraordinary valor in times of stress. He was here for the aftermath of Katrina and the summer of storms. Dan, Michael Quinn. You two might've met years ago. Quinn was with the force for a while."

Dan Petty nodded at the introduction. He started to get up to meet Quinn, then fell back into the chair. As he watched Quinn, a certain expression came into his eyes — a spark of hope.

"Yeah, I remember you!" he said. "You're that football hero who died and then became a cop!"

"I was a cop, and now I'm a private investigator," Quinn responded.

"But you really died, huh?"

"I was resuscitated."

"Yeah, but still . . ." To Petty, it was clearly a good thing. He might have been clinging to the hope that Quinn knew the secrets of the universe.

"Dan, do you want to tell Quinn what happened?" Larue suggested.

"There was something there . . . something in the evidence lockup. Something that wasn't right," Petty said. He swallowed. He'd probably tried to explain himself a few times now and hadn't done well.

Petty grimaced. "It was coming at me . . . It was . . . well, you know how the fog sets over Lake Ponchartrain and it's so damned misty you can't see anything but shapes? The room was filled with the stuff . . . gray, with black shadows. It . . . it touched me. The gunk touched me and it was jerking me around and . . . I couldn't stop it! I couldn't stop it — I couldn't control my own muscles, my own body — it was *in* me, do you understand? The damned gunk was *in* me. I started picking up confiscated knives and guns and then . . ."

"Then?" Quinn encouraged.

"I screamed. I was so damned scared and . . . then I felt that things were on me . . . trying to kill me."

"His fellow officers, at that point." Larue spoke in a low voice.

"They got me out eventually," Petty said, looking at Larue. "I'm sorry. I hope those guys know . . ."

"They know," Larue reassured him. He turned back to Quinn. "The other officers corroborate what Officer Petty just said. They *swear* there was some kind of fog in the evidence lockup."

Quinn nodded. "So, did any of them stay behind?"

"There are men there now, three of them. The fog dissipated."

"You saw it, too?" Quinn asked.

"Don't know what it was, but I saw it, yes."

"All right. I'll talk to these guys, see what they have to say," Quinn said. He patted Officer Petty on the knee. "Something bizarre happened in there. No need to feel like a crazy man. I'll take a look and see if I can figure out what went on."

"You're not just, uh, patronizing me, are you?" Petty asked.

"I don't patronize anyone," Quinn told him. "Did you hear voices? Did you hear anyone speaking? Could you see *anything* in the fog?"

Petty shook his head. "No . . . just black within shadows, if that makes any sense. And — and I couldn't stop myself. I've never had a stroke . . . I'm in great health. I don't know . . . I just don't know."

Quinn glanced over at Larue. He wondered what his friend was thinking and quickly found out when Larue said, "I came in at the tail end when everything was pure chaos. But . . ."

"But?" Quinn prodded.

"But as I said, I saw it, too. Fog. Like the fog you get when the weather's about to change and you know there might be a storm on the horizon. At first, although I couldn't smell smoke, I thought there'd been a fire. It was a mess. Hell, maybe *my* mind's going . . . except that if it was some hallucination, we were all affected."

"Was anything missing?"

"The first assessment we made was on confiscated weapons," Larue said. "All accounted for. The crew in there now is still checking."

"I think I should see the evidence room," Quinn said.

Larue nodded and then returned his attention to Officer Petty. "Dan, you know you'll need to spend an evening in the . . . the hospital for assessment yourself, right?" Larue asked gently.

"A night in the loony bin," Petty said. "I don't care. Anywhere except the evidence lockup."

Larue gestured at the doorway. There was a man in some kind of medical uniform waiting. Petty rose and shook Quinn's hand. "Thank you. Thank you for listening. And you . . . you weren't even here. You didn't see. Thank you for believing."

Quinn nodded gravely.

Petty left the room; one of Larue's men was outside the office, too, ready to accompany the medical man and Officer Petty.

"What do you think?" Larue asked Quinn.

"I think you're going to find something missing from your evidence room. We have to determine exactly what it is."

"You mean someone was trying to break in?"

"Break in — or break out. I'm not sure which," Quinn replied. But he immediately thought of the Garcia murders and the evidence that might have been taken from the house. . . .

"Look for a little glass jar," he said. "Like a vial."

"What's in it?" Larue asked.

"I don't know, since it was empty — except for a trace of . . . something. Anyway, Grace and I felt it needed to be tested. But, whatever it was, I think the killer brought it to the house with him. And I'll bet it's gone."

Danni returned to the shop, but she didn't stay. She smiled cheerfully at Billie and Bo Ray and promised she'd be back — and they should plan for a nice dinner party. Billie just nodded. Bo Ray, relatively new to their team, still looked anxious.

She told them she was going to drop in on Father Ryan and invite him over for dinner. She could call him, of course, but this way, even if he couldn't come that evening, she'd get a chance to see him.

Bo Ray, who'd gained a life thanks to the priest, seemed to like the fact that Father Ryan might be coming to visit.

They'd actually met Bo Ray because he'd been a suspect when people started dying during the Pietro Miro case. Sadly, he'd become caught up in it all, an alcoholic in the early stages of liver failure. Quinn had a good eye for people, just as Father Ryan did. They'd both seen that Bo Ray could be saved. He'd become a great asset to the store — and to their lives, Danni thought.

With Wolf in the car this time, Danni started out.

Father Ryan ministered well to his flock, gave great sermons, tended to the poor and downtrodden and did everything that a priest should do. He even looked like the perfect priest. Middle-aged with snow-white hair, big and brawny but possessing a gentle manner, he seemed to inspire trust. He was also a no-nonsense man, unafraid to take a stand. Willing to confront the unknown . . .

Father John Ryan was standing at the front door of the rectory, almost as if he was waiting for someone, when Danni drove up and parked on the street. He didn't seem surprised when she and Wolf got out of her car and approached him.

"You knew I was coming," she said.

"I did."

Danni offered him a curious half grin. "You speak with the Almighty?"

"I do."

"Oh?"

He smiled ruefully. "I speak with Him the same as you and every other man and woman out there, Danni. Actually, I knew you were coming for a far more mundane reason — Natasha called me."

"Ah! But I didn't tell her I was going to see you."

"That's where instinct kicks in," Father Ryan told her. "But I had a feeling you or Quinn would be by soon enough. I heard about the massacre this morning."

"I believe the police are looking into Garcia's financials and other records," Danni said. "It's the type of thing that could happen if a big drug deal went wrong."

Father Ryan shook his head fiercely. "There was no drug deal gone wrong, Danni. I'm sure of that."

"How?"

"You and Wolf come on in. I'll tell you what I can."

"You know something?"

"Let's have tea, shall we?"

Father Ryan didn't want to be rushed. She and Wolf followed him into the rectory kitchen. First, Wolf got treats; Father Ryan kept them on hand just for him. Then, he put the kettle on and took his time setting out cups. Only when the tea was brewed and they sat down to drink it did he start talking. "James and Andrea Garcia were my parishioners. I've already been called in by social services — I'm helping place the children with relatives. This is a terrible blow. There are three children left behind — a ten-year-old, an eight-year-old and a five-year-old. The two older kids were James and Andrea's and the youngest was the aunt's little girl. Luckily, Andrea has another sister and brother in the city and they're doing their best to comfort and care for the children, but . . . well, the only good thing about the situation is that the children weren't there."

"I'm so sorry. I had no idea you knew these people," Danni murmured.

Father Ryan nodded. "There was no drug deal," he said again. "And don't tell me we don't know what people are really like. James Garcia was a hardworking man. He was with the same company for years. He made deliveries for one of the most trusted services in our city and there was never a single complaint against him. His wife took care of her family — her parents lived with them — and neither Andrea nor James ever minded any burden put upon them. That family did nothing wrong."

"The police are investigating. It won't ease things for the children, but hopefully justice will be done."

"And what are *you* doing about it?" Ryan demanded, looking her hard in the eyes.

"What *can* I do? There's no indication that an object might be involved, not like the Pietro Miro case, Father." Before Father Ryan could protest, she continued. "Quinn just got back last night. He was called to the scene this morning. But that's why I'm here. Can you come to dinner at my place around seven tonight? Quinn wants all of us there to discuss what happened."

"Yes, of course," he said. "I promise you this isn't a random murder. Nor is James Garcia part of it. Something isn't right here — aside from the obvious, I mean. James Garcia was a good man who spent his life hauling packages and received commendations from his employer. His wife was a model of virtue. And the parents . . . hard workers, retired, enjoying their last years with the grandkids. The old man didn't have much time left as it was — cancer. They'd given him six months."

"I'm so sorry, Father Ryan," Danni said again.

He drummed his fingers absently on the table. "What I'm afraid of is that we all may wind up much sorrier. Danni, we *have* to find out what the hell is going on here."

"Dr. Hubert is a descendant of the Hubert who painted the original of the giclée at your friend's gallery," Quinn told Danni, setting plates on the table. The meal Billie had prepared, his version of the classic jambalaya, simmered on the stove.

She stopped patting dry the lettuce she'd just washed and looked over at him. They'd decided to get dinner ready and wait until Natasha and Father Ryan arrived to discuss the situation, so she was surprised that he'd brought up the painting. She'd reported that Father Ryan had known the Garcia family well and that he strenuously denied they could've been doing anything illegal. And Quinn had said only that the autopsy reports had yielded nothing they didn't already know.

"A direct descendant," he added.

"Really? How interesting."

He nodded pensively and didn't say any more.

"You okay?" she asked him.

He gazed at her for a long moment, then smiled, and walked over to her, slipping his arms around her. "I'm going to be more okay later on," he whispered huskily.

They were pressed tightly together. It suddenly felt like months rather than weeks since they'd stood this way. She was acutely aware of his body heat and the strength of his muscles. Memory reflexes were going to kick in hard any minute. The urge to do far more than stand together was almost overwhelming.

They looked into each other's eyes and backed away at the same time. He smiled ruefully. "Sorry." He might have intended to keep his thoughts to himself a while longer, but touching her had obviously changed that.

"We should have scheduled this for . . . any time other than now!" Danni said.

He grinned but then grew serious again. "I don't think we *could* have."

Even as he spoke, Danni heard someone at the courtyard's side entrance. Excusing herself, she went to open the back door. Father Ryan had arrived. She tried to push away her visions of Quinn, naked, as she greeted the priest, but she could feel a flush rise to her cheeks. She had to curb her thoughts about Quinn for the moment.

"Hey, glad you're here," she said. "Come on in, Father."

"Wait up, wait up!" Natasha called, hurrying through the courtyard. Father Ryan turned; the two embraced warmly. An odd couple to many, no doubt — the priest and the voodoo priestess.

Father Ryan had once told her that he was true to his faith, but that, at heart, he and Natasha were kindred souls, seeking the same truth. Which had little to do with the way you sought that truth or the path you took.

She liked his view of the world.

"We're sitting around the little table in the kitchen," Danni said. The *Cheshire Cat* was similar to many places on Royal Street; it had been built as a house but now the shop took up the downstairs, with the small kitchen and one-time pantry on the first floor and her bedroom on the second. Billie's apartment — and now Bo Ray's, too — was located in what had been the attic. Luckily, it was big, and both men had their own rooms and ample space.

And downstairs, in the basement, really the ground level, was her father's office or den and special collection of "curios." Her studio, in the former pantry, was where she worked when she had time for her own art.

"Billie's made jambalaya and cheese grits," Danni announced as she led them in. "And we've got salad."

"Scottish jambalaya!" Father Ryan said. "I can't wait."

Billie was behind them. He threw Father Ryan an evil glare and muttered, "Lucky I didn't get the urge for haggis, friend, that's all I have to say."

When Bo Ray entered a few minutes later, Billie asked them all to grab plates and line up at the stove to help themselves. Natasha designated herself the beverage server and poured tea, lemonade and water, as each person chose. They were still in the act of greeting one another with casual jokes and hugs and getting organized at the table when Danni heard the buzzer at the shop's main door. She excused herself and hurried down the hall, then out to the showroom. Looking through the glass, she saw Jake Larue standing there. He appeared to be tense, worried about something.

When she opened the door, he said, "You're all here?"

Danni nodded. "Yeah. Hi, Jake. How are you?"

"May I?" he asked.

"Of course."

She let him in, wondering why he was here. We're just having dinner," she said. "Hungry?"

"I don't mean to impose," he said.

"We have tons of food," she assured him, leading the way through the darkened showroom to the kitchen.

As he walked in, everyone froze in position.

"Hey, guys. Jake's here," Danni said. "Billie made jambalaya."

"Scottish jambalaya?" Jake's confused words broke the freeze. The others laughed; Billie groaned, "Not again," and shook his head.

"Get a plate and join us," Quinn said. If he was surprised to see Jake, he didn't let on.

Jake started to dish up food, but halfway through he turned to Quinn. "The log-in list disappeared from the evidence room computer. The sign-out sheets are missing, as well."

They all looked at Jake and then back at Quinn. "Nothing there?" he asked.

"It was wiped clean. God knows, we've got our best techs and computer whiz kids on it. They've come up with nothing," Jake said, taking a seat.

Quinn seemed to understand him. The others didn't. But Quinn said, "Jake, sit and we'll figure out what we can."

Squeezing him in meant they were tightly wedged around the table, but they made room. Once Jake was seated, Quinn said, "It's on the news, so we're all aware of what happened to the Garcia family. I went to see Hubert at autopsy, and he said the murders were all different — like a game of Clue, in his words. Nothing at autopsy dispelled his original findings, but we still can't explain why we haven't found a single weapon or worked out exactly what went on. Did James Garcia kill everyone and then slit his own throat? If so, where? Or was there someone else in the house, a person or maybe more than one person, who managed to perform acts of unspeakable horror — and walk away without being seen or leaving a blood trail? Then, before I could return from autopsy, Jake called me and I went down to the police station. There was fog in the evidence room."

"Fog?" Natasha asked hoarsely.

Larue gestured vaguely. "Fog, smoke . . . something. Anyway, an officer on duty went insane, needing help. Help came — and so did I. And the fog or whatever it might've been was still there. The officer said that a shadow went after him. It was all extremely strange. We have *nothing* on the computer anymore — and nothing on the cameras except for the fog or gray smoke that hides the entire area for maybe twenty minutes."

"So they don't know what was taken," Quinn finished. But he was looking curiously at Larue.

"Here's what we do know. A number of things that had been removed from the Garcia house were taken from the evidence room. The vial you mentioned earlier, and three wrapped packages. In other words, things that were spattered with blood or might have given us a clue as to what a murderer was looking for," Jake said.

That caused Father Ryan to thump a fist on the table, which in turn caused all the dishes and glasses and flatware to clatter.

"Sorry," Father Ryan muttered. "But I've told Danni — those people were part of my flock and I *knew* them. I knew them well. There were no drugs, no arms, no implements of any illegality in that house. I'd stake my life on it!"

"I'm not suggesting James Garcia was doing anything illegal," Larue said. "Not *really illegal.*"

"What do you mean?" Father Ryan demanded.

"Garcia was one of the most trusted men in his business," Larue began. "He would pick up items for delivery when he finished for the night so he'd be ready to head out first thing in the morning. This wasn't official policy, but his supervisors have admitted they had an understanding with certain employees and Garcia was one. He'd had packages waiting to go out at his home. Some had blood spatter. We don't know precisely what they were, but one of the crime scene techs who'd been collecting objects from the house for analysis told us the packages weren't in the evidence room. She and a few others were brought down to try to remember. You can knock out a computer, but as long there are still people around, memory serves." He paused. "The only detail she could recall was that one of the packages was large and flat — presumably a piece of art — and another seemed to contain jewelry. . . ."

They all stared at him. "I just wanted to let you know." He shrugged. "Garcia might have been killed over something in his house — something he knew nothing about."

"Are you finding out exactly what packages were being held at Garcia's house?" Quinn asked.

"We'll have a full report from Garcia's company by morning."

"So where are we? What've we got?" Billie asked.

"Five corpses — and a seasoned cop scared out of his wits," Larue said. "That's what we've got."

"Plus missing evidence. And fog, mist, smoke," Quinn added thoughtfully. "Natasha?"

"I haven't heard a thing from the street," she replied. "But . . ."

"But what?" Quinn asked sharply.

Danni stood quickly; she didn't want Quinn trying to read her mind when her thoughts were still so jumbled. If she acted casual and began to clear the table, he might not notice.

Okay, so Natasha had some kind of *sight*. She'd told Danni a dozen times that with most people who came to the shop, she read the *person* more than she ever read a tarot card or tea leaf. And she was very good at it; as a priestess, she knew her followers. She knew when they needed guidance, when they should take a chance and when they should keep their heads down.

But that day, when she'd read Danni's tea leaves, something had been different. Danni had never seen Natasha quite like she'd been that day.

"I'm sensing that this is a situation we all need to be involved in," Natasha said, glancing at Danni.

Danni felt Quinn's eyes on her. Then, when she reached for a plate, she felt his hand. He looked at her as he asked Natasha, "What did you see?"

Natasha seemed to carefully gauge her words. "A very strange sight, and that's why I'm so curious about your 'fog' at the station. I saw Danni standing on a hill, and there was a castle in the background . . . a medieval castle, I believe. She was shouting, warning someone. The fog — the mist or whatever it was — seemed dark and shadowy. Gloomy. But there was something else."

"Like what?" Quinn pressed.

"There was a crimson cast to it. Crimson . . . red . . ." She paused. "I wish I'd seen more. I wish I knew more."

"Crimson. Red," Larue repeated.

"The color of blood," Billie said.

CHAPTER 4

Finally, their guests were gone for the night, each one in a pensive and expectant mood, dreading what the future would hold.

Danni went up to her room first. Quinn — being Quinn — had taken Wolf and gone through the house, assuring himself that the place was securely locked. Since Royal Street was just a block from Bourbon, the faint sounds of music and laughter continued.

The murders had been on the news all day. But visitors to the city — revelers on the streets — probably believed they were a strictly local phenomenon. Still, most people would be more careful that night; when they met in the city's bars or clubs they'd talk about what had happened not far from the French Quarter.

But while they'd react with horror and sympathy, they would tell themselves that it didn't affect them.

Danni usually turned on the television in the evenings. That night, she didn't. She already knew what she'd see on the news.

Quinn came upstairs, quietly opening the door, and just as quietly closing it behind him.

"You asleep?" he asked her.

"Seriously?" she replied.

"I'd rather hoped not," he said.

"Wolf's been relegated to the hall?"

"He doesn't seem to mind. He lets me be the alpha dog."

"And I thought *I* was the alpha dog," Danni said.

He stood in the doorway. "I was thinking —" he began.

"No thinking tonight!" It had been too long. She rose naked from the bed and walked over to him, met his hungry, urgent kiss with her own as she tugged at his shirt.

He kissed her while removing his jacket, shoulder holster and gun, allowing her to play with the buttons on his shirt.

Then he grew impatient and unfastened them himself.

Danni wondered how she'd ever had the strength to let him go. In his arms she immediately felt the inferno between them. His clothing was strewn about the floor and since she hadn't bothered with any . . .

They fell together on her bed. He laughed, rising above her, and then his lips found hers again and they kissed, tongues delving, lips locking and breaking apart so they could gasp for breath, then joining again. She grasped his shoulders, the muscles moving sleekly beneath her touch. He was back; he was with her. It was real, the sheets beneath her were real, the moonlight filtering through the drapes was real. And the force of his body against hers was both solid and dreamlike. For long seconds she was content to feel his flesh, to stroke his shoulders and down his back. But she felt his kiss moving against her, felt his lips on her throat, teasing her collarbones. His hands curved around and caressed her breasts and then his tongue and lips bathed her where his hands had been. She thought she might crawl out of her skin, she was so desperate to be part of him.

He was a tender lover, a careful lover, always wanting to arouse as he was aroused. But she felt the hardness of his erection so swiftly that night, felt him slide into her, and she wanted him so badly, she shared his impatience, entwining her limbs around his, moving with him, arching closer. She felt the frantic rhythm of her heart and his. The music from Bourbon Street seemed to fade away, and even the moon seemed to pale. All that remained was the feel of each other, their desperate, urgent need to be together again.

She rose toward him, the urgency so sweet it was nearly painful, and yet she wanted the moment to go on and on. She saw his eyes, the passion in them, and the wonder he seemed to feel when he was with her, and it was an even greater seduction. She curved her arms around him, and felt the euphoria sweep through her as they shuddered, almost violently, both rocked by their climax.

He half fell and half eased himself to her side. For a minute he was silent. "Whose idea was it that we were better off moving slowly?" he finally asked.

She smiled and turned into him. "Yours."

"No, I think it was yours."

He held her, drawing her to him, and kissed her lovingly. "We won't always need to be apart. When I'm in the city, it just makes sense for me to stay here."

"We . . ." Danni faltered. For her, he was perfect. She'd met him not long after her father died. She'd been at a loss, confused, disbelieving — and Quinn had barreled into her life.

"We what?" he asked her.

She ran her fingers through the lock of hair that fell over his forehead. "You know, I didn't even like you when we met."

"And I wasn't that fond of you, either. Except that I thought you were the sexiest woman I'd ever seen."

"And now?"

"What do you think?"

"I've always thought that actions speak more loudly than words," she said primly.

He grinned. And she smiled as he swept her into his arms. Their world might be going to hell again. But he was with her that night.

She wanted to cling to every moment until morning came.

Quinn could only explain the fact that he hadn't awakened when she left the bed by reminding himself that he hadn't really slept in almost forty-eight hours. He'd barely been back at his house before Larue had called that morning.

He woke now because Wolf was nudging his hand and whining. And if Wolf was in the room, the door was open. But the dog wasn't injured and he wasn't barking; there was no intruder in the house.

He jumped up, grabbing a robe. Then he grabbed a second robe. This had happened before. If the dog wanted him awake but nothing had disturbed the house, Danni was in her studio.

He hurried down the stairs and stopped in the doorway, watching her. He worried when he saw her like this but he was also afraid to startle her. She seemed frenzied and intent, yet she wasn't actually awake.

She sat before the canvas on its easel, her posture completely straight. She made a picture of absolute beauty with her hair flowing down her naked back. Her palette of colors lay next to the canvas where she worked, and she painted as if she were an automaton.

He walked over to stand beside her.

Something inside him seemed to tighten.

She'd copied the Hubert painting he'd seen in the gallery that morning except . . .

There was nothing deceptive about its beauty. The colors drew the eye and compelled the viewer to look more closely. What he saw revealed the emotions hidden in the original work. Her version of the painting made immediately explicit what Hubert's had veiled.

Everyone in this painting had apparently been startled and had turned as if to face a camera. The beautiful woman on the settee or love seat had her dagger out and seemed to be snarling at the man. He'd aimed his gun and moved into position to shoot the woman, an expression of hatred on what you could see of his face. The suits of armor has stepped forward, both holding swords. The chess pieces were running in terror while the children who'd been playing the game were trying to smash them with a large chalice and a medieval shield. Over the fireplace, the man in the portrait was directing the action with a cruel zeal written into his features. The child playing with the guillotine was slicing off the head of another doll — but the doll seemed to be alive and screaming.

That damned giclée. She was creating her own image of the giclée in the shop. Had the horror of it gotten to her?

He knew that wasn't true. Danni was strong; she'd been born with her father's strength. He knew her, and he'd known Angus, so he was sure of that.

Danni's hand paused in midair. He caught her wrist gently and took the paintbrush from her fingers, setting it on the palette. He placed her robe around her shoulders and knelt beside her, shaking her lightly as he said her name. "Danni. Danni, wake up."

She blinked several times and then stared at him with wide eyes. She shivered, and he gathered the robe more tightly around her. Her eyes quickly scanned the studio and then met his again.

"I — I was sleepwalking?"

"Sleep painting," he told her.

She didn't want to look at her creation. He didn't want to let her, but he knew he had to.

She slowly turned and studied the painting. He saw the horror dawn in her expression.

"It's just a painting," she whispered. Anger hardened her voice when she spoke again. "No, not even a painting. A copy of a painting, a giclée."

"We'll have to find the real one," he said.

He had a feeling he knew where the real one was — somewhere in New Orleans.

She shook her head. "Find it? You don't understand. It's a museum piece." She hesitated. "It was just sold. Niles heard a rumor that it's been bought by someone here in the city. But even if we find it . . . we'd need millions to get it!"

He stood and pulled her to her feet, holding her close. "It's coming here?" That rumor confirmed — or at least reinforced — what he already suspected.

"Nothing definite so far," she said.

"We'll get it," he vowed. "Whatever it takes."

She drew away. "How? First, we'd have to identify the new owner — a multimillionaire or billionaire, for sure — and convince him that he's spent a fortune on a killer painting? And you suppose he'll hand it right over?"

He tried to ease her shaking, tried to speak calmly. "We'll have to break in and steal it, then."

"Break in and steal it?" she asked. "You think it *is* here!"

"In the morning," he said. "Come on. We're going back to bed."

"I *can't* go to bed."

"Yes, you can."

"But . . ."

"I'm here, Danni. I'm here. And I'll hold you until you fall asleep, I swear it."

The slightest smile appeared on her lips; she'd needed his strength. Now, she was drawing on her own reserves. "And then you'll let go of me?" she asked. "When I'm asleep?"

"No. Well, not until morning when we wake up and want to get out of bed."

"I guess we *should* get more sleep," she murmured. He could tell that she didn't want to look back at her own work again, but she couldn't help herself. "I don't remember everything I probably learned about Hubert in my art history classes. Tomorrow, I'm going to find out whatever I can about the man." She turned back to Quinn. "Like a lot of artists, he supposedly used people around him to create his characters. I remember that much — and I want to know who they all are. I also want to know *why*. Why there'd be so much evil on every face."

"You might learn something from talking to Dr. Hubert. He admits that he's a descendant, but he doesn't seem very keen on the fact."

"I will talk to him," Danni said.

He cupped her chin in his hands. "Tomorrow," he told her softly.

He heard Wolf whine. The dog had been standing silently in the doorway, waiting for them.

"Oh, Wolf!" Danni hurried forward, kneeling to take the dog's massive head between her hands and plant a kiss on his nose. "Good boy. Good Wolf. Thank you for watching over me."

Wolf wagged his tail and Quinn thought the dog had been one of his best rescues ever. Unconditional love. And protection. Wolf would die for either of them.

"All right, let's get some sleep," he said. "I have a feeling tomorrow will be a long day."

Danni rose, and they started to walk out of the room.

Something brought him back. The canvas, of course, wasn't dry. Despite that, he covered it with one of her artist's sheets.

He didn't want anyone looking at the damned thing. Hell, Billie was old. He could see those faces and have a heart attack!

Quinn knew the desk sergeant on duty when he walked into the station. The officer nodded in acknowledgment. "Larue said to send you right in when I saw you," he said.

"Thanks." Quinn could see Jake Larue through the glass panes of his office. Larue was studying a file; he looked worn and haggard. Quinn assumed he hadn't slept much, either.

He tapped on the door and walked in.

"Quinn. Great. I was hoping you'd be early," Larue said. "I have the list from James Garcia's courier company. He was a trusted employee for sure. He was carrying a package filled with gold and gems that had been valued, signed sports memorabilia for a charity auction and —"

"A painting that recently sold in the millions," Quinn finished for him.

111

Larue frowned at Quinn when he sat down in front of him. "Yes. The painting is called —"

"Ghosts in the Mind," Quinn said. "It's by an artist named Hubert — who, incidentally, was a distant ancestor of our favorite M.E., Dr. Ron Hubert. Hubert the artist was found dead at an old castle in Geneva, still staring at the painting. It was his last work."

Larue picked up the file. "Okay, but here's what you may not know yet. The painting was purchased by a Mrs. Hattie Lamont, who lives in one of the grand old mansions on Esplanade. She's a widow and her husband was a computer genius who built and sold half a dozen companies. Since she's been in NOLA, she's joined every social club and charity foundation in the city, or so it appears. The painting was due to her by ten this morning."

"And it was missing from the evidence lockup after the 'fog'?" Quinn asked, already knowing the answer.

Larue nodded vigorously. "And here's the really curious thing about the three packages that went missing. Our crime scene people swear that we brought all three of them to the evidence room. But they were delivered to their recipients early this morning."

"And we have no idea how? I'm assuming the recipient *has* to sign for a package of that value!" Quinn said.

"In theory. I've already sent sketch artists to all three houses to get them to describe the delivery person," Larue told him. "However, that person didn't exactly make himself known."

"What about the delivery vehicle? Wouldn't the company know if one had been taken? And what about Garcia's truck?"

"Garcia's truck is still at the police impound. Judging by what I've gotten back from my officers in the field, no one saw a delivery truck or remembers seeing one anywhere near them." Larue glanced at his notes again. "But as Tobias Granville — owner of the assessed jewels — said, he was looking at his package and not down the street. He should have signed for the package. He says he didn't, that it was just at his door and he didn't even glance up once he had it in his hands."

Quinn shook his head. "So, a family was brutally murdered. Evidence came into lockup, evidence disappeared from lockup and then it was all delivered where it belonged."

Larue leaned back. "We've retrieved the packaging from Mr. Granville's delivery and from the charity people. Again, the box just showed up at their office door. And of course, the packaging is compromised now. People ripped it up. But we'll try to examine the pieces that have blood spatter."

"No one noticed blood spatter?" Quinn asked dryly.

"There wasn't a lot. Hey, if you're waiting for a fortune in jewelry, are you really going to worry about wrapping paper? Spots of dried blood on brown paper could be anything," Larue pointed out. "Flaw in the paper itself, a drop of coffee, smeared ink. Who knows?"

"What about Mrs. Lamont's package?"

"Well, this is interesting. Her butler — yeah, she has a butler — says he did sign for it."

"And the wrapping paper?"

"She wouldn't give it to us," Larue said sheepishly. "We're still working on that."

Quinn sighed. "Well, let's take a look at that fog or whatever it is — and anything else the cameras caught."

Larue got to his feet. "I can show you what we've got."

■ ■ ■ ■

Henry Sebastian Hubert.

The man had been getting attention recently, and he'd certainly received some during his lifetime, especially because of his connection with Byron, Shelley and their circle. But, alas, like so many writers and artists, he wouldn't actually achieve fame until he died — in front of his last painting, considered his finest, most emotional, most intricate and most disturbing work of art. *Ghosts in the Mind.* Even so, his fame was erratic at best, and he'd never been more than a minor, if talented, painter. Danni sat at the desk in her studio, flipping through art books, Wolf curled at her feet.

When she'd gone through her books, she turned to her computer, keying in book sites to see if anyone had ever done a biography of the man. She found a few slim volumes, as well as several books that included a chapter on Hubert and his work, and ordered them for overnight delivery.

Frustrated, she scratched Wolf's head. "Wolf, I have to leave without you, I'm afraid. I'm going to take a trip to the library. But you'll be fine. Billie and Bo Ray are both here, working at the store."

She stood and started out of her studio, then paused.

She didn't want to look at the painting she'd done the night before. And yet she felt she needed to.

Walking over to her easel, she lifted the sheet from the canvas. The paint had been wet when Quinn covered it, but he'd been careful. There was a little smudging, but nothing that diminished the pure evil that seemed to exist in every stroke.

The faces showed humanity at its absolute worst. They bore hatred, bitterness, maliciousness, cruelty . . . evil. The darkest part of the human soul. These characters were ready to dole out agony without even blinking. This rendition had none of the subtlety or perspective of the Hubert painting, but at a distance, the colors blended together in a way that was striking. She imagined that if it hung in a gallery, people who saw it would be compelled to come closer. . . .

And once they did, they'd be repelled. She studied each face. She'd have to see the Hubert again, but as she examined her own version of it, a sick feeling seemed to lodge in her stomach and stretch out to her limbs.

Had these characters been taken from life? Were they real people?

Wolf didn't like the painting, either; he

whined softly at her side.

She could no longer look at her own work and quickly recovered the canvas.

She turned and left the studio.

The evidence lockup was in a police station; *someone* should've seen *something*. There should have been at least one security camera that picked up what the others didn't. But the fog was there. In every single image. The best techs on the force had searched through them all and found nothing but gray.

"It's like trying to see through an extremely overcast day," Larue commented. "Even where there was no fog, that's what the security cameras recorded. Damnedest thing I've ever seen."

"You got the packaging back on two of the deliveries — but not the objects?" Quinn demanded

"I can't tell you how hard it would be to insist that people return priceless objects that belong to them," Larue said.

"But we could ask."

Larue scowled at him. "Okay, the charity auction — which supports housing in areas that still look like trash bins because of the storms — takes place this afternoon. The man with the jewelry isn't about to let his diamonds and gold go again. And as far as that painting goes . . . well, Mrs. Lamont threatened to bring in the mayor, the governor and the president of the U.S." He shook his head. "She wouldn't even let us have the damn wrapping — said she didn't have time to 'properly devote' to the painting, and until she did, she wasn't unwrapping it."

"I'll go see her," Quinn said.

"And do what?"

"I'll talk to her. Meanwhile, you need to get some kind of court order to get that painting back."

"A judge already slapped my wrist and explained civil rights and property law to me."

"It's evidence!"

"I'm doing everything in my power," Larue insisted.

"Fine. Then I might as well give it a shot. Can't hurt."

Larue apparently agreed. "Hey, I have a suggestion," he said.

"Yeah?"

"Take Danni. That way, maybe Mrs. Lamont will at least let you see the painting."

Quinn nodded. It wasn't a bad idea. Danni had a name as a local artist. Once upon a time — before her father's death — art had been what she wanted in life. And she was good.

Notwithstanding her strange nocturnal frenzies at the canvas.

At the library, Danni leafed through book after book. She'd tried working online, but when it came to art, the best resources — in her opinion, anyway — could be found in a museum or at a library. Some books simply weren't available online or for digital readers; this was especially true of expensive reference books that featured color reproductions.

Much of what she read she was already familiar with. Henry Sebastian Hubert had been born in 1790, making him twenty-six when he had rented a castle, the House of Guillaume, at Lake Geneva in the summer of 1816.

And he'd been twenty-six when he died. Like Shelley, he'd had a wife, a woman named Eloisa, who'd been left behind in England with their toddler son when Hubert had basically deserted her to spend his time on the shores of Lake Geneva. Maybe, had he lived, he would've gone back to her. But that was just Danni's musing. She did love happy endings.

Hubert had not had a happy ending.

He'd created his first well-known work

when he was in his late teens. It had been titled *Graveyard at Night.* It was a sad and oddly arresting piece, showing the facade of a medieval church surrounded by jagged, lichen-covered stones. His next work, more sophisticated, had been called *Hanging Tree.* There was no body hanging from the tree in the painting; the tree itself was the focus, skeletal and bony, seeming to move with the breeze, surrounded by shadow and ghostly images of those who'd met their deaths at the end of that one massive branch. In this painting, he'd begun his work with perspective. Of course, Danni was only looking at the reproductions in the book, but even then, she could see that, at first glance, there was nothing but the tree in the shadows and swirling dust. When she angled the page slightly, the shadows became ghosts.

Hubert had started young and by twenty-six he was well on his way. And then he'd painted *Ghosts in the Mind.*

When he was discovered dead, his wife had been informed, and the authorities had begun to prepare the body for transport to England.

Eloisa hadn't wanted him back, so he'd been interred in the old crypt at the castle. His belongings were packed up and shipped back to her, and according to reputable sources, she hadn't touched any of the paintings he'd done in Switzerland. Apparently, many people had tried to buy them from her — especially *Ghosts in the Mind,* since that painting had been done at the castle while Lord Byron, Shelley and Mary were an influence on his work. But she hadn't unpacked a single crate.

At her death, her son had ordered that his father's belongings be sold. That was in 1888. Henry Hubert's widow had survived until the ripe old age of ninety-three, living happily off her inheritance and the proceeds from his previous artwork. She'd been quite the socialite.

The painting was purchased by a gallery in London. She'd promised the owner that, upon her death, he could buy the piece from her son.

Closing up one night, the owner was murdered. The gallery caught fire. Little attention was paid to the event, since it occurred on the same night as Jack the Ripper's infamous murder of Mary Kelly in Whitechapel.

The painting was found in a thieves' den where the thieves had fought over their ill-gotten gains and taken swords, pistols and knives to one another.

Danni sat back, catching her breath with a

chilling sense of déjà vu.

Death followed the damned thing every-where. Garcia's house had been the scene of a massacre, too. She was more and more convinced that the painting had been in one of the courier packages waiting at his house. Nothing else made sense.

She looked up, gazing around the library. A woman was reading to a group of tod-dlers in the children's section; a number of students were busy at computers. The library was sunny, bright, filled with activ-ity. The world seemed good.

She looked back at the book, determined to pursue the course of the painting's his-tory.

It was locked away again as another twenty years went by, with police trying to sort through ownership. The gallery owner who'd been killed had died with neither wife nor child, so returning it properly became difficult.

Then, as she continued to study the painting's provenance, she learned that an art historian, president of a small but prestigious museum in London, had ac-quired it at an art auction. *Ghosts in the Mind* was given a place of honor at his gal-lery in Surrey. There it was viewed by the public for several years, studied by art students. The place closed before dusk daily — and remained under guard. In January of 1915, the Germans attacked London with their first Zeppelin raids. Five people took shelter in the gallery that night.

All were killed. It was impossible to tell just what had happened; the city had been hard hit. Their bodies were pulled from the wreckage.

But the terror of war meant nothing to a particular French visitor to the city — Jacques Duchanel, who dug through the remains of the bombed gallery and found Hubert's legendary *Ghosts in the Mind.* He saw that the painting was carefully wrapped and carried it back to France, installing it in his private gallery in the city of Nice. The next night, Duchanel was shot dead in front of the painting. The police had heard a commotion, but were never able to identify or track down Duchanel's assailant.

After that, *Ghosts in the Mind* was stored in a warehouse, where it remained until it wound up at a Paris museum right before the beginning of World War II. Then a Nazi general of the occupying force took the painting to the castle where he was staying. It was assumed that he was attacked by the French Resistance. He and seven of his men were murdered. The painting had disappeared.

It next appeared in Central America, arriving on a ghost ship. The author believed the painting had either been found or stolen by the general's friends — Nazis, too — who were fleeing the continent in 1945. They departed on an Italian ship that reached Panama, but by that time they were all dead, by suicide, or because someone had figured out who they were. The painting had again disappeared; however, it eventually made its way to Brazil. It arrived in Rio de Janeiro on a small boat; there were no people on the boat, but there was a great deal of blood. It was assumed that the boat was attacked, the passengers and crew killed and dumped overboard. But there were still a number of Nazi-stolen treasures aboard. If pirates had seized her, they hadn't known much about art.

The information in that book ended, no doubt because it was published in 1949. Frustrated, Danni sat back.

She made copies of the pages that had to do with Henry Sebastian Hubert and *Ghosts in the Mind,* and went onto one of the computers. Using what she'd already learned, she found a site that seemed to have more recent and accurate information.

One headline read Henry Sebastian Hubert's Famous and Infamous *Ghosts in the Mind* Surfaces Again — Sold at Auction in Seven Figure Range!

Danni skimmed the article and focused on the painting's arrival in Brazil. There was a rumor that bad things had happened, even to those who'd just handled the painting. In this case, they were, of course, suspected to have been other Nazis who'd fled, as well, and thus their deaths were put down to revenge.

Then, somehow, a Nazi general safely ensconced in South America got hold of the painting, which he quickly secured in a storage facility. Finally, after his death, it was hung in a major gallery. A few months later, that area of Rio was heavily assaulted by gangs, and there'd been a shoot-out at the museum. A number of men were found dead there. They were suspected of being gang members who'd fought among themselves. The director of the museum, while picking up the pieces, gave a press conference. He said that in the interests of world harmony, he saw fit at this time to return the painting to its rightful place at the West Bank gallery in Paris. The gallery's director thanked the Brazilian director — and promptly put the painting up for auction at a prestigious auction house, where bids immediately began to arrive. The name of the purchaser was withheld at his or her request, but giclée copies were promised so that all could marvel at the talent of this artist who'd perished at such a young age.

Danni sat back again, gazing blankly at the computer screen.

The buyer *had* to be from New Orleans; she was absolutely sure the painting had been at the Garcia house.

But where was it now?

And why was *she* creating images from it?

Danni wasn't home and she wasn't answering her cell. So Quinn called Billie, but all he managed to do was upset him. He tried to reassure Billie that Danni had her phone off or she'd left it in the car. Meanwhile, he made a mental note to beg her to be careful and to have it with her and on while they figured out just what was happening.

He was impatient and worried; the painting had to be found and found fast. It was a miracle that no one had been killed during the chaos at the police station. Quinn didn't know *how* the painting was evil or how it worked. He didn't know if a living person had to chant something or speak to it, invoke a curse or what, but somehow, the painting was a killer.

He drove to Hattie Lamont's house on Esplanade Avenue. Larue had already sent men out to see Lamont and her butler, a sketch artist among them. No one, however, could force her to give the police her work of art, not unless they could prove it was crucial evidence and not without a district attorney weighing in.

He needed to see her himself.

Finding a place on Esplanade where he could wedge his car wasn't easy, but once he had, he leaped out and stared up at the mansion. The home was on a truly grand scale. It had to be at least ten thousand square feet. The house featured a broad front porch with a swing, surrounded by gardens in the few feet of lawn before the street. There was a picket fence, but when he tried it, the gate was locked.

He hopped over it, hoping the woman didn't own a rottweiler.

She didn't. He made it to the porch with no problem and rang the bell.

The door was opened by a regal-looking older woman.

"Mrs. Lamont?"

"No, sir. May I help you?"

"I need to see Mrs. Lamont."

"Hold on." The door closed in his face.

No one came back. He rang the bell again.

This time, the door was opened by a butler. A real, live butler, dressed in livery. He was tall, heavy-set and balding. He could have doubled as a bodyguard. Maybe he did.

"Sir, you have entered the lawn uninvited and are trespassing," the butler said. "Kindly remove yourself from the property."

Quinn stood his ground. "It's imperative that I see Mrs. Lamont."

"Mrs. Lamont deems it imperative that you remove yourself from her property," he repeated.

"You don't understand. Tell her it's a matter of life and death."

"I believe *I* understand, sir. You do not. Mrs. Lamont will shoot you if you trespass on her property."

"I'm referring to this being a matter of *her* life or death," Quinn said.

"Mrs. Lamont is resting. She has been annoyed enough by the police. She is not accepting visitors at this time."

"Let me see someone else, then."

"I am her only live-in employee, sir. Mrs. Lamont handles her own business affairs."

"Please listen. My name is Michael Quinn. I —"

"Mrs. Lamont does not care what your name is."

"She is in possession of property that can kill her."

"Mrs. Lamont thinks you are mentally unstable, sir."

"Mrs. Lamont hasn't met me yet!"

"No, sir. Nor does she intend to. She has informed the police that if they have any thought of demanding she hand over her property, they had best come back with all the proper legal documents."

"So you know why I'm here."

"I assume, sir."

"Five people were brutally murdered over that painting."

"That is regrettable."

"If you'll just let me talk to her —"

"Wait? What's that, Mrs. Lamont?" The butler interrupted him, turning to face the house and cupping a hand to his ear.

"Oh, yes!" the butler said. "Mrs. Lamont says . . ."

The man smiled at Quinn.

And slammed the door.

CHAPTER 5

Leaving the library, Danni dug her phone out of her purse. She grimaced when she saw that Quinn had called five times. Going into the library, she'd set it on silent mode.

She quickly called him back.

"There you are," he answered. "Good thing I don't scare easily — but you'd better give Billie a call because he was concerned when I couldn't reach you."

"I'm sorry, I'm sorry," she said. "I was in the library. I hate people who let their phones ring and . . . Sorry. So what is it? What's wrong? Where are you?"

"Where am I?" he asked in reply. "Hmm. Standing on the street."

"Okay. What street? And why?"

"The things that went missing from the evidence lockup yesterday were delivered to their rightful owners. No one knows how, and a sketch artist was sent to do pictures of the person or persons who made the deliveries. Anyway, I decided to head for *Ghosts in the Mind.* It was bought by a very rich and not terribly pleasant woman named Hattie Lamont who has a very nasty butler," Quinn told her. "And apparently this butler signed for the package, so he's the only one who saw the alleged delivery person."

"Well . . . the police need to get that painting!" Danni said indignantly.

"Yes, I had the same feeling. There has to be a warrant first. And the fact that murders took place and relevant objects disappeared from the police station means very little when it comes to private-property laws. Not only did the objects disappear, the computer logs did, too. And don't tell me nothing disappears from a computer. So, it can't really be *proven* that these things were at the Garcia house from the get-go — despite the fact that the shipping company knew he stored deliveries in his house for early-morning runs. Anyway, Larue's trying to get warrants."

"Hattie Lamont," she said thoughtfully.

"You know her?"

"I believe so. It took me a minute. She bought one of my oil paintings. It's a view of Jackson Square at night."

"Did you get seven figures for it?"

"No."

131

"You should have," he said gruffly. "You know she's got the painting, right? The Hubert."

"Yes, so it seems. I've been researching the history. Quinn! Death has followed that thing since its creation. There's an interesting piece of information I gained from all my reading."

"What's that?"

"It seems the painting can only be, er, *active,* I guess, at night. In any event, that's when all the deaths and relevant crimes took place."

She could almost see him checking his watch; despite the fact that the time was shown on cell phones, Quinn always wore a watch.

"It's almost four, and I didn't have lunch, so I'm hungry. I'll leave my car on Esplanade and meet you at a restaurant." He paused. "Let's go to Port of Call. The house is within easy walking distance from there. Maybe you can get in to see her."

"Maybe," Danni said doubtfully. "But —"

Quinn hung up before she could say anything else.

Danni thought she'd find a place to park on Esplanade. But parking turned out to be more of a problem than she'd expected, and she decided she should just have taken her car home. By the time she reached Quinn at the restaurant, he'd finished his meal and was looking very impatient, although he didn't say anything.

She sat across from him and touched his arm, hoping to erase his scowl. "I'm sorry. It took me a while to park. Big mistake —"

"It's okay. At least you didn't slam a door in my face."

"The mean old woman slammed a door in your face?"

"No, she had the butler do it."

"The butler did it?" She couldn't help giggling. Then she grew serious, wondering how she'd get the woman to let her in. And once she was in . . . what was she going to say?

"Somehow, we have to talk her into giving up that painting," Quinn said.

"She's worth a fortune. I'm sure the place has security up to the rafters," Danni said. She looked at him sharply. "You can't be thinking about breaking into her house!"

"I'm seriously *thinking* about it," Quinn muttered. "Jake Larue did suggest I bring you, but, honestly, I didn't even get a chance to say anything about you. I guess after the police spoke with her this morning, she's holding on to her painting with an iron grip."

Their waitress came, and Danni ordered. A moment later, she received a giant iced tea and a bowl of gumbo. Come to think of it, she hadn't eaten lunch, either. She sipped her tea slowly and enjoyed every spoonful of the gumbo.

"All right," she finally told him. "I'll go to the house."

"With me?"

"Alone. Maybe she won't be as intimidated by a woman."

"I never saw her, just some skinny old broad who opened the door, and then the butler showed up."

"I'm pretty sure Hattie Lamont was your skinny old broad, and I don't think she'd appreciate the description."

"Well, fine. And I don't like doors slammed in my face — especially when I'm trying to save someone's life."

"Hang around on the street. I'll see if I can get in."

She finished her meal, well aware that Quinn was controlling his impatience. He drank another coffee while he waited.

When they were done, they walked down to the beautiful mansion where Hattie Lamont lived. Danni tried the gate.

"You have to hop over it," Quinn explained.

She waved a hand at him and frowned, warning him to get out of sight. Once he'd moved away, she found a small button on the gate and pressed it. From inside the house, she heard a buzzer.

The door opened cautiously. She saw Hattie Lamont peering out.

She knew a little about the woman and what she knew wasn't bad. Hattie was a widow, a very rich one. Her husband had made the *Forbes* top hundred several times; she'd inherited it all. Hattie had fallen in love with New Orleans. She gave to all kinds of projects in the city and had made a huge donation to build a shelter for battered wives and their children — and she'd even seen to it that there was a shelter for battered husbands.

She was slim, yes, although Danni wouldn't call her "skinny." Her hair was iron-gray and perfectly coifed. Danni had heard that a personal trainer went to her house daily and that she was obsessed by fitness, especially with regard to diet. Maybe that was natural; her husband had enjoyed his money, so the story went, by consuming huge quantities of red meat and fried food and bourbon — and then died of a heart attack.

The woman opened the door a little

farther, staring out at Danni, who still stood by the gate.

"Danielle Cafferty?" she asked.

They'd met briefly at an art show. Danni was surprised that Hattie remembered her. However, the woman had actually purchased a piece of her art. Maybe that was why.

"Yes, Mrs. Lamont. May I speak with you for a minute?"

The woman studied her. "It's about the Hubert, isn't it?"

"Yes," Danni said honestly. "I promise I won't take much of your time."

Hattie hesitated a minute longer. Then she hit a buzzer by the door. The white picket gate swung open.

Danni heard Quinn's intake of breath and realized he was standing behind one of the massive old trees on Esplanade, far too close to the house.

She ignored the sound, hoping Hattie Lamont hadn't heard it.

Danni walked into the house.

It rivaled — or surpassed — the finest mansions she'd seen. All her life she'd lived in New Orleans, but the opulence of this house was new to her. Antebellum furniture in perfect condition adorned the entry hallway, and exceptionally fine prints of the city, old and new, lined the walls.

"Come into the parlor," Hattie said.

Danni followed her through a doorway to the right. The parlor was grand and all done in white; the most glorious thing was the one piece of color — a mahogany grand piano set toward the rear of the room. In days gone by, Danni imagined, belles had danced the night away here.

She hoped to see the Hubert. It wasn't in this room.

"Sit down, please. I can have Arnold get you some tea. Hot or cold? I assume you like it swimming with sugar?"

"No, thank you. And, actually, I don't like sugar in it at all."

"I thought that was a Southern thing."

"Sweet tea? Yes, ma'am. I just don't happen to like it."

"But you are from here, are you not? Your painting has a lovely local quality."

"Yes, I am from New Orleans," Danni said.

Hattie pursed her lips. Danni felt slightly guilty, as if she *should've* liked sweet tea.

"Trying to watch the calories, you know," she said, hoping that would appeal to Hattie's obsession with staying fit.

Hattie nodded. "Yes, yes, very good. Most people in this country eat too much sugar and far too much fat."

And none of that's going to matter if you keep that painting in your house! Danni thought.

"So, you're here about the Hubert, as well. I'm not ready to show it. I've begun preparing a special place for it in the gallery upstairs, but I'm not quite finished. And, as it seems you know, I've had a very trying day with the police trying to take my painting from me!"

"Who delivered it?" Danni asked.

"Well, a delivery man, of course! My butler took possession, and he's already worked with a sketch artist." She spoke righteously and with extreme annoyance.

"Mrs. Lamont, do you understand what happened?" Danni asked.

The woman looked at her with shrewd eyes. "I was told about the murders. Absolutely horrible. Beyond horrible. One can only be glad that the children weren't home. But while the murdered man might have worked for the delivery company, he didn't have *my* painting at his house. That's because it's here, in *my* house. It arrived this morning just as it was supposed to. Arnold signed for it. I have it. Period."

"And you're certain it's . . . the original painting?" Danni asked. She'd studied art

138

history, and she knew there were forgeries that even the most renowned experts had difficulty recognizing. Sometimes, in a case such as this one, paint and canvas needed to be analyzed for aging.

Hattie Lamont leaned forward. "You think I spend what I spend on art — and know nothing about it?"

"Of course not!" Danni said immediately. "But, Mrs. Lamont, are you aware of the terrible history of that painting?"

"The artist died. Yes, very sad. But musicians and artists tend to be tortured souls. Look at the fine performers who've died in the past few years. All due to excess. Of drugs and alcohol. Poisons. Overindulgence. It's our greatest killer," Hattie said sternly.

Danni tried again. "It's not just the artist who died, Mrs. Lamont." She reached into her purse and pulled out the copies she'd made at the library earlier. "Death — no, murder, *brutal murder* — follows this painting wherever it goes. Mrs. Lamont, the French museum didn't even want the painting back!"

"My dear girl!" Hattie said. "The museum knew what it could make on the painting. That's why it went up for auction. I'm not afraid of ghosts, Ms. Cafferty. There are far too many people I long to see, and they don't come back. And I'm certainly not frightened by ghost stories — or history, even when it concerns ruffians and bombings and Nazis!"

Danni realized that she needed to proceed carefully. "Mrs. Lamont, you're an incredible asset to the city," she began. "You've done so many wonderful things. But what if there was the slightest chance that there could be something about this painting that attracted the worst kinds of people? Something that brought death, murder, evil . . . Wouldn't you want it out of your house?"

"Did the police send you?" Hattie asked irritably.

"No, I'm here on my own."

Hattie sat back, studying her. After a moment, she spoke again, her voice quiet. "I didn't stay married to my husband all those years by being young and beautiful, Danielle Cafferty. I read the papers, watch the news. I am no one's fool — and I know about you. You were involved in that cult mess or whatever went on. You *are* working with the police."

"No, I'm not. I'm acquainted with a few of them, of course. I know what happened this morning and I know — *I know* — that painting is somehow involved," she said flatly.

140

Hattie smiled. "Look around you. I have cameras everywhere in this house. If anyone tries to gain entry through a window or door, an alarm goes off that could wake people in China. You don't imagine that no one's ever tried to break in, do you? If evil people are a part of this, bring them on. I live my life hoping never to hurt another person. But, my dear, I am no doormat. I'm a crack shot. My husband taught me that if you're going to pull a gun, be prepared to use it. And if you're going to shoot, shoot to kill."

Danni felt a sense of respect for Hattie Lamont, and she didn't want the police to find this woman the way they'd found the Garcia family — viciously murdered.

"I wish you'd reconsider, Mrs. Lamont. That painting is . . . frightening."

She was surprised when Hattie leaned forward again and patted her on the knee. "You're a lovely young woman, Danielle Cafferty. I can tell how earnest you are, and that you're here because you think you can help me. But don't let this facade fool you. I'm a tough old broad."

Danni smiled, remembering Quinn's description of her as a "skinny old broad" and her own objection to it. She liked the woman more and more.

"I believe you," she said. "But I'm not sure you really understand what you're up against."

"And what is that?"

"Like I said, death has accompanied that painting every step of the way. I know that five people were just murdered. I also know that we can't always see everything that's evil in this world."

Hattie Lamont took in her words without betraying any emotion. Then she shook her head. "You're passionate and sincere, Ms. Cafferty. But you don't get where my husband got — and yes, I take some of the credit — without watching what you *can* see, and watching it with a wary eye. No one — and I mean *no one* — is taking that painting from me without a court order. But, be assured, I am listening to you."

The woman was stubborn. She obviously considered her word on the subject final. But Danni couldn't just leave; she couldn't abandon Hattie to what she was sure would come, even if she didn't grasp it herself and couldn't possibly explain it.

She reached into her pocket and took out one of her business cards. She handed it to Hattie Lamont and said, "This is my card. I want to be honest with you. I think you actually met a man named Michael Quinn earlier — before you had your butler slam the door on him. We . . . work together sometimes. You may think we're out to take something from you. We're not. I know how rich you are. I know you can do and have whatever you want. We don't care. From the bottom of my heart, I swear we're trying to help you. If you won't let us take the painting, at least keep this card. It has my number on it and Quinn's. If anything happens — anything that makes you at all nervous — call one of us. Please."

Hattie accepted the card. She glanced at it and then back at Danni. "I have to say, you sound a little crazy. Maybe you've been in this city too long. Too much voodoo."

"For some people, Mrs. Lamont — good people — voodoo is a very real religion. I don't practice it, but I have friends who do. And . . . I'm not crazy."

Hattie Lamont sighed. "I'm sorry. That was rude of me. But I like you, child. Come on up. We'll unwrap the Hubert together."

Danni stared at her. "You haven't unwrapped it yet?"

Hattie Lamont waved a hand. "Oh, the police wanted the wrapping. They said there was blood on it. I told them they were wrong — and to get a warrant!"

Danni realized she wanted to see the

painting in the worst way. The original Hubert! *Ghosts in the Mind.*

She was an artist. As an artist . . .

But she shook her head. "Mrs. Lamont, if you haven't unwrapped the painting yet, I'm begging you — don't. Don't unwrap it."

Hattie Lamont frowned at her curiously. "You don't want to see it?"

"I do. A part of me is dying to see it. To study his every brushstroke. But I know better. I've seen things. . . . So, don't unwrap the painting, okay? Let me leave you this information. Please read it. And don't unwrap the painting, at least until you've read what I've given you. You . . . you don't know what you might unleash. And, again, the card. It has my number and Quinn's. Call if you need us."

Hattie Lamont was obviously listening to her. "I'll keep the card. I do think you're — well, a bit misguided. But, as I said, I like you, and I like your work." She paused, her eyes twinkling. "You're not trying to sell me another painting, are you?"

"No, I'm not!" Hattie smiled. Danni thought it was sad that the woman had no children, by either birth or adoption. Sad because she was such a smart, compassionate and self-possessed person whose outlook on life would have been a wonderful legacy.

Hattie stood up; there was finality in her movements. Danni wasn't going to change her mind.

Only circumstances would.

Danni hoped those circumstances wouldn't leave Hattie Lamont dead.

"I've taken up enough of your time. I don't know how to convince you that the painting — well, frankly, the painting should be destroyed. I'm not telling *you* to destroy it. But I wish you'd get it out of your house. I like you, too, and I don't want bad things to happen to you."

Hattie was watching her with an inscrutable expression.

"I won't give up the painting," she said quietly, "but I'll wait another day or two before I open it. As for your card . . . as I said, I'll hang on to it, although I doubt I'll ever need to use it."

"Thank you. And please, keep it — and your cell phone, of course! — nearby. Just for a few days. If you never need to call us, I'll be delighted," Danni said. As she spoke, the butler returned to the room.

He was there to escort her out. How Mrs. Lamont had summoned him so silently, she didn't know.

"Thank you for seeing me," Danni said.

Mrs. Lamont nodded.

The butler led her to the front door, down the porch steps and out to the street. He hurried back to the house, but Danni didn't stay to watch him. Dusk had come while she was inside, but she still hurried down the street, hoping Quinn wouldn't accost her in front of Mrs. Lamont's house.

He caught up with her by the corner, clasping her arm. "You don't have the painting," he said, clearly disappointed.

"No, I don't have the painting." The woman would never have let her walk out with the painting in a thousand years. The most Danni had hoped for was that Mrs. Lamont might have allowed the police to take it.

"But does Mrs. Lamont have the painting? You didn't get me in there."

"Quinn, *I* barely got in there."

"But when you did, you should've gotten me in!"

"Hey! I did my best with her. You couldn't even get through the front door. I did, and there are times when you can't change the fact that most people think logically and deal with what they see as real."

"I would've made her see what's real."

Danni tried to control her temper. "And what would you have done — beaten it into her?"

He looked down, gritting his teeth. Danni left him there and walked to her car. She'd forgotten he could be so damned stubborn. No less stubborn, in fact, than Mrs. Lamont herself.

He quickly caught up with her again and fell into step beside her. "I'm sorry. It's just that it's getting dark. Hell, it *is* dark. Twilight is now . . . shadow."

"I tried."

"But, Danni, we *have* to get that painting."

"I know that! Remember, I am my father's daughter. Quinn, I'm trying as hard as I can. If we end up in jail — or get shot by a home owner! — we're not going to be any help to anyone."

"Danni, I saw the Garcia house. And come on. You know I don't beat up old ladies! It's just that . . ." He inhaled sharply, holding his breath for a minute. "You didn't see the Garcia house, and I'm glad. No one should've had to see it — ever."

She stopped. They were at the corner of Esplanade and Bourbon. She had walked farther than she'd thought.

As he spoke, her frustration had faded. Quinn was so passionate. But she had no idea what to say, what to do. She searched her mind for an answer, glancing at the old buildings on Esplanade, the grand and the not-so-grand. Even those, like the Lamont house, that were impeccably kept and probably worth millions were close together; Esplanade had been "the" place to build at one time.

Quinn was still staring at her, his eyes intense.

"Yes, she has the painting," she told him. "And she's not giving it up. I'm not sure what else we can do."

Quinn let out a long sigh. "All right. Larue's been trying to get a warrant but it's difficult when we can't prove the packages were in the Garcia house or the evidence room. The records we have only show that the shipping company had them — and they don't explain how any of the packages were delivered. Larue won't drop this. I'd try to break in but you're right — I'd just get arrested. Well, I may still try to break in —"

"Quinn!"

"She'll end up dead if we don't get that painting," he said starkly.

"She did take a card with our cell numbers."

"And it's probably in the trash."

"She liked me, Quinn."

"Good."

"So maybe our numbers aren't in the trash."

"She didn't like *me.*"

"You came at her like a bulldozer."

"I'm trying to save her life!"

"Yes, but she doesn't see that — it makes no logical sense to her. I'm sure she'll appreciate your charm one day," Danni told him. "On the other hand, do you think maybe *we're* wrong? I mean, wrong about the painting itself creating all the violence?"

"Like I said, I saw Garcia's house. You learned about the painting and its history. Put those facts together."

Danni nodded. "What I mean is that maybe the painting needs to be activated. The history of Hubert's painting doesn't come with dozens of senseless murders on a yearly basis. When it was covered and in storage, decades or more went by without any kind of incident. So, either the evil in the painting arises under certain circumstances, or it's . . . activated somehow. Or maybe both . . ."

"You think James Garcia or someone in his family *activated* the painting?" Quinn asked.

"Not necessarily. Possibly. What I'm trying to say is that it might have been James Garcia or a member of his family — *or* someone who was in his house."

Quinn studied her thoughtfully and almost smiled at her garbled explanation. "Hmm. But it was the strangest crime scene I've ever encountered. For one thing, there weren't the blood trails you'd expect."

A group of tourists from one of the bars crossed the street to the corner where Danni and Quinn were standing. They were cheerfully singing "Red Solo Cup" despite the fact that their drinks were in white plastic cups. Danni slipped her arm in Quinn's, and they moved to the side of the road. A young man gave them a sloppy grimace of apology as he brushed by her.

"Sorry!"

She felt Quinn tense, ready to defend her. She didn't need to be defended — not right now, anyway.

She stepped in front of him and spoke to the young man.

"It's fine. But just as a matter of self-preservation, you might want to look when you cross the street. You know, for cars," Danni said.

"We didn't look?" the inebriated young man asked, his expression stricken. One of the girls in the group of four fell against him.

"Charlie, we need to get back to the

hotel," she said.

"We need to get back to the hotel," Charlie agreed. He frowned suddenly and went still, gazing down the street. Danni thought he'd drifted off.

"Where are you staying?" Danni asked.

"What? Oh!" He turned to her. "Weird, huh? Weird. There's a strange light in the sky."

"Charlie, we *need* to go back to the hotel," the girl who seemed to be with Charlie said. "Can you help us?" she asked Danni.

"If we know where you're staying," Quinn said. He was frowning — looking down the street as Charlie had done.

Charlie gave them the name of a small bed-and-breakfast on Royal Street. "You're going the wrong way," Danni told the group. "Go back one block and then right on Royal. Walk down a few blocks and you'll see it."

"Oh. Oh, cool, thanks," Charlie said.

As he spoke, they heard a scream in the night. It was distant, but so loud and piercing it sounded as if a hyena or wolf was shrieking in mortal agony.

It was coming from the direction of the Lamont house.

Chapter 6

Quinn turned and raced down the street, Danni at his heels. Charlie and his friends stared after them, openmouthed with shock. Other people on the street were using their cell phones — calling the police, presumably — or scurrying away.

She was behind Quinn when he leaped over the little gate and she was with him when he reached the front door. By then, sirens were blaring. Police were on their way but Quinn didn't think they had time to wait. A small crowd of onlookers was gathering in the street.

He wasn't sure Hattie Lamont had any time left at all.

The door was bolted, and it was old and heavy. He slammed his shoulder against it but knew before he tried that he wasn't going to break through the thick wooden doors that had been constructed with old-world craftsmanship.

"Back up," he muttered to Danni. Sliding his gun from his shoulder holster, he shot the lower bolt.

The door groaned as he shoved it open, and they stepped into the house.

"Mrs. Lamont!" Danni shouted. "The painting's upstairs in one of her galleries."

They dashed up the stairs and Quinn burst into a bedroom. No one there. Danni was behind him, trying doors. He heard her let out a horrified gasp and ran quickly to where she stood.

The room was a gallery. The walls were covered with paintings. Quinn didn't know what they all were, but he had to assume they were priceless.

They were spattered with blood.

A man lay on the floor in the gallery, his head resting in a pool of blood. Quinn recognized the butler and rushed over to him. He hunkered down, but even before he sought a pulse, he knew he wouldn't find one. The sightless eyes were open and staring.

Quinn was sure the man's jugular had been severed; blood had spurted everywhere before he'd fallen and died. Quinn looked at Danni and shook his head, but Danni, too, had realized that the man was gone.

"Mrs. Lamont!" she cried again. She

backed out of the room. Clearly, no one else was there.

Quinn heard the sirens coming closer. The cops would have been advised by the home's security system, as well as by the bystanders who'd called it in, and in a few minutes, the place would be filled with people. He had to see if the painting was still there. Rising, he scanned the walls and looked for a closet. This room, however, had been designed as a gallery, with walls paneled in fine wood and lighting that had been set to display each piece.

The painting wasn't on any of the walls — nor was there a place it might have been stashed.

"Quinn!" He heard Danni shout his name and rushed down the hallway as he heard police burst in the front door. He was trapped in the upper hallway, just at the top of the stairs, as two officers came through and halted — aiming their guns at him.

He raised his arms. "Michael Quinn, private investigator and ex-NOLA cop. We heard the scream and broke in."

"Yeah?" one of the two men aiming at him asked. "Keep your hands up. Walk down the stairs slowly. No fast motions."

"There's a woman here, too. She just called out for me," Quinn said.

"Hey, Barney, it's Michael Quinn," the other said. "He's Larue's friend."

Quinn couldn't wait; he had to hope Barney wouldn't shoot. He turned and hurried in the direction from which he'd heard Danni's voice. She shouted again.

He threw open the door to another bedroom. Danni had evidently turned on a light. She stood at the closet door.

Hattie Lamont was on the ground, still alive. Danni's arms were around her as she tried to soothe the woman.

"Up here!" he yelled at the cops — Barney and his partner.

They were already on their way up the stairs. When they entered the room, Quinn said, "Mrs. Lamont is alive. Dead man in the other bedroom."

The two uniformed policemen were competent, but they weren't detectives. Barney ordered the second cop to preserve the crime scene and told Quinn to give up his weapon. Quinn did so grudgingly. He was pretty certain the painting was gone, and if the butler had been killed by anyone human, that person was gone, too.

Barney had his radio out. Other officers began to file in and Barney sent the three in the bedroom another glare while he called in the situation and requested further backup.

For several minutes, it was chaos. Danni stayed with Hattie Lamont, her arm still around the woman while Barney barked questions. The only thing Hattie managed was a shake of her head when he asked if anyone else lived in the house.

Hattie was in shock. Quinn knew it, even if Barney and his friends didn't. "She needs an ambulance and medical help immediately. She can't answer questions right now," he said.

"Ambulance should be here any second," Barney announced. "And as for you and the girl —"

"Danielle Cafferty, Officer," Danni said, rising. Hattie clung to her, looking straight ahead at nothing, lips trembling. "We heard the screams from outside and came over right away."

"And broke the door down," Barney added.

"Hell, yes. You hear a scream like that, you break a door down."

Paramedics hurried up the steps. A woman with salt-and-pepper hair seemed to be in charge; she took one look at Hattie and said, "Mrs. Lamont, we're going to get you to a hospital. Can you walk?"

She reached for Hattie, who let out another scream. Like the first scream, it held the sound of primeval terror. Hattie continued to cling to her. The paramedic turned to Danni and asked, "Can you come?"

"Of course," Danni replied. She glanced at Quinn, who nodded. "See you at the hospital," he told her.

"You'll be answering questions at the station!" Barney snapped.

Barney was really starting to get on Quinn's nerves.

"Call Jake Larue," Quinn snapped in response.

But no one needed to call Larue. He'd apparently been close by when the alarm at the Lamont house had sounded. He strode across the upstairs hallway and looked around the room before speaking. "Mrs. Lamont is on her way to the hospital and I have Dr. Hubert coming here to examine the dead man. I want everyone out except for crime scene personnel. Officer Ruggle, I want the sidewalk roped off, a guard on the property and crowd control — you'd think this place was Jackson Square."

"Yes, sir," Barney said. He turned abruptly and went to follow Larue's orders. Others followed him out.

Larue raised his eyebrows at Quinn. "You

happened to be on the doorstep?" he asked.

"Yes. That officer's name is really Barney Ruggle?"

"Don't tease him about it. He won't be amused. And whatever you do, don't go around saying, 'Hey, there's Barney Rubble.' Now, answer me. You just happened to be here?"

"Hey, you told me about the packages and the houses. You were getting a warrant, remember?"

Larue looked at him speculatively. "I guess you were trying in your usual subtle and charming manner to get the painting and you weren't about to wait for a court order."

"Well, we certainly ended up waiting," Quinn said dryly. "And . . . well, the butler is dead."

"You talked to Mrs. Lamont?" Jake asked him. "That's *all* you were supposed to do, may I remind you."

"I couldn't get through the front door," Quinn admitted. "But Danni got in. She gave her our cell numbers, and came back out. We were down the block, talking to a group of rather inebriated tourists, when we heard Hattie Lamont scream."

"You were *down the block* — and you heard her?"

"We heard her, all right."

"Maybe she'll be able to tell us something in a little while," Larue said hopefully.

"Not unless she recovers pretty damn fast."

"I know. I ran into the med techs going out with Hattie Lamont and Danni." Larue sighed. "If there's anything positive here at all — other than the fact that Mrs. Lamont is at least *alive* — it's that she seems to have grown attached to Danni. Which means Danni will be with her and can call us the minute Hattie Lamont starts to speak." He paused for breath, still studying Quinn. "You found her taking refuge in the closet in this room?"

Quinn nodded.

"And the painting?"

"What do you think?"

"It's gone?"

"I can tell you this much. Whoever was here, assuming someone *was* here, didn't go in by the front door. We would've noticed."

"Then there must be a back door," Larue said.

"Yep, or so I assume. Want to check it out while we wait for Dr. Hubert?" Quinn asked.

They did. There *was* a back door, and it wasn't locked. Nor did it show signs of be-

159

ing forced.

"That doesn't seem right. Hattie Lamont has even more money than the rest of the rich people on this street — and there are rough neighborhoods not far from here. We usually have police nearby, but they're more often on Bourbon and the blocks near Canal. She'd make sure that her doors were always locked and the alarm was always on."

"I agree. It doesn't make sense."

"And the butler's dead. . . ."

"Hubert should be here by now," Quinn said.

Hubert was. He was on his knees in Mrs. Lamont's gallery, working on the corpse. Crime scene techs were dusting for prints and searching the surrounding floor.

Hubert looked up as Larue and Quinn entered the room.

"This poor fellow got it in one swipe of the neck," he said. "His throat's sliced almost from ear to ear — and in a very particular way." Hubert stood and demonstrated. "Someone had a blade — an extremely sharp blade — and attacked him from a forward position . . . so." He mimed the attack with an invisible blade. "I believe the dead man approached his assailant but couldn't even put up his arms in a defensive fashion, he was slashed so quickly and with so much force. And why there isn't a mish-mash of bloody prints, I don't know. Obviously, I'll learn more when we've conducted a thorough autopsy, but that won't change the fact that this man's throat was slashed."

"Thank you, Dr. Hubert," Larue said.

"I'd like to take the body now, if I'm cleared to do so."

"Might as well," Quinn said.

"I think he's asking me," Larue told him. "You know, lead detective on the case?"

Quinn heard the amusement in Larue's voice; he hadn't been offended. There was only one reason Quinn ever regretted his decision to work on his own and that reason was Larue. They'd been good partners.

Larue turned back to Hubert, "Fine, Doc. Get him to the morgue."

Hubert looked at them both and asked, "Mrs. Lamont was the rich woman who bought the Henry Hubert painting?"

Quinn was the one to reply. "She was," he said.

"Is it here?"

"I don't think so. It's not on the walls, anyway."

"Maybe she didn't have time to hang it yet," Hubert suggested.

Larue shrugged. "We'll search the house, but Quinn says it's gone."

161

"Search away," Quinn said. "I'm willing to bet that the painting's gone."

"You're a descendant, right?" Larue asked the medical examiner. "It's not exactly a well-known fact."

"Yes, I'm a descendant," Hubert said. "However," he continued indignantly, "I am not running around murdering people over a painting. I wouldn't want the damned thing and its bloody history, that's for sure. Anyway, my artistry is at autopsy and since this follows on the heels of the mass murder at the Garcia house . . . well, I should get moving, gentlemen. If you don't mind."

"Careful to preserve any trace evidence, please," Larue said.

Hubert rolled his eyes. "And when, Detective, am I not?"

He hunkered down by the body again. "Oh," he said, looking up.

"What is it?" Quinn asked.

"There's a cut on the man's finger. He must've sliced it in the kitchen working on something. Actually, I haven't got the faintest idea how or where he cut it. But . . . it almost looks as if the finger was slashed on purpose. You know, like the way boys do when they want to become blood brothers."

"He cut his own finger — and then the killer cut his throat?" Larue scoffed.

"You have extra gloves?" Quinn asked Larue before Hubert could react to his comment. He put on the pair Larue gave him and began to examine the man's clothing.

"His wallet and ID and some change, keys on a chain, plus a few other bits and pieces, are in the evidence bags on that cart," one of the crime scene techs informed them. "His name was Bryson Arnold. He was forty-three, according to his Louisiana driver's license."

"Thanks," Quinn said, studying the bag and its contents.

"He had a box cutter in his pocket. There's blood on it," the tech said.

"The murder weapon?" Larue asked.

"Not for this gash, Detective," Hubert said. "You can see that. But I'd say he could have cut his own finger with the box cutter. Still . . ."

"Still what, Doc?"

"Still, I don't think he cut himself opening boxes. I think he gashed his finger with purpose and intent," Hubert told them.

Being at the hospital was both tedious and tense. Just a year or so ago, her father had died in this same place. It wasn't easy to be there, and yet Danni knew she wouldn't leave. Despite Hattie's vise-grip on Danni, she had to be taken into Emergency on her own and Danni was left to wait. Hattie was suffering from severe shock. First things first; she had to be stabilized. Danni paced the emergency waiting room while physicians attended to Hattie.

Eventually a doctor came out to talk to her. Dr. Dakota appeared to be in his early forties, confident in his movement and with his encouraging smile. Initially he thought she was the older woman's daughter; he knew *of* Hattie Lamont, but not much about her.

Danni explained that she was a friend, but that to the best of her knowledge, there was no immediate family. The police would have to contact her attorney regarding her care.

"Well, she certainly wants you with her," the doctor said. "We have her stabilized. Thankfully, she's a very healthy seventy-seven and her heart is strong. However, we haven't been able to get through to her. She hasn't spoken a word. I understand that her employee was murdered in her house?"

Danni nodded.

"Well, she must've seen or heard something and hidden and . . . well, whatever she saw put her mind into a distant place. We've got her set up for neurology tests and we have Dr. Matthew Boudreaux, one of the finest psychiatrists in the country, coming to speak with the neurologist. Then he'll see if he can breach the wall in her mind. For the moment, she's resting. You're welcome to be with her. They're arranging for a room for her right now. In fact, she was agitated when you two were separated, so I'm pretty sure you're good for her."

"I'm happy to stay with her," Danni said.

Dr. Dakota nodded and moved on to his next emergency.

Danni put a call through to Quinn to let him know what was happening.

"Everyone's anxious to hear what she's got to say," he told her. "Call me the second she's capable of speaking."

"Of course I will, Quinn. But I don't think they have any idea when she'll speak again. There's a neurologist coming to see her, as well as a psychiatrist. Meanwhile, I'll sit with her. What's going on at your end?"

"We're looking for her computer. She has cameras set up everywhere. The butler — his name was Bryson Arnold, by the way — has been taken to the morgue. I'm still at the house, and I guess I'll be here for a while. With any luck there'll be something on the cameras."

"I hope so. When I was talking to Hattie

earlier, she told me how safe her house was because of all the cameras." Danni paused. "Sorry. I should have mentioned it before."

"There was a lot of commotion," Quinn said. "Just see what, if anything, you can get from Mrs. Lamont. Don't forget —"

"Call you the second she starts to speak," Danni finished. "And how about you calling me if there's anything on the cameras? I would think there'd *have* to be."

"Will do." The line went dead. She frowned at the phone for a minute; Quinn had a tendency to hang up before saying goodbye.

A nurse came to tell Danni that Mrs. Lamont was going to be brought to room 228. Danni headed to the elevator, up to Mrs. Lamont's assigned room. She hadn't been brought in yet, so Danni took a chair and checked in with Billie, who promised to keep Father Ryan and Natasha up to date.

As she ended the call, she heard Mrs. Lamont being wheeled in. She rose and looked at her carefully. Hattie had great bone structure. Despite the fact that her gray hair was matted and she was clad in a hospital gown, there was something about her that remained regal, almost pathetically so. She seemed straight and tall even in the bed, but her eyes were open and totally vacant.

166

She barely blinked.

"We'll have her set up in just a minute," a cheerful nurse said. "And don't worry — she's strong. She'll pull through. We're just keeping her hydrated with the IV so don't let that worry you, okay?"

"Thanks," Danni murmured.

"I was told she was very anxious when you two had to be parted. That's a good sign," the nurse said.

Danni drew her chair close to the bed. She took Hattie's hand in her own and held it. The woman's eyes didn't change, although Danni thought she felt Hattie's hand grip hers for a moment. It might have been an involuntary twitch . . . or it might have meant that Hattie knew she was there.

When the nurse left them, Danni tried speaking to Hattie. "I'm here with you." She paused. "I'm sure you know about Mr. Arnold, your butler. I'm so sorry about his death. But you were there, Mrs. Lamont, you were in the house. You saw or heard *something*. But I'm here with you now. You're in the hospital. And you're all right."

The woman didn't look at her. She still didn't blink. She didn't move.

Danni kept talking, but Mrs. Lamont didn't seem to hear. After a while, she leaned her forehead on the edge of the bed.

It had to be very late; she was exhausted.

She must have dozed because she was suddenly aware of being touched. She felt gentle fingers on her hair.

She raised her head and saw Hattie gazing at her with something like tenderness.

"Mrs. Lamont?" Danni said.

"It's so kind of you to be here. I — I don't really understand where I've been, but I know you've stayed with me."

Danni swallowed. "Mrs. Lamont, do you remember . . ."

She nodded sadly. "Bryson is dead. He'd only been with me for about six months. Clara, my housekeeper who'd been with me for years, became very weak. I put her in a beautiful home with a private nurse and then . . . then I hired a young man who'd act as a real butler. We became close. Bryson. My dear Bryson is dead. He . . . is dead. *It* killed him. I saw . . . it. And *it* killed him."

One of Jake Larue's men was brilliant with computers, and he quickly figured out the monitoring system Hattie Lamont had in her house and on her grounds.

There was a camera in every single room, except the bathrooms. Recordings were kept for a week, and then recycled. Mrs. Lamont never came or went from her bathroom without being totally clothed and respectable.

It took the computer officer some time to go through the footage of the front steps, the back, the sides of the house and all the rooms. But he finally found what they were looking for. First, however, there was a lot of fast-motion footage of the butler preparing food, speaking with Hattie, preparing more food and going on errands. There was also a lot of Hattie at her desk in the downstairs study, checking her plants outside, and sleeping.

Quinn saw Danni in the house with the woman, in the parlor. He saw how earnestly Danni had spoken with her.

He saw Danni leave. The butler locked the front door and started up the stairs. Mrs. Lamont sat in the parlor studying the business card Danni had given her. Then she rose, tucked it in a pocket and walked upstairs, too. She went to her bedroom.

"Bring up Mrs. Lamont's room, please," Larue said.

Mrs. Lamont's beautifully appointed bedroom popped onto the screen. Hattie lay down on her bed and closed her eyes, as if she just wanted to rest for a few minutes.

"Could you bring up the back of the

house during these same minutes?" Quinn asked.

The screen went gray, and then another image appeared. The backyard wasn't big; it was easy for the camera to encompass what was there. A charming back porch led out to a small but well-manicured lawn.

Suddenly, there was nothing.

"What happened here?" Quinn asked.

"It's not the computer. Someone did something to the camera," the officer told him. "The lens is . . . dead."

"Was it shot out?" Larue wondered.

"I think I would've heard a shot," Quinn said.

"Paintball," the officer explained. "That's a popular method of knocking out cameras these days. We can check."

"I'll send an officer." Larue reached for his cell.

"Go through every room in the house until you find the butler," Quinn said.

The officer did. They finally saw Bryson Arnold in a small room next to what seemed to be a climate-controlled storage room. He walked toward the rear, and then apparently remembered the camera. He bent down, moving surreptitiously around.

Again, the screen went blank.

"I'm willing to bet something was just

thrown over the camera," Larue murmured.

"Now what?" the officer asked.

"Someone else is in the house. Check out the back entry, the kitchen, the central hall," Quinn said.

"There he is!" The officer pointed at the screen.

There was indeed a man in the house. He wore black pants and a black sweatshirt, the hood pulled low. It was impossible to see his face.

"There's our killer," Larue said.

Quinn wasn't sure if the hooded man was actually the one who'd carried out the killing. He didn't look like someone who could wield a large knife with enough power to nearly sever a head. But he moved up the steps and marched straight to the gallery.

A moment later, Bryson Arnold joined him there, a large, wrapped painting in his hands. He greeted the other man tersely and ripped open the packaging.

Then the screen changed again. It didn't go blank. It fogged over with a gray mist so thick they couldn't see a thing.

And every bit of footage the computer expert went through after that — of every room in the house — showed nothing but what appeared to be heavy gray fog.

Danni called Quinn to tell him that Hattie was speaking — that she seemed to have recovered her senses completely. He didn't answer his phone. She left a message; she was sure the nursing staff had been told to call the police, so she didn't try Larue's number. Instead, she returned her attention to Hattie.

"Hattie, try to describe 'it' for me again," Danni said. "Think carefully and tell me everything that happened after I left."

Hattie was definitely herself again. She gave Danni an impatient look. "I can only tell you what I saw. My story isn't going to change."

"I know, but . . . please. Humor me."

"I was tired, so I went up to my room to rest before dinner. I prefer to eat at about eight-thirty. That's what I'm used to. My husband didn't come home until seven or seven-thirty most nights, so we always dined at eight-thirty."

"That was very caring of you," Danni said, willing herself to be patient.

"And smart," Hattie said, a bit smugly.

"So you went to lie down and rest."

Hattie nodded. "Then . . . I heard a commotion. As if . . . as if there were several people in my house. I was stunned and appalled. Bryson Arnold was a perfect employee — he never let anyone in without my say-so!"

"But there was something going on."

She nodded again. "In the gallery. The door was closed. I opened it and then . . ." She winced. A shudder made its way through her body. "Then I saw it. The *thing*. The darkness . . . like a form, but not a form. It reminded me of a banyan tree with roots everywhere. Or maybe it was more than one thing. Or trying to become more. It was pulsing and moving and —"

"And then what?"

"And then I heard a screeching sound, and suddenly in the midst of all that darkness, I saw Bryson and he yelled at me. He . . . well, he shouted. He shouted one word. *Run.*" She took a breath. "And I tried to run but I couldn't. I can't describe my terror. I felt a sense of fear unlike anything I've ever experienced. I couldn't run, I couldn't breathe. I stood there for a moment and then in all that darkness . . . I saw red. Blood. It was blood flying from Bryson's throat and it seemed brilliant against the darkness that flooded . . . everything. I . . . screamed. And I fell. And then I crawled until I reached a door and I went in and . . . I don't remember anything after that. Sometime later, I'm not sure when, I realized I was still alive. That I was here. And you were with me."

"Mrs. Lamont, did Bryson have the Hubert painting out?" Danni asked.

The older woman smiled. "After all this, call me Hattie. And I don't know if he had the painting out or not. There was so much . . . fog. It was like one of those days when you can't see where you're going because the fog is so thick. I don't even remember Bryson's face. I just remember the blood because the color seemed so ridiculously bright against that fog."

Danni was silent. She wondered what — if anything — Quinn and Larue had found at the house.

"Do you think Bryson had taken the painting out of its packaging?" Danni asked.

"Why?"

"Maybe he wanted to see it?"

"He never asked me. I know what you said about not unwrapping it, but *he* knew that I wanted the lighting fixed before it was hung. That I was waiting for some workers who were due tomorrow. If he'd really wanted to see the painting, he would've asked me."

"Was there anyone else in your house?"

"Besides *it*?"

"Yes."

Hattie shook her head. "If there was, I wasn't aware of it. All I really remember is lying down, then hearing the noise and getting up. I was stupid, I suppose. I mean, even if it was just an art thief, I might've been shot! I should have snuck down the stairs and gotten out."

Danni decided not to mention that she could've grabbed her cell or a bedside phone and called the police or the numbers on the business card.

Hattie seemed to read her mind. "I said I behaved stupidly, didn't I? But do you know how preposterous this all sounds?"

"Of course. But . . . you seem to be doing very well," Danni said.

"And Bryson is dead."

Danni started at the light knock on the door. It opened, although neither she nor Hattie had spoken.

Quinn had come; Jake Larue was with him.

Larue said, "Mrs. Lamont, I don't think you need to shed too many tears for Bryson. Still, I wouldn't have wished such an end on anyone."

"Not shed tears for Bryson!" she retorted.

"The man was quite extraordinary — and an excellent butler!"

Quinn sat in the chair across from Danni, while Larue took a position at the end of the bed.

"Mrs. Lamont," Quinn began. "We have reason to believe that Bryson Arnold was in league with an intruder who entered your house by the rear door."

"The alarm would've gone off!"

"Not if Bryson reset it," Quinn said gently. "And not if he knew your schedule and planned a time for someone to meet him. We have footage of Mr. Arnold in your storage room, Mrs. Lamont. We believe he was taking out the Hubert — and that he'd arranged to steal it and sell it to another man."

Hattie Lamont sat up straighter in her bed and stared at Quinn in disbelief. "No, no, that couldn't be. Bryson was trustworthy."

"Unfortunately not," Quinn went on. "We also have reason to believe he lied about signing for the package and invented a description for the police artist."

"No . . ." Hattie gasped, shaking her head wildly. "Surely not."

"How long had he been with you?" Larue asked.

"Well . . . not that long, but —"

"Did he happen to come into your employ

176

after you found out about the Hubert going up for auction?"

"About six months ago and . . . yes!" Hattie's eyes widened and her face paled. "Yes, I'd just called the auction house. I suppose I'd mentioned in a few of the galleries I visited that I'd heard about it and was interested. I'd been interviewing people during that time and he . . ." She sank back onto the bed. "Bryson Arnold came into my employ then, yes. Our previous butler, Clancy, died about a month before I hired Bryson. I needed someone, and Bryson seemed perfect." Some emotion dimmed her eyes. "There's no fool like an old fool, is there? Money and age. People will take advantage of them every time, won't they?" She seemed to ask the question of herself rather than those gathered around her.

Danni had to argue with that. "Mrs. Lamont — Hattie — Mr. Arnold might have genuinely cared for you. Perhaps he'd made a bargain he couldn't get out of. You said he told you to run. He realized he was in trouble himself, and he told *you* to run."

"His partner killed him," Larue said.

Hattie frowned at Larue. "His partner? I didn't see another man in there. Don't be ridiculous. One man couldn't have caused the fog. And whatever *it* was came out of

177

that fog. No partner killed Bryson Arnold!"

"Then who did?" Larue asked, confused. "What do you mean by *it*? We saw the footage at your house. The back camera was blacked out, but apparently, no one thought of the inside cameras, not at first, anyway. We saw a man in black jeans and a black hoodie come into your house and go up the stairs. He *had* to have killed Bryson Arnold."

"No," Hattie insisted stubbornly. "No, he certainly did not!"

"Then who did?" Larue demanded again.

"I told you. *It* killed him. The thing in the fog. The thing forming there . . . the thing the fog was trying to become." She wagged a finger at Larue. "Do not tell me I'm suffering from any form of shock or dementia, Detective. I'm telling you, and I will swear until my dying day, that *it — the thing in the fog —* killed him!"

CHAPTER 7

Other than Hattie Lamont's insistence on what most people would consider a delusion, she seemed to be in good health. The hospital staff, however, wanted to keep her overnight for observation. That was fine with Larue; he wasn't done with her house and he didn't think it was safe for her to go home, anyway.

For one thing, she no longer had a butler.

"The lady is in great shape," he told Quinn outside the room. "But, still, at her age . . . and with what's just happened, well . . . she's better off here. Tomorrow . . . we'll have to figure out what to do. I can't keep her out of her home. But I'm not sure she should be alone."

"What do you think of her story?" Quinn asked.

Larue twisted his lips wryly. "If I hadn't seen all the fog in the footage at the police station, I'd say she was crazy as a loon." He

179

paused, shrugged. "Quinn, do you suppose there might be a magician involved? Someone who knows how to create fog and illusions and all that?"

Quinn realized that Larue wanted him to say yes. He wanted a *normal* explanation for what had happened. Or at least something that could pass for normal under these very bizarre circumstances.

"Sure," Quinn said, not believing it for a second. "That's a possibility."

"What the hell else is there?" Larue lifted a hand. "Never mind. Don't tell me. I'm headed back to the Lamont house. See if you — or Danni — can get Mrs. Lamont to leave town. Maybe she has relatives somewhere. Hey, maybe she could take a cruise."

"You think someone might still want to hurt her?" Quinn asked.

Larue was thoughtful. "Who knows? You could be right, and it all has to do with that wretched painting. There are *hours* of recorded footage on that house. I'll make some of my guys sit down and watch every second of it. In any case, it looks like the butler was in on it with whoever was in the house. And whoever *that* was seems to have disappeared with the painting. When we've gone through all the footage from the security cameras, we can verify that he left with it." He was quiet for a minute. "Maybe the killing will stop and we'll have a chance to find the thief. You know, maybe he's happy now that he's got the painting."

"Maybe. But I don't think you're going to get Mrs. Lamont out of town," Quinn said. "She's the most stubborn old bird I've ever come across. Are you going to have someone on guard duty here tonight?" If Larue didn't, he knew Danni would insist on staying. But she needed to sleep — or, at the very least, be in her own home.

That was where she'd sleepwalk and paint again — if it happened a second time. Perhaps her vision might give them more clues.

And, selfishly, that was where they'd be together.

Larue nodded. "Yeah, I'd be remiss if I didn't watch out for Mrs. Lamont." He took out his phone and made arrangements for an around-the-clock guard.

"You want to wait until an officer gets here?"

"Of course," Quinn said, relieved.

Larue left him then, hurrying down the hallway, and Quinn walked back into Mrs. Lamont's room. The older woman, who was deep in conversation with Danni, watched him closely as he came back in and took a seat.

He looked from Mrs. Lamont to Danni, arching his brows in silent question.

"We were just discussing the painting," Danni told him.

"Oh?" he murmured politely.

Hattie Lamont was still staring at him. She smiled suddenly. "Danni's been telling me that you're actually a decent young man, Michael Quinn."

"I'm trying," he said.

"Hmph!" Her remark evidently referred to the life he'd been known to lead years before. Not a good one, he had to admit, although he'd never intentionally hurt anyone and the damage he'd done had been mostly to himself.

"I *was* trying to save you," he said.

She nodded. "Obviously I can see that now. And I'm trying to fill in any gaps I can regarding that painting. I've always wanted one of Hubert's works, and this was my opportunity — his most famous painting yet! I love the entire era, and the history of this work especially. Can you imagine what it was like that summer? I think about what the sky must have been like. Mount Tambora erupting in the Dutch East Indies and creating *climate change*! It shows us just how fragile our earth is. And I love imagining what it was like for Mary Shelley growing up — I mean, her mother was the feminist of her day! Even though she died soon after Mary was born, her published works made her famous. She espoused equal rights and women's suffrage, far ahead of her time. And later, Mary would've known about many of the experiments being done with electricity — and with the dead. I'm not losing you, am I, Mr. Quinn?"

Quinn glanced at Danni, who was trying to hide a grin. He smiled at Hattie Lamont. "I'll try to follow along, Mrs. Lamont. I've read *Frankenstein, the Modern Prometheus* by Mary Shelley," he said. "I do admit I'm not really up on the eruption of Mount Tambora, though."

"It was incredibly important," Mrs. Lamont said. "It created the atmosphere! The summer was cold, so cold. Even here, they had snow in New York — in June! Cold, with the ash up there in the atmosphere, blocking the sun, creating a haze . . . a fog."

She stared wide-eyed at Quinn as she repeated the word. "Fog. Like that in my house."

And like that at the police station, Quinn thought.

Danni placed her hand on Hattie's where

it lay on the white sheets. "Hattie, that may mean something. But it's going to take some digging to figure things out."

Hattie looked at Danni approvingly. "You do believe me!" she whispered. "The police think I'm a doddering old woman."

"That's not true, Hattie," Quinn said. "Although they do believe a magician might be the killer."

"Hattie?" she said haughtily.

"I beg your pardon, *Mrs.* Lamont."

He'd just heard Danni call her by her given name! What the hell had he done to the old witch — other than save her life?

"Danielle and I have had time to become friends, and not just acquaintances," she informed him.

"Of course. I'll remember that in the future."

"Am I in danger now, young man?"

"I don't believe so. The killer wanted the painting. He's got it. As far as we can tell, anyway. It was in a storage room next to the gallery?"

"Yes, that's where it is. Or was, if what you're saying is true."

"Mrs. Lamont, I really wouldn't lie to you."

"And you think that whoever — *whatever* — killed Bryson Arnold was after the painting and the painting only and that I'm not in danger?"

"Yes, I *believe* the painting was the reason for the break-in and Mr. Arnold's death," Quinn told her.

"Interesting. So why is there a policeman standing in the doorway?" Hattie Lamont asked.

Quinn turned around and saw that a young officer had arrived. Danni looked curiously at Quinn. He tried to return a look that said they needed every precaution. She seemed to understand.

"Mr. Quinn?"

Quinn walked to the door to shake the officer's hand.

"Connor Gray, sir," the young man said. "Detective Larue gave orders that I was to let you know when I got here. I'll be relieved by Officer Bill Downing at 8:00 a.m. Mrs. Lamont will have one of us in the hallway at all times."

Quinn thanked him and gestured at Danni.

"We're leaving?" she asked.

"It's midnight," he pointed out.

"Oh!" She was clearly surprised that so much time had passed. She smiled at Hattie Lamont with real affection; as Hattie had said, a genuine relationship had grown between the two of them that afternoon. Maybe Danni was looking for the mother who'd died when she was very young and maybe Hattie was looking for the daughter she'd never had.

Hattie Lamont raised a magisterial hand. "Go home and get some sleep. I hope I can sleep, too — although I'm sure they'll give me a sedative. Now, go. And . . . thank you. Thank you for coming here and staying with me."

Danni glanced at Quinn. "I'll be back in the morning. We'll see how you're doing then, and you can figure out what you want to do," she told Mrs. Lamont.

"I'll be quite all right." Hattie Lamont nodded firmly. "I'm a tough old bird," she said, as if she knew the same words had recently passed his lips. But she smiled at him as she spoke.

"We'll see you in the morning," Quinn said. Danni impulsively kissed the old woman on the forehead and came around to the door. Quinn placed a hand at the small of her back. "Good night, Mrs. Lamont."

"Good night," the woman responded. "Oh, and, Mr. Quinn."

"Yes?"

"You may call me Hattie now, if you wish.

And I shall call you?"

Quinn laughed. "Quinn, Hattie. Just Quinn. That's what everyone calls me."

"Fine, then. Sleep well."

Smiling, Quinn urged Danni out of the room.

When they reached The Cheshire Cat, Royal Street was quiet except for the dimly heard sounds of revelry on Bourbon Street. Danni barely heard the noise; she'd lived there since she was born. The Cheshire Cat itself was dark except for the nightlights. She and Quinn let themselves in via the courtyard.

Wolf was waiting when she opened the door, thumping his massive tail, eager to greet them both.

"So?"

She was startled by Billie; he was standing a few feet back in the dark, waiting for them, as well.

"Billie! You scared me!"

"Sorry. We've been sitting in the kitchen, Bo Ray and me. Hate to call you when you're at a hospital, but we haven't heard from either of you in a while now," Billie explained. "So?"

"Got any food?" Quinn asked, looking up. He'd gotten down on the floor to give Wolf a thorough scratching.

"We never don't 'got' food," Billie told Quinn. "I'll 'rustle' some up, as you might put it, but we know hardly anything about what happened today," he said sternly.

"I called you," Danni protested.

"That was hours ago!"

"I feel like I reek of blood," Quinn murmured.

"I'll fill Billie and Bo Ray in, especially since we don't have much more to tell them," Danni said. "You go shower and change."

Quinn shot her a grateful glance and went running up the stairs to the second floor and her room. Billie grabbed her arm — as if he was afraid she'd follow.

"In here, Miss Cafferty, if you will!"

Grinning, Danni followed him into the kitchen. Bo Ray was at the table, reading the paper she still had delivered; they all seemed to like their news in the old-fashioned form — on paper.

"Danni, you okay?" he asked anxiously.

"I'm fine. And I'd love a coffee, even if it is after midnight."

"Gotcha," Billie said, hopping up and switching on their "pod" machine. He knew she liked a special pecan blend and he set about fixing her a cup. Wolf came to rest at her feet. She felt his cold nose and reached down to give him a pat.

She told Billie and Bo Ray everything she knew while Billie reheated their dinner, some kind of chicken and dumplings he'd whipped up. She thought it odd that while the man might have come with her dad from Scotland years before, he'd embraced the New Orleans tradition of throwing hot sauce into everything. Thankfully, he'd decided *not* to dump an entire bottle into the chicken and dumplings.

"One day a slaughter, and the next night a man killed," Bo Ray mused. "Do you think it'll stop now? The person who wanted the painting apparently has the painting. Wouldn't that mean he'd stop killing to get it?"

A reasonable question, the same one Hattie had asked. But . . .

"I don't think the person who has the painting is the one who did the killing," Quinn said from the doorway.

"What do you mean?"

"That the killer is somehow . . . not really human."

"The *painting* is doing the killing?" Bo Ray demanded.

"My turn for a shower," Danni inter-rupted, checking her watch. She'd felt herself growing more tired the longer she sat there. Now it was after one in the morning — early by NOLA standards, perhaps, but it seemed late to her tonight.

She fled up the stairs to shower while Quinn told Billie and Bo Ray everything that had happened while he was at the house.

She meant to shower quickly. She felt exactly as Quinn had described — as though she bore the scent of blood. She hadn't been in the room with Bryson Arnold's body like he had, but she was anxious to wash off all residue of the day.

At last she pulled back the shower curtain . . . and had to swallow a scream. Quinn was standing there, naked, holding a towel for her.

She started to say something. He looked at her, and just shook his head.

She stepped into his arms and he wrapped the towel around her. His mouth found hers. They kissed standing there for a moment, until she didn't need the towel anymore and it dropped to the floor. With their lips still pressed together, they staggered into her bedroom and paused. Moonbeams peeked through slits in the curtains, bathing their bodies in ethereal light. Then they fell onto the bed. She relished the feel of his lips as they moved over her body, igniting her skin and the muscles beneath.

She'd thought she was tired. She *was* tired.

But now she was exhilarated. The entire world was good again.

That night, they made love without ever speaking. They indulged in hot searing kisses before their lips moved on to other erogenous zones, only to meet again. At last they lay quietly together. Danni became aware of the air conditioner's hum; she could even hear distant music and laughter from Bourbon Street. She wanted to drift off in his arms, in the slivers of moonlight that still touched the room.

But she whispered, "Where do we go from here?"

He pulled her more tightly against him. "To sleep," he told her.

"But —"

"Sleep," he said. "Right now, I don't know where we go. All I do know is that we have to find the painting."

"No *object* could cause so much horror. . . ."

"There's still a lot to learn about the history of this painting," he said in a soft voice. "For now . . ."

She grew silent. She let his arms encircle

her and decided that, for this night, she would enjoy the feel of his body against her own.

And she'd pray that the painting had taken its final toll. The painting — and whoever worked for it. Or with it.

She prayed that nothing would happen during the night.

When Danni woke in the morning, she found Quinn leaning up on one elbow, staring at her. "Anything?" she asked warily.

He shook his head. "I'd almost hoped I'd find you painting in the middle of the night," he admitted.

"I didn't . . . I didn't sleepwalk."

"No. I'm going down to study what you did the other night. And I guess we need to get to the hospital as quickly as possible. Before Hattie takes off on her own."

"Seriously, though, why would anyone come after Hattie now? She doesn't have the painting anymore. I'm sure the Garcia family died because the painting was in their house."

"I don't know, but legally she still owns it. That could make her a target," Quinn said.

"Okay, let's look at my painting and then get to the hospital."

"In a minute."

"A minute?"

"Well, a few minutes. We can't take too much time, but there's this very . . . romantic quality about morning. Especially when I'm just getting back in the swing of things with you."

"Romantic?" she asked. "Really?"

He looked at her solemnly for a moment. "You know how I feel about you. I don't think I can even describe it. So, if I'm away from you . . . all I'm doing is dreaming about you. . . ."

"We'd better be fast," she whispered.

"You don't often hear that from a woman!" he said.

Within thirty minutes they were showered, dressed and downstairs. Danni was astonished that it was only eight and that Quinn had woken so easily, since the night before had been late.

But now he seemed to be on a mission.

He studied the painting she'd created herself — her nocturnal interpretation of the Hubert. But he didn't say anything; he told her he was mulling it over. Bo Ray, eating cereal, was eager to know what he should be doing during the day.

"We keep the shop, son. That's what we do. We keep the shop," Billie told him, nodding to Danni as she and Quinn prepared to leave.

"Thanks. We'll be in touch," Danni promised.

Before they went out, she gave Wolf treats. Wolf accepted them but didn't seem mollified. He didn't like being left behind.

They arrived at the hospital just in time; Hattie Lamont was dressed — in yesterday's clothes — and fuming that she needed to be released, but the doctor hadn't signed an order yet.

"Thank God you're here!" Hattie told Danni. "You can help me get out of here!"

"Hattie," Quinn said, "maybe it would be best if you stayed another night."

"Another night?" she challenged. "Hospitals, sir — when you're not in need of medical care — are where they send old people to die. I am not checking out in *that* manner, yet, if you don't mind!"

"Hattie, quite frankly, I think you're far tougher than I am," Quinn said. "But I don't like the idea of you staying at your house alone or even in a hotel."

"Has my house been destroyed?"

"No, the police were careful. Just the one room. You'll need to get a special cleaning crew. There are actually specialists who'll see that . . ."

"All the blood is cleaned up?" Hattie asked.

"Yes," Quinn replied.

Hattie sat on the foot of the hospital bed. "I really prefer my own place. And I don't — oh, it's still so hard to believe that Bryson Arnold plotted against me! But there's no one to plot against me now, and I have locks and alarms and cameras and . . . I want to go home!"

"I have an idea!" Danni said.

Quinn looked at her skeptically.

"Hattie, I have two wonderful employees. Bo Ray is young and industrious and I'd trust him with my life. Billie was with my father back in Scotland, before he came to the States. They can take turns staying with you."

"Billie came with your dad from Scotland, eh?" Hattie snorted in a rather inelegant manner. "He must be even older than I am. He must be older than dirt!"

"Ouch! Don't ever let Billie hear you say that," Quinn teased. "I don't know how old he is, Hattie. I wouldn't dare ask him. He's spry as a young chicken and mean as a hornet when something's up." Quinn turned to Danni. "Brilliant idea!" he said. "I think we —"

"Well, now, wait!" Hattie broke in. "I

haven't met these pillars of virtue yet."

"That's easily done," Quinn said. "I'll see about your discharge papers. Then we'll head over to The Cheshire Cat and you can meet Billie and Bo Ray."

Quinn left the room, moving with a sense of purpose.

"I haven't approved this idea, you know," the old woman muttered.

"Hattie, you shouldn't be alone," Danni said.

Hattie smiled wryly. "A week ago I would've dismissed your fears as if they were flies. Yesterday morning I would've done the same. Last evening, I *did* do the same." She paused. "I'm not afraid often, Danni."

"I realize that, Hattie."

Quinn came back in. "Hattie, the crime scene technicians are giving your house another going-over. And the alarm and security camera people will need to be notified before everything's back in order. But I've thought of another plan you may agree to."

"And what is that, young man?"

"I have a house in the Garden District. It's neat and clean, I swear. I've got a great housekeeper. I'm going to have you stay there, and Billie and Bo Ray can take turns

196

doing guard duty. We're also going to send over someone who's even better at that — Wolf."

"Who is this Wolf person?"

"We'll introduce you," Quinn said.

Crime scene tape still surrounded the mansion on Esplanade, but the officer at the door was expecting them. Hattie entered her house, glanced around and shuddered. "This has been my home for so long. I chose this house. I loved it. I restored it," she said.

"They'll be done soon enough. Then it can be the house you love again," Quinn told her.

"I don't know." Hattie sounded forlorn. "I may never feel the same way about it. Well, I'll just get some things and we can leave."

As she went upstairs, she avoided looking into the room where Bryson Arnold had been killed.

Quinn left Danni downstairs and followed Hattie. As he did, he peered into the gallery. Grace Leon, small, wiry, with short graying curls and a confident manner, was head of the forensic unit still going through the room. He didn't walk in, although he wasn't sure what they still needed to cover.

He didn't intend to risk disturbing their work.

But Grace saw him. "Hey, Quinn."

"Find anything, Grace?"

"Not much. Until whatever happened actually happened, it was spotless. There's no dust. I saw the tapes, and the intruder/ killer was wearing gloves, so I'm not expecting fingerprints. We've only made one little discovery so far — beyond the obvious, I mean. The blood."

"What discovery is that?" he asked.

"A bit of mud that must have been caked on the intruder's shoes." She walked across the room to a cart and returned, holding an evidence bag.

"Can you piece together how Bryson Arnold died?" Quinn asked.

"Sure, come on in. We've tackled the floor already. Avoid the big pool of blood."

"You know, Gracie, that's something I don't need to be told."

"Follow me," Grace said, as if she hadn't heard his tongue-in-cheek comment. "First, our dead man entered dragging something along. Scraps of packaging were found on the floor. He stopped about here and started ripping up the packaging. You can see that by the little pieces of brown paper and bubble wrap, there — where we've put the markers. Then . . . it's the oddest thing."

"What?"

"I think he stopped and cut himself."

"On purpose?" Quinn remembered Dr. Hubert's comments from the night before.

"Yeah, that's what it looks like. I think he used a box cutter to slice his own thumb," Grace told him. "We found the box cutter with his blood on it, but there's none of his blood on the remnants of packaging."

"So, he cut his own hand. What then?"

"Hard to say. The body position is chalked out on the floor. Our intruder came in from that direction." She pointed over her shoulder. "The body's facing the other way. Our intruder should've been in front of him, but it looks like someone came up from behind and cut his throat from left to right, using a very sharp knife and considerable strength. The victim fell — you know where and how, since you were the one to find him. Looking at this room, you'd have thought more than two people were in it, that's for sure," Grace finished.

Quinn nodded; he could see what she meant.

"We'll be done here in a day or two. I left cards with the names of the best crime scene cleanup crews on the counter downstairs."

"Thanks, Gracie."

"You're welcome, Quinn."

He hurried back downstairs. Hattie hadn't returned yet, but Danni was standing in the parlor, pensively studying the room.

She turned to face him. "I like her, Quinn. I really like her."

"Actually, I do, too," he said.

"Do you feel we should just move her to my place?"

"No. She'd be close by, but you never know when some kind of activity might start up at the shop."

The shop had come under attack before.

Danni frowned. "You're right. Did you learn anything from the crime scene people?"

"Grace said that from what they could piece together, it seemed as if someone other than the intruder had gotten behind the victim."

She stared into the fireplace. "So you'd think . . . you'd almost think that someone was stepping out of the painting and bringing a murder weapon along. Or," she added, "*we* might think that."

"Yes."

"How else could it have happened?" she murmured. Then she shook her head. "Let's say that Bryson Arnold purposely took this job because he somehow knew that Hattie was bidding on the painting. He was in collusion with the intruder. That's a sound theory, supported by the footage from the house. It's even possible that someone at the auction house was involved, at least to the extent of providing that information. Or it could be that someone heard her talking about it to a gallery owner somewhere. Hattie said she might have mentioned her interest in acquiring a Hubert painting in one of those conversations. Whoever came in knew that Hattie had bought the painting and he knew its history. Maybe Bryson didn't. Or maybe he'd heard some kind of rumor about it — something we'd need to ferret out. I'm not convinced he was supposed to die. I think he took the initiative and did something that activated the painting, except that . . ." Her voice trailed off for a minute and she looked at Quinn. "Maybe the painting didn't want him?"

"One thing's for sure — we need to learn more about the painting."

"From Dr. Hubert," Danni said. "You suggested that before and I've been wanting to do it. He might have something."

"He might," Quinn agreed. "But I don't think he's too proud of his association with the artist. Still, we can talk to him."

Hattie had come down. "If you would, Quinn, my suitcase is at the top of the stairs."

"I'll get it," he said immediately. They left Hattie's house; the distance to Royal was so short it was almost ridiculous to drive. Danni unlocked the side door and they entered through the courtyard.

Wolf always knew when someone was coming, and he was there to greet them. Seeing the massive dog, Hattie started.

"My God!" she gasped, hanging back.

"This is Wolf, Hattie. He won't hurt you. In fact, he'd die for you once you're his friend," Quinn told her.

For a moment, the older woman remained frozen. Then she said, "I guess I'd better be his friend, then. Hello . . . Wolf."

"Give him a pat," Danni encouraged.

Hattie did so, hesitantly at first. Wolf whined and thumped his tail.

"He *is* quite friendly," Hattie said. "He seems so easygoing."

"He's as easy as a Bourbon Street hooker." Quinn couldn't resist the cheap joke.

Danni rolled her eyes, but Hattie looked shocked. Then she grinned.

"Hattie, we'll see you in the kitchen after we grab Billie and Bo Ray. We'll have you meet them one by one," Danni said.

"That would be lovely. Do you have any tea?"

"Of course." Danni glanced at Quinn.

"You stay with Hattie. I'll explain our situation to the guys." He walked through the showroom, where Bo Ray was busy with a customer, while Billie stood behind the counter. Quinn walked over to him. Billie looked up, a little apprehensive. He was always aware of what could be required — or what could be at stake.

"Billie, I need huge favors from you and Bo Ray."

"All right," he said in a grudging voice. Quinn could tell that Billie already knew he wasn't going to like what he had to say.

"We have Hattie Lamont in the kitchen," he began.

"In *our* kitchen? Ah, the woman is frightened — and therefore slumming?"

"They haven't finished with her house. I don't want her at a hotel or away from . . . well, away from protection."

"She's not staying here!" Billie protested.

"No, I think she should stay at my house," Quinn said.

"It's your house, your choice."

"I need you and Bo Ray to take turns staying with her."

"You want *us* to babysit a society dragon?"

"Billie, I swear, she's not so bad. Come on back and meet her. We'll leave Bo Ray to handle the shop, then I'll let you go and bring him in."

Billie agreed, obviously unhappy. He and Quinn nodded to Bo Ray, who was extolling the virtues of one of their local jewelry designers to a friendly-looking middle-aged couple, and Bo Ray nodded in return. He knew the shop was in his hands.

Billie muttered as they walked through the shop and into the private area downstairs. "Favor. Hmph. *Favor.* You know it's in m'blood to do as you and Danni ask. Favor, indeed."

But before they could reach the kitchen, they heard a scream.

A scream of pure terror.

Quinn could only describe it as déjà vu.

CHAPTER 8

The sound came from Danni's studio.

Quinn rushed in that direction. He threw the door open; Danni's nocturnal rendition of the Hubert painting remained on the easel in all its gory splendor. Hattie Lamont was standing in front of it.

Danni was already there, striding toward the trembling woman. She took Hattie in her arms and turned to Quinn with apologetic eyes. "She was sitting in the kitchen . . . I was making tea and talking, and she wandered in here!"

"Hattie, it's a painting. Just a painting," Quinn said.

"A horrible painting! Lord, it's evil!" Hattie looked at Danni, her eyes wide. "You . . . *you* created this."

"I guess I was trying to figure out what lies beneath the surface of the Hubert," Danni said. "I'm so sorry. I didn't realize you'd left the kitchen and come here."

Hattie seemed to give herself a mental shake as she stood there, very dignified. "Of course, well . . ."

"I'm sorry," Danni said again. "Are you okay?"

"I'm — I'm okay," Hattie whispered. "I was so *startled* . . . and yet it does reveal exactly what's going on in the Hubert, doesn't it? But this doesn't deceive as much. The color draws you to it, and then you see what it really is — ghastly."

"It's only a copy, a different perception of what Hubert was showing, Hattie." Before anyone else could say anything, Wolf started barking and Bo Ray burst into the room. "Don't worry. Everything's fine," Quinn quickly assured him.

"If we have any customers, tell them a friend was just startled," Danni told him.

"Yeah, of course," Bo Ray said.

"Oh — this is Hattie Lamont. Hattie, Bo Ray Tompkins." Once polite greetings were exchanged, Bo Ray returned to the shop.

Wolf whined and set his nose on Hattie's hand. She leaned down to pat the dog. "How embarrassing! In any event, I'm completely recovered. I'll have that tea now if I may."

As if nothing had happened, she sailed out of the studio.

206

They all went into the kitchen, and Danni seated Hattie at the table in front of a steaming cup of tea.

Hattie didn't rise; she studied Billie like a queen inspecting a subject. Then she turned to Quinn, frowning. "*That man* is going to protect me? I'm sorry, but he looks like an escapee from a sixties rock band!"

"And you look like you think your shite smells like roses!" Billie snapped in return.

"Hey!" Danni protested. "Both of you! We're all after the same thing here."

After she'd made introductions, Hattie looked at Quinn. "So, is this Mr. William McDougall going to act as my butler?"

"Now, that's it! I'm *no one's* butler!" Billie insisted.

"No, he's going to be your companion and your guard," Quinn said firmly.

"Society! Och. Only if she remembers her manners!"

"I beg your pardon!" Hattie said, rising to her feet.

"Mrs. Lamont, I will be polite and courteous at all times — if you are capable of doing the same." Billie drew himself up with great dignity.

"Capable!"

"Listen," Quinn said impatiently, "the two of you don't need to become best friends.

You just have to watch out for . . . anything. We'll bring Wolf to the house, as well."

Billie nodded curtly. "Right. I'll go and pack. When does Bo Ray spell me?"

"We'll do one day on and one day off. Does that suit you?"

Billie nodded again.

"Hattie?" Quinn asked.

"I believe, if I value my life, I'm at your mercy, Quinn," Hattie replied. "I shall be quite delighted to have Mr. McDougall as my . . . companion."

"So, let's head over to the Garden District now," Quinn suggested.

"I'll stay with Bo Ray and, uh, bring him up to speed," Danni said.

"Okay." Quinn wasn't sure what, but he sensed that she had something she needed to do.

Then he guessed what it was; she was going to go down and study the book her father, Angus, had left her — along with his other "collectibles."

Billie took a few minutes to pack a small bag. There was no reason to worry about Wolf; Quinn always kept food at his house. Wolf had originally been his; actually, he and Angus Cafferty had been responsible for taking in the one-time police dog — a wolf-shepherd mix — when he'd been seriously injured during a case in Texas.

Quinn had grown up in the Garden District home and eventually purchased it from his parents. He'd been what he could only call a reprobate for so long that it had been a matter of pride for them all when he'd made the money and insisted on paying for the home. His parents had cried.

Dying had been the best thing that had ever happened to him.

Hattie sat silently beside Quinn as he drove, with Wolf and Billie in the back.

"It really is a gorgeous part of the city," Hattie remarked, gazing around.

"Yes, ma'am, I think so, too," Quinn said.

She was just as pleased when they reached his house.

Together with Billie, he inspected the place. Everything was as it should be. "There's one room downstairs that's set up as a bedroom," Quinn told her. "I'm going to have Billie sleep there. Wolf will keep guard in the parlor, and there's a nice guest room upstairs. I think you'll be comfortable there."

Hattie nodded. "Yes, thank you. I'll be just fine. Any minute now, Billie and I are going to turn on the TV and enjoy another cup of tea, while we watch an entertaining musical." She frowned. "You *do* have Netflix, young man?"

Quinn said he did.

When Billie let out a groan, Quinn held back his grin. For a minute there, Billie reminded him of Lurch — the *butler* in the old *Addams Family* television show.

"Don't worry," Hattie said, addressing Billie. "I do know how to brew tea. In fact, I'll be happy to make you a cup right now."

"Lovely," Billie said politely. "I'll turn on the telly."

Quinn left them, sure that they'd get along well enough; frankly, they had no choice. At the door, he spoke to Wolf. "Watch out for them, boy. Okay?"

The dog barked. Quinn had always believed that Wolf knew he'd saved his life, and had given him unstinting loyalty ever since. When the vet had suggested Wolf be put down because of the difficult and lengthy care he'd need, Quinn, with Angus Cafferty's support, had decided to take him on.

He'd never made a better decision.

Back in his car, he called Danni. She answered on the second ring. He told her that his household seemed in order.

"Poor Billie!"

"He'll manage."

"I've gotten accustomed to having Wolf at

my feet."

"We'll manage, too, for a few days, anyway," he said. "Are you in the basement?"

"I am," she answered. "I'm reading. It's slow going. How about you?"

"I'm stopping in at the morgue," he said. "I want to see if we can catch Doc Hubert tonight. Pay him a visit."

"Sounds good.

Quinn hung up and drove to the morgue.

He knew what — or rather, who — Dr. Hubert would be working on.

The massive volume she'd inherited from Angus, written by someone named Millicent Smith — during or soon after the witchcraft trials in Salem — read like a strange cookbook.

Except that the "recipes" were all related to bizarre occurrences in history, objects around which strange events had taken place, or people who'd shown extraordinary behavior, both good and bad.

She searched for references to killer paintings, but she found nothing. The book could be frustrating; sometimes, it took a lot of searching to come up with what she needed.

Sighing loudly, she sat back. Maybe she should bring the book into the modern age — scan the pages and enter them into a computer. That way, she could use the "find" function when she was looking for something specific.

Leaving the book for the moment, she turned to the computer, wondering if she'd been using the wrong key words when she'd tried Google earlier. She'd focused on Hubert and suddenly realized that she hadn't done the obvious — she hadn't looked up *haunted paintings*.

There was a plethora of relevant sites. She felt like a fool; she should've used the right search words from the beginning.

But checking one website after the next, she still couldn't find anything about *Ghosts in the Mind*.

She'd been so elated at what she'd felt would be a breakthrough. Now, nothing.

She thought about the year the painting had been executed. Leaning back, she tried to imagine Lake Geneva and the creepy castle Hubert had rented for the summer. She was certain he'd used the House of Guillaume as the backdrop for *Ghosts in the Mind*. And she wondered, yet again, whether the characters in the painting meant anything. Had he, at some point in his life, known evil children? *Really* evil children — like the ones in *Children of the Corn*?

She turned back to the book. "The answers are in there, aren't they? You're a powerful book. I just haven't learned the right way to read you."

The book had to be read under a special light. Her father had told her about it as he lay dying, but she hadn't understood. She'd had to learn exactly what he'd meant when the bust of Pietro Miro had suddenly appeared in her life.

When Quinn had appeared in her life.

Odd. It hadn't been *that* long ago, but she could barely remember when she hadn't known Quinn.

Or wanted him. Even when he infuriated her.

"Okay, so you're not ready to tell me?" she asked the book. "I'm obviously going about *something* the wrong way."

Danni went to her studio next, determined to study the painting she'd done in her sleep. She tried to recognize the differences between the original and her nocturnal painting, tried to work out what her mind wanted to show her but couldn't express except through the brush.

The real Hubert was so subtle. The painting changed, depending on the distance and angle from which it was seen — perhaps even the person by whom it was seen. It was all about *perspective.* Her own painting was tempting because of the vivid colors, but the ugliness was revealed as soon as the viewer came close.

Danni assumed that her sleepwalk painting had to do with things she saw or suspected in her subconscious mind. But those truths hadn't emerged yet, hadn't entered her *conscious* mind. Studying the picture, she saw that she'd captured the Hubert characters — every one of them.

She found herself looking at the children. No one ever wanted to believe that children could be evil. And yet, most serial killers showed strange traits when they were children. They liked to torture family pets and other animals.

Some started killing at very young ages.

While the great majority of children were innocent and adults tended to protect them, *these children, the ones in the painting,* were definitely different. But in reality, how evil could the child on the floor, playing with the guillotine, have been?

She didn't think she'd ever heard of a two- or three-year-old killer!

So where was the true evil in the painting? Was it the husband? Or the wife? She was well aware that women could be as malicious and evil as men.

She backed away. In the original Hubert,

the evil within was insidious . . . it snuck up on you. Even when you had the right perspective, it took a moment to realize what you were looking at.

In her version, you were drawn in by the color, you came closer, and wham!

She walked up to the painting, and then walked away. Then she moved closer again.

The color, especially the red, so rich, so deep and dark.

Dark, rich, deep red. The color of blood once it was spilled.

She hurried out of the studio, heading down to her father's office in the basement again. Bo Ray called out to her. "Danni? You okay?"

"Yep, I'm fine!" she called back.

She sat behind the desk once more, placing the book beneath the special light. She began to flip through the pages.

She didn't look for *haunted paintings.* She wouldn't find the Hubert, since it was painted more than a century after the book's publication. But she might find information about such works.

She looked for paintings created with *blood.*

Hubert was at autopsy. Quinn found it disturbing that he'd become such a frequent visitor to the morgue these days, he was barely greeted before someone escorted him to Dr. Hubert — whether he was in his office or at autopsy.

The attendant suggested he might want a mask and gown. He accepted.

When he entered, the body of Bryson Arnold had already been cleaned. Still, he was glad of the mask. The tinny scent of blood seemed heavy in the air.

Hubert looked at him through the plastic visor he was wearing; he'd evidently finished the Y incision and measured and inspected the man's organs. He'd taken the saw to the skull and weighed the brain.

Folds of Arnold's skin lay open, leaving a gaping hole as his chest. The skull looked like something out of a horror movie, only it was real. To Hubert, Quinn knew, there was no horror in it. It was science.

"Just in time," Hubert told Quinn.

"For what?"

"For me to tell you that this was a healthy man of forty-three who might have lived to be a hundred. All that blood you saw? It came from one wound. Here's a fact I continue to ponder — the strength needed to cut so swiftly and deeply. Cutting someone's throat might sound easy, but it's not. The throat has muscles and tendons. And severing the spinal column . . . Decapitation is hard."

"Thankfully, I'm not usually looking to decapitate anyone," Quinn muttered.

"I'll be doing tests on the brain, of course," Hubert said. "But I believe we'll find that it's normal. I'm seeing no lesions, cysts or bruising — nothing that would suggest injury or disease. The man was in perfect mental condition."

"Are any of us in perfect mental condition, Doc?" Quinn asked.

"Probably not, my friend. But, as far as our standards go, he was in good physical and mental condition — before he bled out, of course."

"I saw Grace at the crime scene and she demonstrated where Arnold would've been standing when he died. And if the intruder was *in front* of him, someone else had to be there, as well."

"I heard the cameras were knocked out when the intruder got into the room."

"True," Quinn said. "Or more or less true. They weren't knocked out. They just recorded fog."

"Fog? Inside a house? There had to be something wrong with the cameras. Maybe an electrical surge. Whatever happened, it was certainly a convenient malfunction for

217

the intruder."

"The police are still going through the recordings," Quinn said. "And I believe technicians are searching for anything that might have caused such . . . images."

"But you don't think they're going to find an explanation?"

"For the cameras going on the fritz? No. I do think they'll discover that the man who entered the house exited with the painting," Quinn said. "I doubt they'll actually come up with a third person. Oh, there might be footage of Danni and me breaking in and finding Mrs. Lamont. What I mean is, I think there was one person, and he *has* to have been in collusion with Bryson Arnold. Arnold made it possible for the intruder to just walk in. Whether that intruder intended for Bryson to die . . . I'm not sure."

"Well, dead he is," Hubert said flatly.

"Thanks to a sharp blade."

"Yes. Very sharp. Those who set out to do bad things . . . often die badly. I guess the old adage that he who lives by the sword dies by the sword still applies. As you've just said, there's not really much of a mystery. Sad to say, Mr. Arnold here was abusing his position with Mrs. Lamont and making deals with a partner who betrayed him rather than share stolen goods."

218

Quinn was silent.

"So," Hubert continued, "the painting is loose in the city. Or I guess I should say whoever took it is loose in the city."

"That seems to be the gist of it," Quinn said. "I really need help here, Dr. Hubert. What do you know about the painting?"

Hubert shook his head, looking down. "I've never seen the real thing. I've seen likenesses of it in books, that's all. I know very little about it beyond the fact that it's disturbing and ugly. I never cared for it — and never gave it much thought."

"That's it?" Quinn asked. "Come on, you *must* know more. I mean, legends and stories must've come down through your family."

"I know that bad things happened around the painting, yes." He shrugged. "But bad things happened in the world. All wars are dreadful. The painting was caught up in the thievery that went on during the Second World War — but that meant nothing against the multitude of lives lost."

"True, but I have to find that painting, Doc."

"Maybe you shouldn't. Maybe the killer will wallow in it and die himself. Or sell the blasted thing out of the country or dump it in the Mississippi. Better than dumping it in the river, the damned thing should probably be burned."

"Aha! Say what you will, man of science. You believe it *is* evil?"

"I see evil every day, Quinn. I see the evil people do to other people. Gunshot wounds, knife wounds . . . drug deaths."

"You're hedging, Doc."

Hubert paused and sighed deeply. "I'm a medical doctor, Quinn. A scientist. But do I believe perception can create reality? Yes. That painting is bad news. And, yes, I believe it should be destroyed."

"Then help me find it."

For a minute, Quinn thought Hubert was going to ask him how he could possibly help. Then he said, "Come by tonight, after eight. I won't be home until then. Lord, it does seem that I'm married to my work and my work never seems to end. But I do have a home. No wife, no children, no siblings even . . ." He exhaled noisily. "Back to your request, I do have old family papers. I've never shown them to anyone. If you think they'll be of any use, you're welcome to them."

Danni had come across an especially interesting chapter in Millicent Smith's book — "Creations in the Blood of Evil."

Apparently, there'd been a case similar to the one they were working on that had occurred in 1614 in Yorkshire. An artistic young miller had painted a duel between two knights, in which one of the combatants had cleanly sliced the head from the neck of his opponent. Millicent supplied a sketch of the painting. It was gruesome, with the sword still in midair and the head flying. The young miller, who'd been paid by his friend, a local cobbler, to create the painting, died soon after he completed it, suffering from an unknown malady. The painting was taken away by officers in the hamlet; they were soon found dead — decapitated.

James VI of Scotland and I of England was king at the time, and was a huge believer in witchcraft. He ordered the young man exhumed, burned to ash and then the ashes were taken and scattered in the ocean. But the killing didn't stop — until a local priest discovered that the painting remained intact. Through neighbors, who recognized the men in the painting, he learned that the cobbler had commissioned the work. He'd ordered the miller to paint himself as the vanquished knight. When the cobbler was arrested, he admitted giving his blood in the creation of the painting and "awakening" it with more blood.

Goods from several locals who'd been killed were found in his house. Most people assumed the cobbler had done the killing. He was hanged and burned on a pyre, along with the painting.

The killing stopped.

"Those who were innocent, killed for their blood and goods, did not become as demons on earth," Smith commented. "Whatever way men choose to see the Great Power above, innocence is not punished in the afterlife. But those who are seduced to evil will rest with evil. Yet a demon may lie dormant and await the years. Men must take care, for men are weak, and too easily seduced by the demon." Danni drummed her fingers on the table. The seventeenth-century painter had died; his accomplice in the creation of blood-paint had also died.

So, according to what she'd read, the cobbler and perhaps the miller had been willing to dabble in black magic in their quest to gain riches — the riches of the people killed by the painting, which had been activated by blood. The cobbler had given his own blood, starting the whole process, and then continued it by periodically adding blood to the canvas.

She carefully closed the book and rose.

She needed to get a good look at the real *Ghosts in the Mind.* Or at least the copy.

Bo Ray was chatting with an attractive woman at the counter. Danni mouthed to him, "Just going down the street. Back in five!"

He nodded, and she grinned as she left. Healthy and spruced up, Bo Ray was darned cute these days. And he deserved a chance to flirt and maybe get lucky sometime soon.

But she forgot Bo Ray as she hurried down to Image Me This.

She didn't see Niles as she walked in, and Mason was busy extolling the virtues of a local artist's painting of Saint Louis Cathedral to a couple of visitors.

That was good. She didn't want to talk; she wanted to study the giclée of the Hubert painting, *Ghosts in the Mind.*

She positioned herself so she could see the "evil" angle of the painting.

She studied the characters. The man and the woman, presumably the parents, the three children, the two suits of armor, the butler, the two official-looking men who'd just arrived and the medieval knight in the portrait above the hearth.

Of course, the chess pieces were alive at this angle, too, running from the children. And the heads of the decapitated dolls were screaming.

But something still made her believe that the chess pieces and the dolls were victims. It might have been the horror on their faces and the way they were screaming.

That left eleven.

Were the eleven faces pictured the faces of killers? And she had to wonder — did Hubert include himself in the painting?

She asked herself again how a toddler could be a killer. Bad enough to think that children of say eight and ten might have been cold-blooded.

"Ah, you're drawn to it! Fascinating — absolutely fascinating piece!" she heard.

Mason Bradley had come up to her. He was smiling, but rather grimly.

"It's interesting, for sure," Danni said. "How are you doing with it?"

"People are something, aren't they? Since all the hoopla over the original being in the city and people being *killed* so it could be stolen, the giclées have just about jumped off the walls. We have two left — the one on the wall, and one Niles put away for you."

"Wow," Danni said. "I guess we are a gruesome lot."

"So, how's your own work going?"

She thought of the last "painting" she'd done.

"Fine. I'm not ready for another show yet."

Mason was a striking man. He'd have made a great hero on a prime-time drama, so tall, blond and charming. He smiled at her with a rueful curl to his lip — one that, ironically, made him even more attractive.

"Hate to admit it, but I'm not ready, either. You know, Niles mentioned the other day that we should do a show together. Maybe a few months down the line?"

"I'd love to do a show together. Maybe 'Street Scenes' or something like that. When we're both ready, of course."

"I know how hard it can be. And Niles keeps bringing it up." He lowered his voice. "I know he loves me, and I love him — as a friend. A best friend. I'm just not *in* love with him the way he'd like me to be."

Danni nodded sympathetically.

"Anyway, we'll nudge each other every few weeks," Mason said. "I do so much survival work on restoration — it's great to get to my own stuff. Hey, where's that great big pile of dog — Wolf?"

"Oh, he's . . . he's with a friend right now."

"Ah. Don't lend him out often. He's a great accessory for you. Beautiful, tall, long-haired woman, beautiful big wolf-dog at her side — it's a great look."

"Thanks. Dog as fashion accessory. Oh, I'll mention that to Quinn."

Mason laughed. "Hey, would you like your giclée delivered today?"

Yes. She should have it at the house.

No! She hated the damned thing!

"Sure, Mason. Thanks."

"Niles will be back soon and we'll wrap it up. And don't worry — if you're out, we know to deliver it to Billie or Bo Ray," Mason told her.

"Thanks. That's nice of you two. Well, I should get back. Thanks again, Mason."

"Always a pleasure, Danni. Too bad you fell for that good-looking one-time cop," he said, winking. "You and I would've been great together."

She laughed. "Mason, you and I would've been *horrible* together — artistic egos clashing constantly. Not to mention that you're enjoying your life as a . . ."

"Womanizer?"

"Flirt." She gave him a kiss on the cheek. "See you soon."

She fled the store. She wondered why she dreaded having the giclée in the shop.

It was just a copy.

Quinn wouldn't share her apprehension. He'd be glad that they could study it — and try to figure out the evil secrets trapped in the original work.

Bo Ray had new customers when she returned. She interrupted him briefly to smile and welcome the customers — and let him know that the giclée would be arriving some time that evening.

Then she went back to the basement and resumed her study of Millicent Smith's book, hoping she could find more information. Sadly — as she'd already learned — the book offered many answers, but they weren't always easy to find.

Danni was deep into a chapter called "Devils and Demons" when her cell phone rang.

It was Bo Ray.

"Everything okay at the store?" she asked. "You *are* still in the store? I mean, you're calling, but I can't be more than sixty feet from you."

"Yes, I'm in the store. But so are a number of customers. In the interests of no one attempting to take our merchandise without paying for it, I'm calling. I'm just giving you a heads-up. Natasha is on her way down to see you."

Danni thanked him, and a minute later, she heard Natasha on the stairs. "Come in!" she invited.

Natasha did, cracking open the door and

entering the room. She glanced around the "collection" as if she'd expected something to have changed. Nothing had. The Victorian coffin with its glass face plate was still there, along with the sarcophagus, the fortune-telling machine and other mismatched remnants of history.

Natasha took the chair across from her. "I see you're reading Millicent's book," she said with a smile. "Found anything?"

"All kinds of things, but I haven't actually put them together yet. What are you doing here? Everything okay? It's still business hours, and you hardly ever leave your shop when it's open," Danni said.

"I have Jez," she said. "So, Mrs. Lamont is alive, the butler is dead and the painting is gone. What now?"

"Hattie Lamont is staying at Quinn's house in the Garden District. Billie and Wolf are with her. I'm studying the book. The police are following whatever leads they have. Quinn got Hattie and Billie set up, and he's gone to the morgue. He wants to talk to Ron Hubert tonight. We've speculated that the killing will stop now that whoever wanted the painting so badly has it."

She didn't entirely believe that, and Natasha confirmed her fears.

"The killing will *not* stop and you know it. The painting waits for the weak and unwary — those who feel they've been slighted or cheated in life. Or those who — like Henry Sebastian Hubert — so desperately want to be part of the 'in' crowd," she said with unconcealed scorn. "People think they'll use a piece like the painting. They will not. The painting will use them."

"I know you're right," Danni said. "What I'm thinking is that Hubert used blood for his red pigment or mixed it into the paint. Of course, I don't have the painting itself, so I don't know for sure. Ideally, we'd have chemical analysis done. But I also thought maybe he'd painted himself into the scene. I went back to look at the giclée this afternoon, and I've gone through my art books and studied every image of him I could find. He doesn't *seem* to be in it. He's not one of the chess pieces, and he's not one of the decapitated doll heads. He's not in it. Although . . . I can't be a hundred percent sure. All the faces are clearly depicted — except that of the man with the pistol behind his back. We can't really see his face, so I can't tell if that's Hubert himself or someone else. Not only that, I haven't figured out who all the other characters are."

"Then you need to figure that out, don't you?"

"It was painted so long ago — and so far away," Danni murmured.

"That's why I'm here."

"Oh?" Danni threw her a puzzled glance.

"I was doing a reading today for a neighbor. Tarot cards. It was a perfectly normal reading. The cards fell in cycles that fit with her life and the decisions she has to make. Then I was staring at the 'hanged man.' Now, you know that can mean many things. For my client, it's a reversal. She and her husband separated, but they want to be together. They split over money problems and just need to see them through. But there was the card and suddenly . . . I was someplace else. Back on that hillside. There were dark clouds roiling above, and there was a lake churning and white-capped. There was also a castle, an old stone castle, dark and foreboding. The place was just . . . grim. It was meant to repel invaders. I could *feel* that it came with dungeons, that people had suffered there. And, Danni, you were standing on the hill again. You were looking up at the sky and then at the castle. I was terribly afraid for you. It was as if you'd been . . . summoned to the castle. Drawn to it. As if some powerful force wanted you there. And it wasn't good."

Her friend was obviously distraught. Danni stretched her arm across the desk, taking Natasha's hand in hers. "You were reading the hanged man card, which, as you just said, can mean reversal. The painting's taken us on a kind of reversal. It was painted in the distant past, in a castle. That's why you saw . . . what you saw."

Natasha went on as though Danni hadn't spoken. "I kept screaming at you not to go to the castle. You didn't hear me. Or maybe you did, but you ignored me. You started walking toward it and it was . . ."

"What?"

"As if the great gates were a toothed mouth . . . and they were waiting to consume you. Danni, I'm afraid. I don't like this."

"Oh, Natasha, I don't like it, either. But we have to find the painting. You know that."

Natasha nodded fitfully. "Yes, yes, but . . . you *must* hear me out every time I have something to say to you. And I want you to go see Father Ryan tomorrow. I want him to give you a blessing and I . . . I brought you this."

She slipped a medal over her head and handed it to Danni, who studied it. She'd expected a voodoo talisman, but what the priestess had given her was a Saint Jude medallion.

"Saint Jude." Danni raised her eyebrows. "The patron saint of lost causes?"

"Can't hurt," Natasha said, getting to her feet. "I'm heading back to the shop. I just felt I needed to see you right away."

"Thank you. And, Natasha, please don't worry about me. Yes, the painting was created at a castle in Switzerland, but it's in New Orleans now. Six people are dead because of it, and we need to find it — before it really does disappear."

Natasha was silent. "The evil in the painting may go way back, Danni."

"Yes, but the painting itself is here."

Natasha held out her hands. "I see what I see."

"I know, and thank you again. You're a wonderful friend."

"Yes, I am," Natasha said, allowing herself a small smile.

Natasha walked to the door, but once she reached it, she paused. "Don't you even *think* of leaving this city without me."

"I'm not thinking about leaving the city at all."

"You will be," Natasha said. Then, with a swish of her colorful dress, she was gone.

CHAPTER 9

Quinn returned to the shop on Royal Street just as Bo Ray and Danni were locking up. He was glad to see that they'd started making dinner before closing and that the food was almost on the table.

He was famished. "Anything new?" Danni asked him.

"We're going to leave as soon as we've eaten — pay a visit to Dr. Hubert."

Danni nodded, and he realized she seemed a little agitated.

"What's wrong?" he asked. "Do *you* know something?"

"I'll just put plates and the casserole on the table," Bo Ray said. "Don't mind me."

Danni rolled her eyes. "Bo Ray, I've told you everything."

"Yes." Bo Ray turned to Quinn. "She's getting her copy of that blasted painting delivered sometime tonight."

"That's good, Bo Ray. We can study it

when it's here."

Quinn noticed Bo Ray's sardonic expression and smiled. "As far as I know, it's only the real deal that causes trouble. Not a copy."

"Yeah, great. But I'd rather not take any chances. Now you two are going to leave — and I don't even have the damned dog here!"

"I taught you how to shoot," Quinn pointed out. "And we'll be a phone call away. If anything scares you, get the hell out and run up to Bourbon Street. There's always a cop."

"Yeah," Bo Ray muttered. "I'm going to shoot a frickin' painting!"

"I can call and have them not deliver it until morning," Danni offered.

"You don't need to do that. But I'm not unwrapping it," Bo Ray insisted.

"No, you shouldn't. Anyway, you won't be here that long. I'm sure Billie will be switching places with you soon," Danni said.

"Battle-ax Lamont is actually starting to look good!" Bo Ray grumbled.

"The casserole smells delicious," Quinn said, changing the subject.

That remark visibly brightened Bo Ray's spirits. He'd been simmering meat and vegetables in the Crock-Pot all day; it had taken him a few minutes to throw the ingredients in a pan and top them with mashed potatoes and a sprinkling of Parmesan to provide a perfect crust.

The meal was as delicious as it smelled. While they ate, Danni told them both what she'd read in the book and about Natasha's visit. She explained that she'd looked at the giclée again, getting a better sense of the characters in it, including the chess pieces and dolls. "So, in that story I read in the Millicent Smith book, the artist had a friend who paid him to do the painting. He — the friend, a local cobbler — seems to have used his own blood. Then the artist died and there was murder and mayhem. The artist was dug up and burned and his ashes scattered but there was more killing. Turned out that the friend had 'awakened' or 'activated' the painting with *more* of his own blood. He was caught, executed and his ashes were strewn among rocks. The painting was destroyed and the killing stopped. The image was of two knights dueling. According to Smith, they represented the artist and his friend — although I don't quite get why the artist would show himself being killed. But it comes down to what people will do for money, I guess." She took a moment to savor a mouthful of the casserole.

"One thing that scares me is the fact that the Hubert painting is full of people. Eleven of them. I'm almost positive the chess pieces and decapitated dolls are victims."

Bo Ray shuddered. "I plan to turn on every light in this place. And your giclée is going straight to the basement *and* I'm locking the basement door. You two had better not be out too late!"

"Bo Ray, nothing here is worth anyone's life. If you get scared, do what Quinn said — call us and leave immediately," Danni told him.

"Painted with blood," Quinn mused, obviously caught up with his own thoughts. Frowning, he looked at Danni. "When I first went to the Garcia house, I found a small glass container. It had been washed out, but there was some kind of red residue in it. That vial disappeared, along with the other items when the 'fog' was in the evidence room. I'm thinking it might have been . . . blood."

"There would've been blood on the painting already," Danni said.

"Yes, but . . . well, we don't know yet. Whoever broke in might have done it in order to add *more* blood to the painting."

"To wake the dead? The dead in that painting?" Danni murmured.

"It's gone now," Quinn said. "We may never know with certainty. But I'm going to surmise that I'm right . . ."

When they'd finished eating, Quinn was even more anxious to get to Hubert's residence.

"Hey, not to worry. I'll get the dishes," Bo Ray said.

Danni laughed. "I'll make it up to you, I promise."

They escaped with Bo Ray still muttering to himself and reached the Hubert residence at eight-thirty — just in time to find Dr. Hubert out in his yard, despite the fact that it had grown dark.

He was planting a sign that read The Henry Hubert Painting Is Not Here! No Interviews, No Loitering — and Trespassers Will Be Prosecuted to the Full Extent of the Law. At the bottom, an addition had been scrawled: Or Shot!

Getting out of the car, Quinn noticed that there were cars parked up and down the street in the Irish Channel neighborhood.

Ron Hubert seemed almost unfamiliar without his lab coat. He was wearing a tailored shirt and jeans. His hair was ruffled and he resembled a disgruntled modern-day Beethoven. He saw Quinn and Danni and waved them in.

"The media got hold of the information that the police are looking for a killer who stole the painting. Naturally, the reporters just had to do their research and discover that a descendant of the artist lives in the city. I won't even answer my phone anymore, unless I can identify the person trying to reach me. Come in, come in! If I can do anything to help you get that painting back . . ." He shook his head. "People are *dying* over the blasted thing."

He led them into his house, a handsome structure probably built in the late 1800s. He'd been expecting them; there was a large box of documents on the dining room table along with a tea service and a plate of cookies.

"I figured you'd already eaten, but . . ."

"That's very sweet of you, Dr. Hubert," Danni said.

"Ron. You're in my home, young lady. And at this moment, I'm fonder of my first name than my last!"

"So the news is out?" Quinn asked. "I haven't been paying attention to TV, the internet or the radio. Much less a newspaper."

"Larue gave a short press conference to quash the rumors that are flying around. They've been running it constantly on the local news and on the all-news networks. He told the public that the police believe 'an armed and dangerous killer' had attacked the Garcia home where the painting had been awaiting delivery to Mrs. Lamont. And that Mrs. Lamont's home had been broken into and that Bryson Arnold was killed when the painting was stolen." He sighed. "The city's gone art-crazy. So the details about me and my connection to the damn painting . . . Well, you can imagine the sudden interest."

"I'm sorry about that, Ron," Quinn said.

"Well, let's get on with this, shall we? That box there —" he pointed at it "— is filled with family papers. A lot of them are birth, marriage and death certificates. But you'll find one piece of note. Hubert's wife, Eloisa, kept a journal toward the end of her very long life. I haven't read it myself, nor have I read any of the letters stuck inside it. But you might find that useful."

"I'm sure I will," Danni said, sorting through the papers in the box. Quinn knew she was forcing herself to be careful with everything she handled, despite her eagerness to get to the journal.

She lifted it reverently out of the box; it was yellowed and there were loose pages, as well as the letters placed within it. She saw that the handwriting was small and cramped, the ink faded in places, making it difficult to read.

Danni looked up at Hubert. "I'll go through this very carefully. But the way it's written . . . it'll take some time. Did you ever hear anything about your great-great-whatever-grandfather painting with . . . blood?"

Hubert stiffened. He drew in a breath. "Yes."

"What did you hear?" Quinn asked. He thought about the things Danni had told him — starting with the story in Millicent Smith's book. *The* book.

With another long, deep sigh, Hubert sat down, joining them at the table. "First I heard of it was when I was kid. This was in Minneapolis. You know how cruel kids can be to other kids. Anyway, there was a brief piece in a local paper around Halloween, and my family was mentioned — because of the connection to the Hubert painting. The article was about supposedly haunted works of art. Someone called me the devil's child and, after that, various kids started calling me demon boy. I was probably about ten at the time. I socked the hell out of that kid. My mother was called in and rather than yell at me, when we got home she sat me down and we talked. She told me about the painter. To some people, he was brilliant. But certain people liked to think the worst, especially at Halloween. It was really just sad, she told me. Henry Sebastian Hubert had desperately wanted to be with the popular crowd. He'd begun making a name for himself, but he practically hero-worshipped Lord Byron, and when he got into their storytelling game, he wanted to go all out."

"That fits with what I've read," Danni remarked.

Hubert nodded. "My mother did a lot of research on this, although she was a Hubert by marriage, not by birth. According to her, Henry had written in a journal — long ago lost — that his butler, who came with the place, had worked for a total hedonist before him. Apparently this butler was a guy who believed that blood was the essence of everything. . . . So Hubert mixed blood into his paints. That's the first I ever heard of it. I was horrified, of course."

"Then he *did* use blood," Danni breathed.

"How did it go at school after you got into trouble?" Quinn asked.

Hubert grinned wickedly. "Even though I'd been called to the principal's office, I won the fight. The boys left me alone after that. It boosted my standing at the school. And as the years went by, I forgot about the whole situation and so did everyone else." He paused. "Although it might be more accurate to say I *willed* myself to forget."

He poured tea for them. "Have a cookie, Danni."

Quinn was pretty sure Danni was too engrossed in the journal to want a cookie.

She politely took one, anyway, glancing at Quinn.

Then she turned back to Hubert. "From something I've read, I gather your ancestor was buried in the crypt at the House of Guillaume on Lake Geneva, in Switzerland," she said.

"And that I know is true."

"Do you happen to know anything about the House of Guillaume now?" Quinn asked.

Once again, Hubert looked as if he didn't want to speak.

"Ron?" Quinn pressed.

"Yes, I know about it!" Hubert snapped. "I own the damned thing!"

When Hubert escorted them to the door at last, Danni couldn't help noticing that there were even more cars parked around his modest two-story home.

"Quinn," she whispered. "He could be in trouble."

"I don't think tourists — or reporters — are going to go so far as to break into his house," Quinn said.

Danni disagreed. "We can't be sure of that. If nothing else, they'll drive him crazy. *Especially* the snooping journalists."

"Okay, maybe you're right." Quinn tapped at the door to get Hubert back outside while he dialed Jake Larue.

"He's asking for a cop to come out here," Danni explained when Hubert opened the door.

"Not a bad idea. Thank you," Hubert said. "I should've thought of that myself."

Quinn spoke briefly with Larue and then closed his phone. "Jake's going to send a patrol car out here right away," he told Hubert. "It'll sit in front of your house. That should work a little better than your sign, although I do love your final threat. That's a lot more direct than legal action," he said with a laugh.

"I don't even own a gun," Hubert admitted.

"Probably a good thing." Quinn was still smiling. "Okay, Danni, we'll go back inside while we wait for the car to get here. Oh, and I do own a gun," Quinn reminded him.

"*And* I'm licensed to carry it."

"Come in, come in," Hubert said.

They went in, but Quinn hung by the door, looking out the little peephole now and then. "So, you're a Swiss citizen?"

Hubert nodded. "My parents were and I am, too."

"How the hell did you manage that?"

"Right after his death, Hubert was all the rage. The Swiss were particularly fond of him, don't ask me why. He was posthumously granted Swiss citizenship. My family kept it up ever since. I know my parents went over once when I was a child. . . . I've never been there myself, but my mother felt it was very special that we retain dual citizenship. And I guess I never sold the castle out of deference to my parents — and I never needed to sell it for financial reasons." He shrugged. "I'm the last surviving descendant, sad to say, since I don't have any siblings or even cousins. Anyway, Danni will find all the information in the papers there. We — the Hubert family — have owned the property since shortly after Hubert's death. He'd rented it, but his widow bought it from the son of the previous owner. She never did a thing with it. Every few years she had cleaning staff in and ordered that the integrity of the building be maintained. My parents did even less than those before them . . . and I haven't done a damned thing. Except I carry an insurance policy, just in case some idiot tourist goes in and gets himself hurt or killed."

Danni felt a creeping sensation crawl up her spine. She knew Quinn was already planning their trip to Switzerland.

He looked at her, just as the thought entered her mind.

"Your passport is up to date, right?"

"Yes," she said dully.

Quinn walked over to where Ron Hubert had taken a seat in his parlor. "Ron, you know I'm going to the castle, don't you? *We're* going to the castle. I'd like your permission to dig up your ancestor."

Ron Hubert shuddered visibly. He was an M.E.; he dealt with dead bodies all the time. Finally he looked up at Quinn. "I'm a scientist, remember? A dead body is a dead body. I don't believe in supernatural phenomena. But as to your request — don't we need more than my permission?"

"Not the way we're going to do it," Quinn said wryly.

"Ah."

"You're the only one I'm worried about."

"So we're going to do illegal things. In a

foreign country."

"Probably, but don't worry — I don't intend to announce what we're doing, not to anyone. Humor me? Give me your blessing to travel to the House of Guillaume."

"You want to dig up my ancestor's bones and burn them and scatter the ashes somewhere?"

"That's the gist of it, yes," he said.

Danni heard a small sound escape her lips. Both men turned to her. "The way we see it, Ron, that would work. Except . . ."

"Except what?" Quinn frowned.

"What if he wasn't painting with his own blood?"

"Whose blood would he have used?" Quinn asked.

"Well, you'd imagine he'd have *started* with his own, at least," Hubert said. "It would be right at hand, so to speak. Prick a finger and you've got blood."

"That's logical," Danni put in.

"But it goes further than that," Quinn said. "You told us the cut on Bryson Arnold's thumb was self-inflicted. So that must be how the painting is 'activated,' as you called it. Maybe he touched it up with blood?"

"That falls in line with what we've seen so far," Danni said.

246

"And it's out there somewhere — in the city of New Orleans." Quinn gestured at the window.

"If you were to destroy the painting, wouldn't that be good enough?" Hubert asked.

"Possibly," Danni replied. "I just don't know where we'd begin to look for it."

"Follow the blood," Quinn said morosely.

They went straight to Father Ryan's rectory when they left Dr. Hubert's house. They'd carefully placed the box containing the Hubert family papers in the trunk of Quinn's car.

Father Ryan was evidently expecting them.

"Natasha called me," he explained. "Said you were going to Ron's and would be dropping by here when you were done."

"Henry Hubert is buried in the castle that belonged to Guillaume and we have one huge piece of luck in our favor. Ron now owns the castle. The widow bought the property from the son of the dead owner, who was apparently quite the hedonist. The son lived in England, just like Eloisa Hubert. Neither of them wanted anything to do with it, but Eloisa did want to own it. It — and Swiss citizenship — have stayed in the family ever since," Quinn said.

"Very curious, and yet not really," Father Ryan murmured. "The widow must have known — or sensed — something. She never rented it out?" he asked.

"Not according to Dr. Hubert," Danni told him.

"So, you can find the painting — or dig up the bones and bury them. Or burn them. But while you're gone, searching for the body, anything could happen here," Father Ryan said.

"Look," Quinn began impatiently. "We don't know where the painting is, but we *do* know where to find Hubert's body."

"Well, I can only assume you're going to get into trouble, no matter what you plan to do." Father Ryan walked into the dining room. Danni and Quinn followed him.

He took what appeared to be large garish gold medals off a shelf and gave one to Danni and another to Quinn.

They were heavy and didn't depict any saints. "These have holy water in them," Father Ryan said. "Not enough to drown a host of whatever you find, but enough to cause a retreat, perhaps. I have more for you in small flasks. Yes, sorry, flasks — they're easily sealed and easily carried. They'll pass through airport security, like contact solution. Keep one in your pocket,

Quinn, and, Danni, just make sure you have your bag, purse or whatever nearby."

"And you believe the holy water will . . . take down whatever this is?" Quinn asked.

"What do *you* believe?" Father Ryan asked.

Quinn smiled slowly. "I believe it will."

Danni hoped they were right.

"Oh, and one more thing," Father Ryan said. "If you do decide to fly to Geneva, you're taking Natasha and me with you. You understand that, don't you? And fair warning would be nice, since I'm going to have to get a substitute for any time I'm gone. The Lord is never on vacation, you know."

"I'd look for a substitute, then, Father," Quinn said.

Father Ryan nodded. "Well, then, you'd best go home. Get some sleep. And call me about the arrangements as soon as you can."

"We'll do that, Father," Danni promised.

Father Ryan shooed them out. On the way to the car, Danni remembered Billie — and Hattie Lamont.

"Oh! I've got to call Billie!" she said. "He's probably ready to tear his hair out by now. It's getting late, but I should probably call Bo Ray, too, and ask him to get over to your house so Billie can have a reprieve."

She dialed Billie's number.

"Eh, Danni?" he said, answering his cell on the third ring.

"Billie. I'm sorry. I should've gotten in touch earlier —"

"If I'd needed you, lass, I'd have called you."

"Okay, well, I wanted to tell you I'm going to call Bo Ray right now —"

"No need. I'm settled in for the night. Hattie is in the guest room. I'm on the sofa in the parlor and Wolf is guarding the front door. We're good for the evening."

Danni almost dropped the phone, she was so surprised.

"Oh. All right, then. Call me in the morning and let me know how you want to proceed, okay?"

"Aye, lass. Have a good night."

"Thanks. You, too."

She hit the end button and looked at Quinn. "We don't need to send Bo Ray over. Billie says he's fine and they're in for the night."

Quinn smiled. "Circumstances make for strange bedfellows," he said. "And speaking of bed, I'm all for it, Ms. Cafferty. It's been a long couple of days."

When they reached Danni's place, they discovered that Bo Ray had waited up for them.

And it seemed that he'd kept his promise — every single light was on.

"So, you're okay. Did the giclée get here?" Danni asked, shifting the box filled with Hubert's papers in her arms. She'd insisted on carrying it herself.

"Yeah, it got here," Bo Ray said.

"Niles brought it?"

"Actually, Mason Bradley brought it first and then Niles came over later to check that it got here okay. Mason is a nice guy. We talked for a while. He said he wants to do a show with you sometime in the future."

"I know," Danni said. "But I'm not sure when."

"Actually, I don't understand why he's an artist. He could make a fortune as a model. He's a good-looking guy. I think that — and I'm straight," Bo Ray said with a shrug.

"Yes, he's a very good-looking man," Danni agreed. "What about the giclée?"

"It's down in the basement, in the office, and I locked the door. It's still wrapped up. Mason was pretty fussy about handling it just right, but you know I don't let anyone into the basement. And I didn't let Mason down — or Niles. I know the score. If you're not here and it's not Quinn or Natasha or Father Ryan, *no one* goes down. I handled that sucker all by myself and very carefully, too!" Bo Ray said proudly.

"But you stayed awake and waited for us," Quinn teased.

"Hey. I just wanted to make sure you got home safe. And I was expecting to go out to your house, Quinn."

"Billie's in for the night," Danni said. "I should've called. You don't have to change places with him."

"Wow!" Bo Ray whistled in amazement. "I guess he's getting along with the old battle-ax. Hmm. And I was ready to face her, too!"

"Hattie Lamont can be incredibly nice," Danni said.

Quinn made a sound that was something like a snort.

"Okay, well, you two are here, and I'm exhausted. Now I can sleep." Bo Ray yawned. He headed up to the apartment in the attic.

"I'm going to have a look around," Quinn said. "And turn off a few lights."

"I'm going to see that the basement door's locked." Danni put the box of Hubert papers on the kitchen table.

"Good idea."

The basement door *was* locked; Billie had been thorough. She could hear Quinn moving through the first floor, double-checking the doors and the alarm system. She waited for him at the foot of the stairs. As he approached her with a thumbs-up that meant they were all locked in, she heard his phone ring.

He answered it, didn't say another word, then frowned and hurried to the courtyard door.

"Quinn?"

"Lock yourself in, Danni."

He keyed the alarm again and opened the door. She ran behind him.

"What is it?"

"Trouble at Dr. Hubert's house."

"What trouble?"

"I don't know. He just whispered into the phone that *we* needed to come back." Quinn was already out the door. He was moving quickly, and she ran to keep up with him.

"Danni, I can take this alone. Stay here."

"No! You said he whispered that *we* should come back."

"I don't know what we'll find —"

"So let's go see!" she said. "Quinn, I'm going with you."

She locked the door carefully as they left; Bo Ray was still in the house.

Once they set off, she was glad it was late — and that most of the revelers had gone home or to their hotels for the night. At the speed Quinn was driving, she pitied any poor drunk who might wander into the street.

He jerked to a halt behind the patrol car parked in front of the Hubert house. They could both see that there was no officer in the car.

Quinn raced up the steps to the front door, with Danni on his heels.

The door was ajar, and they walked cautiously into the house.

The first thing she noticed was the fog.

Fog. Inside his house. There was none outside.

"Ron!" Quinn called.

No answer.

"Stay close behind me," he told Danni, drawing his weapon. "Call 9-1-1. We need cops. Backup."

She did, making an effort to speak slowly and clearly — and asked that Detective Jake Larue be notified, as well.

"Come on. Stay right behind me," Quinn repeated.

She nodded, which, of course, he couldn't see. She wanted to remind him that he'd taken her to the shooting range back when they'd first found themselves working together, and that he'd bought her a Smith &

Wesson 642 and taught her how to use it. She'd put the revolver in her shoulder bag that morning, Father Ryan's flask nestled beside it. Quinn moved forward, but even though they'd been there only a few hours earlier, everything seemed to have changed — not to mention that it was like walking into a thick haze. Quinn groped his way through the parlor, the dining room and into the back.

"We need to find the lights and turn them on," he whispered.

"Quinn, I think the lights *are* on."

He swore as he banged into a wall. "I'm going to try upstairs."

"Should we split up?" she asked.

"Hell, no!"

"I . . . I have my gun."

"No splitting up," he said firmly.

She was glad.

But at the same time she wondered if their guns would do a damn thing. It was hard to shoot when you were aiming at . . . fog.

She nodded again, uselessly, and followed him.

As they came to the bottom step, she suddenly felt she was being watched. As if there was something behind her.

She could hear breathing . . . and feel breath, misty and hot and menacing, against the back of her neck.

An instinctive chill settled over her, threatening to paralyze her with fear, and she spun around.

There *was* something there.

Something within the fog, or part of the fog. It seemed to become darker and darker, a whirling mass of darkness that was trying to take shape.

And it was moving toward her.

And . . .

There was a face within the whirling mass.

A face taking form, becoming clearer in the mist.

Yes . . .

Evil had a face.

CHAPTER 10

Danni felt mesmerized by it. She blinked; it was still there. She blinked again and found her voice.

"Quinn." She spoke his name. It came out in a low whisper.

He swiveled around, and she knew he was taking aim with his Glock 22.

A gun wasn't going to stop this, she thought.

With trembling fingers she grasped the medallion around her neck. She pulled out the tiny stopper, and as the darkness approached, she threw out the holy water.

A sound filled the room. It wasn't a cry of distress; it was low, guttural, angry, and . . .

Not human.

The face was gone. She didn't know if Quinn had seen it.

He thrust her behind him again. But even as he did, the fog began to dissipate. There was no face — and there was no fog.

She was incredibly grateful for Father Ryan.

"What the hell?" Quinn muttered.

Danni looked around. As she'd assumed, the lights were on in the house and she could see a fallen body in uniform on the parlor floor. "The cop!" Danni gasped, pointing at the edge of the sofa.

The man was on the ground so close to the sofa that they'd missed him before when they felt their way through the room.

Quinn and Danni rushed over, crouching beside him. Quinn touched the man's throat, seeking a pulse. "He's alive, just unconscious."

"I don't see any injuries," Danni said.

Quinn nodded. "He's not bleeding. He must have fallen and hit his head. I can hear sirens. The cops will be here any minute."

Danni heard them, too, with more than a little relief.

"I've got to find Dr. Hubert," Quinn said, and then shouted. "Ron? Where the hell are you?"

He rose. "Stay with him," he told Danni, pointing at the cop, and strode toward the stairs.

Stay with him! In the parlor alone?

Quinn was already gone. She remained with the officer, looking around the room that had felt so welcoming not long before. She tried to fathom what could have happened.

The painting wasn't here — so what was going on?

She blinked; it seemed that a mist was growing in the room again. She couldn't tell if it was real or if her mind was playing tricks out of fear. She fumbled in her shoulder bag for the flask of holy water Father Ryan had given her. "I'm armed with the right stuff, you know," she said inanely to nothing. "Come near me, and you'll wish you hadn't!"

Real or imagined? The mist receded again.

She stared at the spot where it had been, wondering how mist could just appear — and how it could be so insidious, so menacing.

Time seemed to stop as she continued to stare . . . and then everything happened at once.

Quinn came running back down the stairs — and to Danni's gratitude, Ron Hubert was with him. The police arrived, an officer thrusting the door farther open and shouting, "It's the police! Throw down your weapons."

Quinn shouted out in return, identifying himself. The first two officers on the scene were followed by two others.

Danni could hear more sirens in the street. Within a few minutes, med techs were hurrying to the side of the downed officer, searching as Quinn and Danni had done, but finding nothing. And while they worked on him, she rose, trying to hear the officers as they questioned Dr. Hubert, anxious to learn what had happened at the house. He stood with Quinn and the senior officer who'd come while the others were going through the residence, searching from room to room, making sure that no intruders remained. Hubert had stopped and started his story several times when Larue reached the scene.

He started again.

"I'd gone up to my room to call it a night when I heard something. I don't even know how to describe *what* I heard, but . . . I knew someone was in the house. Maybe more than one person. They entered through the back. I grabbed my baseball bat — we have a medical examiners' team that plays at the park. I don't have an alarm system. I never needed one. I know my closest neighbors, and this is a safe area. But I'd locked the door, I'm positive of that."

"What did you see? Or who did you see?" Larue demanded.

Ron Hubert was quiet for a moment, looking at them with pursed lips.

"A magician?" Ron Hubert said, but it was more of a question than a statement. He shook his head. "All right, I seriously think it had to be a magician. Or someone who works with special effects. He — she, they? — filled the place with smog or fog or something. I couldn't see a thing, but I knew it was too late to get out. I couldn't make it to the bottom of the stairs and out the front door. I raced back up to my room and into my closet. I should keep a gun. Maybe I *will* keep a gun —"

"Wait," Larue interrupted. "You didn't actually see anyone? Or hear anything else?"

"Once I was in the closet, I heard the front door being broken open and assumed it was the cop from outside. I was about to go back downstairs but then . . . I heard him shout, and I heard a thump. And I knew he was down. I stayed where I was." His gaze flashed nervously toward Quinn. "When I'd first thought something was wrong, I called Quinn. I should've called 9-1-1, too, except . . . at that point I heard that noise at the back of the house. And when I headed for the stairs in the dark, I dropped my phone, so I couldn't make another call. I admit I was afraid to come out and try to

261

find it." He winced. "I'm a doctor. I'm sorry. I'm not a cop or an investigator."

"No one expects you to be, Ron," Quinn told him.

"No, I just wish . . ." Larue's voice trailed off.

"Your officer's alive," Quinn said. "Maybe he'll be able to tell us something."

"He's coming to," one of the med techs announced.

They had the patrol officer sitting up, still on the floor, his back braced against the sofa.

Quinn and Larue made their way over. "What's wrong with him?" Larue asked the EMT.

"Nothing. Nothing we can see, anyway," the young woman replied.

The officer opened his eyes. He looked straight ahead and let out a scream. It was so loud and piercing that everyone around him started.

"Hey, Officer, it's all right," Quinn said. "You're not hurt. We have cops here and medical help and you're fine. Can you tell us what happened?"

The man's eyes were wide, his pupils dilated as if he'd been out in bright sunlight. He didn't speak for a moment. He glanced at the faces surrounding him and then lurched, looking over his shoulder as though he expected to be grabbed from behind.

Danni came forward, kneeling beside him. "You're safe. The fog's gone. Whatever was in the fog is gone," she said gently.

He finally focused on her. He was a man in his mid-thirties, and the uniform he wore was crisp and well-tended. Danni estimated that he was about six-three. He had broad shoulders and appeared to be fit and muscular. Not the kind of man you'd expect to be easily intimidated.

"There's something in this house," he said hoarsely, staring at Danni.

"Officer Franklin," Larue said, crouching next to him. "Whoever's doing this is using a fog machine or some device like that. We seem to have a magician or special effects wizard on our hands. But the house is crawling with your fellow officers right now. If there's *anything* in here, they'll find it. Now, what exactly happened to you?"

"Happened?" The officer's eyes were still focused on Danni.

"Officer Franklin," Larue urged.

Franklin turned to face Larue. "I broke in. I'd heard a commotion. I . . . I called the doc's name. But I was blinded when I got inside, couldn't see. And then . . . I did."

"*What* did you see?" Danni persisted softly.

He turned to look at her again. "Demon eyes," he said in a solemn voice. "Red eyes. They were fire eyes — like portals to hell."

Larue uttered a little sound of impatience. Danni was surprised to catch herself elbowing him in the ribs and glaring in disapproval.

Larue was surprised, too. He glanced up at Quinn, who merely shrugged.

"Did the eyes hurt you? How did you wind up on the floor?" Danni asked Officer Franklin. "You were unconscious. Were you hurt?"

"I don't know."

"You saw the eyes. Then what?"

His gaze went blank, as if he was trying to see into the past. But he shook his head. "I don't know," he repeated. "I just don't know."

"At the very least," Quinn said, speaking to Larue, "he had a nasty fall. Want to let the EMTs take him?"

Larue sighed in frustration. "Yeah, might as well. Okay, Officer Franklin, they're going to bring you to the hospital now." He spoke to one of the EMTs. "See that they keep him there for observation overnight, will you?"

"I'll give Emergency your message, Detective," the young woman promised.

Another policeman reported to Larue. "Back door was jimmied open, sir. Front door was broken, but from what I understand, that was Officer Franklin's doing."

Larue nodded. "Keep searching. Doc — Ron — can you go through the house with my officers? Try not to handle any objects or touch walls or other surfaces, but see if anything's missing."

"Of course," Hubert said. He moved off, accompanied by several police officers.

When everyone else had left, Larue addressed Danni and Quinn. "Let's get to the point. Why attack the doc? Yeah, his name is Hubert, but he doesn't own the painting and never did. Whoever wanted the painting *has* the painting, or so we assume."

"I don't have an answer," Quinn said.

"I might," Danni murmured.

They both looked at her. "The intruder might have been after his family records." She didn't say that those same records were now sitting on her kitchen table.

"Why?" Larue asked bluntly.

"There could be something in them that explains what's going on."

Larue's voice was gravelly when he said, "What's going on is that people are being

265

killed. You need to tell me everything you know about this . . . magician."

"If we told you what we suspect, you wouldn't believe it, anyway," Quinn told him.

"Hmph," Larue said. "Then, answer me this. Why didn't the killer finish off Officer Franklin and kill Ron Hubert?"

"Maybe Hubert's not supposed to be a victim," Quinn suggested. "After all, he is a descendant."

"And maybe we got here before the killing began," Danni added.

"Or," Larue said, "perhaps because of who he is, Hubert might still be on the hit list."

That was possible, too, Danni thought. Just as it remained possible that the killer or killers would come after Hattie Lamont again, since she was the legal owner of the painting.

Maybe the damned thing was lethal — but vulnerable, as well.

"It's your turn," Danni said. "You have to convince Ron Hubert that he can't stay here — or anywhere — alone."

"My place or yours?" he asked dryly.

Danni shook her head. "I'm starting to think we need —"

"To gather everyone in one place," Quinn

finished. "I was thinking the same thing."

"Do you suppose that'll work with Hattie Lamont?" Quinn grimaced as he spoke. "And maybe not so well with Ron Hubert, either. But it may be a case of listening to us and staying alive or —"

"You don't think an officer posted here will be enough?" Larue interrupted.

"After this?" Quinn asked.

"The first officer was outside. If we put a man *in* the house, he can prevent a back door break-in," Jake said.

Quinn shrugged. "Better yet if I can convince Hubert to come with us."

Apparently, Ron Hubert did want to stay alive. When they asked him to temporarily move in with them, he agreed. "I'm not married, no kids to worry about. So . . . whatever you feel is best."

Within half an hour, they were in Quinn's car, on their way to Danni's house. By then it was after two. Quinn figured that until a final decision was made regarding their next step, it would be best for all of them to stay together. But if Hattie and Billie were managing, with Wolf on guard, he'd leave them until morning.

Danni called Billie. Hattie was sleeping; Billie was fine. He'd dozed off a bit, well aware that Wolf would bark at the slightest change in the house.

Danni told Quinn, "Billie said Father Ryan visited him, too. He's supplied with 'ammo.' Father Ryan left him half a dozen twenty-two-ounce soda bottles filled with holy water. Billie is happy."

"You really think all of this is necessary?" Ron asked incredulously. "A priest running around doling out holy water?"

"You're in the backseat of my car, aren't you?" Quinn asked him.

"Yeah, I guess I am," Hubert muttered.

They'd just reached the shop on Royal Street. Once again, every light in the place was on.

"My God, now what?" Danni groaned. She leaped from the car, racing out of the garage and through the courtyard. Quinn came up behind her as she was fumbling with her keys.

"Bo Ray's fine," he assured her. "He's a smart young man."

"But we left him here alone!"

Quinn got the door open and she dashed in. He followed her quickly, aware that Ron Hubert was behind him — so close they both almost tripped.

There was nothing out of order in the house, no sign of damage. It was easy to tell, and easy to get around, since every light was on. Danni bolted up the stairs. "Hey, be careful!" Quinn called.

She didn't answer.

He caught up with her, and they searched together. But a thorough scrutiny of the second floor yielded nothing, and neither did a search of the attic. *Where was Bo Ray?*

They tried Danni's studio next, and then the shop. Hubert shivered as they headed down to the basement. But when they unlocked the door and went in, they saw nothing there, either.

Danni's giclée copy of the Hubert painting, still wrapped, leaned against the wall.

Her cell rang and she pulled it out.

Despite the hour, music blasted so loudly through the phone that Quinn could hear it.

"Bo Ray!" she gasped.

But whatever Bo Ray said, Quinn couldn't make out.

Then he heard Danni say, "We're back. You can come home. You didn't . . . you didn't . . ."

Danni gave a sigh of relief and closed her phone. "He said he woke up feeling as though someone was calling him. He got scared, discovered that we weren't here and went to Bourbon Street." Bo Ray was an addict; he'd been in recovery a long time, but Quinn could see that Danni was praying the situation hadn't been a trigger, hadn't driven him to hit the streets in search of drugs or go sit in a bar to drown his sorrows.

"He sound okay?" Quinn asked, purposely keeping his voice casual.

She smiled. "He sounded angry. We left without telling him."

A few minutes later, Bo Ray was back. Bourbon was just a street up and he'd gone to the Cat's Meow, which was another block down once you got to Bourbon.

They introduced Ron Hubert to Bo Ray and vice versa, then went to sit in the kitchen. While Quinn carried Ron's box of family documents to the studio, Danni prepared tea. She'd learned about the calming properties of tea from Billie and from her father; it was obvious that none of them would be going to sleep right away, and a cup of tea might relax them.

"Why didn't you call me?" Danni demanded, turning to Bo Ray.

"I was scared. I was worried that you were on a real mission," Bo Ray explained. He glanced at her hopefully. "Nobody . . . died tonight, did they?"

"No. Now, tell me *exactly* what happened here!"

"You said that if I got scared, I should leave. So I did," Bo Ray said simply.

"But *why* did you get scared?" Quinn asked him as he entered the kitchen.

"I don't know," Bo Ray said slowly. "I was sound asleep and I suddenly woke up and it felt like . . . something was in my head. I got up and went down to the second floor — I thought you guys were sleeping there," he told them reproachfully.

"I'm sorry, Bo Ray," Danni said. "We didn't want to wake you, and . . . well, it sounded like the danger was at Doc Hubert's place."

Bo Ray studied Hubert. "You really a descendant of that artist?"

"Yeah, I really am," Hubert said.

Bo Ray continued to watch him closely. "And you're a medical examiner? Huh. Weird."

"Young man," Hubert said, drawing himself up. "Medical examiner is an honorable profession and I'm darned good at what I do."

Danni set a hand on Hubert's arm. "Of course you are."

"Yeah, I didn't mean anything by that!" Bo Ray mumbled. "I, uh, it's just that I'm

271

sure it's really hard and you must be, uh, incredibly brilliant."

"Flattery, son, will not get you anywhere — especially since you seem to think there's something creepy about me," Hubert said, grinning slightly.

Bo Ray grinned back. "Nah, honestly — I think you're kind of cool. Really. But that painting's definitely creepy and so is the way it came back into the limelight."

"No denying that," Ron said.

"Get back to what scared you, Bo Ray," Quinn insisted.

"There's not much to tell. I felt like someone was in my head, calling me. That was it. It was sort of like . . . *Come to me, come to me* . . . Like out of a vampire movie! Anyway, I was scared, turned on all the lights everywhere and started running like a maniac — right out the courtyard door. Not to worry. I made sure I locked it before I left."

Danni frowned. "A voice in your head," she murmured.

"I'm okay now," Bo Ray said. "I just scared myself. I'm kind of new to this stuff and I'm not . . ." He hesitated, lowered his head and then grimaced as he looked up again. "I'm not like Quinn," he said quietly.

"Ready to face anything — like a super-hero."

"You're doing fine, Bo Ray," Quinn said in a reassuring voice. "Hey, there are people in this city who still remember that I was a successful college football player — and then a no-good entitled jerk. So, we all move along our own paths. I had to die to straighten out — to find my way. And it didn't make me a superhero, just a man who's prepared to fight some of the bad things that happen in this world. Some of them not so easily explained . . . Perhaps like death itself."

"How does one define death?" Ron Hubert asked philosophically. "In your case, you did flatline. I remember that clearly because your case was in medical journals. The hospital did a fantastic job with CPR. You were damn lucky."

"I know," Quinn said quietly. "All right. I suggest we get some sleep. Now. Tomorrow, we have decisions to make. Danni, where are we putting Ron for the night?"

"The guest room," she replied. "Come with me, Ron. I'll take you up there."

Bo Ray got to his feet. "Hey, I did a Led Zeppelin tune tonight and I was *good*!"

"When this is all over," Danni said, "we'll go back to the Cat's Meow and you can do

273

it again for all of us!"

Bo Ray went ahead of Danni and Ron. Quinn walked around the premises, pausing to see if he saw, heard or *felt* anything. He didn't. He turned off most of the lights, reset the alarm and went on up the stairs; they were well into the wee hours of the morning.

It was almost 4:00 a.m.

He slipped into Danni's room to join her at last. She was stretched out in her clothes, sound asleep.

He didn't disturb her. When he lay down beside her, she eased against him, and he placed an arm around her, pulling her close.

To his amazement, he didn't lie awake trying to puzzle out the situation — or the right way to put the pieces together.

He slept.

Danni was at the kitchen table, carefully going through Ron Hubert's family records, when Quinn came down. She had piles of paper in neat stacks. Some of the pages were yellowed and curling with age. Others were newer, some obviously recent copies, while the rest were the real thing.

He poured himself a coffee. "Where's our guest?" he asked.

"Bo Ray drove him to work." Danni's

forehead wrinkled in a frown. "That's okay, isn't it?"

"Yeah, he should be fine at work. At least, I hope so. I still don't know why there was a break-in at his house."

"I think someone wants these. I really do," Danni said.

"You could be right. It's just that . . . well, I thought the bad stuff only happened where the painting was. That the painting had to be activated or 'awakened' as you said. But it wasn't, and never has been, at Hubert's place."

Danni looked pensive. "Yes, but if someone was after these papers . . . They do reveal a lot about the artist. So, say the painting was awakened. Maybe our *living* intruder and/or murderer, whoever he is, was able to 'wake' the painting and bring whatever evil is in it with him on . . . on a house call," she said. "Or maybe, although this seems unlikely, he brought the painting itself. To get these papers back."

"Could be," Quinn agreed. "The question is how someone knew about the papers. But I suppose if he did his research, it wouldn't be that hard to figure out. All of which means it's a good thing *we* have the papers — and that we need to keep them with us wherever we go."

"You really want to go to Switzerland?" she asked. "You believe that destroying Hubert's body, burning it, will be the end we need?"

"I honestly don't know," he answered. "But we haven't got a clue as to where the painting is. We'll probably follow a trail of blood. We'll learn more when the next person's killed. I'm sure it's going to happen, but we don't know when — or where — that'll take place. But as I told Ron, we *do* know where to find Henry Hubert's body."

They heard footsteps in the courtyard, and Quinn walked to the door. Billie, Bo Ray and Hattie Lamont were standing there. Bo Ray was carrying Hattie's bag again, while Billie clutched Wolf's leash, with the dog wagging his tail excitedly.

Quinn realized Danni was behind him. He turned to face her, a question in his eyes.

"Oh, I asked Bo Ray to pick them up. You said earlier that we all need to be together under one roof," she reminded him.

"So I did," he agreed. "And here we are."

When he opened the door, Hattie sailed in. "This moving about is quite tiresome, Quinn. Billie and I were actually settling in nicely. Your home is lovely. You're a lucky young man to have your parents give you such a house."

"I bought the house," Quinn said, trying not to bristle at her tone. "I'll admit my folks sold it to me at a good price. But I bought it." He bent down to rub Wolf's ears, greeting the dog, then ordering him to sit.

"That *is* commendable," Hattie said. "Your industriousness, I mean." She glanced at the closed door to Danni's studio and shivered. "If you consider it important, I shall make do here."

"Kind of you," Danni said wryly, crouching to hug Wolf and whisper endearments to him.

"Oh, my dear, you keep a charming place, it's just that . . . well, it does also function as a shop," Hattie said.

"Gotta live somehow," Danni murmured.

"I'll bring Hattie's things upstairs. Where am I putting her?"

"Let Hattie have my father's room," Danni said. Quinn looked at her curiously. To the best of his knowledge, Danni hadn't let anyone in her father's room. He sensed that it was something of a shrine, although she'd never said as much.

He supposed this was progress. They'd all loved Angus, but Angus was gone.

"I'm opening the shop," Bo Ray announced.

"Is there coffee?" Hattie asked.

"Yes, of course. Quinn and I were just in the kitchen —"

"I should *love* some coffee," Hattie said imperiously. "And then you can tell me about your plans. This must be stopped. Billie told me there was an incident at a medical examiner's house, and I understand this medical examiner is a direct descendant of Henry Hubert. Do you think *he's* causing all of this somehow? *Pretending* to be under attack when he's the culprit himself?"

"No, I don't." Quinn shook his head. "I've known Ron Hubert a very long time. He's a good man."

Maybe it was natural that someone might suspect Ron; still, Hattie's voice — and her attitude — grated on him.

"Let's go back and have some coffee, shall we?" Danni suggested.

She led the way. Quinn made an exaggerated bow, sweeping his arm to indicate that Hattie should go ahead of him. As Danni made coffee for her, Quinn pulled out a chair.

He'd been raised to be polite; he would have pulled out the chair for anyone. Somehow, though, with this woman, he felt that she expected it, that she had delusions of her own importance.

He took his own chair and gulped down his coffee as if he were a drunk in need of a shot. Danni tried to hide a smile and poured him another cup before resuming her seat.

"We don't know if it'll work or not, Hattie," Danni began. "But . . . it just might. We're planning to take a trip to Switzerland."

"Lake Geneva?"

"Yes. And to tell you the truth, we're afraid to leave you here, in the city, alone," Danni said.

"Shall I accompany you? That's probably best. There's English spoken almost everywhere, but you may, at times, need someone with a thorough understanding of the French language," Hattie said.

"I'm not exactly fluent," Danni explained, "but I did grow up in the French Quarter with a number of Cajun friends —"

"Oh, my dear! Cajun French is . . . Cajun French," Hattie said, patting her hand sympathetically.

Danni bit her lip and sent Quinn a sly glance. He almost laughed out loud.

"Well, it doesn't really matter," Danni said cheerfully. "I'm sure your linguistic abilities will come in handy."

"We'll be traveling with a rather large party," Quinn pointed out.

"Oh?" Hattie said.

"Natasha will be with us — oh, she's a voodoo priestess." Quinn couldn't help smiling. "Also Father Ryan. He's a Catholic priest. And Billie, who's been working this type of situation longer than either Danni or me. And, of course, after last night, I'm not leaving Bo Ray alone." He paused. "I'm also going to do my best to talk Ron Hubert into joining us."

"A voodoo priestess?" Hattie demanded, obviously fixated on that one description.

"Yeah, she snake dances and everything!" Quinn said. Danni shot him a frown.

"How remarkable — and exciting!" Hattie said, to his surprise. "I look forward to meeting this Natasha. And, my smart-aleck young friend, I happen to know your Father Ryan, or *a* Father Ryan, at any rate. Big, handsome man, quite a waste as a Catholic priest, I must say. His genes would do the world gene pool some good, and not just because of his looks. Now, where do we stay while we're in Geneva? I do know some of the most charming boutique hotels. Geneva is a beautiful city, but arrangements can be a bit difficult, you know. There are constantly UN and other conventions going on, so booking on short notice could be a problem."

"And very expensive," Danni added.

Hattie turned to her and smiled. "My dear, surely you're aware that while my personality can be a bit prickly, I'm very grateful for my life. If there's one thing I do have, it's a generous supply of funds, thanks to my late husband. I shall be happy to make our travel arrangements. If you'll be so good as to give me a list with the legal names and dates of birth for all your friends, I will call my travel agent."

"Oh, Hattie, that's sweet," Danni said. "But we really couldn't —"

"Yes, we could," Quinn interrupted. "Thank you, Hattie. We'll be very grateful if you'd do that for us."

"Now, where shall we stay?"

"Oh, that's taken care of," Quinn said.

"Oh?"

"We'll be staying at the castle."

"The castle? The House of Guillaume? But . . . how?"

"Dr. Ronald Hubert owns it." He thought she would tell him she was afraid to stay at the grim and foreboding castle where the painting had been created.

She didn't.

To his shock, she said, "Where better! So, when do you wish to leave?"

CHAPTER 11

The second hardest thing for Danni was making a decision about the *shop*.

She hated closing it. But she decided she had to. She wanted the shop — and her home — locked and the alarm on for the entire time they were gone, however long that turned out to be. She ran over to see Niles Villiers and Mason Bradley at the gallery, but didn't tell them where she was going. They both assumed that she and Quinn were taking off for a romantic tryst, and she blushed and let them think that was the case. She also said she'd given her staff a brief vacation and merely wanted to inform Niles and Mason that she'd be away for a few days. She asked if they'd walk down the block to check on the shop now and then.

"Of course!" Niles promised her. "This is the French Quarter — Royal Street! We look after one another."

"I'll walk by the shop every day," Mason

had vowed.

Closing the shop was the *second* hardest thing she had to do.

The hardest was leaving Wolf. But Natasha helped her solve that dilemma. Her assistant, Jez, loved the dog and would happily take care of him.

Danni knew that, for Quinn, the most difficult task had been explaining to Jake Larue that going to Geneva wasn't irresponsible, but the most important move he could make. He'd also asked Larue to keep an eye on the store.

As Quinn expected, Ron Hubert had balked at going, claiming he was "needed here, for God's sake!"

But, in the end, he was convinced.

Bo Ray was thrilled — until he discovered they were staying at a real medieval castle with dungeons and darkness. A place no one had lived in for over a century.

Not a castle-turned-bed-and-breakfast.

When Hattie and Ron met, they made a strange and interesting pair. Ron Hubert was somewhat fascinated by the stern but attractive society matron, while Hattie seemed to appreciate Ron Hubert's intelligence and perspective on life. She'd arranged for a cleaning crew, a large one — twenty people would be sent out! — to ensure that the castle was *livable* when they arrived. Hattie might've had any number of servants for years, but she was extremely capable herself. She made a number of calls to Switzerland, dealing not just with cleaning crews, but with food delivery and other necessities.

Hattie's wealth was useful, Danni thought. She'd also arranged for generators so they'd have light and other electrical conveniences. As she told Danni, "I'm *far* too old to enjoy burned marshmallows over a fire!"

So, by the time they boarded their plane to France a week later, *everything* for their stay had been set in motion.

Danni had decided that despite their destination and their purpose, she was going to enjoy the "getting there" part of it.

Hattie hadn't just booked them flights. She'd booked the eight of them first class all the way. And she'd worked with the passport office to expedite passports for those who needed them, namely Bo Ray and Natasha.

Danni had gotten upgraded with her dad a few times in their travels, so it wasn't as if she'd never been in first class, although she was much more accustomed to coach. She'd stayed in some nice places — and also camped out, sleeping on the ground. Worst were probably the budget motels where she turned the lights out quickly rather than wonder if roaches were scurrying around.

But this . . .

They were on one of the new planes that had private first-class seats that reclined to become beds. She had a workstation, a setup for a computer, pillows, champagne, blankets . . . it was a piece of heaven.

Danni was impressed that Hattie had pulled this off in such a short time. The eight of them took up the entire business-class section, which was cordoned off from coach. Danni was in the second of the middle seats, with Quinn to her left and Bo Ray to her right.

Bo Ray's eyes were still huge. He was happily playing with the video and stereo system.

Hattie, seated in front of Quinn, closed her eyes and rested. Billie did the same. Behind Quinn, Father Ryan read from a religious text and Ron was also reading, frowning as he did so. Natasha was in front of Danni, smiling as she sipped champagne.

Danni knew she had to use the time to finish Eloisa Hubert's journal and the letters that had been stuck between the pages, but for the first thirty minutes of the flight, she just wanted to revel in the luxurious experience of being on this plane.

Danni thought it was a pity they hadn't been able to let Hattie make hotel reservations for them; she could only imagine the accommodations they might have had. . . .

As she carefully took the journal out of her bag, she noticed that Quinn was watching her from across the aisle. "I can help," he told her.

She nodded and shook the journal gently, letting some of the letters fall out. She passed them over to him.

Danni began to read where she'd left off. She was starting to get used to Eloisa's small, cramped handwriting and found herself trying to picture what her life had been like. She imagined Eloisa sitting by a cozy fire. . . .

The solicitor called again today. The castle was packed up immediately after Henry's death but he wanted me to know that he'd had six requests from would-be buyers for the heinous painting my foolhardy husband had created. Apparently, the fact that he died in front of it has made it valuable. The solicitor is quite astonished that I am refusing all offers and that I want the thing wrapped and stored. Everything that Henry painted is now worth a great deal — dead artists seem exceedingly more valuable than living ones. I will never sell that horrid painting, nor shall I ever set eyes on it. The creating of it killed Henry.

I do believe that, in his way, he loved me and our son. But there was something that burned in him, a hunger to be like Lord Byron. Perhaps I couldn't give him the life he longed for; I couldn't give him a certain freedom. Or perhaps he longed for brilliance and didn't believe it existed within him. But I am convinced that in joining with Byron's circle, he indeed sold his soul to the devil.

Most of the Swiss authorities believe he committed suicide, but some claim he was murdered. The one undeniable fact is that there was poison found in his system. I have little recourse except to trust that those in Switzerland are doing everything in their power to discover the truth.

However, I doubt they will ever know with certainty. Henry's servant, a man named Raoul Messine, found my poor husband and brought in the police. He wrote me a lovely letter of condolence.

It was then that I began to think of that wretched dark castle Henry had rented. I knew about Lord Guillaume; word of the man's perversions and killings spread through newspapers across Europe. It was a blessed thing that he was killed by the Swiss authorities. The more I thought about everything that had happened — and that my poor son, Henry William, would grow up without a father, the more distressed I became.

I felt great relief when I made my decision; the painting would go into storage. And I would buy the House of Guillaume from the man's son, a delightful fellow who eschewed his father's evil ways! Young Guillaume wanted nothing to do with his father's memory or the castle. Our deal was quickly made and the young man was pleased to hear that I mean to keep the castle, never to sell it, and that I don't intend to visit or to let it to tenants. He applauded my decision wholeheartedly.

Danni sighed loudly, then realized that Quinn was watching her.

"I just read about Hubert's wife, Eloisa, buying the castle from Guillaume's son," she said. "What did you learn?"

"I found the bill of sale from when the painting was sold to the gallery owner in London — and a newspaper clipping from March 15, 1891, describing his death. Which leads me to think . . ."

"What?"

"That you're right. That whatever is in the painting can only be awakened at night. It appears that nothing happened until the gallery owner was there *at night.* He must have read something about the painting's history and was curious. Or he was somehow compelled to see what would happen if he touched the thing up with a few drops of his own blood," Quinn said.

"The painting's not at the castle, but on the other hand that place *is* where Hubert created it. So it's at night that we need to be wary."

Quinn nodded. "At least we'll get to the castle in daylight. We arrive in Paris at 7:00 a.m., and it's a quick hop to Geneva, and then a short drive from the city."

"I'm glad," Danni said. "Quinn, do you think the castle itself could be evil?"

He was quiet for a minute. "I think *men* can be evil and that's how objects become evil," he replied. "I'm not sure I can really answer that. Why?"

"I read that Eloisa began to heal — I guess that's how I'd put it — or at any rate make her peace with Henry's death, only when she decided to store the painting and to buy the castle and see that no one used it. And she mentions that when she bought it from the hedonist Guillaume's son, he didn't question her plan never to let anyone stay there again," Danni explained.

"Interesting . . ." Quinn said. "We certainly won't take any chances while *we're* there."

Hattie, who'd appeared to be sleeping, turned around at that. "Good thing we have a priest *and* a voodoo priestess with us, isn't it?" She was actually smiling as she said it.

Quinn laughed, obviously pleased by her reaction.

"Good thing," Danni agreed.

Their flight attendants began to serve dinner. Danni worried about spilling something on the journal, so she put it away.

Dinner was surf and turf — lobster and filet — accompanied by a salad, a cheese course and their choice of wines.

"This is *too* cool," Bo Ray said.

Danni smiled. "Yeah, just don't get used to it!"

After dinner, their flight attendants converted their seats into bed compartments. Danni lay down, comfortable in her leggings and sweatshirt, determined to read more of the journal.

Eloisa continued with the business arrangements that had to be made after Henry's death. Danni kept reading, but her eyes were growing heavy.

Then she was wide awake again as she read:

The Swiss authorities have reached me through Scotland Yard's Lieutenant Morrison, a man who has been a great comfort to me. They have questioned every member of staff at the castle with the help of Raoul Messine, but they haven't been able to discover anyone who would have had motive to hurt my Henry. He was well-liked, according to Messine, and the only time any member of the staff was disgruntled was when Lord Byron and his party came to stay. When they were gone and Henry worked alone in his attic, he was faultlessly kind to those who cleaned, cooked and saw to his needs.

Farther down on the same page she read:

My dear Lieutenant Morrison came to see me today with bad news. Apparently, in the midst of packing Henry's belongings, Raoul Messine passed away. His heart, so it seemed, seized as he most tenderly cared for my Henry's last work. Alas, no one was there to help him. The man fell in the midst of glass and china being packed, as well; he was bloody and bruised by the fall, and lay there dying all alone. I will pray for the man who tried so hard to help me.

Danni hadn't seen the information about the butler named Messine anywhere else. She'd only known that the painting had been packaged and stored — and not until Eloisa had died and the painting was sold had there been more deaths. Was the butler, Messine, a victim of the painting, too?

She closed the journal and held it close. The silence of the plane was soothing.

"Danni?" She heard Quinn's soft whisper.

Leaning up on one elbow, she opened her compartment door. He'd opened his own door across the aisle, a grin on his face.

"Yes?"

"Nice digs, huh?"

"Very."

"I'd rather be next to you, though. In a real bed somewhere."

"Excuse me!" They could hear Hattie from the seat in front of Quinn. "I'm still awake. So if you two wouldn't mind!"

Danni smiled and Quinn grimaced. " 'Night," he told her.

" 'Night."

"Good night, Hattie," Quinn said with excessive formality.

"Indeed!"

Danni lay down and went to sleep, still smiling and cradling the journal.

They arrived in Paris feeling surprisingly rested after their night on the plane.

They had an hour's layover — not much time, but Quinn made use of it to purchase European cell phones so they could stay in touch with one another. He texted the numbers to Larue so the New Orleans detective could reach him easily.

The next flight was brief. They deplaned in Geneva where Bo Ray, who'd never been out of the States before, was wide-eyed with wonder. He was so busy looking at the bustle of people moving around him that he walked into a post when they went to line up for customs. Hattie seemed touched by his wonderment and took it upon herself to guide him. She'd gone into her European mode and she did speak French like a native.

With their carry-on luggage, they headed to their rental car. Hattie had seen to it that they had a van — but it was a Mercedes. Generous of her, Quinn thought.

He was definitely starting to like the old battle-ax, as Billie and Bo Ray had called her.

While she had no desire to drive, the others automatically deferred to her and she sat in the front passenger seat while Quinn did the driving.

"It's a pity that we can't at least stop for lunch in the city," Hattie said. "Geneva is charming — absolutely charming!"

Quinn shook his head. "We haven't got time."

"Ah, but the scenery! The mountains, the lake —"

"We'll see the lake," Quinn reminded her.

Hattie chatted on about the attractions of Geneva as they drove. Quinn gave his complete attention to the road, but even so, he saw enough to be impressed. The mountains, beautifully snow-capped, rose around them. The water of the lake was the bluest he'd ever seen. They passed cathedrals and villas — and lots of sheep and cattle and goats, grazing in green and flower-strewn fields.

And then they came to the castle. The House of Guillaume.

Quinn wondered again if Danni was right, if a structure of stone and wood could be evil.

They were met first by the walls, rising twenty feet above the ground. There was a huge iron fence; Bo Ray, by the door in the second row, said, "I've got it."

Hopping from the van, he trotted over to the gate. It didn't creak — not that Quinn could hear — but opened easily.

He drove in and parked in the large courtyard. One by one, they all piled out of the van and gazed up at the foreboding building.

The castle had four towers, heavy wooden doors and a gloomy gray facade that seemed jarringly out of place with the pristine beauty of the nearby mountains and the lake. There were no real windows in the wall surrounding the castle, only arrow slits. The place had been built for defense; it was supposed to be unwelcoming — and it was.

"Well," Ron murmured. "Welcome to my . . . house."

"You've owned this, and you've never been here?" Hattie asked him.

"No," Ron said. "It's not like my parents showed me pretty pictures of a villa somewhere. I've just — well, I've just never had the inclination to come here. I've paid the taxes and arranged for the upkeep. That's all."

He turned to face them all. "I never wanted to be associated with the artist. That's just the way it is." His words were followed by an awkward silence.

"Let's go in, shall we?" Danni finally suggested.

"Wait! I think a prayer for help won't go amiss," Father Ryan said.

"Sounds reasonable to me!" Hattie responded.

Father Ryan walked to the door. He stared at it — as if he was staring at something that had a heartbeat, something that lived.

"Dear Lord," he began, "protect us, we beg You, as we enter unknown realms. Give us strength against Your enemies and ours. Help us be the best we can be, and let us move in the assurance that You will guide us. Amen."

"You have anything?" he asked Natasha.

"I can add a little good gris-gris," she told him. "I will say a prayer for protection and sprinkle herbs for goodness and light."

Father Ryan nodded with a smile.

"I'm for all the gris-gris anyone's got," Hattie said.

"Hear, hear, I do agree!" Billie said. "Bo Ray, give me a hand. We'll get the bags." Billie knew damned well that Quinn and everyone else would gladly help with the bags, but to Billie's mind, Quinn and Danni needed to get into the castle first.

Quinn strode ahead. There was a massive lock on the doors, but while they were driving, Hattie had been in touch with the cleaning crew and learned that they were just finishing up. She'd instructed them to leave the door open when they left.

Quinn entered. He could feel Danni behind him — and hear her gasp as they walked into the massive great hall.

It was exactly as it was in the Hubert painting.

Minus the people, of course. But the full medieval suits of armor were off to the far right; a painting of a medieval knight, minus helmet, hung above the huge hearth. The family crest of Guillaume, with crossed swords beneath, sat to either side of the painting.

A plush red love seat was off in a corner near the stone stairs that led to a gallery and the halls above. A wooden-planked table stood in the middle of the room, perhaps fifteen feet from the love seat.

"Well . . . oh, my," Billie said, coming in behind them.

"Paint what you see," Natasha murmured.

"Or paint what you see in the mind's eye," Danni said. "He worked in the south tower. And he was found dead in the south tower."

For a moment, they all stood there, surveying the room.

"Perhaps we should get organized," Hattie

said briskly. "I don't know about you people, but I'm careful to eat three healthful meals per day and we should choose our rooms and then find the kitchenette the cleaners set up for us. We should square ourselves away, and then get cracking on what needs to be done."

Danni started up the stairs. Quinn, looking down at the castle's great hall as he walked up the stairs, followed her.

There were several doors along the gallery hallway. "We'll take the room closest to the stairs," he said.

"Billie," Bo Ray began. "If we can find a room with two beds . . ."

"Aye, lad, we'll take it," Billie said patiently.

Quinn opened the door at the top of the stairs. A full-size four-poster bed sat on a raised dais. Large windows overlooked the twenty-foot stone wall that surrounded the castle.

Danni headed straight for the window. "It opens up onto a balcony," she told him.

"I guess if invaders breached the wall, you could mount a defense from here," Quinn said.

Danni opened the window. "I have to admit I'm glad Hattie hired a cleaning crew."

"Thank goodness, since I doubt anyone's stayed here in years. More than a century . . ."

"If I hadn't seen *Ghosts in the Mind,* I'd think visiting a castle like this would be wonderful. Especially a castle we have all to ourselves. That *is* pretty remarkable," Danni said.

"I'll bet no one cleaned up in the crypt."

"No, that probably didn't occur to Hattie — and I'm sure it's for the best."

"We should go back down," Quinn said. "I know Father Ryan will be helping Billie and Bo Ray, but I want to give a hand getting the luggage up the stairs. And we should investigate the kitchenette, for what it's worth."

As it turned out, the kitchenette — within the original kitchen — wasn't bad. They reached it by going through the arched doorway, passing the two knights in armor.

He noted that Danni shuddered as she walked by them. The others, though not as visibly disturbed, also reacted to the pair of sentinels.

There was a massive heavy wooden table in the middle of the room; a giant hearth still had utensils and roasting spits on the tile apron around it, and there was a giant cauldron suspended from chains over the fire pit.

New to the kitchen was a generator that hummed away, an electric stovetop and a small refrigerator.

"Did we think about running water?" Father Ryan asked.

"Yes, Father, we did. There's a pump by that small boarded window. It was in use when Henry Hubert was here and, as far as I know, it's remained in fine working order," Ron told him.

"I'll check it out right now," Father Ryan said.

He used the pump to wash his hands with a smile on his face. "Excellent. The water is fresh and cold."

"Let's make ourselves some lunch, shall we?" Hattie suggested. "I ordered salads, vegetables, cheeses and cold cuts — they should be . . . yes! Everything's in the refrigerator and on that table near the pump."

"I'm going to call Larue." Quinn glanced at his watch. "Should be seven or so back home."

"I'll make you a sandwich," Danni said.

He left them in the kitchen and walked back out to the great hall. Just standing there was eerie; he could all too easily picture the scene depicted in the painting.

The woman with her knife.

The man with his pistol.

The servant at the door.

The children with the screaming chess pieces at the great planked table.

The toddler beheading dolls on the floor . . .

"This ain't nothing yet," he told himself, punching in Larue's cell phone number. "We haven't even gotten to the crypt."

Jake answered his phone on the first ring, sounding tense. "I was about to call you," he said wearily. "There's been another killing."

Quinn stayed on the phone for a long time.

The kitchen didn't have chairs, but it had plenty of stools.

Somewhat to Danni's surprise, Hattie didn't expect to be served. She immediately got involved in finding the plastic cutlery and plates their hired staff had provided, and setting up an assembly line to prepare sandwiches.

When Quinn had rejoined them and the sandwiches had been consumed, they all sat around the large wooden table. They weren't talking about the painting or the murders; they were talking about the castle, imagining the era when it was built — and what it was like in the early 1800s when Henry Sebastian Hubert had rented it.

Danni found herself studying another archway at the end of the kitchen. She rose, unnoticed. The others were deep in a discussion about Switzerland's history.

Danni wandered through the archway — no scary men in armor here — and into the room behind the kitchen. She assumed it had served as a pantry or storeroom.

But it also offered another gaping archway to the rear. Stone steps led downward.

Into darkness.

It had to be the entry to the crypt.

And while the gaping darkness sent a chill sweeping through her . . .

It seemed to beckon her, as well.

Come . . .

Chapter 12

Danni told herself sternly that darkness didn't speak. She frequently tried to convince herself that it was her own subconscious mind that tugged at her — especially after an episode of nocturnal painting. But she knew damned well that they had to go down to the crypt.

Still, the castle was creepy. Maybe it really *was* true that the violence of the past lived on in the stone walls of the place.

She hated the great hall.

Naturally; it was the setting for Hubert's incredibly disturbing picture.

Thankfully, he hadn't painted an image of the crypt.

She was certain that if they were visiting a preserved castle now functioning as a museum, she would've seen a chain across the crypt opening and a sign that warned Entrance Strictly Forbidden! Staff Members Only.

But they weren't in a museum. They *were* in a castle — owned by a New Orleans medical examiner.

And nothing here was forbidden to them.

"Wish it was," she murmured aloud.

Digging in her pocket, Danni pulled out the little penlight she usually carried. She started down the steps; she was only going so far and no farther. She just wanted to know what lay beyond once she got to the bottom.

There were a lot of steps. She began counting them — twenty-two until she reached the ground. And when she did, she felt as if she'd walked into an old horror film; Vincent Price should've been there saying something like, "I've been expecting you, my dear."

Vincent Price wasn't there.

What she found was more archways. She assumed they were all part of the support structure of the castle. Cobwebs clung to them like decorations for a wild Halloween party. It was dark and dank.

There were gates, also covered in cobwebs, to the largest archway. They, too, looked as if they hadn't been touched in years. Even before she got to the gates that actually led to the tombs, she saw a number of stone sarcophagi scattered along the way.

The words on them were timeworn, but she had the feeling they might be the latest ones brought to the crypt — which still made them two centuries old. This was farther than she'd meant to go, but she walked toward them, seeking names. One was for a Marie Lisbet Jordain, another for Tomas L'Enfant. The third was smaller than the others; it touched her heart. This tomb was for Jacques Benoit Jordain, 1816. She dusted the tomb to read that he was the son of Marie, who died in childbirth. Danni wondered whether Marie might have been a servant at the castle. If Eloisa Hubert had purchased the castle that same year, then it stood to reason that these people had been interred here before ownership had changed.

She glanced back at the gates. They stood ajar. There was a large metal plaque with the Guillaume coat of arms and a warning in French. She translated as best she could, reading aloud. "Rest in darkness, rest from the light. Take care when mourning the dead, for dead we all shall be. May the spirit rest with the weariness of the body spent and gone. Take care lest you wake the dead."

"Not very charming *or* religious."

Danni nearly jumped sky-high. She hadn't heard Father Ryan come down the steps behind her.

"Sorry," he apologized quickly. "Thanks for reading that. My own French is rusty — oh, wait. I don't know any," he told her, smiling.

"I *think* it's a strange epitaph. Or maybe a prayer of some kind," she said, and read the words again.

"A strange epitaph indeed," Hattie said, walking carefully down the steps. "And you do have it right, Danni. 'May the spirit rest with the weariness of the body spent and gone. Take care lest you wake the dead.' The last part seems to be more of a warning," she noted.

"That's what I thought, too," Danni said.

"I don't like it. I don't like it one bit," Billie muttered, joining them.

"Well, one doesn't like to think of death," Hattie said. "But . . . we've come to this place with a purpose. Where's Quinn?"

"Here." He was on his way down the stairs; Bo Ray, Natasha and Ron were with him.

They were all armed with big, heavy flashlights that revealed the crypt beyond the gates.

It seemed to stretch on forever.

Danni looked over at Quinn. His expression was grim and stoic but he didn't say anything as he studied the long hallway of the dead. "Everything okay with Larue?" she asked.

He didn't respond, and Danni decided she'd ask him again later, in privacy. "Let's get this done, shall we?" he said softly.

"The bad thing here," Ron told them, "is that I have no idea where Henry Sebastian Hubert's interred in this crypt."

"Hopefully, there'll be engraving on a tomb or a plaque or something," Quinn said. "You don't all have to be down here. Father Ryan and Billie and I can handle finding him and getting him out, and then, of course, we'll have Natasha and Father Ryan say words over the burning bones."

"You want the rest of us to go upstairs and wait?" Hattie demanded. "No, no. I'm just fine down here. I'd rather we were together in this place."

Danni frowned at Quinn. "You know I'm going wherever you go."

Bo Ray said, "Hey, Natasha, I'm willing *not* to be here!"

Natasha shook her head. "No, my boy, we're meant to do this as a team. Quinn, you'll need all of us to find the dead man you're seeking."

The iron gates made a screaming sound as Quinn pulled them fully open.

"This isn't good," Bo Ray said. "Ohhh, this isn't good."

"The dead in their tombs offer no danger, son," Father Ryan reassured him.

"Yeah? How do I know they're all really in their tombs?"

Quinn ignored their conversation. "I'm pretty sure he should be toward the front," he said. "Usually, the first interments would be at the end, and the crypt would be filled from the back to the front. Or, at least, that's what I assume."

"Me, too," Danni commented. "So, we start looking in the front." She used her light and went down the line. The wall of tombs — set one upon the other — was sealed. She saw only a few cracks and chips as she walked in, shining her penlight over the engraving and small plaques that identified the dead.

She found more Jordains and thought that perhaps the family had worked for the Guillaumes for several generations.

"The castle was in the Guillaume family for years and I believe they were respected. They prospered until Alain Guillaume, who apparently destroyed the family — well, certainly the family holding — with his wickedness."

"I'm not finding any family members yet

— oh, wait! Here's one." Billie pointed at it. "Yvonne Chambeau Guillaume, 1811!"

"She must have been Alain's wife, poor woman," Danni said.

"Or a daughter . . . no, probably not. She died at the age of thirty-five. I imagine that would make her the man's wife," Billie agreed.

Danni was across from him. She took a few steps and suddenly felt a keen sense of the darkness and dankness within the crypt. She was chilled and wanted to run back and touch another human being.

She swallowed, glancing around. Everyone was close by; there was no reason to be afraid.

Danni inhaled and then exhaled and moved toward the wall. As she did, she slammed into something in her way. She gasped for breath.

"Danni?" Quinn called.

In a second he was behind her. She felt his warmth and his strength, a bulwark against her own fear.

"Walked into a sarcophagus," she said.

"A free-standing tomb. Maybe this is it — let's see . . ." Quinn shone his light over the tomb. "No, this isn't it. It's Alain Guillaume," he read.

"The hedonist himself." Ron shrugged.

"But not my ancestor."

"Okay, we keep going. I guess it's natural that he'd be near his wife," Quinn said.

"Do you think *she'd* be so pleased?" Natasha asked.

"Probably not," Ron said. "He must've made her life hell."

They kept moving, each calling out more and more names, but none of the names was *Hubert.*

Danni paused. They'd come to yet another archway. Rows and rows of funerary slabs stretched out before her. These interments weren't walled.

The decaying dead lay in fragmented shrouds.

She turned around. Quinn and the others seemed far away.

And the feeling of fear and darkness began to sweep over her again.

Wait! she told herself.

But she sensed that it was important to keep moving forward.

She even felt *compelled* to do so.

The others receded behind her. She was alone.

And she *had* to move forward. Into greater darkness.

Deeper into the realm of the dead.

Shelf after shelf, row after row, of coffins. Quinn was astonished by the sheer number.

There were a lot of dead in the Guillaume crypt, that was for sure. But the castle was old; there'd been a lot of Guillaume family members — as well as servants, friends, neighbors. . . . It was impossible to tell just who'd been brought down here and why they'd been interred at the castle.

Studying one of the tombs, he suddenly realized that Danni had moved ahead of them. She was far deeper into the crypt.

"Danni?" he called out.

She stopped, turned back and smiled at him. He thought she smiled, anyway. Their flashlights, against the darkness of the tomb, created a strange and eerie light.

She was as pale as a ghost herself. But then he looked through the next archway, where she seemed to be headed. It was a chilling sight. He guessed that when the crypt was first created, perhaps the living hadn't worried quite so much about the dead. These "shelving" tombs had not been sealed.

Bones broke through the shrouds that had frayed with time. Everything was covered in the dust of the stone and brick that formed the basement, the foundation of the castle, and had become an enormous graveyard within its walls.

"Are you all right?" he asked her.

"Sure, I'm fine."

"Don't move so quickly," Quinn warned her. "Don't get too far ahead of us."

"She's not all right and neither am I," Hattie said. She'd evidently followed Quinn. "There's really only so long that any of us should breathe down here. We need to make some kind of masks before we inhale all this dust, mold and rot."

"She's got a good point, Quinn," Ron told him.

"I think so, too," Natasha said.

Quinn knew they were right. He was angry with himself for not planning better. He should've arranged for masks before they spent any time in the crypts.

But this was urgent. People had been killed.

He was afraid that more could be killed. He wanted to find the damned body and burn it!

"We could use a break, anyway." It wasn't going to help if one of them got ill in the process of doing what needed to be done. "Let's take half an hour, get something to drink, step outside and breathe."

"No, we should go on," Danni pleaded. "Continue what we're doing."

"We will," Natasha said in a calm voice. "Danni, the crypt isn't going away. It's been here all these years, and it'll still be here after we take a few minutes to breathe some fresh air."

"Yes, we need a break," Father Ryan said. "Quinn, you lead. Your light seems to be the strongest. I'll bring up the rear."

Not surprisingly, it didn't take half as long to retrace their steps.

Only Danni seemed to lag. Quinn was about to go back for her, but Father Ryan took her by the arm and hurried her along.

Quinn wanted to make sure none of them remained down there alone. He waited at the top of the steps, watching until everyone had passed him.

Back in the kitchen area, he was pleased to hear Danni laughing. He realized the others were laughing, as well.

When he came closer, he understood why.

"We all look like ghosts!" Bo Ray said. "Tomb dust!"

"Great. And no lovely shower with dual heads and steaming water," Hattie complained. But she didn't seem too distressed about the situation. Quinn had to admit he was impressed by the woman. At her age —

and with her wealth and social standing —
she was a pretty good sport. He'd bet the
last thing she'd expected when she bought
that damn painting was that she'd be crawling through a crypt.

"Let's step outside. The road's across
from the lake. We can avoid a rush at the
pump and see how the waters of Lake
Geneva feel," Bo Ray suggested.

"Yes," Hattie said. "Let's go outside.
Beautiful, fresh, clean air would be such a
treat right now."

When the others headed for the door,
Danni hung back. "What did Larue tell
you?" she asked.

He'd been waiting for this question; she'd
recognized that something was wrong,
something he hadn't told them.

"Three people were killed last night. Two
middle-aged men and a woman, friends
from Ohio. They were attacked on a side
street, heading down to their hotel on Royal
from a night of partying on Bourbon."

Danni's breath caught in her throat.
"Killed — how?"

"Slashed."

"Like with . . . a sword?"

He nodded.

She started past him, as if she was going
to tackle the crypt on her own.

He clasped her gently by the shoulders. "No, Danni. Hattie and Ron were right. We needed to come back up. Staying down there too long would be dangerous without masks. We'll have to make some because there's just too much dust. I mean, look at yourself. Well, that would be hard," he joked. "Look at me."

She didn't smile.

"Come on, let's go outside. We'll get some air. Then we'll rip up some fabric and make masks. Okay?"

After a moment she nodded. He slipped his arm around her shoulders and they walked back through the great hall.

Danni paused there, looking up at the painting above the hearth.

"I wonder if he was the lord who built the castle," she said.

"He isn't wearing a helmet and it's hard to judge by the armor, but I'm thinking maybe early 1600s."

"Like the suits of armor." She frowned. "I thought that kind of armor more or less went out at the end of the 1500s."

"Breast and back plates were used into the 1700s," Quinn said. "That's a full suit he's wearing, other than the helmet. The advent of more powerful guns — bullets with greater impact and velocity — made changes in armor necessary. Eventually more modern guns rendered it almost useless. That," he said, pointing at it, "might have been dress armor."

Danni was still staring at the painting. She shivered. "I don't like him."

Quinn laughed. "Oh, he looks okay in that portrait. Now, in the Hubert, on the other hand . . . Anyway, let's not stare at him. Shall we go outside now?"

"You have to tell the others, you know. About the deaths at home."

"I know. But I thought I'd wait until we found our body — and burned it to cinders."

"Okay," she said softly.

They finally headed out to join the others. Father Ryan stood with Ron by the gates, which were wide open. The others had crossed the road and were walking up a green hillock that led down to the other side.

Danni followed Quinn as he strolled over to join the two men.

"We were just imagining what it was like before this road was put in," Father Ryan said.

Ron nodded. "This road is fairly new, from what I understand. At one time, the only road came around the corner from the hill on the other side of the castle. I believe that when they built the castle, the entrance was to the water side because they could go up into the towers and see the lake clearly — and attack intruders attempting to take the castle. If they were coming by land, they'd have to circle the castle to get to the entrance. This road was probably put in sometime around 1910 to provide for the 'horseless' carriage that was becoming so popular."

"So," Father Ryan said, "I was trying to imagine that summer of 1816. Henry Hubert's guests would've come by water. They were staying just over there." He pointed across the lake. "I'm surprised they made the effort. It rained almost every day that summer and the sky was overcast and wind was whipping around on a daily basis."

"The world is a fragile place," Danni added. "All of that was caused by an explosion of Mount Tambora — far, far away."

"I think scientists decided that it was also a year in which solar flares were inactive — and that would've meant much less sun and heat, too," Ron said. "I can just see them, though — Lord Byron and his party! There would've been five of them. Dr. Polidori, Claire, Mary, Percy and Lord Byron. They would've pulled their boat up on the shore somewhere over that little rise. They would have been full of life, laughing at the wind and rain, and yet eager to get in. And my ancestor — so in love with how 'cool' he was, how popular — would have been anxiously waiting. He'd have filled the house with alcohol and food and done everything in his power to welcome such guests."

"The lake is beautiful," Danni murmured. She left them, hurrying over the rise toward the water.

Uneasy, Quinn followed.

But Danni merely walked down by the lake and joined Natasha, Hattie, Billie and Bo Ray. Bo Ray was still in travel heaven.

"Have you ever seen anything as blue as the lake? And the mountains are so . . . awesome!" he said, plainly bereft of a more expressive vocabulary.

"France is over there, Bo Ray," Hattie said, gesturing. "I think you're right, though. This must be one of the most beautiful regions in the world."

Danni looked out across the water. "We should get back. We need to find that tomb."

"Yeah," Quinn said. "We should."

"A few more minutes," Bo Ray begged.

"Just a few," Hattie agreed. She seemed to enjoy the fact that Bo Ray marveled at the snowcapped mountains around them, the greenery that grew so lush, the color of the lake.

Focused as he was on the other side of the lake, Quinn hadn't noticed that Danni had left them. When he turned, he saw that she was standing on the top of the hillock, staring at the castle.

The castle created a scene of discord, jarring the peace of the day. Time had aged the stone so that it seemed to be like a black rip or tear, a schism in the scenery. A lovely villa should have stood on the site, complete with manicured gardens and flowers blooming everywhere.

As he watched Danni, standing there, gazing pensively at the castle, the day suddenly began to change. Clouds moved across the lake as if they'd been thrown. The sun disappeared; the bright afternoon faded. Darkness seemed to be coming at an accelerated rate.

"Time to go!" Father Ryan shouted.

"Wait!" Natasha said, pointing.

They all looked at Danni. She stood on the hill, long hair flowing in the wind. She continued to stare at the castle — and started walking toward it.

Quinn began to move, but Natasha grabbed his arm. "Follow her, but stay well behind. Let her lead us."

He wanted to jerk free from Natasha so he could run forward and put an arm around Danni. He didn't want her walking alone. The weather, the day, had changed so quickly. From light to darkness. She headed toward the stark and foreboding castle as though in a trance.

"Not *too* far behind," he muttered to Natasha.

They all followed Danni back to the castle. It was going to rain, Quinn thought. He turned back to the lake for a moment.

Spring still seemed to remain there. He realized that sun still dappled the water.

The darkness was over the castle.

Just as they made it back inside, a tremendous brilliance lit up the world around them. It was a flash of lightning, succeeded almost instantly by a clap of thunder that seemed to shake the very earth and stone of the castle's foundation.

"Good thing we don't have any electricity to lose," Bo Ray said. "We're okay — aren't we?"

"We're fine in here," Billie reassured him. "Generators don't go out because of lightning and we've flashlights aplenty and batteries to keep them blazing."

"Yeah, of course," Bo Ray said.

Quinn barely heard them.

Danni paused in the great hall, looking up at the portrait of the medieval knight above the great stone fireplace. She studied it curiously, but there was no emotion in her features. She walked through to the kitchen and then the pantry — and straight to the archway and the stone steps that led down to the crypt.

Quinn felt Natasha's hand on his arm. "Stay close, but follow her lead," Natasha said again.

He turned to Father Ryan, who nodded grimly.

Danni walked down the steps; she hadn't stopped for a flashlight. Billie came hurrying forward, supplying Quinn with one of their largest lanterns. He whispered his thanks, throwing light ahead of Danni. Maybe, in her current state, she could see in the dark.

And maybe not.

He was hardly aware of the others behind him as he tried to keep his distance — while staying no more than an arm's length from Danni.

She passed the crypt that had been sealed, came to those that were broken and crumbling and moved into the oldest part of the crypt, where decaying and yellowed linen covered what was left of the mortal remains of the dead.

The air was filled with a dank scent, not so much of rot, but of time and decay and death. Perhaps because of the depth they were at or the cold that permeated the underground tomb here, some of the bodies had naturally mummified. From somewhere far behind him, he heard a muffled groan of horror.

Bones protruded here and there where the linen of a shroud had completely desiccated. Half of an eyeless, mummified face seemed to watch them as they moved closer.

Danni paid no attention to the bodies on their final beds. She walked until she could go no farther and stopped at the wall.

She turned to speak to Quinn as if she hadn't been in a trance at all. "Quinn, I think he's in the wall. Someone put up new — well, new two hundred years ago — plaster or some other building material."

Quinn looked at her and then at the wall. He stepped forward, tapping the end of the giant flashlight against it.

A hollow sound greeted him.

He didn't ask her how she'd known. He gestured at Billie. "Can you go up and grab a poker from the fireplace?"

"Aye, Quinn."

"I'll go with him," Father Ryan said.

"None of us should be anywhere in this place alone."

Quinn was surprised that no one else said a word. No one asked Danni how she could possibly have known to come to the far back of the crypt to look for the body of a man who should've been in one of the newer sarcophagi toward the front.

Billie and Father Ryan hurried off. They returned with two pokers and an ash broom. Quinn lifted one of the pokers and slammed it hard against the plaster that covered the rear wall.

It gave quickly.

Father Ryan, big and heavily muscled, picked up another poker. Between them, they worked at the wall, and white plaster began to crumble around them. Only the support beams remained intact.

Billie took the broom and swept the floor, trying to clear away the rubble.

They all stood back.

The corpse had been positioned against the support beams for the false wall, held there with clamps. He appeared to be standing.

His arms were folded over his chest, frozen there by death or time.

He had mummified. Tight, almost black, skin was stretched across the bone; the eyes were closed and sunken.

And yet they appeared to watch. To stare at them with mockery and loathing.

And . . . evil.

Had the man been evil? He'd been vain — he had desperately wanted friendship with Byron and Mary and Percy. Had that covetous desire turned him evil? Or had he unleashed something terrible without knowing it? Had he somehow taken on the depravity of the man who had lived in the castle before him?

Quinn didn't know the answers. He felt that what they were about to do was the right thing.

They had found him.

Henry Sebastian Hubert.

CHAPTER 13

In death, Hubert had been dressed in a poet's shirt, now shredded and covered with the tomb's dust. A rich silk coat was worn over the shirt and his breeches were tucked into leather boots, adding to the impression that he stood there, watching them.

As the seconds ticked past, Quinn realized he was staring at the corpse, wondering how so much evil could have been embodied in one man.

Wondering how it could seem that the man was somehow still alive, staring back at them in such a mocking fury.

Finally, he heard Hattie's loud, shaky breath. "Oh, my God," she said.

"Wait! How . . . how do we know it's him?" Bo Ray asked.

Quinn told himself the man was a corpse — just a corpse.

He walked closer, studying it.

There was no resemblance to images he'd

seen of Henry, and he found it difficult to tell one mummified corpse from another.

"The clothing is right for the era," Natasha said.

Quinn bent down; something had fallen to the stone floor within the wall. He picked it up. It was a brass plaque.

Dusting it off, he read aloud, " 'Henry Sebastian Hubert. Disturb not the dead, nor shall any man awaken the soul that rests in peace and darkness.' "

"This plaque with his name is a pretty good sign, I'd say," Hattie suggested dryly.

"Let's get him out of here," Quinn said, looking at Billie.

"Wait." Father Ryan made the sign of the cross.

Natasha might have been a voodoo priestess worshipping gods with other names, but she made the sign of the cross, as well.

Father Ryan beseeched God's blessing and begged His protection, for they now walked through the valley of the shadow of death.

He finished with an "Amen" that they all echoed.

"Natasha?" Father Ryan said next.

Natasha nodded and stepped forward. She clasped one of the talismans she wore around her neck and began to chant in singsong Creole. Finally, she, too, stepped back and said, "Now. Take him. Billie, come with me. I want gas and accelerant to be used. We want him to burn and then we'll send his ashes to the four corners of the world."

"I'll help," Bo Ray cried, following her. He was obviously eager to leave the crypt behind.

Ron Hubert was motionless, staring at the corpse of his ancestor.

Danni, who was just fine now, took Ron by the arm. "We've found him. Now all we have to do is *really* bury the past," she said. "Or put an end to it, anyway."

Ron nodded, still staring at the corpse. Then he blinked. "Yes, yes, of course. It's just a little . . ."

"A little shocking to see a corpse like this — especially when that corpse is an ancestor. I can only imagine," Danni said. "Let's get out of here. Hattie? Will you come with us?"

"Of course."

Danni led Ron Hubert and Hattie out.

"Father, help me?" Quinn asked as the others left, their footsteps loud in the quiet of the crypt. "Billie, if you'll position yourself so . . ."

As they disappeared, Natasha said matter-of-factly, "I've got the light and I'll keep it trained on the wall if you gentlemen will disengage the body."

"Billie, please stand in front," Quinn said.

Billie stood braced to catch the corpse if it fell as Father Ryan and Quinn struggled to remove it from the beams set in to create the false wall.

Quinn was glad Ron Hubert was gone. When they dislocated the corpse from its position, it was so dry an arm and a foot snapped off.

"Make sure we have all the pieces," Natasha said.

Quinn scowled at her. *As if he didn't know that.*

She smiled, reading his mind. "Sorry. I'll see that nothing . . . is left behind," she said.

He nodded.

He'd had no idea just how hard it would be to carry a broken corpse. They didn't get more than a few feet before the brittle neck broke and the head fell off.

They stood there, gaping at one another.

"You men," Natasha said. "You stay here. I'll get a sheet or something to wrap it in."

"Hey, you didn't figure on this, either!" Quinn called after her.

They all suddenly noticed that she was the only one who'd had a flashlight on —

just as she left with it.

Quinn searched for where he'd set down his own light, but Father Ryan had already found it, as well as his own.

"Human nature to fear the dark," Ryan said cheerfully. "Our ancestors had to fear the nightly predators, so naturally they preferred light."

"Good logic, Father," Billie agreed. Quinn saw the older man's face. Billie didn't rattle easily, any more than he did, but they were all somewhat spooked at being in the crypt, with decaying corpses on slabs around them — and the mummified and now-broken body of Henry Sebastian Hubert in their keeping.

At least they didn't have to wait long; Natasha hurried back with a large sheet, Danni on her heels. "Billie and Hubert built up a nice fire outside. They found some old crating to lie the . . . the corpse on."

"Good," Quinn said. "Well, let's get these, uh, pieces together."

They carefully collected the body, the larger disjointed bones and leathered skin and any bits that had fallen off the corpse. A grotesque task but a necessary one . . . When it was wrapped in the sheet, the corpse didn't weigh much at all. Quinn carried the bundle. He didn't look around as they walked out of the crypt.

They passed through the pantry, the kitchen and the great hall.

When they stepped outside, Quinn immediately felt the chill. He glanced up; the sky was roiling. Black clouds seemed to burst upon black clouds. A gust of wind struck him, and he worried that they might burn down half of Geneva if they didn't get it taken care of quickly.

As Danni had said, Bo Ray and Ron had created a good fire — and they'd been aware of the wind and the danger. They'd found a nook in the stone structure of the castle; the wind blew toward it, so there was little risk of the fire sweeping at them backward. They had some kind of leftover packing crate ready for the corpse. Quinn laid his bundle on it and, with Father Ryan, lifted the entire crate-turned-brazier and set it over the fire.

The flames snapped and soared, an eerie blue color. Hattie stepped back, but then moved forward again, wearing a determined expression.

They grouped around the fire. Father Ryan let Natasha intone the first words. He went next, praying that Henry Sebastian Hubert could now rest in peace and cease any evil he sought to perpetrate on earth.

The corpse, in its deteriorated condition,

burned fast. The flames began to subside, but Quinn could still identify remnants of bone . . . and other things.

He wanted it all gone. Completely gone.

He fed more gasoline to the flames from the can Bo Ray and Ron had used.

They watched again. As the fire once more subsided, they saw that there was nothing left but ash; Quinn couldn't even see the remnants of bone.

Then they heard a rumbling overhead. Quinn expected it to be the sound of distant thunder. It wasn't, though, and he couldn't tell what had caused the noise, since the clouds over the castle had dispersed. The sky was darkening, but that was because night was coming on.

"Let's keep going," he said to the others.

Bo Ray had seen to it that they had a bucket to collect the ash — whatever was left of the wooden crate and the body, now mixed in a pile. When that task was finished, they headed to the lake, where they divided the ashes, sending them in different directions, into the wind and the water.

Done. It was done.

Quinn should have felt a massive sense of relief. A feeling that it was over.

He didn't. Looking at Danni, he thought she was puzzled, as well — certain that she should've felt the sense of a burden being lifted. He knew, of course, that the painting still existed, presumably in New Orleans somewhere, and thought perhaps that explained his continued discomfort.

"So, we did it, and we all look as if we've been mud wrestling in plaster," Hattie observed.

"There are some old tubs, and we can heat water," Billie said grudgingly.

"That would be quite nice, Mr. McDougall. And sincerely appreciated," Hattie told him.

"Mrs. Lamont?" Father Ryan asked. "Would it be presumptuous of me to hope that you ordered a good Irish whiskey delivered with the food supplies?"

"Not at all, Father Ryan. Not at all. Besides our baths, a drink would seem to be in order."

"Well, speaking of those baths," Bo Ray said, "guess I'm hauling the water, huh?"

"Only if you want to," Hattie replied.

Bo Ray grinned at her. "After that plane trip over here . . . yeah! I want to haul water!"

"If we all help, it won't take long," Quinn said.

"Shall we head in?" Father Ryan suggested. "I'm ready for a shot of whiskey."

"I was thinking of jumping in the lake," Bo Ray admitted. He shrugged and turned to follow Father Ryan, Hattie and Billie back to the castle.

Ron and Natasha stayed with Quinn and Danni by the lake.

"It *is* done, right?" Ron asked. "He's gone."

"He is gone," Natasha agreed.

"Then why are you all acting like you expected something to be different?" Ron asked.

Quinn figured it was an appropriate time to tell him what had happened in NOLA. "There were other deaths back home," he said. "Three of them."

Natasha's beautiful features were stoic.

Ron paled. "Before we did this, obviously."

"Yes."

Natasha said, "Maybe one day we'll discover the *science* behind what we don't understand. *Science* once claimed that the sun revolved around a flat earth, you'll recall, Doctor."

"There are eight of us," Danni said, changing the subject abruptly. "If we're all going to halfway clean up — and I don't feel like wearing crypt dust when we board a plane tomorrow — we'll have to get going on the whole water-hauling event."

As they walked back toward the castle, Natasha and Quinn hung back for a moment.

"You don't think it's really over, do you?" he asked quietly.

She shook her head and glanced at Danni's retreating back. "No. Neither does Danni. And neither do you."

"Why?" Quinn asked. "We did what we should have done. From any work I ever did with Angus and from the pages of his Millicent Smith book, this is how we end it."

Natasha shook her head again. "Maybe I'm wrong. We *did* do everything we were supposed to. Except . . ."

"Except the painting's still out there." Quinn finished her sentence. "And whoever *killed* to get that painting is still out there."

She nodded, and Quinn set an arm around her shoulders. "Okay, tomorrow we go home and find the painting. But if Hubert created it with his blood, he shouldn't be able to inhabit the painting anymore."

"I know Hattie Lamont won't have a problem destroying it. I'm certain of that," Natasha said.

"True, but for now . . ."

"Yes?"

"I'm with Hattie. This crypt dust and dirt is . . ."

"Creepy?" Natasha asked.

He laughed. "Creepy — and disgusting."

Together they walked back to the castle.

Danni couldn't help being amused that they managed to make something of a game out of supplying water to the massive tubs in the guest rooms upstairs.

Everyone joined in — except Hattie.

That wasn't because she was unwilling. They'd all tacitly agreed that, despite the fact that she was so fit, they weren't letting a woman her age haul buckets up and down the stairs.

She insisted, however, that she'd take care of the cleaning up.

"Really?" Ron teased her.

"Well, of course. I'll order in a crew after we leave," she told him.

Getting everyone bathed took two and a half hours. But those who'd gone first had started working in the kitchen. Sometime around 9:30 p.m. they'd concocted a meal of chicken and pasta, salad and vegetables; they even had a box of delightful French pastries for dessert.

Danni didn't understand why she still felt so worried — apart from the one obvious reality. The painting hadn't been destroyed yet. She knew that she and Quinn would talk later, when they had time.

She wasn't sure if it was logic — or something else — that had told her where to find Henry Hubert. Instinct. Logic *and* instinct.

His wife hadn't wanted his body. She'd wanted the castle kept in the family — but never occupied.

Where would you put someone you thought should disappear into the earth as deeply as possible? At the far end of the crypt. You wouldn't leave any outward sign of him because you wouldn't want idiotic devil worshippers digging him up. Eloisa's journal had been obscure about her instructions for his burial, but she'd revealed enough to lead Danni to his final resting place.

Just as she was thinking about the body, Bo Ray, licking his fingers after finishing what must have been an especially delicious éclair, said, "I get the impression Hubert's wife really wanted nothing to do with him — or his body. And I guess she couldn't cremate him because it wasn't done in Christian societies at the time."

Father Ryan nodded. "It's only recently that the Catholic Church began to condone cremation."

"Well, she buried him, all right," Natasha said. "Or had him buried. We're lucky Danni found him."

"It wasn't that hard. I was remembering a vague comment in his wife's journal," Danni said. She didn't want to think about being in the crypt. She'd been in cemeteries and catacombs, and she'd never felt as uncomfortable as she'd felt in that crypt. It almost seemed as if the walls were infused with evil.

Quinn chose that moment to tell the group at large that three more people had died in their absence.

"And I'm not there," Ron moaned. "I should've been there. I need to see the bodies. I need to know if the killings were related. The only way to figure that out is . . . well, I'd have to compare them." He paused. "Not that we don't have a number of talented medical examiners. I'll just have to look at the autopsy reports tomorrow."

"Where'd it happen?" Bo Ray demanded.

There was silence for a minute.

"Quinn, where were they killed?" Bo Ray persisted.

Quinn told him.

"That's the corner down the street from the Cheshire Cat!" he said.

"Yes. The three of them were staying at a hotel on Royal. They were going back there from Bourbon."

Bo Ray shuddered. "But that was *before* we burned the body, right?"

"Yes," Ron answered, and Quinn nodded.

"Bo Ray, we acted as quickly as we could," Father Ryan said. "We're doing everything we can to stop this evil."

"I guess I was thinking that as creepy as this castle is, I'm glad I'm here, and not at home. I know I'm being selfish, but . . . that's too close."

"We can't undo what's been done," Natasha said. "We can only hope to right the present and safeguard the future."

The room fell silent again.

Father Ryan raised his glass and said, "As Natasha says, all we can do is move forward and act to the best of our abilities. We've done what we needed to do — but more work lies ahead. And I wish to thank Dr. Ronald Hubert and Mrs. Hattie Lamont. Without your help, Ron, we couldn't be here. And, Hattie, without your brilliant planning as well as your generous financing, it would've been a far more wretched trip."

"A toast to you both!" Billie cried, holding his tumbler of whiskey aloft.

"Ah, thank you." Hattie lifted her wineglass. "Without *you,* I wouldn't be alive."

Quinn was drinking water. He raised his own glass in a toast to the others. "To all of us, because everyone's put in what was needed, and I'm grateful, too."

"Can't find many water haulers better than me," Bo Ray said in a mock-boastful tone that made Danni smile.

"You know," Hattie said, "it's really too bad that we're here under such circumstances. It would be fun to experience this place more as tourists. I can imagine Mary Shelley and Claire, both beautiful in their Empire gowns, reclining on the sofa. And Byron. I wonder what it was like to hear the man speak. Was he as brilliant as we believe? Or was he just a dilettante? Do you think Shelley was morose — or charming and seductive?"

For a moment, Danni could almost hear the people who would've been in this room nearly two hundred years earlier. She saw Mary move about, her hair pulled back, a few curls escaping. In her imagination, Mary laughed easily. Claire, an absolute beauty, would have been pining after Lord Byron. And Henry Hubert . . .

Had he been jealous of Byron's friendships with Polidori and Shelley?

Had he joined in the conversation, and

yet watched them carefully, yearning to really be one of them?

Natasha stood and walked over to the hearth, gazing up at the painting. "There were many reasons the tale of Frankenstein's monster came to Mary Shelley's mind. Remember, there were scientists all over the world conducting experiments with electricity. Her father's home was open to the greatest minds of her day."

"Not to mention the experiments being done on corpses!" Ron said. "It was a pretty macabre time in medical research. But all over Europe and beyond, graveyards were being plundered for corpses. Medical schools needed them. More importantly for our purposes, several men had used frogs and other small creatures to prove that electricity could cause movement in the dead when shot through the nervous system and into the muscles."

"Mary knew all that. And then, while they were at Villa Diodati, they read German ghost stories," Hattie said, adding, "I've been researching all this and even reading some of those stories. Can't you just hear her talking to Henry Hubert, telling him about her nightmares?"

"They probably sat in this very room on their visit to Hubert," Bo Ray said, "talking about everything they were doing. All the stuff they'd learned . . ."

"And fantasized about," Ron threw in.

"Hubert would've felt the need to keep up," Hattie said thoughtfully. "Those beautiful people! So bright and shining to Hubert!"

"Hedonists," Ron said in a sardonic voice. "Even if they weren't hedonists on the order of Alain Guillaume. From what I've heard, he took village girls, had his way with them as they said back then — and murdered them. But one girl who'd gone missing had a father in local government. That's when the authorities became involved. He tried to kill the local police who came after him . . . and got himself killed. Beautiful people or not, I can't imagine anything too edifying going on here!"

Hattie laughed. "Well, on that cheerful note, I'm off to bed," she said, rising. "I've had all the fun I can take for the moment."

"I'll walk you up," Ron offered.

"We should all call it a night," Quinn said. "I'll just pick up."

"Cleaning crew when we leave," Hattie reminded him.

"I'm a creature of habit," Quinn told her. "I will, at least, throw away the paper and plastic we've been using."

Natasha and Father Ryan stayed down-stairs with them, and Danni wasn't going up without Quinn. There was something about the castle that made her feel she shouldn't be alone in it. As they collected the dishes and leftovers, Danni noticed that he didn't seem to care about using up the generator; he wasn't turning off any of the lights they'd set up to illuminate the place. Natasha and Father Ryan started up the stairs to the second floor. Quinn took Danni's hand, and they followed soon after. Halfway up the stairs, Danni paused. She had the sensation that someone was behind her, watching her.

She shivered and looked back. Had there been movement in the room?

But nothing seemed different. Then she sensed it again. Movement. Somewhere . . . on the wall?

She stared up at the portrait of the knight, the man they all assumed to be the first Lord Guillaume. The painting hadn't changed.

Neither had the coat of arms or the crossed swords beneath.

Her eyes shot to the suits of armor guard-ing the archway to the kitchen.

Nothing had moved. Nothing at all.

"Danni?" Quinn asked worriedly.

She shook her head. "This whole place is . . . repulsive. Thank God we're finished and flying home in the morning!"

"I'm here with you," he said. "I won't leave your side."

He slipped his arm around her and they continued up the stairs. Still, as they neared the top, she looked back a final time.

She just couldn't shake the feeling of being watched.

Of being watched by . . .

Something evil.

They'd killed *the evil!* she told herself. They'd followed everything they knew about destroying the essence of evil that could survive after a man's death. Body burned to ash. They'd seen the body; they'd burned it themselves and scattered the ashes to the four winds.

Yes, they'd burned Hubert. Nothing remained of him — except his painting. *Ghosts in the Mind.* Perhaps his most candid expression of evil.

It also seemed to her, more intensely than ever, that the castle itself, the very walls, the structure and everything in it, was somehow permeated with that same evil.

She shivered, forced herself to look forward.

To feel the warmth of Quinn's arm.
She would not let the castle claim her.

CHAPTER 14

Quinn lay awake a long time after Danni had fallen asleep.

He should have felt good. Exhausted, perhaps, but good. He'd meant to be a gentleman — old-fashioned term though it was — and do nothing but hold Danni until they slept. To his surprise, she'd wanted more. So they'd made love, and for those moments, they'd left the foreboding castle behind. Through their bodies, through sheer sensation and pure emotion, they'd escaped into blissful new regions.

No eerie ghosts had shrieked in the night; no werewolves on distant hills had howled at the moon.

The castle was just brick and mortar, wood and stone.

But they were all bothered by the sense of something unfinished, he knew. At least he, Danni, Father Ryan and Natasha were.

Father Ryan was behaving almost jovially.

Quinn believed he was putting up a front for the others. After all, by 11:00 a.m. the next day, they'd be on a plane heading home and this would all be behind them.

Lying awake, he was glad they'd have a pleasant trip back the next morning; he intended to sleep the entire way.

Now, when they got home . . .

That would be the time to worry again. Despite the fact that Hubert was dead — more than dead — they had to find and destroy his painting.

His thoughts continued to plague him but eventually jet lag, the day, the week, took hold, and he fell into a fitful sleep.

He awoke abruptly to discover that Danni wasn't at his side.

Leaping out of bed, he slid into his jeans, grabbed his Glock, plus a robe for Danni, and ran out of the room. He raced down the stairs, calling her name.

She wasn't in the great hall. The pale light created by naked bulbs cast an eerie glow now that the room was empty, a glow in which all kinds of things could be seen — or *perceived.*

Movement.

Yes, the suits of armor shifting just slightly.

The eyes in the portrait above the fire, moving, following him.

Something alive in every shadow, in every corner.

None of that mattered. Danni wasn't here.

He feared that she'd gone to the crypt.

Quinn picked up one of the heavy lantern-size flashlights they'd been using and made his way into the kitchen and through the pantry — and the maw of darkness that was the stairs down to the crypt. The light blazed before him.

At least the crypt was no darker now than it had been during the day. And yet, it seemed worse as he hurried along the sealed shelving, passing the few stone sarcophagi that had been set on the ground.

He entered through the archway that led to the far reaches of the crypt, the oldest area. The corpses seemed alive as he passed them, bones protruding from ancient shrouds, sightless eyes in half-exposed skulls.

He steeled himself against imagination and fear, and proceeded to the back wall of the crypt, now destroyed by their efforts.

It was as if he could hear mocking laughter in the silence of the night.

We've taken her. She's one of us now.

She wasn't there, either. He turned and ran back as fast as he could. He had to wake the others. He'd hoped to find her himself because she was probably seeking a canvas. Her nocturnal wandering usually resulted from her need to paint — either something that came to her mind when it was at rest, or something she sensed, knew or feared in some unknown way.

Paint!

Henry Sebastian Hubert had painted in the south tower. They hadn't even explored any of the towers; they'd chosen bedrooms and gone immediately to the crypts.

He raced back to the second floor and stood still for a minute, orienting himself. Then he dashed down the main hallway and found the winding staircase. Without his flashlight, he didn't think he could have managed the stairs. He moved swiftly and yet watched every step he took. *How had she negotiated the stairs in the dark?*

He reached the tower. His light played over the room.

And then he saw her.

There was no canvas here now, and no paints to work with.

Danni sat, very straight, in a richly tapestried wingback chair, staring at the wall. She might have been posing for another artist or photographer, she was so beautifully seated, hair spilling down her back in wild, sensual waves, head high, hands resting lightly on her knees.

He walked carefully to her side, wrapped the robe around her naked body and knelt by her, taking her hands. At first, she didn't respond to him. It was as if she really *saw* something there. He noticed the angle of her gaze as he held her hands.

If there'd been a canvas in the room, she would've been staring straight at it. He could tell because of the location of the arrow slits and the small observation window.

She faced the direction from which the best light of day would have fallen, whatever light there was that summer when Hubert had painted.

"Danni," he said firmly.

She still didn't respond.

He took her head between his hands and turned it toward him. "Danni!" he said again.

She blinked; then she saw him.

"Quinn . . ."

She blinked a second time, looked around the tower room and shivered fiercely. "No . . . oh, Quinn!" she gasped.

"Let's get out of here." He drew her to her feet; she pulled back a little, looking around again. There was almost nothing in the room, just the chair where she'd sat, a taller stool shoved against the wall and a small table beside the chair.

There were no signs that anyone had ever worked on a canvas here.

"Danni," he said urgently. "Come on, let's go."

A tremor shook its way through her. He brought her into his arms, holding her close. He felt the thunder of her heart and tried to warm her and reassure her with his embrace. "The others?" she whispered.

"Still sleeping," he said.

"Thank God," she murmured, following as he shone his light on the entrance and the winding stairs. "I guess you didn't happen to come up here with a full outfit and shoes, huh?" she asked.

"Silly me. I forgot. Just brought the robe."

She smiled wryly. "I should learn to get dressed before sleepwalking."

They made it down the stairs and hurried back to the room they'd chosen. When they reached it, he snatched the blanket off the bed and wrapped it around her. She sank onto the foot of the bed, then looked up at him. "How do I stop this?" she whispered, a little desperately.

He went down on one knee, clasping her hands, rubbing them between his own, restoring warmth. "Danni . . . I'm not sure you can. I guess I need to become better at keeping an eye on you. Or," he teased, "I could tie you next to me when we go to bed."

That brought a weak smile. "Maybe not such a bad idea," she said.

"Kinky." He laughed. "Could be fun, you know."

She tried to smile again. "Quinn, the painting. It has to be burned to ash — just like Hubert himself."

"We'll find it," he pledged, "and that's what we'll do."

"There were no more calls from Larue, were there?" she asked anxiously.

Three dead since they'd left; that seemed bad enough.

"No," he told her. "No more calls." He smoothed back her hair. "Let's try to sleep."

She was still trembling, and he held her close as they lay back down.

The night passed.

The only negative to riding in a first-class cabin was the fact that the seats were divided from one another. Quinn wanted to have a private talk with Hattie, but that wouldn't be easy.

He didn't even try on their first short flight from Geneva to Paris. He waited until they'd boarded at Paris and been airborne for an hour. Then he went to her seat and perched on the side of her chair.

"I still don't want you to be alone," he said without preamble.

"But . . . we burned the body."

"I know, but as we've discussed, the painting's still out there," Quinn reminded her in a low voice, "and people are still dying."

"And I own the painting," Hattie said. "That's your point, isn't it?"

He nodded.

"Well, I own it legally. But possession is the real law, isn't it?"

"Especially in a case like this."

"You want me to stay at Danni's place?"

"A little longer. Until this is completely over."

She studied him for a moment and smiled. "Other than being scared nearly to death, I've had some nice times with you and your friends, Quinn. I'm grateful that you care about my life. I'll be happy to remain at The Cheshire Cat."

Relieved, Quinn astonished himself by giving her a kiss on the cheek.

And *she* astonished him by accepting it.

"And," she promised, "when we find that wretched painting, I shall be the first to light a match."

He rose and went to Ron's seat next. He needed Ron to stay at Danni's place awhile longer, too.

"What about my work?" he asked dully. "You know how we say a medical examiner speaks for the dead? I believe that, and it actually means a lot to me. Being an M.E. is my profession, yes, but it's not just a job to me."

"I'm not suggesting you stop working. All the evidence is that these killings only happen at night," Quinn told him. "Stay at Danni's for a few more days — just until we find the painting."

Ron nodded. "If there's one thing this whole ordeal has taught me it's that I like living," he said, not for the first time.

Satisfied, Quinn resumed his own seat.

He saw that Danni was deep into Eloisa's journal once again. Her forehead was puckered in a frown, but when she sensed him watching her, she looked up. "Interesting material," she said. "I suppose it's not really necessary to keep reading. This won't help us find the painting, but . . ."

"Can't hurt," he assured her.

She returned to the journal, and he allowed the quiet hum of the engines to lull him to sleep.

■ ■ ■ ■

Quinn wasn't really surprised that Larue was waiting for them at the terminal when they arrived in New Orleans. He was hovering just beyond the TSA official who guarded the exit — making sure no one used it as an entrance.

At first, Quinn was afraid that Larue had come because something else had happened.

He hurried past security to Larue and asked, "My God, not more — not another murder?"

"No, not since I called you," Larue said. "But I thought you and Ron might want to drive to the morgue with me, study the autopsy reports." Ron had reached them by then and nodded vigorously.

"Did the crime scene investigators get anything on the street?" Quinn asked.

"Nothing," Larue said with disgust. "Seriously, what the hell would you get off a street between Bourbon and Royal? Hundreds of footprints, cigarette butts, you name it. Even though the streets are cleaned in the wee hours every morning . . . Well, the street's a veritable hotbed of DNA evidence — but it's DNA evidence that comes from hundreds of people. If not thousands."

Father Ryan set a hand on Quinn's shoulder. "You and Hubert go in with Larue. I'll get everyone back to The Cheshire Cat."

"You're going to stay there, too?" Quinn asked him.

"Only until you return," Father Ryan replied.

"Maybe we should *all* stay there," Quinn said. "Including you. Just until this situation is . . . resolved."

Father Ryan shook his head. "I've never had anything to do with the painting. I never possessed the painting. And I'm a man of God. My parishioners need me. For one thing, the Garcia family's bodies were released for burial just before we left. I'm their priest and must see to their funerals. My faith is with me," he added quietly. "But I won't leave until you're back. And I'm always close at hand."

"Quinn, we'll be fine," Danni assured him. "Hey, it's daylight. And we'll be together."

She didn't say anything else, but she seemed pensive, as if she'd had a new thought or idea.

"All right, Ron and I are going with you," Quinn told Larue.

They followed him out. He knew that

Danni would see that their bags got home. "What time were the three tourists killed?" Quinn asked as they walked to Larue's unmarked car, left outside the door at arrivals.

"Around 3:30 a.m.," Larue said. "It was late enough that the streets were starting to slow down a bit. The victims couldn't have been dead long when they were discovered. Some girls on their way back from a bachelorette evening stumbled on them. The girls are still pretty traumatized. Oh, and two officers from the Bourbon Street mounted patrol had just gone by about ten minutes before, so the three were killed *in full view* of Bourbon in a matter of minutes." Larue paused to look at Quinn. "I'm sure you were doing something that you needed to do on your jaunt to the Old World, but you know as well as I do that there's someone flesh-and-blood and very much alive causing these murders."

"Yes," Quinn agreed.

"We can't find any forensic evidence, not on the bodies and not on the streets," Ron Hubert said in a hopeless voice. "Think I'll be able to keep living in the city after all this?"

"You can't help who your ancestors are," Quinn said. "And like Jake said, regardless of the role of that damned painting, these murders were committed by a living, breathing human being."

"We need you," Larue added. "Don't even *think* about leaving the city."

When they got to the morgue, Quinn figured Ron should feel relieved; he was greeted with affection and respect, as if he'd been gone a long time rather than a few days.

Another medical examiner, Gerry Vassery, had performed the autopsies on the three who'd been killed while they were gone. He was waiting for Ron, his reports ready. The bodies were on steel gurneys in the chilled room. Quinn stood with Larue while the two medical examiners talked.

When Ron had finished questioning the other M.E., he came back to where Quinn waited with Larue.

"Lynn and Marty Seabold and their friend, Justin Ottaway. Ages sixty-two, sixty-four and sixty-six, respectively. At least they'd had some time to live," Ron Hubert said with chagrin. "Come on over and you can see how the wounds were inflicted."

They went from body to body. "Mrs. Seabold probably died first and almost instantly," Ron said. "It looks as if an executioner swung a sword to behead someone, even though he didn't quite decapitate her. The other two . . . Mr. Seabold's arm is nearly severed — he put it up like this. . . ." Ron demonstrated. "A defensive wound. Then he was slashed across the stomach. Half his internal organs are damaged. Death wouldn't have been as instantaneous, but it would've come quickly. Mr. Ottaway has several defensive wounds, too — and he tried to run. He was slashed from his neck downward at an angle. His spinal column was severed."

Quinn pictured a medieval horseman riding down the street — slashing, slashing, slashing. Killing as quickly as possible.

Of course, there'd been no medieval horseman. Whoever had come to the street had done it stealthily — taking a chance on not being seen or heard.

"These people weren't murdered the way Mrs. Lamont's butler, Bryson Arnold, was," Quinn mused aloud, "but very much like Andrea Garcia, Mr. Garcia's wife, who was killed in the kitchen at their home."

"My thoughts exactly," Larue murmured.

"Can I speak with the girls who found them?" Quinn asked.

"I'll take you to them now," Larue replied.

"I'm going to stay here, catch up on all the notes . . . go back over everything," Ron told them.

"Call when you're ready to leave for the night," Quinn said. "Someone will come and get you and bring you back to Danni's."

Ron didn't argue with him, and Quinn and Jake headed out.

The three young women who'd come across the bodies were staying not far from The Cheshire Cat, at one of the grand old hotels off Royal.

Larue called them before they reached the hotel, and the three were waiting for them. They had a small suite on the third floor and Quinn and Larue went directly there.

The young women were all in their early twenties. Katie Dobinsky, the bride-to-be, was still nervous and shaky. The other two were Sissy Dobinsky, a cousin, and Julia Seton, a close friend.

Katie, although she swallowed a lot when she spoke, seemed to be the calmest and to have the best memory of the night.

"I can't tell you how horrible it was," she said. "We were laughing . . . we were, I will admit, pretty drunk. I mean, it was my wild and crazy bachelorette night for the three of us. Jimmy — my fiancé — was home in Pittsburgh."

Sissy placed an arm around her shoulders. "He's here now," she said.

"He ran out a few minutes ago to buy us some takeout meals," Julia explained. "We . . . we're not really up to going out. We would've gone back home already except that Detective Larue asked us to stay for a couple of days."

"Thank you," Quinn said sincerely. "Can you tell me anything else?"

"Like I was saying," Katie began, "we were . . . smashed. We were walking down the street arm-in-arm, and then . . ."

"I remember thinking some drunks had passed out on the street," Sissy put in.

"But then we saw the blood," Julia said.

Katie cleared her throat. "It was even worse than that. We couldn't see the blood at first. Then we did see it. I mean, I almost tripped over the woman. . . . But when I saw all the blood, I started screaming. And then the cops on their horses came . . . and, oh, God! So much blood!"

Quinn patted her hand. "Thank you. You just said, 'It was even worse than that.' What did you mean? And don't apologize — lots of brides-to-be have been inebriated on the streets of New Orleans." He gave her what he hoped was an understanding smile.

She tried to smile back. "What was even worse . . . was the reason we couldn't see."

"The fog," Sissy clarified. "So bizarre! We

walked off Bourbon, and suddenly there was fog everywhere. Heavy fog. Like pea soup. We couldn't see at all for a few minutes. You can ask the officers. It was just beginning to lift when they arrived on the scene."

Eyebrows raised, Quinn looked at Larue, who returned his stare.

Larue had known about the "fog" the young women had seen.

He'd wanted Quinn to hear it for himself.

It should've felt good to get home. And, of course, it did.

They reached the shop on Royal and she opened it up. In a few minutes, the bags, including Quinn's and Ron's, were inside, and Natasha had called Jez to tell him they were back. Natasha was going to stay a while, so Bo Ray walked down to retrieve Wolf, while Danni and the others carried the various pieces of luggage to the rooms where they needed to go.

She should've felt comfortable, she kept telling herself; she should've felt relieved.

She didn't. Not really. And she knew why.

When she discussed the situation with Natasha, her friend said, "Don't worry so. We'll track down the painting. Anyway, it's lost some of its power. We *will* find it."

"Yeah?" Danni asked. "Why don't you

sound convinced?"

Natasha shrugged. "It's going to be difficult to find, that's all."

"But it still *has* power," Danni argued. "If whoever has it uses his own blood to 'feed' it . . ."

That was when Bo Ray returned with the dog.

Wolf whimpered when he saw Danni. She was so happy to see him that she forgot her misgivings — for about a minute.

But even after greeting her and then everyone else, Wolf seemed restless, too. He kept pacing the kitchen, as if there was something he should be doing, something he should be hunting down, but he didn't know what.

Danni gave him treats and he settled on the floor at her feet.

"We're not opening the store, are we?" Bo Ray asked.

"No, it's almost closing time." They'd left Geneva at 11:00 a.m. and Paris at 2:00 p.m. But because of the time change and despite the eight-hour flight, it was only four when they touched down in New Orleans. Now, however, after driving into the city and settling in, it was after six.

"Let's get some dinner going, shall we?" Hattie said cheerfully. "Believe it or not, children, I'm an excellent cook. Shall I see what's in the larder?"

"Oh, Hattie, we can take care of the cooking. You don't have to," Danni told her.

"I'm delighted to show off my prowess in the kitchen," Hattie insisted. "If you don't mind, I'll go through what we have."

"There's a grocery down the street," Bo Ray said. "I can run out and get anything you need."

Hattie smiled. "What a sweet offer. Thank you, Bo Ray."

"I'll just take a gander at the shop, see that everything's all right," Billie said.

"Much as I'd like to stay for your meal, Mrs. Lamont, I should go back to my own place." Natasha gathered up her bags as she spoke.

"I'll walk you home, Natasha," Father Ryan said.

"There's no need," she protested.

"Nonsense. I'll enjoy the fresh air and I could use the exercise," Father Ryan said, and Natasha agreed to his company.

Danni decided she should take the journal down to her father's office. There was something she felt she should be seeing in the painting — *understanding* about the painting. Something she just hadn't figured out.

"I'll be downstairs," she announced. "Just call if you need me, anyone."

"And I'm only a holler away," Natasha said. "A loud holler, but . . . I'll be there in no time."

Hugs goodbye were exchanged, then Father Ryan left with Natasha, and Danni headed down to the basement. The door to the office was locked, and she remembered Billie had done that after bringing in her giclée copy of the Hubert.

Wolf was at her side. He whined when she pulled out her keys and opened the door, clearly not wanting her to go in. He sat in the little hallway at the foot of the stairs, refusing to enter the room.

"Wolf, I don't like the damned thing, either. But it's only a copy, and we need to read the rest of that journal. There might be information in it that'll direct me to Millicent Smith's book, so . . ."

She went inside, flicking on the light.

Wolf stayed in the hall for a minute, but then seemed to feel he couldn't let her enter alone.

She paused at the door, thinking that something was awry. But nothing had changed about the office or her father's collection.

Except, of course, the presence of the gi-clée.

It leaned against the far wall. Danni walked closer to it.

She was surprised to see that the brown paper wrapping was falling off. Niles was usually so meticulous.

Faulty tape, she thought. She could see where it had given way.

She was about to rewrap it; she still had a sense of discomfort in her own home — a home she loved — and she sure didn't want to look at the giclée. Not even a corner of it.

But before she could approach it, Wolf began to bark loudly and excitedly.

He ran to the door, whined, then ran back to her.

She realized she was hearing voices from the kitchen above.

"Ah, Quinn's back!" she told the dog. "And you have to go and see your Quinn, don't you? Let's go up and maybe have some dinner, and then we'll come down again, okay?"

Wolf barked, apparently delighted with her decision, and sprinted up the stairs.

She was about to turn off the light when she glanced back at the painting.

Now the wrapping had fallen almost

completely off.

She'd ask Billie to repackage the damned thing later.

Flicking off the light switch, she hurried out of the room and up the stairs.

CHAPTER 15

Quinn wondered how he could be so tired when all he'd really done was fly in a very comfortable seat, dozing for much of the trip.

But when he reached The Cheshire Cat, he *was* tired. Maybe they were all just drained; they'd done a lot in a very short time, and events around them had been traumatic.

When he entered the kitchen, greeted Hattie and Bo Ray, and then had Wolf run up to greet him as if he were long-lost and dearly beloved, he felt better.

Danni followed the dog. There was a tense expression on her face, probably because she was hoping he'd learned something by going off with Larue.

"Anything?" she asked breathlessly.

"They were killed much like one of the previous victims," Quinn said.

"Bryson?" Hattie paused, a skillet in her hands.

"No, a member of the Garcia family."

"No weapons, no clues?" Danni asked.

"Fog," he said. "That's all."

"Fog!" Hattie repeated. Then she shook her head firmly. "No more talk of this right now! Let's sit down to a lovely meal. Yes, lovely, if I do say so myself. It's not just about the food, it's about the company. Danni, my dear, give Bo Ray a hand setting the table, will you? Quinn, wash up. I believe Father Ryan will be back any minute. Natasha had to go and see about her own affairs, but the five of us can have a little downtime here."

They obediently set to work as she'd instructed. Wolf curled up in a corner, watching them, waiting to see where Danni and Quinn would land so he could lie at their feet.

Father Ryan returned soon after, and Billie came in from the shop. The five of them sat down to Hattie's cooking; she'd created a nice meal of chicken, pasta with a delicious sauce, as well as a big salad.

"So," Hattie began, after Father Ryan had said grace, "no talk of the murders tonight. Let's get to know one another better, shall we?"

"Ah, sure," Bo Ray mumbled.

"We'll start with you," Hattie told him. "How do you come to be here?"

"Um . . ." Bo Ray looked around the table and shrugged. "I was an addict, involved in all kinds of bad things and with bad people. Then Quinn and Danni found me. After that, Father Ryan helped me and now I'm clean. I live here and I work at The Cheshire Cat."

"Very good." Hattie nodded approvingly. "Oh, not good that you had such a hard time. But that you're clean and working at the shop. Billie, how about you?"

"I was born in Scotland. . . ."

"Shocking!" Hattie teased.

"I was Angus Cafferty's best friend. He came to the States, so I came to the States. He moved to New Orleans because of his wife, and I came to New Orleans. And when he died . . . well, now I'm with Danni," Billie said.

"Father Ryan?"

Father Ryan grinned. "Actually, I was going to become a boxer. I went into the military, I came out . . . and I knew my place was in the church. There you have it."

"A fighting father!" Hattie said, smiling. "And let's see . . . Danni. You grew up in the city with your loving father, became an artist . . . and took over your father's very strange work, collecting — and destroying! — things."

"More or less," Danni responded.

Quinn knew the question was coming his way next.

"And Mr. Michael Quinn. Oh, yes, I heard about you, sir! A college football player like we'd rarely seen in this city before. All but worshipped. Everyone wanted you for endorsements, so money was yours. Women threw themselves at you — and everything became too easy."

"That's it in a nutshell," Quinn said. "I got so much that I abused drugs and alcohol . . . and managed to die."

"Ah, but you came back as an avenging angel. The doctors saved you on the emergency-room table. And you became . . ."

"Not an avenging angel, just a man," Quinn told her. "But I was given a second chance. So, I move along, trying to make the second go-round better than the first."

"Quite commendable, Mr. Quinn."

"What about you, Hattie?" Danni asked. "We know the rich widow part — and that you donate to so many charities in the city. But where did you begin?"

"In a trailer park in Georgia." Hattie gave

them a small smile. "I was born in one. I didn't want to die in one. I took a job as a waitress and worked and went to school part-time — and met my blessed husband, who didn't care where I was born or anything about my past. I spent my every waking hour loving the man. Sometimes I wonder if I should've made more of an effort to get him to live a healthier life, but I never tried to change him and he never tried to change me. So I'm grateful for the good years we had."

"That's a beautiful story, Hattie!" Danni said.

"Thank you. Eat up. What about Dr. Hubert? It's quite late. Should we be worried about him? Perhaps you ought to call him, Quinn."

"If it'll make you feel better, I will," Quinn said.

Hattie was staring at him, so he assumed he was supposed to call Ron right then and there. He did. The medical examiner sounded surprised to hear his voice and even more surprised to realize how late it was. He told Quinn he was ready to leave the morgue; he'd gone over the notes for so long his vision was blurring.

Billie said he'd go and pick him up. Meanwhile, Hattie fixed a plate to put in the microwave for Ron as soon as he got back to the house.

Father Ryan asked Billie to drop him off at the rectory on his way, and bade them all good night.

Quinn wasn't happy was about his leaving, but Father Ryan was determined.

When the two men had left, Danni ordered Hattie to relax; she and Quinn would clean up. Bo Ray told her he was a wicked Uno player, and the two of them decided on a game.

Danni and Quinn had finished clearing away the dishes when Billie returned with Ron, and Hattie took a break in her game to warm his meal.

Danni went down to the office to retrieve the journal; she wanted to read in bed.

She hurried down the stairs.

Quinn noticed that Wolf didn't go with her. The dog, knowing his duty, usually followed Danni anywhere she went.

"What's up, boy?" he asked.

Wolf barked and sat down at the head of the basement stairs. Then, wagging his tail, he came back for Quinn. Curious, Quinn walked over to the stairs, and the dog seemed noticeably happier that he was coming along.

Danni was collecting Ron Hubert's family

journal when he reached the door.

"You okay?"

"Jumpy," she admitted. "Oh, the wrapping on that stupid giclée is coming off. I'm surprised, since Niles usually wraps things so expertly. Maybe he thought the thing was just going down the street so he didn't bother. Anyway, I'll get Billie to seal it up tomorrow. I don't even want to look at it. Still, I do feel there's something I haven't figured out yet. But maybe I'll feel that way forever and everything really is over."

He didn't respond; she knew as well as he did that the situation *wasn't* over.

"You heading up now?" he asked.

"Yes."

"I'll come with you."

Danni smiled.

Upstairs, they both realized they hadn't had a steaming hot shower in days. Danni went in first, but she knew he'd be following her. And he did.

Naturally, a shower led to other things . . .

Like kissing each other's lips in the thunder of the spray — very, very nice.

Kissing various other body parts was also very . . .

Nice wasn't the word.

Exotic, erotic, explosive.

Stumbling around in the bathroom, wearing towels while trying to get to the bed . . . Just a little wet, but . . .

Finding the bed. And making love . . .

The world felt as if it had been cleansed in the spray of the water. For long moments he forgot the dark cloud that seemed to hang over them.

For those moments, there was nothing in the world but Danni, and the feelings she woke in his heart, his soul, his entire being.

She nudged him as they lay, just feeling the cool air moving over their heated bodies.

"I was going to try to finish Eloisa's journal tonight," she whispered. "But . . . I think I'm going to sleep."

"Sleep," he told her.

He pulled her closer and stroked her hair.

And he wished the feeling of dread wasn't slipping back.

It had to be about 3:00 a.m. when Danni roused. She wondered what had awakened her; then she knew. It was Wolf. He was barking insanely. The noise seemed to come from far away, but she realized he was just downstairs, on the first floor.

Quinn was already up, pulling on jeans and grabbing his gun. He was at the bedroom door before she could scramble into a robe and sweep up one of the flasks Father

Ryan had given her — filled with holy water.

She knew from past experience that it was a viable weapon. At least when it came to a particular kind of enemy . . .

He threw open the door. Both Hattie and Ron were out of their rooms; Billie and Bo Ray were running down from the attic.

"Stay here, Hattie, Ron, please. Bo Ray and Billie will be with you. Danni," he began.

"I'm coming. I have my medal — and my flask." He hurried down the stairs. Wolf was in the center of the hall, still barking.

A quick look around yielded nothing.

"The store?" Danni asked. She hit a switch that illuminated The Cheshire Cat.

Nothing out of the ordinary. Not that there was anything ordinary about the shop. But they saw nothing that shouldn't have been there.

Quinn walked toward the kitchen but instead went into Danni's studio. He glanced around, then closed the door.

"I don't see anything out of order," he said, puzzled.

Wolf barked at the two of them again.

As he did, Quinn's phone started to ring, the sound loud and discordant.

He answered it, and Danni saw his face darken.

"On my way," he said.

He closed his phone. "Another incident," he muttered. "Down toward Chartres."

Another . . .

Just a block or so away.

"I'll get dressed," she told him.

"I'm going to throw on a shirt and go ahead. Get Billie to come with you. I mean it. Get Billie," he said. He was already halfway up the stairs and more or less burst past the small crowd who'd gathered to wait for them there. Danni stopped to explain, but before she'd finished, Quinn was back, buttoning his shirt as he raced down the stairs on his way out. At the bottom he paused. "Billie, you go with Danni. Bo Ray, you watch over our guests."

Bo Ray nodded, apparently speechless.

"We'll be fine," Hattie said. "As long as you leave us the dog. You *can* leave us the dog?"

"Yes," Danni said. Wolf wouldn't be happy; he'd known something was wrong — a couple of blocks away! But he had to stay here to guard the house.

She hurried up to her room to dress. By the time she got downstairs again, the others were back in the kitchen and the teakettle was steaming.

Bo Ray was explaining the game of Uno

to Ron, while Hattie set out cups.

"We'll be right here," Hattie said. "Don't worry about us."

Wolf barked, running toward Danni, and she crouched down beside him. "Wolf, you have to stay here and look after everyone. Okay? I need you, my man. You understand that, right?"

But for once, Wolf didn't seem to understand. He ran to the stairs that led down to the basement.

"He hates that giclée," Bo Ray said. "So do I. Danni, honest to God, can't we just get rid of it? I swear, I don't even like being in the house with that thing!"

"I must admit, just knowing it's down there makes me uncomfortable, too," Ron said. "And I work with dead people!"

"Perhaps . . . perhaps we could put it out in the courtyard," Hattie suggested.

Danni looked at Billie, who'd come up behind her, pulling on a jacket. "Let me put it out," he said. "Then we won't worry so much, all right?"

She nodded. She ran down the stairs, Billie and Wolf right behind her.

Billie walked across the room for the giclée. More of the packaging had fallen off. He swore beneath his breath, something with a long rolling burr, and threw an old piano cover over the print before picking it up. "I'll set it next to the garage," he told her.

"Thanks," she said gratefully. "That should do for now. But when you get a chance . . ."

"Aye. I'll wrap it up solid."

She locked the office door and led Billie, carrying his burden, and Wolf back upstairs.

Bo Ray was waiting; he had the courtyard door open. Billie took the giclée out and leaned it against the garage wall.

Everyone in the house seemed relieved — and she could tell that Wolf thoroughly approved. He licked Danni's hand and settled by the back door.

Now he was on guard duty.

"It's just a copy," she murmured. "Lock us out and set the alarm, Bo Ray!"

"You bet!"

She and Billie ran down the street to make the right turn to Chartres.

Quinn reached the location on Chartres to learn that this time, miraculously, no one had been killed.

The area around the doorway of the Zombies Here and Now shop had been cordoned off with crime scene tape, but there was no one around.

Larue told Quinn that a couple of locals had been attacked. The Reverend Cosby Tournier, a Haitian *Houngan,* had been walking down to meet friends at Café du Monde after a meeting at his house. He was with two young pupils who were learning the ways of the *loa* — those who intercede with God on behalf of the faithful.

They'd been studying talismans, holding them in their hands and talking as they walked. They'd been astounded to encounter a fog bank in the middle of the street. When Cosby Tournier was attacked — by some degenerate wielding a knife in the middle of the street — one of the pupils had pulled out his own knife while the other had begun reciting chants.

"Are either of the pupils here?" Quinn asked Larue. "I'm assuming Cosby Tournier has been taken to the hospital?"

"Yes, he's at the hospital. One of the men went with him. The other is right there in the street. His name is Michel Dumont. He's Haitian and he's only been in the country about six months, but his English is pretty decent. I'll bring you over," Larue said.

Larue performed the introductions. Michel Dumont was a good six-three, lean and muscled, and in Quinn's eyes, not a man to be taken lightly. His build suggested that he studied mixed martial arts — something that was confirmed when Quinn asked him. Larue left the two of them to talk, going to speak with one of the crime scene investigators by the doorway where Cosby Tournier had been attacked.

Dumont studied Quinn for a moment, waiting for him to speak.

"You walked into a fog bank?" Quinn asked.

"Yes, we walked into what looked like a fog bank," Dumont said.

Quinn heard his name called; Danni had arrived with Billie. She was slightly out of breath and Billie was gasping. Quinn had the feeling she'd started running the minute she'd left The Cheshire Cat.

"Monsieur Dumont, my friends, Danielle Cafferty and William McDougall. We search together for . . . for what is hard to find."

Dumont said something, looking at Danni. Quinn didn't catch the words.

"Les chimères," Danni said. "Yes," she added softly. "Monsters."

Dumont nodded. He turned to Quinn again. "It was fog, but it was not fog. We knew we had walked into something different, something that wasn't right. There was movement in the fog. There was a woman

— and then there wasn't a woman. But I saw a deep gash on Teacher's arm, and Pierre — my cousin — and I know when fog is not a fog. Pierre began a chant to his *loa,* and I took out my own knife. Then the fog began to fade. We screamed for the police and they came quickly."

Larue had returned and heard the end of Dumont's description. "It's a damned psychotic magician! An illusionist. How the hell someone's walking around the city with a fog machine . . ."

"Ah, Lieutenant," Dumont said. "This city? I have seen everything since I've been here. Except what I saw tonight."

"Lieutenant!" someone called from the narrow alley that ran behind the Zombies Here and Now shop.

"Excuse me," Larue muttered. He left them again, responding to the summons.

"It wasn't a magician," Quinn said to Dumont.

Dumont shook his head. "No, I agree. The fog was not an illusion, although the woman . . . she was strange. She looked . . . faded."

"Old?" Billie asked.

"No," Dumont said. "*Faded.* As if she was not real. As if she was . . . projected. She faded when the chants began. When I lashed out."

"*La chimère,*" Danni repeated. "Or chimera, as we call it," she told Dumont. "A monster — who faded into the fog."

Dumont nodded. He turned back to Quinn. "But there *was* a man. A flesh-and-blood man. I nicked him with my knife," he said proudly.

"And you know that he was real?" Quinn asked.

Dumont nodded again. "Oh, yes. And I have given the lieutenant my knife. He says they can get DNA from my knife."

"Yes, they can," Quinn said. "Thank you, Monsieur Dumont. Thank you."

"I wish to go to see Cosby Tournier now, if I may?" Dumont asked.

"Of course," Quinn said. "You've been extremely helpful."

"It is for all of us to fight monsters," he said. "Some are entrusted by the *loa.*"

"The lieutenant will get an officer to drive you to the hospital." Quinn looked for Larue, but his ex-partner was still in the alley. He saw another officer and arranged a ride for Dumont. The officer beckoned him and escorted him to a car.

Danni touched Quinn's arm. "It's a break, a real break," she whispered.

"Yes," he agreed cautiously. "Larue will have the lab process the DNA from the blood."

"Will they be able to do it quickly?"

"Yes. And if we're lucky, whoever's behind this is in the system. Then we're golden. But if the guy's *not* in the system . . ."

"But if we find a suspect, we can get his DNA and have it tested, right?" Danni asked. "Maybe it'll match the DNA on the knife."

"Yes."

"And then we have to pray that catching the suspect can stop this," Billie said. "Especially if that DNA doesn't match *anything.*" He paused, a somber look on his face. "The sense we all had in Switzerland — that we're not done — was justified. The killing will go on."

Quinn couldn't help wincing. Billie was right. And as long as the murders continued, Hubert's soul, Hubert's evil, was being kept alive by the blood of others.

Larue came back from the alley.

"Whoever it was went that way," he said, pointing. "There are scratches against the wall and drops of blood. Whether they're the killer's — he has to be bleeding, since Dumont nicked him — or Cosby Tournier's, who knows? Meanwhile, the techs will keep sweeping the alley."

"Mind if I look, too?" Quinn asked.

"Suit up before you go too far," Larue warned, "I don't want you leaving more traces than you find."

"Billie and I will go to the hospital," Danni said, "and see if we're allowed to visit Cosby Tournier."

Quinn nodded. Billie and Danni left, heading back to Royal Street to get a car for the drive to the hospital.

"Danni!" he shouted as they walked away.

She turned back to him.

"Call me. Call me if there's anything. Keep in close touch."

She sent him a thumbs-up.

He watched them as far as Royal, until they disappeared around the corner.

Quinn studied the narrow alley by Zombies Here and Now. It was scarcely the width of two men, but he knew it opened up to the back of one of the hotels.

Someone escaping could have run back up to Royal, or down to Chartres and then Decatur.

Whoever it had been was long gone.

Quinn hoped he'd left *something* of himself in the alley.

Dumont had seen a woman who wasn't

real. She'd been a monster.

That made a certain kind of sense . . . and it was scary as hell.

Danni remembered counting the people in the painting who had weapons — and the children who'd been torturing the dolls and the chess pieces.

"What if there are eleven of them?" she asked Billie.

"Pardon?" Billie was concentrating on the road, but once they were past Canal, the driving was easier. There were no partiers out with their red plastic cups, other than a few gamblers making their way out of the casino.

"I studied the giclée and the copy I made of it," Danni said. "There are the husband and the wife, the three children, the two suits of armor, the butler and two officials at the door. I'm including that wretched painting over the hearth."

He turned to her briefly. "You think the painting might be infused with the blood of *all* those people?" he asked, horrified. "Not just Henry?"

"We're not sure if he's represented himself in the painting or not. But what if the other faces were those of despicable murderers throughout the history of the house or even the area?"

"How would he acquire their blood? The dead don't bleed."

"He could probably get blood from the recently dead," Danni said. "I'll have to ask Ron. Embalming wasn't really done at the time, right? In this country, it only became popular during the Civil War, when people wanted to return fallen soldiers to their rightful homes for burial."

Billie looked at her, a fierce frown on his face. "*Eleven* people? Och, girl, I pray not! How will we find eleven people to put to fire and ash?"

"There has to be a way," Danni murmured thoughtfully. "I'm just trying to think it through. . . ."

She was still pondering the possibilities when they reached the hospital. At first, they weren't permitted to see Cosby Tournier. Then Danni called Jake Larue, who in turn called the hospital.

She learned that Cosby Tournier had been stitched up. He'd received a gash across his chest and was groggy from sedation, but he was a strong man and he would survive.

Danni shouldn't have been surprised, but when they entered Tournier's room, Natasha was already there. She was sitting with Michel Dumont and another handsome young black man. The three chanted together, talismans in their hands.

Natasha finished an incantation, then excused herself and rose to meet Danni and Billie.

"Cosby is a friend, a fellow," she explained.

"Of course," Danni said. She added awkwardly, "I'm grateful that your friend will survive the attack."

Dumont nodded to the two of them but didn't stop his chants.

"We were hoping he could tell us more," Danni said.

"Cosby is extremely tired, but I know he'll talk to you." Natasha led her to the man's bedside, speaking softly in Creole.

Cosby Tournier opened his eyes and looked directly at Danni. She instantly believed he was probably a good priest — and a good man. He had beautiful eyes, green with gold flecks, eyes that spoke of his mixed New Orleans heritage.

"Sir, I'm Danni Cafferty," she said. "We're trying very hard to catch *les chimères.*"

Cosby managed a smile for her. He took her hand, his grip surprisingly strong. *"L'ange,"* he said.

Danni shook her head. "I'm not an angel. But my friends and I are trying to help."

He looked at Natasha and repeated,

387

"L'ange."

Natasha shrugged with a smile. "What can he tell you?" she asked Danni.

"What he saw, what he felt. Monsieur Dumont told me there was a woman — *la chimère* — who disappeared. But that there was a flesh-and-blood man who disappeared, as well."

Cosby Tournier understood her perfectly. He addressed her in English. "She was beautiful, except for her eyes. They were demon's eyes. She was a monster, but . . . she can be stopped. Our faith is strong. She will be stopped by belief in a greater power, by the Father who watches over us all. The man who lives . . . he is a coward. He fears pain. He ran quickly, but perhaps you will find him. Unless the monsters attack again, you will not find *them.* But the one who follows their command . . . yes. He can be stopped. Where the monsters have breached the veil, I do not know."

"We think we do," Danni told him.

He had a wonderful smile, despite the pain he was obviously feeling even under sedation. "You believe me. The police will not. That's all right. They will seek the living. You must seek the dead."

Danni thanked him and said she'd pray for his speedy recovery. Then she hugged

Natasha and waved to Cosby and his two friends as they continued their chanting.

She and Billie left the hospital.

"And now?" Billie asked.

"Home," she replied. "I don't like being away from home. Quinn will come as soon as he's done. I think I have work to do at the house."

There were narrow Dumpsters down the alley; it provided too little space for the regular-size ones and no truck would be getting down that way to empty them.

Quinn worked along with the crime scene specialists, carefully searching the ground and the debris. The techs didn't seem to mind that he was there, but that could've been because Grace Leon was head of the unit that night and, thankfully, Grace liked him.

The smell of urine in the alley was strong.

It wasn't a place frequented by tourists. The alley was used mainly by the various businesses — the hotels, shops and restaurants — that backed on to it. Quinn turned into the small area behind the beautiful and historic hotel that fronted Royal Street.

There was a larger Dumpster there.

Curious, he walked toward it, noticing that none of the crime scene techs had gotten this far yet.

He opened the Dumpster.

He froze, seeing what looked up at him.

CHAPTER 16

Danni and Billie arrived at the shop on Royal Street, parked and walked through the courtyard.

The morning sun was just starting to rise.

"Sleep," Billie grumbled. "Seems it's a real luxury these days."

"What's that saying, Billie? You can sleep when you're dead."

"Some do and some don't!" he muttered darkly.

As they approached the courtyard door, Danni glanced around. She flinched, seeing the giclée by the garage door. She was going to have to look at it again — and she didn't want to.

Just the fact that it was in the courtyard bothered her.

"I don't like it, either," Billie said, as if she'd spoken aloud.

Danni had her keys, but knocked at the door to let the others know they were back.

Wolf, of course, had already signaled their arrival. He'd started his excited bark as soon as they'd driven the car into the garage. The sound was very different from his warning bark or the bark he used to scare off would-be intruders.

Bo Ray opened the door. He peered through the peephole first, surprising, since Wolf was really notice enough.

"So, I take it all of you stayed up, huh?" Danni asked, stretching as she walked in.

"We stayed up. You bet. We've all been twitchy since you left," Bo Ray said.

"Did anything happen here?" she asked, coming into the kitchen.

"Nothing," Ron told her. "We were just nervous as hell and waiting for the light!"

Danni turned to Hattie, who shrugged.

"Everything feels . . . off, Danni," Bo Ray said. "Wolf prowled in front of the door — growling now and then. He's a good dog — fantastic guard dog — but I've got to admit, he was setting my nerves on edge."

"Tell us what happened," Ron said evenly. "Do I have a new corpse this morning, thanks to that painting?"

Danni shook her head and described the whole scenario, from the attack on Cosby Tournier to the chimera and the fog. "Cosby Tournier's a voodoo priest. I think his religion is a little different from Natasha's. But I got the same thing from him that I always get from her and Father Ryan — there's really just one Higher Power, and we all see Him a little differently. Anyway, Cosby was with two of his students, and their chanting, their faith, is what got them through. And fortunately, as it turns out, one of the men had a knife and nicked the attacker, who then disappeared." Danni hesitated. "The bad thing is —"

She broke off. There was a commotion at the door; Wolf was barking frantically.

But in his good way.

Quinn was back.

Danni ran to the door and opened it. He entered the house, looking worn, yet somehow triumphant.

"What? What? Did you find him? Catch him?" Danni asked.

"No, but I found something better," he said.

"What?" they all demanded.

"The painting," he told them. "The Henry Sebastian Hubert titled *Ghosts in the Mind*. It's at the police station now. Hattie, I need to bring you down there to claim your stolen property. Then we can take care of it."

"You found it where?" Danni asked urgently.

"In a trash bin. I opened it and the damned thing was staring straight up at me. I would've just taken it — except that the entire forensics team was there with me. Then I realized that daylight was breaking and we were going to be all right. It should be held for evidence, but I went through a whole argument with Larue, and if I bring Hattie down, she can simply claim it as her property. I think — whether he wants to or not — Larue understands that there's something really wrong with the painting. He's eager to have us destroy it. Of course, it *is* Hattie's property, so it has to go into her hands before we burn it."

"You found it in a *trash bin*?" Danni said incredulously.

He nodded.

She closed her eyes for a moment. "Quinn, it might be one of the giclées. Niles had two hundred of them for sale. And there are others across the country, right, Hattie?" She turned to the older woman. "How many did you allow them to create?"

"Two thousand," Hattie replied.

"But we don't have to destroy all the giclées," Billie said. "Just the real thing."

"Hattie? Will you come to the station with

me to retrieve it? Danni, can you call Father Ryan? I'd like to take it to the church and see that it's burned properly. Then we can bring the ashes to the river and cast them to the wind."

"Quinn, did you —"

"Danni!" Quinn said. "I've actually learned something from you. I looked for the number on the giclée and there wasn't one. It's not a numbered copy. Hubert's signature is the only thing on it. You can check. But for now, will you call Father Ryan and collect Natasha? She should come for this."

"Natasha's still at the hospital with Cosby Tournier."

"Call her, anyway. I think she'll want to be there," Quinn said. "Ready, Hattie?"

"Getting my bag!" Hattie responded, hurrying to the stairs.

"I should go to work," Ron said. "Except I don't want to miss this, either!"

Hattie came back down with her handbag. "Let's go! Let's do this!" she declared.

Quinn was happy; Danni remained doubtful. "This is too easy," she murmured.

"Maybe. But . . . Danni, it's a real oil painting. It's no giclée, I guarantee it." He patted the dog's head. "Come on, Wolf. You can join us on this trip. Jake's used to you, and the good Father loves to see you. Not to mention that you and I need a little bonding time."

A moment later, he and Hattie were gone. Danni and the others left shortly afterward.

Once again, as she walked through her own courtyard, Danni felt uneasy. And once again she glanced at the packaged giclée by the wall. To her gratitude, Billie had found time to rewrap it, resting it neatly on the folded-up piano cover. If Quinn was right and he'd discovered the real deal, she was going to burn this sucker that night.

She made her calls to Father Ryan and Natasha as Billie drove.

By the time they reached the church, Father Ryan was prepared.

He'd set up a brazier in front of the main altar and he had large crucifixes for them to wear. He'd brought out one of his prayer books and was anxious to get going.

While they waited outside for Natasha, and for Quinn and Hattie to show up with the painting, Danni told Father Ryan what had happened in the middle of the night.

He nodded slowly. "I heartily believe that most men are good, just as I believe that faith and goodness will always prevail in the end. Not that evil doesn't have a strong hold on the world. Whatever the reason, some people are just . . . bad."

"What about children, Father Ryan?" Danni asked. "Do you think a child can be evil? I mean, can you be *born* evil?"

"Ah, Danni, that question is far too difficult for me to answer. I do believe that babies are born innocent. Yes, I'm a priest, but not terribly fond of the concept of original sin. But can we be born with faulty minds? Yes. We can be born with any number of physical birth defects, and it's possible to have mental defects, as well. Look at the various forms of psychopathy. But is it nature or nurture? Or both? No one's been able to completely answer that question. As far as specific examples . . ." Father Ryan paused for a minute. "I know there was a Boston boy named Jesse Pomeroy who was arrested for murder in 1874 when he was just fourteen. He'd tortured boys before that but only been sent to reform school. In England in the late sixties, Mary Flora Bell with the help of a friend became a killer at the age of eleven. Even more recently, in 1998 a fourteen-year-old was convicted of first-degree murder in Florida. He beat up an old woman — which was an accident, or so he claimed — but then stabbed her eleven times. None of us wants to think of such things, but . . . yes, children have murdered other children *and* adults throughout history. Carl Newton Mahan was only six when he killed his best friend. The boys were fighting over scrap metal and Carl wound up shooting the other boy with his father's shotgun. That was in Kentucky, 1929."

"You're a priest and you know all this stuff?" Billie asked, grimacing.

"Yeah, how come?" Bo Ray added.

"I've studied both psychology and criminology," Father Ryan told them, his mouth set in a grim line.

Natasha arrived. They greeted her, asking about Cosby Tournier.

He was still doing well, Natasha said, and would be released in a day or two.

Then Quinn showed up with Wolf, Hattie — and the painting.

"No coming in, no tea and crumpets. Straight to the church!" Father Ryan ordered. Danni loved Father Ryan's church; it had been built in the mid-1800s. Stained-glass windows portrayed gentle pictures of Christ and the Apostles. There was a classic image of the Holy Trinity above the sanctuary; marble statues of Mary and Gabriel and other saints and angels sat about on their podiums.

Quinn brought the painting up to Father

Ryan, who lit the brazier and suggested they fan out.

It was while they all did that — most trying *not* to see the Henry Hubert painting — that Danni decided that she had to look at it.

"Wait," she said, and walked over to the painting. She studied it for a long moment.

Quinn was correct. It wasn't a giclée.

But . . .

"Father, everyone. Quinn! I'm really sorry, but I have to see this in better light."

Bo Ray groaned. "Danni, Quinn's sure it's not a giclée!" he said.

"No, it's not," Danni agreed. Quinn and Billie, somewhat reluctantly, carried the painting to the front door, where Danni asked that they step outside, into the natural light.

And when they did, when they stood in the bright sunshine, she knew.

"This isn't the original," she said.

"Danni, at Niles's shop you two showed me the numbering," Quinn argued.

"It isn't one of the giclées," Danni repeated. "But it isn't the original."

"How can you tell?" Quinn demanded.

"Well, we'd probably have to test the paint, but trust me, I've studied the giclée and I've looked at images of the original in enough art books by now. That's not *quite* Hubert's signature. The *B* isn't right. And, if you examine the portrait over the fire, you'll see there's a difference — very slight, but the kind of mistake a forger might make — in the way the face is angled."

"You're positive?" Quinn asked, his voice filled with disappointment and weariness.

"I'm sorry, Quinn."

"When I touched the color — the red on the sofa — it was damp. I was sure my fingers had touched . . . blood," Quinn said. "It might have been the blood of a victim or blood from the killer. Maybe it was an attempt to activate the painting — to 'awaken' it. Whether or not that would be successful, since this isn't the real thing . . . I don't know." He turned to Danni. "I *can* tell the difference between blood and red paint."

"I know you can, Quinn," she said, trying to calm his agitation. "It's even possible that blood was used in creating the actual painting."

"Oh." Hattie Lamont, deflated, walked back into the church and took a seat in the rear pew.

"Burn the copy," Natasha said decisively. "Burn the copy."

"What if there's evidence on it?" Quinn

asked. "If someone's tried feeding the copy with blood, it could be the killer's." He shook his head. "I should've told Larue about this. I should've had it tested. I've become so aware of the *evil* that can't always be touched — or explained — that I sometimes forget about actual police work."

"It doesn't matter. Natasha is right," Father Ryan chimed in. "We need to get rid of it, just get rid of it. I have to believe it was left where it was for a reason. You were *supposed* to find it. Maybe so you'd believe this was all over, that you'd solved it." He paused. "Nonetheless, the intent was evil. We have to destroy the thing."

Quinn was silent. "Okay," he finally said. "I guess that's for the best. We burn it and keep quiet about it. Hell, one reason I didn't take it for testing is that I was afraid to leave it with anyone else. That's when I thought it *was* the real thing. Still, this one scares me almost as much." He looked at Danni again, and the weariness in his eyes made her feel sad — and guilty. "You're sure, *really* sure, it's not Hubert's painting?"

"Quinn, like you said, we can have it tested. But I'm just as worried as you are about exposing anyone else to it. . . . Anyway, this is a good copy. But it *is* a copy."

"So, Father, that's what you all think we should do? Burn it?"

They did. They trooped back into the church. Father Ryan held the service; they all participated. The copy of the painting was burned.

"Now, I need everyone out," Father Ryan said. "I have a Mass later this evening. Quinn, you want to dump the ashes in the river? We'll scatter them in the wind just over the water."

"Sure. Yep, sure," Quinn said.

Billie, Quinn and Father Ryan swept up the ashes. Danni didn't want to tell him what she was beginning to suspect, but she knew she'd have to.

The painting had been full of people. Evil people.

"Do you want to come with me?" he asked her.

She shook her head. "I need to go back home. And I really have to get the shop open again. But I need to speak with you as soon as you're done."

She glanced toward the church. Hattie was still inside; she'd been exceptionally generous about financing their activities, but Danni didn't like depending on others. For the moment, though, she had no choice.

Her father had told her never to close the

402

shop, except in the most dire of circumstances.

And she needed the shop; she survived on the proceeds from it.

Quinn understood. "I'll take Bo Ray with me for this. You go ahead and bring Billie and Hattie back to the store. Ron's going to want to get to work, so I'll ask Natasha to drop him off."

Danni nodded. "May I have Wolf for the time being?"

"Of course," Quinn said. "You can have him anytime you want, you know that. Is there a particular reason right now?"

"Yes. When you're not there . . . oh, I don't know. I don't even feel safe in my own place lately. So hurry back, okay?"

"I will," Quinn promised her.

They all left, going their separate ways.

Danni hoped she'd feel differently once she got back home; she didn't. And it didn't help that Wolf growled menacingly when they arrived. But then he was eager to get inside, barking at the door until she opened it.

When she, Hattie and Billie had gone in, Wolf took up a position at the courtyard door, as if this was where he needed to make a stand.

"I'll get the shop open," Billie told Danni.

403

"Is there a way for me to help you?" Hattie asked Danni.

"Oh, Hattie, no, but thank you," Danni said. Then she rethought her answer. "Wait, maybe. Hattie, how familiar are you with computers?"

Hattie laughed. "Ah, yes, old people know nothing about technology, is that it?"

"No!" Danni protested, but flushed.

"My husband was a tech genius, remember?" Hattie said. "I can easily handle a computer."

"Great. Then come with me. I'm going to keep reading Eloisa Hubert's journal — and I need you to search for serial killers or especially cruel people who might have lived or visited the Geneva area around the same time Henry Hubert did."

Hattie looked at her, startled. "Oh. Certainly. But do you really think there were that many serial killers running around Lake Geneva in one summer?"

"I hope not," Danni said. "But . . . see what you can find."

"Will do."

"I'll get you a computer."

"I have my own — and it's a new, top-of-the-line, state-of-the-art laptop," Hattie assured her.

Danni smiled. "Okay. I'm getting the

journal and my art books. You grab your computer."

"Where shall we work?"

Danni didn't want to go back down to the basement just then. She wanted the daylight to surround her. Light came to the basement, too, since it was really the ground floor. But not the way it streamed into the kitchen.

"Right here. Kitchen table. Seems like that's our place these days," she told Hattie.

Ten minutes later, they sat at opposite ends of the table. Danni noticed that Hattie seemed, not surprisingly, extremely competent as she clicked through a number of websites.

Danni turned her attention to the journal, reading about Eloisa Hubert and her relationship with the young Herman, Lord Guillaume.

She'd barely started when Billie came into the kitchen. "Niles Villiers is here. Says not to bother you if you're busy. He just wanted to say hello. Shall I tell him you're otherwise engaged?"

"No, no, let me at least thank him for stopping by!" Danni said. "I'll be right back," she promised Hattie.

Hattie gave her a distracted wave, deeply involved in something she was reading on her computer.

Danni hurried into the shop. Niles was looking at some of the leather bracelets she'd displayed on a plastic wrist on the counter. He turned when she came in.

"Danni!" Walking over to her, he kissed her on both cheeks. "Glad to see you home, although you didn't take much of a vacation."

"Hey, *you* never take a vacation," she reminded him.

He shrugged comically, but then his smile faded. "There were more bad things happening while you were away. I guess Quinn knows all about that," he said. He shook his head. "Maybe you should've *stayed* away. I don't think they got the guy yet."

"Oh, we needed to be home, Niles," she said. "But thank you so much for keeping an eye on the place."

"Of course, Danni, anytime. I know you'd do the same for me." That brought a smile to his lips again. "You got the giclée, didn't you?"

"Oh, yes, thank you very much. I'll write you a check —"

"Don't be ridiculous. It's a gift."

"Oh, Niles, I couldn't . . ."

"Danni, you gave me your exquisite painting of the river! It's a fair trade."

She laughed. "Hardly. I'm not exactly as well-known as Hubert — or at least as well-known as he is now," she added wryly.

"But you will be one day!" he said cheerfully, ignoring her reference to the recent horrors. "And you gave me a painting. All I gave you is a giclée."

"Well, then, thank you."

"Guess I'll get back to the gallery," Niles said. "Good to see you, Danni."

"You, too, Niles." She waved as he left the store.

Billie groaned and rolled his eyes. "You couldn't figure out a way to return that wretched giclée to him, eh?"

"We might need it yet."

Billie shuddered. "As you say, lass."

"Thanks, Billie. I'm going back to my reading. You okay out here?"

"Right as rain, girl. Right as rain."

She hurried into the kitchen, smiling at Hattie as she took her seat and started to read again.

She quickly became immersed in the material. She discovered that the hedonist's son and the artist's wife had formed a strong friendship.

In fact, Danni wondered if it had been more than a friendship, although Eloisa had never remarried.

At first, her journal entries concerning Herman were casual, about the two of them meeting for chocolate or coffee. Soon after that, the two of them began to have dinners, and then they "paid call upon each other" at their homes.

Eventually Eloisa began to confide a number of their conversations to her journal — if not their emotional or possibly physical relationship.

My dear Herman was quite appalled by his father's exploits, and, of course, shamed by his ignoble end. Herman had lost his mother years before, but had come to live with her family in England, avoiding his father. Alain Guillaume wanted his son to "be a man," to learn to enjoy life as he did — hunting, drinking and enjoying depraved relationships with women. Herman had noted once, when he was still young, that a serving girl had gone missing. He'd seen her with his father, and then she'd disappeared. That was long before the man was suspected of murdering those poor, wretched innocents he seduced. Herman was quite sure that his father kept company with other men of his social standing who had like tastes and similar proclivities. How far their interest in depravity went, he didn't know.

Hattie suddenly gasped.

Danni jerked her head up. "What is it?"

"Lady Mimette Lamere!"

Danni stared at her blankly.

"I've found someone who might be one of those you're looking for, my dear. Lady Mimette Lamere. She was known to keep company with Alain Guillaume at his castle. In fact, after his wife's death, the two were supposed to be . . . having an affair. This is a site from a Swiss university. They've done some research on her. She joined him at the castle the summer before he died. In fact, the goings-on of that pair were part of what alerted the authorities to the man's atrocities!"

Danni stood up and walked around to Hattie's computer. She skimmed the information — and held her breath as she studied a painting of the woman.

"Can you enlarge that?" Danni asked tensely.

Hattie did. The face sprang up large and clear on the screen.

Danni stood back. "We've found one," she announced.

"What do you mean?" Hattie asked.

Danni still didn't want to touch the giclée by the garage. Instead, she led Hattie to her studio and went in, uncovering her own work. Her rendition of the painting.

The face of the woman on the divan was the same face they'd just seen.

Hubert had indeed used the faces of people he'd known or known of in his painting; he'd put a pistol into the hands of Mimette Lamere, a woman with whom Alain Guillaume had probably tortured and killed some of his victims.

Hattie, behind her, gasped again.

"How many?" she whispered.

"Eleven," Danni said. "I believe we have to identify and find eleven people in all and then we have to figure out where they're all buried."

Quinn returned from his trip to the river with Bo Ray to see Hattie and Danni feverishly at work; they had notes spread all over the table.

"We're finding them. We're finding so many!" Hattie told him excitedly.

"So many what?"

"Horrible people!" Hattie exclaimed.

Quinn looked at Danni for an explanation.

"Remember how Michel Dumont was

410

saying that there'd been a woman, but she disappeared?"

"Into the fog," he said, nodding.

"I think Hubert was just the tip of the iceberg when it comes to this painting. All of the characters in it are based on actual killers — I'm convinced of it. I started thinking about this a while ago. Remember when we talked about the fact that he was believed to have taken all his characters from real life? Well, Hattie and I are proving that's true — and more than that, everyone in the painting was a killer, a murderer who really existed, including the child on the floor." Danni paused. "I don't know if he managed to find and use their blood or ripped skin or . . . or tissue, maybe from remains in the crypt, for his pigments, but I'm absolutely sure we're right about this," Danni said.

"How would he have known what they looked like?" Quinn asked.

"From sketches in the newspapers or paintings done during their lifetimes. In some cases, maybe even the bodies themselves — or their remains. He was a trained artist. He would've had the ability to create remarkable likenesses based on whatever images or descriptions he found."

"But the child," Quinn said. "The child

411

looks to be about three —"

"A little artistic license was taken there. The child was actually six. He was Jermaine Wasser, the son of a local carpenter. He killed his baby sister with a hammer and went on to stab his mother with a pick. His father killed himself. At that time, Alain Guillaume was applauded for being such a great and giving man. He took the child in — using the argument, of course, that the boy hadn't known what he was doing."

"The two at the table," Hattie continued, "are Solange and Gérard Rastira, children of an Italian nobleman who often visited Guillaume. After a time, they disappeared, and it was discovered that they'd amused themselves in a particularly horrendous way. The boy would tell unwary peasants that his sister was hurt — then club the peasants to death when they came to give aid."

"You're saying," Quinn said, "that every face in that painting is part of the evil within it?"

She nodded, biting her lower lip.

He found a chair at the kitchen table and sank into it.

"Can that be true?" he asked.

Danni nudged Eloisa's journal toward him. "A lot of the details are corroborated here," she said, "but it seems that after buy-

ing the castle from Herman Guillaume —
son of the despot who'd owned it before
Hubert rented it for the summer of 1816 —
Eloisa continued to see him. I think they
were in love. He told her something about
his past — and his father."

"Who else is in there?" he asked.

"It's hard to know about the suits of
armor," Danni said.

"Well," Hattie began, "I did learn that,
aside from Henry's butler, Raoul Messine
— inherited from Guillaume! — Henry had
a groom and someone called 'the keeper of
the keys.' They were also, by the way,
original employees of Alain Guillaume.
When all those horrible things were being
done at the castle, they *must* have known.
There were even rumors that Guillaume's
servants went out and procured women and
children for him to torture."

Quinn felt a sick tightening in his gut. It
all explained so much. The killing at the
Garcia house — so many people, killed in
so many different ways.

Slashed, bludgeoned, shot . . .

"How do we end this?" he asked. "We still
don't have the real *Ghosts in the Mind* —
and we don't know who in this city
'awakened' the dead in that painting. And
how on earth do we find the graves of all

these people?"

He didn't know why he'd bothered to ask the question; he was pretty sure he already knew.

He looked at Danni. "We can chase the painting all over the city. Or . . ."

"Or?"

"I know what he's thinking," Hattie murmured. "These people . . . they were all with him at the castle. The child he took in . . . the children of the Italian nobleman. The woman he was sleeping with. The others . . . I don't think we have all of them yet, but . . ."

"But?" Danni echoed, dread in her voice.

"It would make sense that they're still at the castle. We must've passed every interment in that crypt. There's only one thing to do. Return to the House of Guillaume."

CHAPTER 17

Natasha arrived soon after Quinn got home. She'd left Jez to close up for the day and came after another visit with her friend Cosby Tournier.

Billie and Bo Ray were closing The Cheshire Cat, and Hattie had gone upstairs to handle the travel arrangements again; she was good at it, as they all knew and as she'd informed them.

"There's got to be some reason for *la chimère,* the woman who disappears in the fog," Natasha announced, bursting into the kitchen and setting her bag on the table. She frowned at all the notes spread out there. "After talking with Cosby today, I believe there *is* a woman involved."

Quinn glanced at Danni. "There's always a woman involved . . . somehow," he said.

Danni rolled her eyes. "Ah, but there's just one woman," she said. "We won't count the girl."

"What are you talking about?" Natasha asked.

"We know who she is," Danni told her. "Or at least we think we do." She showed Natasha the people they'd aligned with faces in the painting. "We're assuming that the suits of armor cover Alain Guillaume's other servants — the groom and the keeper of the keys," Danni said. "So, we have the children, the woman, the suits of armor — and I believe that Hubert himself was the husband with the pistol at his back — the man with his face turned away. That leaves the butler and the two officials at the door — and the man in the portrait above the fireplace."

"I thought he was supposed to be the original Guillaume?" Natasha asked.

"We're not sure. We also aren't sure if blood was used for every character," Quinn said. "Danni suggested that Hubert might have . . . might have dug up the dead — *these* dead people, Mimette and so on — and used their skin or rotting flesh in some kind of paint mix."

Natasha shuddered. "I didn't feel we were done here."

"Messine," Quinn said suddenly. "The butler . . . Is the butler —"

"Yes! That must be right," Danni agreed.

"That would be natural! And Messine worked for Alain Guillaume before he worked for Hubert, so Hubert could very well have heard rumors — or worse — about him."

Natasha pulled out her cell phone. She said, "I'm just letting Jez know that he's going to be watching Wolf again. He'll be thrilled. He loves the dog. Have you told Father Ryan we're leaving again?"

"Yes, he knows, and so does Ron."

"Hattie's up in my dad's room, making arrangements," Danni said.

"So, we're definitely going." Natasha took a seat at the table. "I felt it, I'm afraid."

"I believe it's the best thing we can do," Quinn said. "We haven't found the painting. Although we might have a lead on the person involved at this end — thanks to the blood on Michel Dumont's knife."

"When do we go back to Switzerland?" Natasha asked.

"We won't be able to leave until tomorrow night — unless Hattie just ups and buys us a jet," Quinn said.

"She did suggest it, I think," Danni murmured.

Natasha smiled. "Well, if we have to do all this travelling, it's great that the woman's so generous and that —"

"The woman is fond of living," Hattie cut in, coming back to the kitchen. "We're all set. We leave at 8:00 p.m. tomorrow."

"Larue has a rush on the DNA. Top priority," Quinn said.

"How are we finding the bodies?" Natasha asked.

"The Guillaume servants were interred at the castle," Danni replied. "So that part's easy. And if Guillaume brought in the children and then killed them — which he must have, since they disappeared — then they're in the crypt, too."

"Let's hope we're that lucky," Natasha said. "One down . . . ten to go. If you're right."

Danni laid her head on her arms. "I'm positive I'm right. I've looked at that damn painting so often, I can see it with my eyes closed. I'm afraid I'll never get it out of my mind."

Natasha nodded sympathetically. "Well, then, I'm off," she said. "I'll be ready to leave tomorrow night."

"I guess I should do something about dinner," Danni said, rising.

"We'll order in," Quinn told her. "Okay?"

"Sure. Thanks." Danni returned her attention to the notes while Quinn asked

Hattie, Billie and Bo Ray what they'd like to eat.

She thought she had it nearly all figured out. The children, the woman, the man. The butler and the men in the suits of armor. The officials at the door were still a mystery; they had to be friends of Guillaume's. One might well be the Italian nobleman who'd fathered the two murderous children, Solange and Gérard Rastira.

"Hattie, would you mind looking up 'Rastira' again? See what you can find out about the father."

"Quinn, meat and vegetables, please," Hattie said in response to his question about dinner, "and I don't care what kind. Fish would be lovely." Hattie resumed her seat at the computer.

"Danni?" Quinn asked.

"Whatever you order for Hattie is fine."

"You're brilliant, Danni!" Hattie was looking at her across the table. "I'm reading straight from an article on Antonio Rastira! It's unproven, but he was rumored to have been interred at the castle. Some people said he killed himself because of his children. Regardless of how he perished, there was a secret ceremony at the castle — according to this long-dead and very obscure art historian, anyway — presided over by

Guillaume. The historian heard about it through village gossip. Apparently there were servants at the castle who weren't included in the ceremony but still knew something was going on."

"And when we're there, I suppose, we'll have to find the original Guillaume," Danni murmured.

"He should be at the far end of the crypt, near the wall where we found Hubert," Quinn said. "The interments started there, and the crypt grew out as more people died."

Danni nodded. "You're right. I'm going to keep reading. Maybe Herman told Eloisa more about his father's wicked dealings."

Quinn stopped beside her, setting a hand softly on her hair. "Someone else can read, if you like, Danni."

She looked up. "I'm on a mission," she told him. "I want to continue."

"All right, then. I guess I'll be helpful and place our dinner orders." He glanced at the takeout brochure. "But I'm going to call Ron first."

"Bo Ray and I can pick him up and then get dinner," Billie offered.

Quinn thanked him, then took out his cell.

Quinn walked around while he was talking to Ron, but Danni hardly noticed him;

she'd become engrossed in Eloisa Hubert's journal again.

She had to skim several pages about a new restaurant that Eloisa and Guillaume had tried in Kensington.

Immediately after that, she found what she was searching for.

Tonight the poor man bared more of his soul to me. He told me about waking up and hearing a woman scream. He wandered into the hall. There was a man there, dragging a half-naked woman back into a room; the man paused, staring at him. Then Herman saw his father come from behind the other man. His father had laughed. "Ah, we should bring the little bugger in — he needs a taste of what it is to be a man! My son, what you have yet to learn!" Later, my poor dear Herman heard the woman screaming again. The next day his father's visitor was gone and so was the woman. That week, there was much bustling about the castle. There was to be a "ceremony" for Count Fabre Clairmonte; alas, the poor fellow had apparently drunk himself silly and fallen from the tower. Herman told me all this, controlling his sobs, for while he didn't share his father's wretched tastes, he would not cry, for he believed that crying did not befit a man. My heart ached for him. I promised him once more that no one would ever live at the castle again.

Danni raised her eyes to Hattie. "Fabre Clairemont," she said. "Check him out, please. His name is in the journal."

"Yes . . . yes." Hattie began keying in the name.

She looked up at Danni and nodded slowly.

Meanwhile Billie and Bo Ray went to retrieve Ron Hubert from work and pick up their food. Danni and Hattie organized their notes.

When Ron arrived, he didn't object to a second trip across the Atlantic in a matter of days, but he wasn't happy about it, either. He seemed weary and depressed. "Imagine," he said. "It actually felt like a relief to autopsy a man who died pathetically of a drug overdose today. I am becoming numb. To have had such . . . an obscene ancestor weighs on me now like a dozen anchors."

"Ron, my dear man!" Hattie protested. "You mustn't feel that way. From what Danni and I have discovered, Henry Hubert himself wasn't cruel. He lived at that dreadful castle. The place was imbued with the cruelty of that horrible Alain Guillaume — a man who truly *was* obscene. I don't believe your ancestor had much of a chance once he walked in."

Ron Hubert smiled at her. "Well, thank you for that. It helps a little."

Danni went back to the journal, trying to hide a smile of her own. Hattie, she thought, was older than Ron Hubert, but she was in beautiful shape and they seemed to get on very well.

Perhaps a romance was budding between them — or might, once this situation was over and they were no longer under stress.

They all ate and decided they'd make it an early night. Danni was glad of it. She was delighted to go to bed early.

Wolf, however, didn't accompany her and Quinn up the stairs to take his position outside the bedroom door.

He curled up by the door to the courtyard, keeping sentinel there again.

Quinn shrugged. "He's protecting the whole household tonight, I suppose."

It felt good to close the door, to be alone. To have time together — except that they were both so exhausted, they fell asleep in each other's arms.

Quinn sensed it when Danni rose that night;

he hadn't been deeply asleep. He stirred when she moved, and then realized that she'd started to rise.

That she was sleepwalking.

He threw on his jeans and draped a blanket around her shoulders without waking her. Then he followed her as she walked down the stairs to the studio.

She removed the painting she'd *really* been working on — a view of Saint Louis Cathedral — from the easel and replaced it with a blank canvas.

Wolf came to join them, whining nervously.

"It's all right, boy. Let her be," Quinn said.

He watched Danni get out a palette and sit in front of her canvas, brush in hand. At first, he couldn't tell what she was creating, her brush moved so quickly. She chose color after color, and eventually the painting began to emerge.

As it did, she went still.

He took the brush from her fingers and laid it on the palette. Then he turned her toward him and shook her gently. "Danni. Danni. Wake up."

She did, and her eyes widened. She cringed, immediately grasping where she was and what she was doing. She didn't look at the canvas.

"What . . ."

"It's the painting."

"The Hubert?" she asked in confusion.

"No. The one above the fireplace in Switzerland," Quinn told her.

She finally looked at her rendering and shuddered.

"It's not the *original* Guillaume," she said. "Not the Guillaume who built the castle, the medieval patriarch as we've all thought. I think Alain put his own portrait there — he was that self-centered. A true psychopath believing *his* wants and needs mattered more than everyone and everything else. Herman was lucky to survive at all with a father like that. I think he would've killed his own son." She paused for a few seconds. "I'm sure it's him."

"I hope so," Quinn said.

"Why?"

"We know exactly where he is." Quinn reached out for her. "Come on. Let's go back to sleep. We'll need whatever rest we can get."

She rose and slid into his arms, and he began to lead her away. As they left the studio, Quinn bent to stroke Wolf. The dog still didn't follow them upstairs but returned to his position by the door.

They stayed awake for hours, not speaking. Quinn just held her close.

The both dreaded a return to Switzerland.

Sometime during the night, he slept. He knew, because it took him a minute to register the fact that his cell phone was ringing.

He'd plugged it in on his side of the bed. He glanced over, about to apologize to Danni for waking her, but she wasn't there. Then he remembered that she'd woken earlier, kissed him lightly and said she was going to make coffee.

Reaching over, he groaned aloud when he saw his caller ID.

Larue.

He had to answer it, of course.

"Hey," he said into the receiver. He wondered if Larue could tell how much he feared more bad news.

"No, no bodies," Larue said instantly. "I have something for you, though."

"Yeah?"

"We've got him — got him dead to rights. We pulled a DNA match to the blood on Michel Dumont's knife."

"Well, go on! Tell me. Who the hell are we looking for?"

Danni wished she could have slept longer,

as the rest of her household seemed to be doing.

It was too early to open the store. She wandered through, making sure everything was set for the day, but it was in perfect shape. Of course, Billie McDougall had run The Cheshire Cat with her father while she'd been blithely growing up, making her way through college, working at becoming an artist.

Now, with or without her participation, Billie — and Bo Ray, too — kept the shop in superb condition.

Wolf trailed her through the store.

Glancing at her watch, she saw that it was only eight-thirty. She'd showered, dressed, brewed coffee and checked the store.

She didn't want to look at last night's painting and she didn't want to paint and she couldn't bear the idea of picking up the giclée outside.

"How about a walk in the Quarter?" she asked Wolf. The morning was pleasant, a flawless midspring day. "Let's see what our neighbors are doing with their windows, huh?"

Evidently Wolf agreed; he barked excitedly.

First Danni wandered down to the George Rodrigue Gallery. She loved *Blue Dog* —

and every painting the artist did in this series. For a moment, she felt like an artist again. She studied the many paintings of *Blue Dog* on display, considering how Rodrigue had created the charm in every one of these images.

Eventually she moved on.

She came to Image Me This.

Niles Villiers hadn't placed his last Hubert giclée in the window. His display was enchanting, filled with different paintings by different artists that took the viewer on a tour of the Quarter. It was an effective presentation, one that caused people to stop and study the windows — and it intrigued them into coming through the doors.

Wolf suddenly tugged at the leash, pulling her toward the entry.

"Wolf, it's too early. This is New Orleans, remember? They're not open yet."

But Wolf seemed anxious to get inside. He ran to the door, dragging her with him.

"Wolf!" she chastised. Then she noticed that the door was slightly ajar.

She opened it more fully. "Niles — hey, Niles? Mason? Anyone in there?"

Wolf darted through the door. "Wolf! What's the matter with you?" Danni demanded.

Clutching his leash, she slipped into the

gallery, too.

For a moment, she paused.

Don't go in alone! What's the matter with you?

Technically, she wasn't alone; she was with Wolf. And it was broad daylight. Besides, this was Niles's gallery and she'd been here dozens if not hundreds of times.

"Niles! Your door is open," she called.

There was no answer. Wolf stood in the middle of the floor as if he was confused. Then he leaped forward and around one of the display walls, moving toward the back.

And Danni followed.

Quinn rode with Larue, who'd already been on his way to get him when he called.

Backup teams were behind them, and the closest car in the vicinity of the house had already been sent to secure the Tremé neighborhood house where Mason Bradley lived.

Quinn felt like a fool. The first place to search for someone connected to the painting, someone other than Hattie, should have been the gallery. Of course, that would've meant taking a careful look at Niles Villiers, but Danni had known Niles a long time; she'd done shows at his gallery.

And it wasn't Niles Villiers's DNA they'd

found on the knife.

It had been Mason Bradley's.

Mason Bradley — an artist known for his exceptional work restoring the art of others!

The presence of his DNA in the system — because of a DUI several years before — was fortuitous, to say the least. Mason must've forgotten about that little transgression. . . .

As they drove, Quinn took out his phone and tried Danni's cell again. She didn't answer but Billie did.

"Danni is still out, Quinn. And she left her phone behind."

"Where the hell did she go?" Quinn muttered.

"Since Wolf's gone, too, I'm assuming that she's got him out for a walk — just like I told you ten minutes ago when you left."

He quickly explained to Billie what he'd learned and then said, "She doesn't know, Billie. She doesn't know about Mason Bradley or what forensics have shown."

"She can handle it, Quinn. I'll have her call you. Or I'll ask her to stay here and wait for you — or . . . I could just tell her. Whatever you want."

"Just tell her. She'd be furious if you knew something and didn't spit it out. We're not going to play guessing games. But . . . don't let her run down to see Niles, okay? Ask her to stay in the house."

"It's bad news about Mason, but she can handle it," Billie repeated.

"Danni's going to be fine," Larue told him, making a sharp turn.

"Yeah. I know. I'm sorry, though. She considered the guy a friend."

Larue pulled his unmarked car up to the curb, jumping out, armed and ready. Quinn was on the sidewalk just as fast. There was already a patrol car there, and an officer hurried to tell Larue that he had a man around back.

As the backup cars jerked to a halt on the sidewalk, street and lawn, Larue shouted orders for them to take their positions, two teams on either side of the house, backup for the rear door. Larue walked to the front door, banging on it, and shouted, "Bradley! Mason Bradley, this is Lieutenant Jake Larue, NOPD. Open up!"

Larue waited, glancing at Quinn.

Larue knew his duty and his job, and he'd always been a courageous cop. But they both understood that a cop without a sense of fear was a dangerous cop.

And they had every reason to suspect that Mason had either killed — or been an accomplice in killing — many times over.

Silence greeted them from the house. Jake shouted out his identity again, warning that they'd break in. "You're surrounded, Bradley! Open the door."

They waited some more. Again, no response.

Larue offered Quinn a tight-lipped grimace. They'd done this together in the past. They'd been partners. Now, in an odd way, they still were.

Larue counted silently. On three, Quinn threw his shoulder and all his weight against the door, smashing it open.

Larue moved ahead of him, ready to shoot.

But there was no one there.

The men at the rear of the small house had heard their entry and responded by breaking through the back door. Quinn obeyed Larue's hand signals, moving from room to room.

Shouts of "clear" resonated through the house.

Mason Bradley wasn't home.

It was, however, an interesting house.

There were canvases everywhere, all in different states of completion. Mason Bradley hadn't kept a studio, per se. He'd worked anywhere and everywhere. There were easels set up in the parlor, dining room and kitchen and in the three small bedrooms upstairs. Palettes filled with different colors and shelves of paint lined every room. Some canvases were covered; most were not. Some were beautiful images of historic buildings caught in the perfect light. Some were likenesses of people, including well-known historical figures, and others who were probably alive and well and walking the streets of New Orleans. Bradley was good at faces.

Larue didn't hide his disappointment. "Where the hell is Bradley? It's too early for him to be at work," he muttered.

"Maybe not," Quinn said. "On the other hand, he might have headed out and stopped for breakfast, gone for a walk or to watch the sunrise over the Mississippi."

"*Or* maybe he knew we had evidence on him — and he's skipped out," Larue said disgustedly.

"Maybe. You have officers stationed around the Quarter?"

"Yeah, and they've been watching the gallery on Royal since I called you."

"Then we'd better get over there."

"I have a feeling he's gone, lit out," Larue said. "Damn, and we moved so fast! I can't believe he's not here."

"You know what else isn't here?" Quinn asked.

Larue shook his head.

"The Hubert — the Henry Sebastian Hubert painting, *Ghosts in the Mind*," Quinn said. "The real one, I mean," he added wryly. He'd explained their earlier mistake on the drive over.

"You thought it would be here?"

"I'd hoped . . ."

"Yeah, I know you want it, and you want to . . . whatever. But Mason is a killer. A flesh-and-blood killer," Larue said.

Quinn didn't disagree; he'd never be able to entirely convince Larue that a painting could play havoc with human lives.

"Well, let's get moving." Jake nodded and ordered one of his officers to keep a team on the house, just in case Mason Bradley returned.

He and Quinn started back to his car.

As they reached it, Larue's phone rang. He answered it and listened in terse silence. "On my way" was all he said.

When he ended the call, he looked at Quinn. "There's some trouble on Royal Street. There's —" He broke off, then said, "There's someone dead in the Image Me This gallery."

■ ■ ■ ■

Wolf would never have *led* her into danger, Danni knew.

He was too good a dog, too good a guardian.

He had led her forward because the danger was gone. It had come, taken its toll and now it was gone.

Death had come.

And the killer had gone.

Danni sat on the back gallery floor next to the corpse of Mason Bradley. If the killer had remained in the gallery, Wolf would have warned her — and led her out.

He sat dutifully a few feet off, waiting. He knew not to trample a crime scene; he'd been a police dog at one time.

He wouldn't leave her — unless he was forced to. And then, Danni thought, pity the person who tried to force him.

But there was a dead man here. And Wolf knew that the dead had to be discovered.

She hadn't brought her cell. Finding the body, she'd used the store phone to dial 9-1-1 and she'd also tried to reach Quinn. There must've been officers close by, since there was always a police presence in the Quarter, and with what had been happening, she was sure that Larue had doubled their numbers. Within a few seconds, the gallery was crowded with police. Then they backed out, securing the crime scene.

She didn't move; she was still sitting in the same spot where she'd waited for the officers. The woman in charge of the forensics unit was Grace Leon and Danni knew her; she was a friend of Quinn's. She told Danni just to sit tight while they put some controls in place.

It was then that Niles Villiers arrived at his gallery. The police, Danni was certain, had tried to keep him out, but Niles made it in. He gasped and went dead silent looking at his friend and employee on the floor. The horror on his face was unmistakable.

The next arrivals on the scene were Quinn and Larue. Quinn's eyes sought hers and she gave him a nod, telling him she was okay. She thought she was; she hadn't become hysterical and run shrieking into the street. She'd called the police. Maybe it hadn't registered yet that a friend had been brutally killed.

Viciously knifed. Slashed to ribbons.
She hadn't realized the extent of his wounds at first. Her initial instinct had been to try to save Mason, which was why she was down on the floor next to him.

There had been no saving him.

Mason stared up at her with only one eye; the other had been slashed into a dark crimson and black pool. She had touched him, his shoulders, his back, moving him when she was trying to see if he could be saved.

At the moment, she just felt numb.

Her friend was dead. Butchered.

Quinn and Larue and the first officer on the scene were talking but she couldn't seem to make out their words. Grace Leon came over to her, giving her a hand to help her rise, walking her carefully from the scene — making sure she didn't step in any of the congealing blood.

Grace brought her over to Quinn and Larue.

"How did you happen to find him?" Larue asked.

"I was walking Wolf," she said dully. "The door to the gallery was slightly open. I called out when I entered . . . but no one answered. I probably would've just left if Wolf hadn't been so insistent. I didn't immediately see the body — Mason — because he was behind the wall where paintings are hung. Wolf charged forward — and I went with him. And I found Mason. . . . I called 9-1-1 and I tried to call Quinn but his line was busy."

"I was probably calling *you,*" Quinn murmured.

"This just beats all to hell," Larue said.

"The killer is out there." Danni turned to Quinn. "A . . . living killer." She turned to Larue next. "Have you gotten anything yet? Anything at all from the alley, Cosby Tournier or his friends?"

Larue shot Quinn a quick glance. "She doesn't know?" he asked.

"I hadn't reached her," Quinn said. "I was with you! Remember?"

Danni looked from one of them to the other. They were behaving very strangely.

Another man had been killed.

A man who'd been a friend of hers . . .

"Doesn't know what?" she demanded. "Tell me!"

"We were out trying to arrest Mason Bradley this morning," Quinn said quietly.

"The blood on Michel Dumont's knife was Mason's, Danni." Larue was also keeping his voice low.

Danni blinked. That was . . . not right. Mason was lying on the floor. Dead.

She heard a cry. Niles Villiers suddenly went down on his knees, shaking with sobs. Perhaps he'd been in shock, too numb to react at first.

And now it was sinking in.

Danni walked up to Niles and placed a consoling hand on his shoulder. She shook her head at Quinn. *"Mason?"* she mouthed.

"I'm sorry, Danni."

"But . . . he's dead now. A victim, too."

"I don't know who killed Mason Bradley, Danni," Larue told her. "But I do know that Mason Bradley was in that alley, that he attacked Cosby Tournier and in that attack, he was wounded.

She stared at them both, wide-eyed. "A test could have been compromised. It could have been faulty. Something must've been wrong with it. Mason is *dead.*"

"Yes, and I'm the investigator working on his death," Larue said. "Tell me again *exactly* what happened this morning."

Danni glared at him, her anger rising. Her emotions were heightened now. Sooner or later, numbness wore off and then . . .

She felt like screaming, just as Niles had screamed.

"I was walking Wolf. He started getting agitated when we reached the gallery. Like I said, the door was ajar — so I went in, calling out to Niles and Mason. Wolf ran to the back and . . . I found Mason. I did move him slightly, trying to check for a pulse, a heartbeat. I called the police. I tried to call

Quinn. I've already *told* you all this. I went back to sit with Mason, because —" She broke off. She had to inhale deeply. "Because I couldn't believe he was dead."

As she finished speaking, Ron Hubert arrived with his bag and a crew. His face was gray. As he approached, a female officer and a paramedic led Niles away, presumably to be treated for shock. Danni gave him a final hug.

"Another one?" Ron said once the small group had passed by. "Mason Bradley. Slashed to death."

Larue nodded. "The rest of the facts about his death will come from you."

"No murder weapon?" Ron Hubert asked.

Larue shook his head.

Ron walked toward the body but stopped abruptly.

Danni realized that he was standing in front of the last giclée copy of *Ghosts in the Mind.*

She hadn't even noticed it.

And now she couldn't bear to look at it. Neither, it seemed, could Ron. He turned away, muttering to himself. "Blasted thing — should've been lost forever after World War II."

"Mason was knifed to death," Danni said. "Maybe the woman in the 'fog' instigated

Mason to kill and then 'disappeared.' She had a knife. She tried to kill Cosby last night." Danni closed her eyes. "Mason is . . . dead. I don't understand why . . ."

"Could be revenge," Larue told her. "Or vigilante justice. Perhaps someone who suspected he was the killer — and was afraid we'd never catch him. Danni, I don't know what's going on. But I'm sorry to say I believe your friend was involved in the other killings. It also seems that he wasn't alone. Now we have to find out who killed him."

"Do you need us anymore?" Quinn asked.

"I'll need a statement."

"She's given you her statement. I want to get Danni out of here now. You don't make others stand over a damned body once they've reported it, Jake. Come on. We'll just be down the block."

"Go," Larue said.

Ron looked up from the body. He nodded solemnly at Quinn.

"What did that mean?" Danni asked, speaking to him alone as they walked toward the gallery entrance.

"It means he's going to get that autopsy done quickly so we can leave on time tonight. Wolf, come on, boy — let's go."

An officer in uniform let them duck beneath the crime scene tape stretched across the doorway.

"We're still going to Switzerland — tonight?"

Quinn took her by the shoulders and said, "Tonight. Danni, it's more important than ever that we burn the bodies of the dead at the House of Guillaume. Now that we understand a little more about how the painting works . . . We know its evil comes from the people portrayed in it. They have to be destroyed, and quickly."

CHAPTER 18

There was no real opportunity for Danni to discuss anything with Quinn alone. Ron was, of course, aware that Mason Bradley was dead; he'd been at the scene. But they had to let Father Ryan and Natasha know, as well as the others. None of them seemed to grasp the fact that forensic evidence proved Mason had been the one with the fog/woman/ghost who'd attacked Cosby Tournier.

"It makes no sense," Natasha argued. She and Jez had arrived together.

This time, Danni really wanted to cry when Wolf left with Jez. She'd come to realize how much she hated being away from the dog.

But Wolf couldn't go with them.

It seemed incredible, even bizarre, that they were still taking off, still going to Europe, when she'd just found a friend dead. In a pool of blood. And even though she recognized that Mason Bradley certainly had the talent to paint the excellent copy of *Ghosts in the Mind* that had deceived Quinn, she didn't want to accept that he could've done what everyone seemed to believe he'd done.

"He wanted to be famous," Billie told her. "He *desperately* wanted to be famous. Maybe that was the promise in the painting for him. And it's logical in a way. As we know, Hubert wanted to be famous, too. He was getting there, but probably felt it wasn't happening quickly enough. He wanted to be part of the 'in crowd' that meant so much to him. Play ghost games with Byron and friends. Fame would do that for him. Mason was similar, I think. He was tired of working on other people's art — the painting promised him his own rise to fame."

She knew that Billie was right. She'd often complimented Mason on his restoration work and the copies he did of renowned paintings, marveling at his ability to imitate others.

"True artistry is in *new* style and individual creation," Mason had said.

He'd wanted to create for himself — and he had done so. He'd somehow, ironically, created *life*. Or a form of life.

Just as Mary Shelley had created her

Frankenstein — from nightmares and the world that surrounded her.

When Jez had taken Wolf, and Ron had arrived and they were only waiting for Father Ryan, Quinn came up to Danni's room as she packed a few last-minute toiletries.

He slid his arms around her. "I'm really sorry."

She was surprised to find herself easing away from him; she didn't want more sympathy. She wanted to understand.

"So, did he have the original? Did he steal the painting and hide it in his house somewhere?"

"No."

"Someone else has the painting — and that means someone else is really behind these killings."

He hesitated before answering her. "Danni, obviously I don't think the characters in the painting can run amok on their own. I do think that requires an ongoing supply of blood. So, they need a willing assistant — just as Stoker's Dracula did. But whether it was *his* hunger, desire and cruelty behind the 'awakening' of the painting, I don't know. Either the painting turned on him — perhaps because he'd failed it somehow. Or his . . . accomplice failed him.

Like I said, Danni, I'm sorry about all of this. But I'm absolutely convinced that Mason Bradley was involved."

She wished she wasn't leaving. She wasn't Niles's best friend, but she figured he'd need a lot of support. He had trusted Mason and depended on him.

"What do you suppose we're going to accomplish if there's still a living person out there who instigated all of this? Someone still *feeding* the painting to awaken or activate it?" Danni asked.

"Danni, you're the one who pointed out that we have to find every dead person in that painting. Every one of them can be awakened. Every one is a potential killer. One down — Henry Hubert. We have ten to go. According to everything we've learned, if the killers who come to life in fog or mist or whatever are sent to hell or purgatory or wherever it is are completely destroyed, burned to ashes, the killing will stop — at least the killing that can't be explained, that leaves no clues. Maybe Mason wasn't the real bad guy in this. Maybe he wanted fame so much that he let himself be seduced into feeding the painting, activating it."

Danni nodded. She felt guilty about the distance she needed right now.

"I think I hear Father Ryan. We'd better get going," she said.

They took two cars to the airport and left them in long-term parking.

Hattie had spun her magic again, and they were off to Europe first class once more. Danni spent most of the evening trying to read about the last few years described in Eloisa's journal, but that night, the words seemed to spin before her eyes. She couldn't find the name of another friend who'd been close to Alain Guillaume, who might have shared his sick desires — or been interred at the castle. What they were doing was a crap shoot.

Then again, how would it hurt anyone if they burned the wrong corpses?

They changed planes in Paris again for the short flight to Geneva and rented a van.

Getting to the castle was different this time, Danni thought. Now, they knew what they'd see.

They would walk into the Hubert painting, more or less.

"We have to move quickly. We want the daylight," Quinn said, "because the *activated* evil seems to need the night. That's when the dead in that painting awake, at night and only at night. So I suggest we leave the luggage in the hall and get it up to the rooms later."

"Makes sense," Billie murmured, to agreement all around.

"We know exactly where Alain Guillaume is interred," Quinn went on, "so we'll get him out first. Father Ryan, Billie and Bo Ray can help me break into the sarcophagus and the coffin. Danni, you, Hattie, Natasha and Ron can start looking for people we believe to be in the tombs here."

Everyone was touched and impressed that Hattie had provided medical masks to protect them from breathing in the tomb dust. She'd also supplied them with gloves, heavy mallets, sledgehammers — and dress bags for transporting what was left of the corpses. "I thought it might look a little strange if I ordered body bags," Hattie told them, and they managed to smile.

Within twenty minutes of arriving at the castle, they were masked, armed with flashlights and tools and heading down into the crypt.

"Everybody has the list of the names we're looking for?" Quinn asked.

"We should just burn this whole place down to the ground," Natasha said. "But even if we did that," Quinn reminded her, "we might completely miss destroying the right corpse. If the castle burned, there'd still be ruins. And in those ruins . . . remains could be intact."

"Not to mention the likelihood of us being arrested by the Swiss government," Ron added. "It's my property, but there is insurance and it's number seventeen on some list of historic landmarks." He grimaced. "I wish we *could* burn it to the ground. I wish it more than ever now that I've been here."

"Yeah. Well, we're going to do what we have to do," Quinn said. "Maybe everything will be sunshine and roses after we're done."

He turned to go through the archway and the stairs down to the crypt. When Quinn stopped at the tomb clearly labeled with Alain Guillaume's name, Danni moved on, studying each of the sealed interments she passed, checking the names.

She heard Quinn whack the hammer into the crowbar as he worked to unseal Alain Guillaume's tomb. The sound seemed deafening in the musty corridors of the crypt — almost as if they were pounding nails into a coffin, rather than trying to demolish one.

Danni turned around, shining her light behind her. "Ron, why don't you search the right side with me, and, Hattie, follow along with Natasha," she suggested.

"Thorough and organized. I like it," Hattie said.

Natasha paused and shone her own light on the list she carried. "I've found one . . . no, three!" she said, looking at Danni. "They're here," she said, her voice incredulous. "They're actually here. This may be the answer."

Danni walked over to the tombs Natasha had indicated; they were one on top of another on the shelving. Small metal plaques affixed to the concrete seals bore their names and birth dates; there was nothing else written — including their dates of death.

"Solange, Gérard and Antonio Rastira, one on top of the other . . ." Natasha breathed.

"So, the children *did* die here — along with their father. I wonder how," Danni murmured.

Father Ryan had heard them. He came striding down the medieval corridor between the tombs, a sledgehammer in his hands.

"Stand back," he warned.

They did.

With a mighty swing, he broke the first seal.

Decaying linen and silk stretched across the decomposed body of a boy.

"He didn't even give them funeral

shrouds, much less coffins," Father Ryan said. He paused for a minute, gazing down at the boy. He made the sign of the cross, then swung the sledgehammer again.

.The second tomb revealed the remains of a girl, her flesh mostly gone. Father Ryan said something in Latin and made the sign of the cross once more — then brought the sledgehammer down a third time.

Antonio Rastira had been interred with a black mask over his face. Danni stared at it and at a whip that lay at his side.

"Well, I'd venture to say the knife still in his chest is a clue to his death," Ron muttered.

"You think?" Hattie muttered back.

"No one seemed to be safe around Guillaume," Danni said. She jumped; the sound of Quinn hammering at the sarcophagus holding Alain was so loud it seemed to shake the walls, the shelves and archways of the crypt. Her flashlight jiggled; the light played eerily on the dead.

"Three ready for the fire," Natasha said. "I'll get the bags."

"Quinn!" Father Ryan called toward the entry where Quinn was hard at work. "We have three!"

Quinn, caught in the light, looked back at them. His shirtsleeves were rolled up; breaking the sarcophagus seal was heavy labor.

He wiped his forehead with one arm and nodded. "I'll send Bo Ray. Get those in body bags and take them up. And keep searching."

Danni turned away. She could hear Bo Ray making disgusted noises as he dealt with the corpses. Not a pleasant task. "I hope we're not all going to die of some weird disease like the people who opened King Tut's tomb," he said.

"I hope not, too," Father Ryan responded with a chuckle.

"You were supposed to tell me that couldn't happen for some reason or other," Bo Ray told him.

"It's doubtful, Bo Ray. Tut's tomb had been completely sealed and was thousands of years old," Hattie said.

"I like her!" Bo Ray pointed at Hattie.

Danni listened to their patter, searching for more of the names they were seeking.

As she neared one, she knew even before she got there that she'd found someone.

It almost seemed as if heat were radiating from the tomb. As if an ancient fury was reaching out for her.

She paused for a moment, unwilling to go farther. Then she felt Hattie behind her.

"Who did you find?" Hattie asked.

Danni forced herself to move forward. She envisioned a skeletal claw shooting from the burial shelf to pull her inside — into some form of hell.

Using one gloved hand, she dusted off the brass name plate. This one was embellished — set there with care.

"Mimette Lamere. Guillaume's mistress."

"Father Ryan and Bo Ray dragged out the first three bodies," Hattie said. "All the remains fit into one bag, and Father Ryan said it wasn't that heavy. He'll be down in a minute. We should get this wretched creature out quickly!"

When Father Ryan returned, his face was smudged. He shrugged when he saw them. "I didn't want to leave them up there untended and Bo Ray wouldn't stay unless I started them burning," he explained.

"That might be a wise decision," Danni said. "This is the mistress, Mimette Lamere."

Father Ryan raised the sledgehammer once and then again. The seal crumbled into pieces on the second slam.

Mimette Lamere was on a stone shelf; no shroud or coffin covered her. A black miasma seemed to rise from her body.

A body that didn't seem to have decayed.

Father Ryan immediately began praying

in Latin. Danni heard Natasha behind him, intoning her own prayers.

Something cloying and sickly sweet, like old perfume, filled the air. Danni swallowed hard, terrified that the woman would open her eyes.

Father Ryan anointed the corpse with holy water from the flask he carried.

Danni could have sworn that steam rose from her. She thought she heard a scream of fury.

"Get me a dress bag, please," Father Ryan said calmly.

Danni didn't want to, but she had to turn away. Ron helped Father Ryan get the corpse into the bag.

That one apparently was heavy; Father Ryan grunted as he made for the stairs. She shivered as he left — and hoped that, outside, Bo Ray had kept the flames burning high.

She glanced at her watch and wondered if she'd changed the time correctly. Two-thirty now, Swiss time. They had five or so hours before dark. They were doing well.

She moved deeper into the crypt.

Hattie was the next to make a discovery. She found Jermaine Wasser, the youngest of the murdering lot within the painting.

Danni knew what the boy had done and

yet when his tomb was opened — the seal had already cracked and part of it was missing — the bones and bits of hair and fabric still seemed to tug at her heart.

How did such a young child come to kill?

Apparently, the small and fragile bones touched them all. They were silent for a moment; Father Ryan and Natasha prayed softly.

Then the boy, too, went into a bag.

She came upon a plaque that read Jacques, Groom to His Lordship, Alain Guillaume.

Jacques didn't rate a surname on his memorial. Danni thought the "keeper of the keys" might be near the groom, and he was. Very near, they discovered. He was on the same shelf. They only knew they'd found him because there was a plaque; it had been set on his chest and now protruded from his rib cage.

He had been Louis. No last name, either. He was simply Louis, Keeper of the Keys.

"Two in one." Ron must have noticed Danni's expression because he said, "Danni, don't look so sad. It's how we all got our surnames. We're someone's son, or we're named after towns or locations or the work our fathers did. Louis — they knew who he was because he was the keeper of the keys."

"Yes, but by this time it was the nineteenth

century. Surely he would've had a name!"

"True," Ron said. "But let's face it. Guillaume was a depraved murderer. He probably figured it didn't matter if he was politically correct or not."

Danni smiled. "Well, at any rate, we did find two more of them."

From far down the tomb, she heard Quinn's cry of triumph.

He'd finally reached the coffin that held Alain Guillaume.

They all moved closer to watch Quinn.

When they'd gathered around, Quinn was working a crowbar at one end while Billie struggled at the other.

The seals broke and the coffin finally opened.

Danni backed away. She'd thought Mimette Lamere was well preserved, but her appearance seemed less striking beside that of Alain.

"I guess we can say it's really him," Quinn murmured.

"Indeed." Natasha had out a bag of her gris-gris. She began chanting and tossing herbs onto the corpse.

Father Ryan stared at it, silent; he seemed entranced.

Alain truly looked as if he were asleep. His mustache and beard were perfectly clipped, his clothing strangely clean and fresh, as though he'd just dressed for an evening out.

Danni wondered why she felt so disturbed. Yes, he was a corpse. Yes, he was so well preserved he might've sat up and spoken. . . .

But it wasn't any of that. She didn't understand what it was.

"Father," Ron said. There was a hardness in his voice. "No matter how he looks, he's dead. A corpse that must be burned to ash."

Father Ryan started visibly as Ron spoke his name. He nodded. "Just a corpse. A man who is dead before Almighty God." He pulled out his flask of holy water. As he began to speak over the body, Danni was sure she saw it twitch. When he poured holy water on it, they all heard a hiss, and steam rose from the corpse.

"Let's get him out of here fast," Quinn said.

Even he seemed loath to touch the body, Danni thought.

But he did. He picked it up and threw it over his shoulder, then headed straight for the stairs. Father Ryan followed him quickly. Danni watched them go and suddenly felt as if the darkness and the arched support beams that ran down the aisle of the dead were closing in on her. She blinked hard.

We're almost done! But Quinn, Father Ryan and Bo Ray were up above. She, Natasha, Billie, Ron and Hattie were alone in the crypt.

Four people, she told herself. She was with four other people.

Not enough!

Natasha read aloud from her notes. "The three children in the painting — Solange, Gérard and Jermaine. The two at the door — the groom and the keeper of the keys. The husband, Hubert himself. The lady, Mimette. Guillaume's close friends — we've found Antonio, and we still need to find Fabre Clairmonte." She glanced up at Danni. "They've just disinterred Guillaume himself."

"We have to find Fabre Clairmonte — and Raoul Messine, the butler," Danni said.

"Yes, yes . . . yes . . ." Natasha walked toward the back of the tomb to resume searching.

Danni followed her, turning back to her side of the aisle. She knew that Hattie was right behind her. Suddenly, she felt as if there'd been an earthquake.

Hattie fell against a tomb but caught herself. They looked at each other.

"That was Alain Guillaume, his flesh being consumed by the fire," Natasha told them. "We must hurry now."

"We still have a few hours," Danni said.

"Time's slipping by," Natasha insisted.

"And," Hattie added dryly, "a local might drive by and report us to the police. They just might notice what we're doing."

"We're almost at the end of the crypt. The last ones couldn't be this far back, could they?" Ron asked.

"Doesn't matter. We'll find them," Billie vowed. "You mark my words. We *will* find them."

They did. Just before they reached the archway that became the oldest section of the crypts, Danni saw the name Clairmonte.

"Thank goodness," Billie muttered.

"We're still missing Messine," Danni said, perplexed.

"Father Ryan and Quinn are back. Let's get the rest of 'em out and put 'em on the fire. Then we'll search, every one of us, for Messine," Billie vowed.

He turned to speak with Quinn. Evidently, Quinn agreed. He, Father Ryan and Billie started breaking the seals and dragging out the corpses.

Natasha touched Danni's shoulder. "We all need to go outside, to the fire, for this," she said.

Danni managed a smile beneath her mask. "Did you think I was staying down here *alone*?"

When she followed the others out, she was shocked by the appearance of the sky. If it had seemed to roil before, now it billowed and waved darkly. The threat of rain was strong.

But not strong enough to douse the fire the men had going.

The last of the corpses they'd discovered so far burned on the braziers. Father Ryan stood before the fire, speaking in Latin first, saying prayers he knew well. Then he switched to English, begging that good swiftly triumph over evil — and that God help them all. He invited Natasha next; she spoke in Creole, ready with more of her magic herbs to toss upon the flames. She asked the *loa* of goodness to see them through the darkness and into the light of the sun.

Billie kept feeding the fire, kept burning the corpses. Finally, there was nothing but ash. It was scooped up and Bo Ray and Billie took it to the river.

Danni nervously checked her watch. Almost five.

They still had to find Raoul Messine.

She looked up at the sky. Some of the

violence that seemed to send gray clouds bursting against other gray clouds had eased.

But the sky remained dark.

"We need to hurry," she said.

Quinn watched her, apparently puzzled. "Just one more, Danni. I'd been afraid we weren't going to get them all today. We've done well. We just have one to go."

"But not much time," she whispered.

He nodded. "Let's get down there. At least we did find Guillaume — the master of evil."

She felt better. "His corpse . . ."

"Frightening that it was so well pre-served," he said. "But there's nothing now. He's gone."

They returned to the crypt. Billie and Bo Ray weren't away long, and soon they all were continuing the search for the grave of Raoul Messine.

No one could find any mention of the butler anywhere.

"Maybe we need to just burn them all!" Danni announced.

From wherever they were in the crypt, the others stopped what they were doing and looked at her.

"Danni, we have tomorrow. And the next day," Ron said. "I'll stay here until we find him." He inhaled deeply. "My family started this. I will see that it's ended."

"Ron, your family *didn't* start this! The horror began with Alain Guillaume."

Quinn walked over to put his hands on her shoulders. "We both know this isn't easy," he told her. "For any of us."

She lowered her head. "Yes, I know. We have to call it quits for now. Everyone's exhausted. We did . . . we did take care of Guillaume. And even though we thought at first that we only needed to burn Henry Hubert, well . . . now we know what we're doing."

They left the crypt.

Upstairs, while Hattie and Ron tried to be cheerful and Bo Ray worked hard at it, too, they were a somber group.

It had grown late. No one wanted to deal with the luggage or preparing the wonderful baths they'd enjoyed before.

"We'll all just crash as we are, I guess," Quinn said after they'd made sandwiches and eaten.

They kept the generator running so the castle would be somewhat illuminated.

Then they went to bed.

Danni found herself pausing on the stairs and studying the great hall. Coming to the castle the first time had been a déjà vu experience; it still felt that way. The great hall was exactly like the painting Hubert had done. Naturally. He'd used what he saw — and what he knew.

The castle — and the people within it.

But there was nothing that disturbed her as much as the portrait above the fire. They'd found Guillaume's body that day. They'd burned it to ash.

And yet . . .

The painting still seemed to watch her. Almost as if it had power over her.

It wasn't what they were looking for, of course. But she hated the damned thing. In the morning, she'd ask Ron if they could burn that painting, too. She didn't think he'd mind.

In the room she and Quinn shared, Danni threw herself onto the bed. She stared at the ceiling. "Quinn, I'm sorry. I know I'm being difficult today. Acting a bit funny . . ."

He stretched out next to her. "You're funny-looking, too," he said, obviously trying to coax a laugh out of her. She glared up at him as he hovered over her on one elbow.

"It's all the white stuff on you."

"We've been handling graves and corpses — and we haven't had baths."

"We'll be going back down there in the

morning. We'll find Raoul Messine — and then we'll get Hattie to take us all to a five-star hotel." She smiled at last. He wrapped her in his arms, and they lay there quietly, both hoping for sleep.

CHAPTER 19

How?

Quinn had barely closed his eyes; he was so afraid Danni would wander.

Somehow he'd slept.

And somehow, she'd escaped him.

Something hadn't been right that day.

It hadn't felt completely off like last time, and he figured it was because they still had one to go. Raoul Messine.

But now . . .

Danni wasn't with him. And she'd been more on edge than any of them.

He shot out of bed, heedless of the fact that he had no shoes. Because of his last experience, he raced to the south tower — to the room where Hubert had created that damned painting.

Where Danni had gone before.

But she wasn't there.

Cursing himself for every wasted second, he raced for the steps to the ground floor.

He was halfway down when he found himself lifted and thrown back hard. He crashed against the wall and fell onto the steps, tumbling down to land hard on the stone ground.

Wincing, looking up, he blinked. The room was alive with fog. It was silver in places, darker in others.

Danni stood in the center of the great hall. She stared up at the painting above the hearth. The portrait they'd assumed to be of the original Guillaume. The man in knight's armor.

The portrait they'd later come to believe was that of Alain, so narcissistic that he assumed himself to be the creator of life — and life within death.

She seemed to be talking to the man in the painting.

Quinn blinked; the painting was speaking to her. Within the canvas, the man moved and spoke, as if he was chatting through an open window.

Quinn couldn't make out the words. His French was decent, but the man was speaking very quickly.

"Danni!" Quinn shouted her name, afraid. Something was forming beneath the painting; something was coming to life. Out of the fog, out of the shadows.

She didn't hear him. She was still staring at the painting.

Hypnotized. Mesmerized.

"Danni!" He struggled to his feet. Inside the painting, the man lifted an arm — and Quinn flew backward again.

Danni turned. She didn't see Quinn. She walked within the strange fog, walked to where they'd left the sledgehammers.

She picked one up; the man in the portrait pointed to Quinn.

She looked at Quinn and walked toward him.

Holding the sledgehammer.

Ready to use it.

Danni knew the voice of the man in the painting, felt it in her head. She'd felt its strange enticement in the crypt when she'd first gone down there — the very first time.

The voice in her head — the *entity* — had power over her. It had summoned her from the bedroom.

Now she walked in the fog, feeling the terror that still shivered within her. The fog was a miasma, rich with death and blood, torture and misery.

They'd all been such fools.

They hadn't seen . . .

It was never Hubert who was calling the shots.

It had never even been Guillaume.

Guillaume, Hubert, all of them — they'd just been pawns, playthings to order about. They'd been quietly manipulated by a man who'd been truly evil. Like a puppet master, he'd made them all dance, marionettes on strings.

And now . . .

Now she knew the secret. Hubert himself hadn't been evil; he'd been ensnared by the evil in another man — a man who hadn't been noble or artistically talented. But this man's evil had provided the cover of fog and darkness. Still provided it. Through the medium of Hubert's painting, he offered the promise that anything could be accomplished, any dream touched and held. And all the painting wanted in return . . .

Was a little blood.

She stopped in front of Quinn.

"I know the answers," she said. "I know what happened." She hefted the sledgehammer, shifting it from hand to hand. "In New Orleans, I believe it started with Mason. He knew the painting was for sale. Maybe Hattie said something when she was at their gallery so he knew she was interested. He must've had a contact at the auction house and through that person, he found out that Hattie had bought it. He investigated some more and managed to find out that James Garcia kept packages at home. All he had to do was get into the Garcia house sometime before dawn with a few drops of blood to touch up the painting — *to awaken it again* — and then the painting came to life. For some reason, he wrapped it up again and left it behind, and it was taken to the police evidence room. From which it disappeared . . . in the midst of all that fog."

"The characters in the painting committed those murders," Quinn murmured.

She nodded. "Let's see . . . it was Antonio who bludgeoned the one victim, Mimette who chopped up the poor grandmother . . . well, you understand." She glanced at the painting. "But now, you see, the true maestro behind all of this is watching. He's very, very angry. We've just destroyed everything. . . ."

Quinn stared up at Danni.

"He takes what he wants. He takes *who* he wants. He called me tonight. I'm to be the one . . ."

She'd reached Quinn. He could take the sledgehammer from her without straining a muscle. Except that the evil soul in the portrait was extending his force. His power

469

was in the air.

She had to be careful. . . .

And believe.

Believe in Quinn's faith in her.

"Danni," Quinn said softly.

It was time. Now or never.

"The portrait," she whispered to him, pretending to lift the sledgehammer and aim it. "Quinn, it's the portrait. It all *began* with that portrait, not with the Hubert. Get it down . . . reach up and take it down. You have to get it!"

She moved as if she'd bring the sledgehammer down on Quinn. It landed on the ground.

Quinn grabbed it and leaped to his feet. As he ran to the massive hearth, she saw the strain in his face, in his muscles. The wind, the darkness of the world during a long-ago summer, seemed to whirl within the great hall of the castle.

"Get thee gone, spawn of Satan!"

The thunderous cry sounded in the room — so loud that the heavens might have opened up.

Father Ryan stood at the top of the stairs. He had found them. He carried a large wooden cross and directed it at the painting.

Quinn felt as though he'd received a sudden boost; he grasped hold of the stone mantel on the giant hearth and pulled himself up high enough to seize the painting.

He yanked it from the wall, then half jumped and half slid down, crashing onto the floor with the thing. Danni was at his side by then, and Father Ryan and Natasha, with the others behind them, came running down the stairs.

Danni seized one of the fireplace pokers and drew it across the canvas, ripping with all her strength. She was so angry — she'd been so scared! — that she began to beat it over and over again.

She didn't realize what she was doing until Quinn got to his feet, walked over to her and took the poker.

"I think you've killed it," he said. She wouldn't have thought it possible for a painting to be torn into so many pieces.

"Ah, lass, that's a lot for me to sweep up and burn now, you know," Billie said, smiling as he came forward to get the ash broom.

There was no more fog. It was completely gone.

She looked back at Quinn. "The portrait was of *Raoul Messine*! He instigated Guillaume's depravity — and when Guillaume was killed for the transgressions Messine taught him to perform, he found another easy mark in Hubert. I believe Messine was the man in this painting. His reign of evil began with Guillaume, and when Guillaume was gone, he meant to continue. He didn't have a title or riches, so he had to prey on those who did. I believe the portrait was done for him by Hubert when he first came to the castle. Messine, through this painting, was the one who could lure anyone who came to the castle, seduce them. . . ." She shook her head. "And somehow, without understanding why, Hubert's widow knew the castle was evil."

"But do we really *know* he created that painting?" Quinn asked.

"Not for sure — and we won't find a signature now. Maybe there never was one. But I believe Henry Sebastian Hubert painted it."

"So Messine appears twice in *Ghosts in the Mind*? As the butler *and* as the man in the portrait?"

"Yes, I think so. Raoul Messine was evil. He worked with Guillaume, worked *on* him. He convinced him he was entitled to do what he wanted, to anyone he wanted, and Messine procured victims for him. That much history records — or at least oral histories of the time strongly suggest it. When Guillaume was taken down by the authorities, Hubert entered the scene. I imagine that this trusted servant could have gotten quite a lot from Hubert. And maybe Hubert didn't know there was blood mixed into his paints. Maybe not at first, anyway. It could've been an idea Messine put in his head, even *before* Byron's group showed up at the castle. And blood was definitely used to create that painting of Messine over the fire."

"And now it's destroyed. A good night's work, Danni," Father Ryan said. "The evil revenant of Messine tried to reach you. If you'd fallen in with it, the rest of us would've been in trouble. You were stronger than the painting."

"And I'm grateful, Danni. You're stronger than you know," Quinn told her.

She let out a soft sigh. "We're . . . we're strong together," she said.

Ron Hubert spoke up. "There's just one problem," he began.

They all turned to him.

"We still haven't found Messine's body."

And it was true.

"We start again at daylight," Quinn said. "We'll burn anyone we so much as suspect might be Messine."

"We need a big fire in this hearth right now. The remnants of this painting need to be swept up and destroyed," Danni insisted.

And so it was done. The hour had grown late — and yet there was still time to sleep.

Shaken, somewhat shell-shocked, they all went back up to bed.

"You still trust me enough to sleep with me?" Danni asked Quinn in a low voice.

"Sleep with, live with you — die with you, if need be," he whispered back. "Of course, I'm rather fond of living!"

Danni was astonished at how well she slept. The darkness that had settled over the castle was gone. It was still night, but it felt as if the sun shone eternally within her heart.

They searched frantically the next day. Danni no longer felt the urgency she had the night before — but then, the painting above the fire had unnerved her from the beginning.

Now it was gone.

It was Ron who came through in the end. He surmised that Messine would've seen to it that he *wasn't* found.

Where, then, would his body lie?

"I doubt it's Guillaume's long-suffering wife lying in the tomb with him. Or if she is, she's not the only one in there. I bet that's where Messine is. No one would think to disturb the woman who'd endured marriage to Alain Guillaume."

They all agreed with his theory. They used the sledgehammer and crowbars to muscle open the sarcophagus and the coffin inside it.

They all stared.

They presumed the woman broken and shoved to one side of the coffin was Alain's wife.

But the man who'd been in the coffin on top of her . . .

"Let's assume it *is* Messine," Quinn said. "Ron, the logic sounds right."

Messine was taken out and burned.

And when the rites were performed, Danni finally felt good.

Afterward, Hattie Lamont dusted off her hands. "You have a shop, of course, Danni," she said. "As do you, Natasha. And you have the congregation you serve, too. Ron, you'll always have more corpses to deal with — sad, but true. And, Father Ryan, you have your flock. But humor an old lady. I really need a good bath. I say we leave this wretched castle and enjoy one night in Geneva."

Danni smiled at Quinn, wondering if he'd

suggested the idea or Hattie had come up with it herself.

"I'm in," he told Hattie.

"Me, too," Danni said.

So that was what they did.

And it was a wonderful day — and night.

When they returned to the city, Danni set to work cleaning out her studio. She destroyed her own version of *Ghosts in the Mind,* the one she'd painted in a trance a few weeks ago.

That same day, Quinn answered a call from Larue. He went down to the station and took a chair in front of Jake's desk.

"Oddest thing happened the other night," Larue told him. "We had another attack — no killing, but another attack. Or an almost-attack." He spun around in his chair and picked up a folder on his desk. "Two sorority girls were heading back to Conti and Decatur. One of our mounted patrolmen heard a scream and rushed to the scene. The two girls were in an absolute panic. They said, 'Everything was suddenly foggy,' " he read from the report on his desk, " 'and we saw a man, a horrible man — he had a sword. A sword! And he was coming at us and then . . .' "

"And then?" Quinn asked.

"Then the officer assumed they'd seen things because they were drunk. But he filled out a complete report." He pointed at the paper.

"Well, what else was in the report?"

"They believe the officer saved them. But they also believe that the man coming through the fog with a sword disappeared into thin air — in a puff of smoke. That's what one of the girls said."

"Interesting," Quinn murmured. *They'd burned someone in the nick of time.*

"So it's over?" Larue asked him.

In a way, it was. None of the characters from the painting were left, none could come to life and wield their weapons of choice. And Messine, the man who'd started it all, was gone.

"Yes," Quinn said slowly.

But . . . it wasn't *quite* over. The real Hubert painting was still missing.

And someone had killed Mason Bradley. Someone had done that, apparently in league with the beings from the painting. Or maybe they'd acted on their own. . . . One fact that was undeniable: Mason Bradley had been with them, the beings in the painting, that night in the alley.

The painting had remained active until they'd burned the bodies of all the characters depicted within it.

Or *had* it gained a power of its own?

Quinn didn't think so. The portrait in the castle had to enter the minds of others in order to act. He thought the Hubert painting was the same. The painting itself lured the right people to it. . . . People willing to feed it with their own blood — to wake the dead it portrayed.

"Mostly over," Quinn amended.

"The painting remains missing," Larue said.

"Like Mason Bradley's killer," Quinn reminded him.

Quinn was at the police station, Ron was back at work and even Hattie had insisted on returning home.

She wasn't going to have another butler, she decided. She was going to hire a live-in secretary and a housekeeper.

"If one of them is evil, chances are the other won't be!" Hattie had told Danni cheerfully. Billie had gone to take her home and get her settled back in.

It was just Bo Ray and Danni for the moment. Wolf wasn't home yet because Jez had asked if he could take him on a fundraising walk for the animal shelter. He'd secured pledges from all of them for the cause.

Danni was happy to contribute — and glad to let Wolf and Jez continue to bond. Jez had looked after him for her and she wasn't going to wrench him right back.

Bo Ray had been thrilled to open the shop by himself.

Natasha was back at her own store and Father Ryan was at his church.

Danni had been so relieved when she destroyed the painting in her studio, her version of the Hubert. Then she remembered the giclée that Niles had given her.

Poor Niles was still devastated by Mason's death. Regardless, she was going to destroy that giclée, even though it had been a gift. Even though she might hurt his feelings.

She headed out to the garage. They'd pulled the giclee inside when they took out the cars to leave for the airport.

Danni opened the garage.

She blinked as her eyes adjusted to the lower light. She saw the giclée — with its wrapping torn once again — at the rear of the garage.

As she started toward it, she came to a sudden halt. A trick of the eyes? Or had she seen something move?

Just get out, her instincts warned.

She turned to leave.

"Stop, Danni."

She *had* seen something move. *Someone.*

"Turn around." She did.

A man walked toward her. Holding a gun.

Quinn had taken her to the shooting range; she still didn't know enough about guns to recognize what kind it was.

All she knew was that it was big — and it had a long barrel.

It was the man holding the gun who surprised her. He surprised her so much that for a moment, she was oddly relieved.

"Niles, it's you! What are you doing in my garage — and . . . and with a gun?"

"I'm going to kill you, Danni," Niles Villiers told her.

Any relief she felt drained out of her. And it hit her all at once.

Of course. Niles. Niles had been so thrilled to have the giclées. Niles had known that the original had been purchased — and that it was coming to New Orleans. *He* must've been the one who'd heard Hattie, the one who had a contact at the auction house, and then shared the information with Mason.

Not only that, Niles knew art.

"You woke the dead," she said quietly. "You woke the dead — and you brought Mason in on it." She shook her head. "Oh, and the way you cried when you saw his body! I really believed you were heartbroken. The hell with art, Niles. You should have been an actor."

Was there a way out of this? Wolf wasn't home to attack the man. Bo Ray was probably flirting and charming tourists in the shop. Quinn was at the station.

And it took about a second to fire a gun . . . and seconds for a bullet to hit her heart.

"I wasn't acting, Danni. I never thought I'd lose Mason. But he's dead — because of you. I needed Mason in my life."

"He's not dead because of *me.* Because of *you.* And the painting. Don't you know that evil spirits can't be trusted, Niles? They turn on you."

He smiled. "No. The painting won't turn on me. But . . . it should've taken you. It should've seen the danger in you. You're the one who caused everything to go badly. You chased down Hattie. You were there. You got her butler killed. Bryson Arnold. He was helping Mason and me. Oh, Danni. You ruined everything. You just *had* to come into my gallery that day. If you hadn't, you would never have seen the giclée, you wouldn't have suspected that the painting could be involved. But you saw it. And then you went after the real painting. You even went to Switzerland. You and Quinn. You ruined everything for me."

"What was the plan?"

"The plan?" Niles repeated. "Well, I'd touch up the painting with blood, I'd bring it to life when I needed it. And then Mason would've become a brilliant artist. He didn't know . . . how I felt about him, except that we were friends. He would've realized that he . . . that he cared, too. We'd be happy together. And once he became famous, he'd . . . he'd realize how much I'd done for him and how much I loved him. He'd want to be with me. He was never really happy being someone who restored the work of others or just made copies. He hardly had time for his own work. But now Mason's dead. My life is ruined. So, I'm going to ruin everything for *you.* I'm going to shoot you. Then I'm going to wait for Quinn — and I'm going to shoot him as he bends over your body in horror and agony. I'm going to make you both pay."

"And then they'll arrest you. And when they piece it all together, you'll get the death penalty. Or you'll sit and rot in a cell for the rest of your life. That would probably be worse for you."

"It doesn't matter anymore, Danni. It's . . . it's over for me. The painting . . . it would've given me everything. I could have made it work, *they* would've made it work."

"Niles, you were fooled. Seduced. The painting, the dead people in it, wanted nothing except immortality. Don't you understand that? I believe, when Hubert started the painting, it was just to be part of the 'ghost' bet that was going on within Byron's circle. But he had no idea how *evil* Raoul Messine would prove to be. Between them, they dug up killers and used their blood. And when *you* got hold of the painting, when you stole the thing, it got away from you. The killers in that painting wanted blood in exchange for what they'd do, the murders they'd commit and the chaos they'd create. You thought you could control the painting, but it controlled you. People in this city were killed — people who had nothing to do with ownership of the painting."

"I *did* control the painting — I would have controlled the painting," Niles protested. "You brought in the police. You and Quinn . . . The Garcia family had to die. He had the painting — I needed it. I went there. I didn't have a chance to take it that day — a neighbor came to the door and I couldn't risk being seen with the package. But then I got it back from the police station. The painting, it helped me do that . . ."

"It thrives on blood," Danni said, not ignoring his self-congratulatory tone. "A drop gets it started, gets *them* started, and suddenly the fog is all around — fog, blinding fog like the weather that settled over Geneva and the world that year. Then the evil souls captured in the painting come to life and walk within the fog — seeking death to stay awake. You helped the painting — *you* prowled the streets, trying to let the souls within it make kills. And in exchange you asked for power and success. For yourself and Mason. You involved other people, too. Like Mason himself. And Bryson."

"You . . ."

"Know more than you do," Danni said quietly. "Blood — and more blood. You would've been consumed. And you — did you *mean* to start this bloodbath? Regardless, you let it happen. And what about the fake painting? You had Mason do that painting — and you made sure Quinn found it, hoping you could deflect his attention. But don't you see? It destroys *everyone* who comes in contact with it. When it was finished with you, it would've consumed you. It killed Mason, which means *you* were responsible for his death. Not anyone else! Don't you see that yet? They'll arrest you, Niles."

Niles nodded. "Yes, they will now. I don't care anymore. I just want you and Quinn dead. Because that's the way it has to be now. You were supposed to die, but not by my hand. I would've had an alibi. Ah, Danni, I'd love to have seen it — the fog rising and the hungriest one, the cruelest one, coming after you. It would've been so . . . so right. But you didn't appreciate art, Danni." He seemed to puff up with indignation. "You put a painting *outside*. You leaned it against the garage wall!"

A chill settled over Danni. She'd just figured out where the real Hubert had landed.

At her home!

The painting had been masquerading as a giclée all this time — it had been at her house since the day it was delivered.

And with its torn wrapping . . .

The evil had been able to seep out into the streets, create the fog from two centuries before and hide within it to seek fresh blood.

Miraculously, it had scared Bo Ray before ever becoming active; miraculously, they'd all survived it. Because they'd never completely unwrapped it. Billie had even refastened the original wrapping. And they'd locked it up — and gotten it out of the house.

Wolf had known, she thought.

"So that's the real Hubert," she said.

Niles nodded. "Useless now. And all I have is . . . revenge."

He smiled. Danni heard something click. The trigger of the gun that was aimed straight at her?

"You brought it all on yourself, Danni."

She wasn't even sure what she felt. Fear? Or regret? If only she could live . . .

If she survived this, she'd let Quinn know that he meant everything to her. She'd hug Natasha and tell her what an important friend she was. She'd ask Father Ryan more about his life. She'd tell Billie he was the best man ever, that she wouldn't have done so many things in life, nor would her father, if it hadn't been for Billie.

She was going to die.

"No, you idiot! *You* brought it all on yourself!" she heard.

Niles Villiers twisted, startled by the sound of Quinn's voice booming in the garage.

Niles fired.

His shot went wild.

Quinn's didn't.

Niles Villiers spun around and then slammed onto the floor.

Danni discovered that her knees had no

strength. She sank to the floor of the garage, too.

But she didn't fall. Quinn caught her.

Shuddering, she held him. She held him so tightly that he smoothed back her hair and said, "I think you're breaking one of my ribs, Danni. But, hey, it's just a rib," he joked. "I have more."

Despite herself and the horror of what had happened, she gulped out a laugh. She eased her hold and met his eyes.

"Oh, Quinn, it was Niles. *Niles.* He brought Mason in, he —"

"I heard a lot of it, trying to get an angle on him from outside the door."

"We've had the real Hubert all along!" she said.

"And we can burn it now, and it finally will be over."

Trembling, she turned to look at Niles. He lay facedown, blood streaming from beneath him.

She heard sirens and shouts from the street. Someone had called 9-1-1 after hearing the gunshot.

They had only seconds before the world would burst in on them.

Quinn lifted her chin, bringing her face back to his.

"This isn't the time or the place, here in

the garage with . . . with a dead man, but . . . I love you, Quinn. I really love you."

He smiled. "I love you, too, Danni. Really love you."

She swallowed and nodded. "And . . ."

"Yes?"

"When the police are gone, I have to see Billie. And Natasha and Father Ryan and . . ."

"And?"

"Dog treats. We need to buy more dog treats."

Quinn gazed down at her with quizzical affection. "Whatever you want, Danni. Whatever you want. Just realize it's over. We're safe."

For now, at least. But, of course, they never knew when a new object would need collecting.

Or when someone else might find a way to wake the dead.

ABOUT THE AUTHOR

New York Times bestselling author **Heather Graham** has written more than one hundred fifty novels and novellas, has been published in nearly twenty-five languages, and has over seventy-five million copies in print. An avid scuba diver, ballroom dancer, and mother of five, she still enjoys her south Florida home, but loves to travel as well. Reading, however, is the pastime she still loves best, and is a member of many writing groups. For more information, check out her Web site, theoriginalheathergraham .com.

The employees of Thorndike Press hope you have enjoyed this Large Print book. All our Thorndike, Wheeler, and Kennebec Large Print titles are designed for easy reading, and all our books are made to last. Other Thorndike Press Large Print books are available at your library, through selected bookstores, or directly from us.

For information about titles, please call:
(800) 223-1244

or visit our Web site at:

gale.cengage.com/thorndike

To share your comments, please write:

Publisher
Thorndike Press
10 Water St., Suite 310
Waterville, ME 04901